THE STOLEN GIRLS

JEFF STETSON

Storm
PUBLISHING

Copyright © Jeff Stetson, 2024

The moral right of the author has been asserted.

Ebook ISBN: 978-1-80508-469-3
Paperback ISBN: 978-1-80508-471-6

Cover design: Blacksheep
Cover images: Shutterstock

Published by Storm Publishing.
For further information, visit:
www.stormpublishing.co

Raoul, forever my hero
Fabiana, for your love, continuing concerns, and embodying the spirit of my brother
All my family for your love and building the foundation of my life
And to my friends, for forgiving my mistakes but still helping me to be better

PROLOGUE

The footsteps drew closer, muffled by the recently installed three-quarter-inch-thick carpet. The boy sensed the shadow long before he saw it lurking at the base of his bedroom door, creeping underneath, flickering with every drunken, staggered movement. Then he heard that familiar noise, the terrible fumbling at the bronze knob, a secret turn made more desperate with each futile attempt to violate his safety.

Immediately after he had prayed, he wedged the back of his wooden chair against the door, stuck it below the handle, a discovery made after watching an old horror movie. He didn't expect it would deter the monster from eventually entering, but it might provide precious time and occasionally that was enough to offer sanctuary, a respite leading to a much-needed reprieve, no matter how fleeting.

The boy pulled up his blanket over his head. If he couldn't make himself disappear, perhaps he could eliminate the noise. Sometimes that had been sufficient to make the nightmare more bearable. In the past, he had feigned sleep hoping that would drive the monster away or convince it to wait another night. It had worked on one or two occasions, why not now? Suddenly, the noise ceased. The boy peeked from under his improvised shelter, grabbed his teddy bear and hugged it tightly. Maybe the prayer, in combination with his makeshift barricade, had discouraged the intruder. He listened intently, then whispered something to his protector.

"We're safe," he said, then relaxed his grip. He placed his arm around the bear and smiled nervously. He gazed outside his window; the night seemed peaceful. He was about to say "Thank you" when the chair crashed to the floor, causing him to drop his stuffed animal. Unable to protect himself, he quickly reached for his fallen friend and shoved it underneath his bed where he hoped it wouldn't be harmed.

ONE

TUESDAY APRIL 4TH

A radio alarm blasted an intermittent buzzer that could wake the dead and kill the living. Ron Butler's head shot straight up, but his body wouldn't follow. He stared at the digital numbers flashing the same three hypnotic numbers—6:15 A.M. His arm snaked its way beneath the sheet and around the pillow until it reached the nightstand. The fingers of his left hand fumbled, striking small switches and tiny knobs on the radio until a frantic energy overtook his palm. He bashed the top and sides of the machine. After several failed attempts, he shut off the alarm but activated an F.M. station, forcing music and static to compete at full volume. His fingers quickly shifted, turning the music off.

Ron sat on the edge of his bed and gently rubbed both eyes. He remained motionless for several moments and then began counting. He took a deep breath, glanced at the radio, waited for the unavoidable passage of time. When the last digit changed to "7," he shook his head resignedly and left the room.

He proceeded down a hallway, made a brief stop at the bathroom, washed his hands ignoring the mirror, and then headed to the kitchen in darkness. He opened the refrigerator and adjusted his eyes to the light. Searching inside, he removed a carton of orange juice, shook it side to side, then poured a glass. Once it was full, he placed the container to his lips, drank whatever remained, and threw the empty carton into the trash. He closed the refrigerator door, allowed his eyes to become readjusted to the dark, and left the kitchen carrying the glass of juice.

He yawned while keeping his focus on the glass. He'd poured too much, and the juice threatened to overflow. It would join a host of other carpet stains: apple, strawberry, banana, peanut butter and grape jam, and the dreaded tomato juice that no amount of scrubbing could eliminate. Last month, he received an estimate for a new carpet and as an alternative also obtained a quote on the cost of ripping it up and replacing it with tile. He couldn't afford either option and instead opted for a fresh coat of paint on the hallway walls which only caused the stains to become more pronounced. To rectify the problem, he changed the overhead light bulb from one hundred watts to sixty, believing it improved the "ambiance."

He'd succeeded in reaching his daughter's bedroom and managed to open the door while keeping the juice safely contained. He observed the silhouette of his child, her blanket pulled over her head, her arms surrounding her stuffed elephant in a mutual embrace. Her legs were posed like a wishbone, one leg hanging off the edge, the other propped against the wall. He moved carefully until he reached her bedside, found a magazine, placed it on her night table, and put the glass of juice on the paper coaster.

Sitting on the edge of the bed, he gently nudged her leg. "Jenny," he said softly and then stared at her sleeping which, as always, caused him to smile. He slid down the blanket a few inches until it revealed a mat of light brown hair, followed by a face the color of caramel with features that resembled a perfect doll.

Looking at her was like watching a younger version of himself—large almond-shaped brown eyes, smooth light chocolate skin, a nose that leaned ever so slightly to the left. The mouth, however, belonged to her mother, although Jennifer had no way of knowing that, other than from the photos stored in the family album locked away in the closet. Ron had considered removing a few, perhaps framing the wedding pictures or the one that showed her pregnant, bulging like a small woman concealing an oversized bag stuffed beneath her loosely fitting blouse. He loved the one he'd snapped of her as she was entering the hospital's maternity ward over eleven years ago. She had such a beautiful smile that afternoon. Why wouldn't she? She had waited for that moment all her life. They both had. In a few hours they would be given a gift from God, but it would come at a terrible price. He should have destroyed the photo, but how could he? One day, he would take it out and show it to his daughter. She, more than anyone, had a right to see it.

"Jenny," he repeated, then leaned close, kissed her on the cheek, lay down next to her, and rested his head near the fluffy animal she had named "Dumbo" in tribute to her favorite cartoon character. He had taken her to see the movie on her fourth birthday and had the elephant waiting for her when she arrived home. She had a collection of stuffed animals for every classic Disney movie they had seen together, and they had seen them all, enough to fill two bookcases with lions and dragons and deer alongside Peter Pan, Aladdin, Snow White, and six of the seven dwarfs. He couldn't remember which dwarf was missing or when it managed to escape from the group.

Opposite the bookcases was a large toy chest holding the entire collection of *Thomas the Tank Engine* trains, wooden clackety-clack tracks, bridges, tunnels, flashing lights, and whistles that, when blown properly, could mimic the television show's theme song. She used to sing that damn thing a hundred times a day. How did it go? He sang softly. "Thomas the Tank... you're the one." The one what? He tried to remember but his singing must have awakened Jennifer. He gave her another gentle nudge which caused her to smile. He pointed to the juice. She immediately drank it as she had done every morning.

He watched her ease herself out of the bed and cross to her closet where she removed the clothes she had selected the night before, which included her favorite brown sweater. He smiled at how organized she kept everything. It made him think of her mother who spent hours making sure outfits were color coordinated. His eyes closed and his smile slowly disappeared. It would be a while before he realized that his daughter had covered him with her blanket that went no higher than his shoulders, just the way he liked it.

TWO

The bedroom door crashed open, and Rebecca rushed inside, startling her parents, Todd and Elizabeth Roth, who were still in bed but awake. "Don't forget this afternoon," Rebecca insisted. "You promised."

"How many times do I have to tell you not to barge in on us without knocking," her father warned. Although he knew she wouldn't be interrupting anything. He and his wife shared the same bed but little else.

Rebecca left the room, closed the door, then knocked on it several times. Todd shook his head, conveying a weak surrender as Liz smiled. "Come in," she said.

Rebecca entered with a slight curtsey. "Don't forget this af—"

"He'll be there," her mother said, grabbing a pillow in a threatening manner and holding it above her husband's head. "Or else." She swung the pillow striking Todd's face to Rebecca's delight.

* * *

Rebecca placed her schoolbooks in her backpack and observed her parents finishing breakfast. As usual, they sat at opposite ends of the rosewood table with inlaid imported marble that, had it been any longer, would have placed them in different rooms. As it was, they might as well have been in different worlds, with Rebecca caught in between, either waiting for a truce or a war that would declare a victor.

"You prepared for the test?" asked Liz.

"Who uses fractions?" responded Rebecca, pulling back her reddish-blond hair and keeping it in place with a silver barrette. "If you can't get the whole thing, why bother?" She kissed her mother.

Todd read his newspaper and addressed his daughter without looking at her. "Sometimes you have to discover things one small piece at a time."

Rebecca moved toward her father and patiently stood next to him, waiting for some type of recognition.

Liz studied the situation for a moment, cleared her throat once and then a second time before finally taking matters into her own hands. She joined Rebecca, both now standing on either side of the preoccupied reader of the business section. She glanced at her daughter who raised her eyebrows and shrugged helplessly. Then, in a united front, they both pushed down the newspaper.

"Hey!" said Todd, more annoyed than startled. "You almost tore the paper."

"Well, that certainly would have been a tragedy of monumental proportions," stated Liz. "Hate to think you'd have to rely on NPR for your financial news."

She nodded toward Rebecca. Todd positioned his cheek so that his daughter could plant a kiss, which she did as an unappreciated formality. He returned to his reading. Rebecca looked at her father, wanting more, but received no further recognition. She looked at her mother who smiled reassuringly.

"You get an 'A' on those fractions," said Liz, and then looked at her husband, now lost in an article about a bank merger. "Sooner or later, they come together to make a remarkable whole."

Rebecca rushed toward the side door held open by Neil, the family's chauffeur, who was dressed in his black uniform with a crisp, heavily starched white shirt, his hat in hand.

"Mr. Roth, what time do you want me to pick you up this afternoon?"

"I'll be driving myself."

Liz exchanged an annoyed glance with Rebecca who couldn't conceal her concern which changed to disappointment.

"But, Daddy, if—"

"I know how to find your school, Becky," he said more sharply than he had intended. He placed the paper onto the table and displayed a business-like smile. "I'll be there." The smile changed to warm, almost genuine.

Rebecca, unconvinced, left with Neil, but not before giving her mother one last apprehensive look.

Liz poured herself some coffee and studied her husband, who ignored her. "You know how important this is for her," she said, not noticing that the coffee overflowed into the saucer.

"I'll be there," he repeated, but demonstrated little conviction.

"You better be," she said, conveying more of a plea than an ultimatum. She had long ago given up on making threats and, in any event, no longer had the will nor the inclination to enforce them. She let her bathrobe open slightly, then loosened the thin velvet belt, allowing more of her upper body to be revealed. Once, so very long ago, that's all it would take to have her husband delay his plans and make new ones. He would skip work and gladly miss appointments, to remain with her an hour or two longer. She waited for him to put down the paper, which over the years had become a flexible but impenetrable wall between them. She hoped his attention would turn to her as easily as it did to the pages of that artificial barrier. The story of their marriage was printed not on the page of a newspaper, but on her silent and lonely expression that he wouldn't see even though he sat a few feet away in a space she could no longer enter, and a place reserved for memories, not the future. She wrapped herself in the comfort of her robe and left the room.

THREE

Ron rolled over onto his back and sprawled out on his daughter's bed, relaxed, comfortable, not a care in the world. Suddenly he awoke, desperately searching the empty room until his eyes fixed on a *Thomas the Tank Engine* clock. The tiny engine's hands pointed to 7:30. The clock made a soft loco-motion sound followed by a train whistle and three weak "Toot... toot... toots."

He froze for a moment. "Shit!" He jumped out of bed. "Jenny! Jennifer!" He ran out of the bedroom, stubbing his toe against the door on the way. Hopping one foot down the hall-way, he lost his balance and crashed his left shoulder into the wall.

"You all right, Dad?" He heard his daughter's voice coming from the kitchen. Muttering a few uncharitable words, he limped through the living room and collapsed onto the imitation suede chair at the breakfast table. He rubbed his foot and noticed blood on his big toe. Jennifer brought him a bowl of cereal and two slices of wheat toast with butter and raspberry preserves.

"Jenny! Why'd you let me sleep?" he asked, more concerned than angry, a distinction without a difference.

"You looked so tired."

"Tired is better than fired, which is what I'm going to be if I miss my meeting!" He massaged his forehead to avoid a migraine, unsuccessfully. She opened a cabinet, removed a bottle of Excedrin, and gave it to her father along with a glass of water. He removed two capsules and popped them into his mouth.

"I can take the bus to school," offered Jennifer.

"Not with those baggy-pants-snot-nose kids with God-knows-what in their backpacks!" He swallowed hard and sipped water.

"Dad, you're supposed to drink the water first. It helps the aspirin go down better."

"Need a metal detector just to ride a damn school bus!" He took two quick spoonfuls of cereal.

"You swore," she gently reminded him.

"I did not," he said calmly and took a bite of toast.

"You said 'damn'," she offered, expressing noticeable enjoyment.

Ron stared at his daughter. "No music, no television, no video games next two nights."

"Why?"

"You swore."

She turned away in disbelief and mouthed the word, "Damn."

He took a napkin and wiped the blood off his foot.

Ron paced back and forth by his car. He reached through the driver's window and tapped the horn twice, then held it down for what seemed an eternity to Mrs. Newman, his elderly neighbor whom he fondly thought of as "the snoop on the stoop." He noticed her obvious displeasure and released his hand from the horn. He gave her an insincere smile which she didn't bother to return. Instead, she drew her beloved cat, Belle, closer to her chest.

Jennifer opened the door to the apartment building and headed halfway down the steps, stopping for a moment to rub Belle underneath her willing chin, eliciting a grateful purring sound which was quickly interrupted by her frustrated father.

"Jenny, would you leave that thing alone and hurry up!"

Clearly affronted, Mrs. Newman appeared devastated at the thought that her precious Belle had been insulted and defined as "that thing."

Ron held open the door to the driver's seat, which had become the entry to the passenger seat, being the only door that opened and closed on a somewhat consistent basis. Jennifer tossed her backpack into the car, climbed across the seat without disturbing the steering wheel, and took her place by the cracked window. He climbed in after her and slammed the door, causing Mrs. Newman to raise her eyes in disgust.

Ron put the key into the ignition and turned it enough to receive an unhealthy whine followed by a sick, sputtering cough and then silence. He tried again. The whine produced by this effort made the first one sound like an expensive European sports car.

He slammed both fists against the steering wheel, striking the horn with such force that it stuck and blared throughout the neighborhood for several moments. Belle's back arched as far as it could go, and it was even money who or what would explode first, the cat or her owner.

Ron massaged his forehead and muttered, "Goddamn it."

The horn went dead, the result of being either unstuck or broken.

"You said damn again," proclaimed Jennifer. "Only this time you put God before it."

"Grounded for the weekend," he declared softly.

Jennifer folded her arms across her chest defiantly. "That's not fair," she unequivocally stated.

"Neither is life," replied her father who exited the disabled automobile, leaving the door wide opened. "Stay in the car," he ordered, then proceeded toward the apartment building and climbed the steps. Halfway up, he stopped; a strange look appeared on his face as he stood eye to eye with Mrs. Newman and Belle.

He slowly lifted his right foot and studied the bottom of his shoe, discovering cat poop. He scraped the shoe against the step while giving Belle an accusatory stare. He then looked at Mrs. Newman who didn't appreciate the implication.

"I thought cats were supposed to clean up their own shit?"

"Well, I never," huffed Mrs. Newman, who dropped her cat to the stoop and marched down the street, Belle following behind with elegant, graceful strides.

Ron turned and looked at his daughter who had placed both hands over her mouth to conceal her laughter, but he could still hear a giggle or two. He gave her an annoyed glance, then continued up the steps, a smile beginning to form on his lips.

FOUR

Ron's Volvo sputtered to a stop in front of the Culver City school building. A security cop glanced at his watch, then stood guard near the administration entrance.

He stepped out of the vehicle and waited for Jennifer to complete her journey from one side of the car to the other. She climbed out, grabbing her backpack on the way.

"When are you gonna get the door fixed?"

"Nothing's wrong with my door."

"It's been broken forever."

"It stays closed just fine," he grumbled. Ron leaned down to reenter the car when Jenny nudged him aside and headed back in, reaching for something near the passenger seat.

"Jenny, for Christ sake's what are you doing?"

"I forgot something."

"Get it later! I'm already a half-hour late and—"

"I need to get it now."

The security cop took a few steps toward the car, motioning Ron to move it.

Jennifer searched the car floor. Ron, totally exasperated, looked at his watch, and reached into the automobile to expedite the matter. He tugged her arm, attempting to pull her out of the vehicle, but she resisted until she was able to accomplish her goal.

"I found it!" she shrieked.

Ron backed out of the car, striking his head on the door frame "Owww! See what you've done!" He rubbed the damaged spot while the school guard looked on unsympatheti-cally. "Are you happy now? Get your stuff and get out!"

She exited the car, stunned by her father's uncharacteristic outburst and disappointed that her effort to bring him a little happiness did just the opposite. They looked at each other awkwardly as the security cop observed them for a moment before entering the building. Ron felt ashamed and embarrassed and all the other emotions he always felt on those rare occasions when he directed his own frustration at his daughter. He tenderly placed his hand on her shoulder, which was sufficient to change her sadness and regret to a hopeful smile.

"I'm sorry, sweetheart. It just seems like I've screwed up this day before it even started. Might as well kiss that promotion goodbye."

She handed him a card which he studied uncomfortably. "What's this for?"

"It's a good-luck card," she answered proudly. "I know how important that job is to you. But whether you get it or not, you're still the best dad, ever."

He felt an overpowering fear that all the frustration he had stored up would be released in tears of gratitude, and once those floodgates opened, being late to his job would be the least of his problems. Fortunately, the lump in his throat couldn't block the words he found so difficult to form.

"The only important thing in my life is you." He felt the tears well up in his eyes and the lump grow larger in his throat. "You know that don't you?"

She shrugged and shuffled one foot, pushing dirt side to side. "Am I still grounded?"

"When I was eleven, I wasn't allowed weekends."

"I didn't think there was anything to do back-in-the-day, so you couldn't have missed that much." She kissed him on the cheek and ran toward the school entrance. He watched her disappear behind the large door. He stood perfectly still, interrupted for a moment by a slight smile that made him feel inexplicably lonely. But he was comforted by the knowledge that his loneliness would end in a few hours when the school bell rang for the last time this afternoon and he'd be reunited with his Jenny.

He looked at his card, but before opening the envelope, glanced at his watch and realized that whatever message his daughter had written would have to wait. He climbed back into his car, stepped slowly on the accelerator, and prayed that his vehicle wouldn't fail him, just this once.

FIVE

Sheldon Miller picked at a scab on his wrist. On most days Ron would have turned away in disgust or despair, but this time he couldn't afford that escape from his obnoxious boss. He had no choice but to pay special attention, to search for a clue, some small signal that his desperate appeal had a chance of working. He needed to make as much eye contact as possible in an effort to read this man's body language, to find a hint of a heart. He was prepared to beg if necessary, although it never should have gotten to this point. His work record and performance had earned him the promotion. Everyone in the office knew he deserved it. But Miller enjoyed tormenting him, making him plead his case, giving him a glimmer of hope only to snatch it away with a condescending smile and an unwelcome pat on the back.

"Ronald, it's not your work," Miller said, drawing blood from the open wound, which he smeared with his index finger. He then licked the stain and repeated the gesture. "When you're here, you're as good as—"

"When I'm here?" Ron restrained the anger, but just barely. "I'm here every day."

"Hey, I appreciate you're a single parent and you've got obligations. I admire that. I really do." Miller had gotten a trace of blood on his shirtsleeve, already stained with black powder from a failed attempt to insert an ink cartridge into a laser printer. He insisted on doing this not in an effort to be helpful to the staff, but rather to ensure that the last drop of ink was shaken out of the previous cartridge before being replaced.

"Then what's the problem?" Ron asked, knowing full well the answer would be as disingenuous as the fake smile frozen on Miller's face.

"I need to count on my supervisor to be here longer than I am. And I don't have a life. Consider yourself lucky. You've got a reason to go home. You may get paid less, but, in the end, you'll gain a lot more than a title and a set of bullshit responsibilities."

"I'll also have a lot of bills that will go unpaid." Ron stopped himself from providing more details. He had no intention of opening his life and his financial problems to this man. "Look, Mr. Miller—"

"I've made my decision."

"But I really need the extra money and I—"

"I've promoted William."

"William? I trained him!"

"Then I'm sure you won't mind being supervised by him. It'll be like reporting to yourself." Having done enough damage to his wrist as well as Ron's sense of worth, Miller pulled his sleeve over the wound.

Ron headed for the door without further argument or loss of dignity. He stopped and forced himself to turn around to face Miller, hoping his request concealed the anger building inside. "I'd like to leave an hour early. I've got something special I want to do with my daughter."

"Ask William if it's all right. If he has no problem, you can leave a half-hour early."

He wished he had the courage to quit. If he hadn't had any obligations, courage or not, he'd walk out and never come back.

"It's Penny, isn't it?"

"What?"

"Your daughter, Penny?"

Mangling his daughter's name and reducing it to the lowest form of compensation was about all Ron could endure, but he found solace in a short silent prayer and acquired the strength necessary to politely correct the man who controlled his future paychecks. "Jennifer, but she prefers to be called Jenny."

"Pretty name."

Miller went back to work with his face not smashed—a small miracle that proved restraint could remain possible under the most difficult of circumstances. Ron glanced at his watch, the first of many such efforts to anticipate the time when he would be reunited with the only person on this earth who made his job tolerable.

SIX

It was hard to believe that these were mere middle school children. The exquisite costumes made them appear so much older. Silk, satin, embroidered lace—a luxury for most students, but no expense was ever spared for school recitals. The sons and daughters of the country's elite had the added advantage of performing on an elaborate stage with the benefit of musicians that rivaled the state's best symphony orchestras. The young girls and boys showcased their talent in front of an adoring audience comprised of parents, friends, and teachers who were proud and privileged to be a part of a private school that ranked in the top one percent of all elementary and secondary educational institutions in the nation, a training ground for future leaders. Its alumni held powerful and influential positions in society, politics, business, law, the arts, and finance. Students were expected to excel, and the counseling office had several psychologists on staff to support their efforts and manage levels of stress that would have overwhelmed most adults.

Trustees, politicians, film, and sports celebrities, along with major benefactors, filled the first six rows of a packed auditorium recently renovated to house fifteen hundred comfortably.

Liz Roth, vice-chair of the board, sat next to the principal of this elegant Bel-Air school situated on nearly twenty-five acres of some of the most valuable real estate in Southern California.

In recognition of the seventy-fifth anniversary of the school's founding, this summer the gold circle members, led by Liz and her husband Todd, had raised more than five million dollars for a landscaping beautification project, a new Olympic-sized pool, an archery area, and an annual endowment to be used to fund full scholarships for three to five needy students from an inner-city environment, to be implemented once guidelines were finalized by a parent—teacher advisory committee and approved by the full board.

The recital encompassed a variety of music and dance, a bit of ballet, a touch of jazz, even a blues number that generated the first of many standing ovations and its fair share of laughter. But there was one child, in particular, who had become an audience favorite the moment she leaped onto the stage, arms gracefully raised above her head, spinning with a mesmerizing confidence that captured the attention and admiration of her fellow performers.

The principal leaned close to Mrs. Roth and whispered, "Your daughter is as talented as she is stunning."

Liz smiled and lightly rubbed her purse which rested next to her in the only empty seat in the auditorium.

* * *

Jennifer watched the last school bus leave the long circular driveway. Alone, she leaned against the wall of the administration building, removed a book from her backpack, and got a head start on her homework. She wanted to finish as much as she could before her father arrived. That way, she would have time to celebrate his promotion. And if he didn't get one, she would convince him to watch one of their favorite movies, something funny and stupid that would help him laugh and ease his disappointment. She heard a man's voice, calling out from behind overgrown bushes that blocked a pathway to the parking lot near the athletic field. The voice sounded increasingly desperate. The pleas turned into whistling, the type used to gain attention or issue a command. Then the man appeared, dressed like a college student but older. He placed his right hand over his mouth as if considering something important or perhaps not wanting to confront the possibility of something dreadful. He lowered his hand about the same time as they made eye contact. The way he looked at her made Jennifer feel sorry for him. He looked like a lost soul, sad, in need of help. When he walked toward her, she noticed his left hand holding a dog's leash dangling by his side. He smiled at her, his first hopeful expression.

* * *

The orchestra reached a crescendo, matched by cheers and applause from the audience. The students took their curtain calls like seasoned professionals forming two lines, an honor guard with arms lifted to celebrate Rebecca who pirouetted to center stage where she accepted a bouquet of roses and the adoration of all in attendance. Despite the overflowing support, Rebecca displayed no emotion, no trace of a smile. She searched the auditorium until she discovered her mother applauding, tears of pride glistening on her face. Her gaze shifted slightly left to concentrate on the space, a void that should have been filled by the other most important person in her life.

The students joined hands, forming a single line to take their final bows. They extended their arms over their heads in appreciation and triumph, but Rebecca never joined them. She dropped the roses and ran off, stumbling once, the only misstep she had made all afternoon.

SEVEN

Ron had checked in the administration building, the library, the gymnasium, and with the help of the security guard, several girls' restrooms. As the search became more frantic, he asked the secretary in the principal's office if he could use the phone to call the police. She felt that unnecessary, but he took the phone and dialed nine-one-one despite her protestations.

Two police officers arrived within ten minutes.

"You sure she wouldn't have gone home with a friend?" asked Officer Sanchez, who made it clear he didn't consider this an emergency.

"Maybe a parent gave her a lift," suggested the officer's female partner, Jill Nelson, who appeared more understanding if not empathetic.

"There's no way she would have left on her own or with anyone else but me. I've drilled that into her since... since she was just a baby."

"No brothers or sisters?" Sanchez asked.

"She's my only child."

"Your wife," Nelson intervened, "has she been notified?"

"Died soon after Jenny was born. My daughter's the only family I have."

Sanchez glanced at his watch. "Mr. Butler, there's nothing more we can do here. It's best you get home. With any luck she'll be there waiting for you with an upset stomach from eating too much popcorn at the movies."

"Jenny wouldn't have done that. There's no way she—"

"I've notified my office," said Sanchez. "I'm sure detectives have already been assigned the case." He handed Ron a card. "Call that number when you get home. If your daughter's not there, you'll need to make a more extensive report which will trigger an Amber alert. Let's hope this is only a matter of your daughter deciding to take the bus with her friends. The worst that will happen is for you to put her on punishment for a week."

"You want to try calling your home again?" asked Nelson, who had already taken out her cell phone and offered it to Ron. He nodded appreciation and started dialing.

Sanchez studied him for a moment, then said, "It's unusual nowadays not to have a cell phone. It's almost standard practice for all schoolkids to carry their own."

"Service was cancelled last month." Ron finished dialing and placed the phone to his ear. "A luxury I can't afford, not with my budget."

Sanchez looked at his partner and jotted something in his notepad.

Ron listened to the phone ringing. It would go unanswered.

EIGHT

The five minutes of silence had turned into an argument ten minutes ago and quickly escalated into a heated exchange.

"Liz, I'll make it up to her!"

"How are you gonna do that, Todd?" Liz moved closer to her recalcitrant husband. "Are you going to have her dance here? Maybe we can create the illusion that there's an adoring audience she searches through until she finds her father who joins with them in applauding her, in appreciating the incredible gift she has, the gift she wanted to share with you, for you." She formed two fists but kept her hands firmly pressed against the sides of her legs. "Damn it, you should have been there! You should have seen her! She was so proud until she looked out and found the only empty seat in the place, the only seat that mattered!"

"What do you want me to do? I told you it couldn't be helped. I needed to get those construction plans into City Hall before the close of day or it would have cost us almost—"

"What the hell is wrong with you? That's your daughter, not another one of your drawings for a building that no one will ever live in! You treat her like she's a damn stranger. You always have. But I swear to God, Todd, if you hurt her one more time, I—"

"Hi, Dad."

Both Liz and Todd turned their attention to Rebecca, who gave a weak smile that failed to conceal a face puffy and red and still moist from tears. She closed the front door behind her, cradling the bouquet of roses and carrying over her shoulder a garment bag that contained her costume.

Todd took a step toward his daughter but then stopped. "Becky, I'm sorry. I really tried my best to—"

"I'm glad you didn't come." She tossed the bag onto the couch. "I wasn't very good. Couldn't even hold onto some dumb flowers." She shifted her weight from one leg to the other, bit down lightly on her lower lip but couldn't prevent it from trembling. "I've been thinking, maybe, I should quit dancing and—"

"Rebecca, you were wonderful." Her mother offered the best encouragement she could under the circumstances. "Everyone in that auditorium cheered you. They loved you."

"Loved me?" Rebecca replied in disbelief. "They weren't there for me, Mommy. They're parents. They were there for their kids. That's who they loved. Not me. I was just up on that stage making a fool of myself. But I won't do it again. I swear I won't!" Rebecca slammed the bouquet of flowers on the table and ran out of the room.

Liz looked at Todd with more disappointment than anger. Just before she could speak, he walked away, leaving her to pick up the roses and cradle them in her arms.

Face down on her bed, Rebecca didn't move when her father entered and sat on the edge. He reached for her shoulder, came very close to touching her, but pulled back before he could. He searched for the right words, wanted to say her name, but listened to her voice instead.

"What did I do wrong?" The voice was soft, not accusatory, and if not broken, then surely cracked.

"Becky, you—"

"Why don't you love me?" She finally turned and addressed her father. "I'll do whatever you want me to, but please, Daddy, please Daddy... just..." She sounded like a drowning child, gasping for breath. The air that filled her chest was released through the force of shoulders heaving back and forth. Her sobbing vibrated against his body. He wanted to comfort her, attempted to hold her. An awkward effort at best.

He noticed her favorite teddy bear, old and tattered, a gift she had given herself after a scavenger hunt through dozens of boxes untouched for years and stacked against the walls of a storage room adjacent to the garage. He'd promised to buy her a new one, but she refused. She insisted on keeping the one she had found. She'd argued it had a history and a character all its own and smelled like her father. Gradually, he touched her hair, stroked it gently, and then stopped. He rose quickly from the bed.

"Your mother's worried about you. Come on downstairs and get something to eat."

She watched him cross to the door and then stop. He edged back toward her but never completed the turn.

"This weekend we'll do whatever you want to do. Disneyland. Magic Mountain. The circus is in town. Or we could do a movie, take in a Lakers game." He waited for a response, then placed his hand on the doorknob.

"Venice Beach."

"What?"

She sat up, more in control of her emotions. "For rollerblading." She stood and took a step toward him, then two more confident strides. "Just you and me."

He thought about it for a moment. "But I don't know how to—"

"I'll teach you," she interrupted before he could find an excuse to say no. "It's easy, like riding a bike without sitting down."

"I haven't ridden a bike in more than—"

"Once you know how, you never forget."

He stared at her, waiting for her to come to her senses, offer an alternative. But instead of a change of heart, she touched her index finger to her tongue, then moved it against an imaginary chalkboard. After a moment of resignation, he did the same and then pointed his finger at her, acknowledging her victory. He left, closing the door behind him.

She stood motionless for almost a minute, then returned to the bed where she picked up her teddy bear, held it closely, and smiled for the first time all day.

NINE

WEDNESDAY APRIL 5TH

A single night light filtered through the kitchen area creating small shadows that appeared to end too soon. Ron sat at the breakfast table, numb, paralyzed by fear and tormented by the many thoughts that he couldn't control. He held a portable phone, rested it on his lap. He pushed a button to check the dial tone, then quickly hung up. He buried his face into his hands and prayed for the first time in many years, but cried before he could finish. Where was she? Where was his daughter?

* * *

She lay still, violated by darkness, terrified by her own vivid imagination that, until now, had always comforted her. Her hands were bound, her legs shackled at the ankles, but fear rather than any iron restraints held her in place. It immobilized everything except her heart pounding against her chest as her mind searched for a solution that would bring her home. Where was the light? It must be somewhere, a sliver to provide a hint of the nature and condition of her captivity. She tried counting, tapping her finger against the wall or her foot against the floor, but it only added to a sense of dread, a feeling that the world had deserted her.

"You can scream if you want to," said the peculiar voice, filtering through a cheap speaker that hissed and crackled. "But it won't do you any good." The mouth had come too close to the microphone, causing static and an occasional screeching sound followed by an electronic hiss. The breathing was labored, but as awkward and frightening as the voice sounded, it was oddly soothing at the same time. Perhaps any noise was better than the silence that permitted her mind to conjure up sounds and images more terrifying than any known horror, even this one.

"This is your home now," declared the voice trickling down from the ceiling or from some high-up crevice in the wall in front of her.

Home... For the first time in her brief existence, that word brought her great sadness. She didn't know if she'd ever see it again. But this much was certain: This place would never become the home she now missed most, whatever the voice demanded.

"You will come to love it. Then you will come to love me."

And now the word *love* would have a new meaning, too. How could the most magical and beautiful word in the world, the one that left her father's lips each night, sound so terrifying?

Who was this man behind the voice and darkness? She remembered a damp cloth placed over her mouth and nose; it smelled like laundry detergent. She'd struggled, at least she thought she had, but it wasn't long before she drifted into a dreamlike state, not fully asleep, a sense of floating. Whatever drug he had used had not fully worn off and it made her thirsty and ill, although the uneasiness in her stomach was caused more by fear of the unknown than anything else.

Her father had warned her so many times, "Don't talk to strangers" followed by "Don't ever, ever walk off with someone you don't know." How could she be that stupid? He looked

normal, actually quite nice, so it seemed reasonable, even chari-
table for her to help him find a beloved pet. Still, he was a
stranger and that meant she had violated her father's most
adamant rule, one of the few he had ever imposed on her. He
hated establishing rules for her, almost as much as he hated
punishing her. He had never spanked her. He didn't believe in
that, although there were times she had tested those beliefs
enough for him to reach for his belt, but never unbuckled it. It
was rare for him to yell, which was why she was surprised he
had lost his temper when he dropped her off at school. He must
have been more nervous about his job interview than she had
originally imagined. He told her that people who shouted had a
limited vocabulary. As an insurance policy, she had given him a
pocket dictionary for his last birthday. Sometimes it really is
better to give than receive. The only thing she feared was letting
down her dad, disappointing him. Now this was the ultimate
failure.

As afraid as she was for herself, she was much more frightened for him. Her father was her best friend, but she was his
only friend. He'd given up so much for her, everything, made
one sacrifice after another, fulfilled the roles of father and
mother, and excelled at both. What must he be feeling now?
She knew he would blame himself, never forgive himself if it
turned out the way these things usually turned out. She didn't
want to think about that now. She had to find a way to save
herself, to save him from a lifetime of living without her.

She thought of him attending her third-grade poetry reading. When she'd read her poem entitled "Poem for my Father,"
he'd cried before she completed the first verse. He never missed
anything she did, stage plays, recitals, concerts, singing in the
church choir. Even when she didn't perform solo or have a
speaking part, he'd tear up. She'd played a tree once, covered in
branches and leaves, and she could hear him sniffling from his
center seat in the third row, his favorite spot. Her friends had

told her they had seen him get all choked up on the way to his seat. Someone had pointed out her name in the program and that was all it took for the emotions to be released.

When she was chosen for one of the two leads in her first musical, he attended all the rehearsals by volunteering to be house photographer. He was there early and left late, snapping photos for the school newspaper. They would pay for the copies, which allowed him the chance to keep duplicates for himself without straining the family budget. Opening night, he stood at the head of the line to order a videotape of the production even though he couldn't afford it. He had unsuccessfully attempted to purchase an outdated camcorder, so he'd have a permanent record of her events. Unfortunately, he didn't have sufficient credit on his maxed-out Visa and his cheap smartphone was useless.

He'd once said that his love for her, unlike his charge cards, had no limit. His love had saved her so many times. Now her love for him would need to be strong enough to save them both. That's what she had to believe. That's what she was thinking when her concentration was broken by a shuffling sound, followed by a sad, desperate moan.

She was not alone.

TEN

Ron hadn't cried in an hour, nor had he moved from the corner chair in his daughter's bedroom during the same period. Perhaps the two events were related. If he had moved, gotten up or walked to another spot, the floodgates would have opened. As long as he remained perfectly still, he had a chance to contain the emotions, but any movement, no matter how slight, and the tears would follow the violent shaking that always began deep inside his stomach and worked its way up to his throat, releasing a sound he didn't recognize as his own. He wanted to say her name out loud, Jennifer, but he refused to call her with terror in his voice; that association he could not bear, not tonight, not ever.

He knew every inch of this room, knew where everything should be placed. His daughter had suffered from allergies until she was seven which forced him to encase her pillows, mattress, and box spring with a special covering. He'd removed the carpeting and replaced it with linoleum and then eliminated the drapes and installed wooden shutters. Two air-purifiers ran twenty-four hours a day, tripling his electric bill. He'd dusted, vacuumed, and polished every week. She loved stuffed animals, so he'd selected the ones without much fur and made sure all her dolls had short hair, which he helped her manage until she had gotten old enough to appear indignant at his interference.

His wife had taught him that it was possible to love someone so much that you cried at the very thought of them. That's the love he maintained for Jennifer, his daughter, the child who carried the D.N.A. of his beloved wife Nikki, taken so soon. He was surprised he could love her so much, particularly when her birth coincided with her mother's death, actually caused it, he used to think. He once believed those tears were the result of that tragic connection. He'd look at her sleeping and be reminded of Nikki and then the tears would fall, usually in silence, but occasionally followed by the sound of heartache and pain filtering throughout his body before eventually escaping between trembling lips.

But then at other times he'd think only of Jennifer and the tears would still flow and he knew, right then and there, it couldn't be contained, this feeling he had for her. He wanted to blame her for taking away the woman of his dreams, the one he'd known he would marry the moment she turned around and they made instant eye contact and found themselves laughing for no apparent reason. It didn't take long to realize they didn't need a reason. Being together was sufficient explanation for the joy they shared, and they shared it often and so well.

The desire to blame an infant for the loss of that joy changed the first time Jennifer cried and he discovered she needed him as much as he needed her. They were both helpless. He knew that even if she didn't. As he learned to comfort her better, the pain he felt became more manageable until eventually it was soothed well enough that he believed he could face the future. And when she smiled, displayed a toothless grin that leaped onto his soul, he understood and accepted that his life had changed forever, it would never be his alone.

Ron knew he shouldn't be here, but the room had never

failed to bring him comfort. If he wasn't smiling when he entered, he'd find a reason to before he left. He'd shed his share of tears here, too. When she slept and he stood over her wondering how he could fill the void that her mother had left. Or when he doubted he could give her everything she needed, feared that whatever he had wouldn't be enough. And those tears that occasionally flowed simply from realizing his unconditional love? Those were the healing tears, the ones that purified—to love so much and so completely that you cried at the mere thought of your child. He'd smile at some inconsequential memory of her sleeping or playing with her friends or watching television with him and his eyes would turn misty. While driving home from work, he'd recall how she sounded when she giggled, and it always made him smile. As an infant, she'd wrap her tiny hand around his finger and wouldn't let go. If he tried to put her into her crib, she'd emit such a terrifying wail that he'd quickly forsake the task and hold her until she slept.

It was hard to believe now, but he had wanted a son, even planned for one, decided to decorate the bedroom with sports paraphernalia: a basketball lamp, a baseball throw rug, a crib that could be converted to a racing car bed with sheets, pillowcases, and a blanket that had the Raiders silver and black insignia. (Yes, they were currently losers but by the time his son reached grade school, he was convinced the commitment to excellence would have returned in spades. *Just win, baby!*) And then she was born, and the room would need nothing more than her to make it special, no banners or favorite teams. Her presence alone was sufficient to generate dreams of glory, achieving the ultimate victory. She had made him feel like a champion without ever having to compete for her love, and she had done so with the very first breath she took that had nearly taken his away.

Those cops at the school who had interviewed him could never understand how important she was to him, how she had changed his life, made his life worth continuing when he didn't want to go on. He feared they were treating her like just another Black girl who had run off to have some fun and would be back. They had told him there was nothing more they could do. Wanted him to go home and just wait a reasonable time. *Reasonable?* He had called the number they had given him several times that afternoon to update them, let them know she hadn't returned home. Tried to convince them she would never go off on her own. They treated the whole thing as if he shouldn't be concerned since she was probably with a friend eating popcorn and the worst thing that could happen is she'd have a stomachache.

The worst thing that could happen. How many times had he thought about that? Could anything ever be as bad as the evening he lost his wife? Now the question had confronted him again and provided the answer that drove him to his knees in prayer, a place he'd vowed never to return to. He'd had his battles with God in the past, exhausting conflicts that left him drained and weary. He wanted God to lose, to admit to a horrific mistake, but the best he could manage was a truce. *I won't question why you took her as long as you allow me to keep the child she saved with her dying breath.* That was the agreement, the reason he had stopped fighting, stopped cursing the things he couldn't understand.

Now, it had happened again. His daughter, her daughter, snatched away, a dream stolen before it could be fully realized. His fault. Not the car's. Not the job's. Not the promotion that didn't come or the boss that didn't care about anything but the bottom line. Not even the God that fought him to a draw. His... His! No one else was to blame. He looked around the room. It was much larger now, yet somehow managed to feel claustrophobic, as if being crushed by the pressure of an enormous emptiness, a vacuum that absorbs all your oxygen and leaves you inhaling your own terror and choking on a grief more powerful than the love you thought you'd never lose.

He wanted to think of all the happy times, the special moments committed to memory stored as much in his heart as in his mind. Recalling them never failed to bring a sense of fulfillment, gave him a purpose that would allow him to endure any frustration, transcend any pain. No matter how hard he tried to conjure the magic, all he could think of were the times she was sick, the visits to the emergency room that always came late at night; the ear infections that always occurred on the weekend when the doctor was unavailable until Monday. How he hated the sound of her cries, they made him feel completely helpless. He would have gladly absorbed her anguish, made it his own. What parent wouldn't relieve his child of any illness, at any cost? What kind of anguish was she experiencing now, assuming she was still a... No. He would not complete that thought even though he'd been advised that the longer this went on, the less likely it would end well. He'd give up everything else, but not hope, not the love that kept that hope alive. He knew now why his pleasant memories had betrayed him, replaced them with trips to the hospital and cries late at night. She needed him then as she needed him now, and he could not, would not fail her. She would be found. She must be saved.

ELEVEN

The teardrop fell to the floor and joined the others that preceded it. Jennifer hadn't wanted to cry, hadn't wanted to give that much power to her captor, but after she heard the girl unsuccessfully stifle her sobs, she couldn't stop herself from crying, too. Perhaps it was empathy or a reflex, like a yawn coming from a stranger across the room forcing the same response.

"What's your name?" The question frightened her, then almost as quickly brought her comfort. The voice belonged to a young girl, maybe the same age.

"Jennifer... Jenny."

"I'm Selena," she spoke in a hushed voice, in sporadic phrases. "But some folks call me Sara... which they shouldn't... because it's not short for Selena... not even close."

She sounded as if she would cry after each few words, afraid to speak too loudly or too much. *What had he done to her to make her sound like that?*

"Did he take you, too?"

"Yes."

"How long have you been here?"

"I don't know... I think a week... Maybe longer." Her voice broke, followed by a sad whimper as if the words were causing her pain.

Jennifer hesitated before asking the next question, but she needed to know the answer. "Has he hurt you?"

There was a long silence and Jennifer closed her eyes and lowered her head. If he had taken another girl and let her live this long, then maybe she was safe for a while. She had a million questions, but all of them would be overwhelmed with the next unexpected words.

"My name is Mei Lin," said a voice from the opposite side of the room. "As far as I can tell, I've been here almost a month. But it's hard to tell."

Fluorescent lights sputtered to life and Jennifer saw the room for the first time: large, twice the size of a normal living room and colorless, like a giant storage area or warehouse. Not knowing how long the lights would remain on, she absorbed as many details as she could. Cement walls padded with a thick insulation going from the floor to several inches below the ceiling, which must have been at least ten to twelve feet high. Video cameras are positioned in every corner. No windows that she could discover. There were two toilets, one on either side of the room. Each had a thin silk screen that served as partition, offering minimal privacy. She noticed a sink, a small refrigerator, a Styrofoam container the size of a picnic cooler, a portable floor fan in one corner, and a larger one on a stand in the center. She couldn't tell for sure, but the room appeared to be below ground level, some type of basement which one of her teachers had told her was illegal in California. Although given the situation confronting her and the two girls who shared the accommodations, thinking about building code violations didn't seem terribly useful.

Mei Lin and Selena were opposite each other, lying on narrow cots set against the wall. Unlike her, the other girls had chains around their waists long enough for them to move six feet or so to reach the toilets but not each other. She was confined directly across from them, near the middle of the wall, shackled around both ankles and wrists.

Who abducted them? Was it more than one person? Did the girls ever leave the room? How often did he visit and why? Did he bring food? Did he take them outside? Why did he take them? Should she ask all those questions now or wait until later, when she could learn more about the girls and maybe the man who—

She heard noises at the door: A lock turned, metal scraped a surface, and a heavy bolt lifted then dropped into place. The other two girls instantly tensed up, like frightened animals in a cage. A door, metal, or wood heavily reinforced with steel bars, slid open, slamming with a loud thud. A man stood at the doorway, holding what seemed to be a long chain. It wasn't a leash, and when he approached her, she knew he wouldn't be using it on a dog. She recognized him as the man who had lied to her, taken her away from her father. Except he didn't look as nice, and he certainly didn't exhibit any helplessness.

"You're safe now," he said. His voice was surprisingly calm, almost sympathetic. If she didn't know better, she would have thought he was trying to help, apologize for someone else's behavior.

"I won't let anyone hurt you." He placed the chain around her waist, similar to the ones around Selena and Mei Lin but much longer. She assumed she needed extra length to use the makeshift bathroom and reach the appliances. Whatever else she would learn about her captor, one thing was certain: He had been planning this for some time.

"Children killing children. Predators everywhere." He removed the chains around her ankles and the constraints around her wrists.

"It will all end soon. To begin again. A new world." He

looked at all three girls, studied them for a moment as if admiring paintings in a museum. "Our world." He went to stroke Jennifer's hair, but she pulled back, pressed herself against the wall.

"Jennifer," he said softly. How did he know her name? She looked at the cameras in all four corners and realized small microphones were attached. He could see and listen to everything. She wondered if he was recording them and would play the tapes at night like some sick—

"Or would you prefer I call you Jenny?" He interrupted her thoughts or more likely confirmed them. "There's no need to fear me," he leaned closer to her, "unless you defy me, which I know you won't, at least, not more than once." He moved a step away from her, giving her enough space to breathe again.

"Why did you take me? What do you want with me?" She hoped her questions hadn't conveyed fear, even though she knew her upper body trembled when she delivered the final few words.

"You will know all there is to know in due time."

"When?" she asked and realized by the body language of her fellow captives that she was being warned to stop.

"Soon," he answered. "When my task is done, we will move to a better place. A place without fear or ignorance." He stared at Jennifer. His piercing blue eyes had darkness in the center, a strange void, as if something had died there and been removed, but not before it was left to rot and stain. "And where there is no further need for questions, only answers to be revealed and rejoiced."

A better place... A place without fear. Was he talking about death? Was he planning on killing them, sacrificing them to some bizarre faith he had? And if so, what was he waiting for?

"I have to leave you, but I won't be away long. I want you to get to know each other. I insist that you do. You're family now. It's important that you behave as such. We're all we have, and we must depend on each other. I know you won't disappoint me."

His assurance came as both a command and a threat.

Jennifer watched him walk toward the metal door and step outside. He slid the door shut halfway. "I'll bring you food in an hour. You must all be hungry... Especially you, Jenny. I must admit, I prefer Jennifer, there's a certain lyrical quality to it, musical and poetic. But I want to satisfy you, and if calling you Jenny brings you happiness, then that's how you'll be known."

The door shut and Jennifer could hear a deadbolt drop into place. *I want to satisfy you* rang in her ears. It wasn't an offering of support. Even at her tender age she knew that much. And it made her feel dirty. She looked at the two girls for answers, a response that would make sense of this whole situation. She started to speak when she realized for the first time, there was a fourth cot across from her. Empty for now. She wondered how long it would take before the square would be completed. The lights went out and the girls were left to whisper in the darkness, except now Jennifer had nothing to say.

TWELVE

FRIDAY APRIL 7TH

Mrs. Newman held her cat Belle close to her chest as if she feared that one of the two detectives would snatch her away. The temperature had dropped in the last few minutes, an uncomfortable chill in the air that compromised the health of her feline who suffered from the peculiar climate changes associated with the Santa Ana winds. Belle had developed the same allergies which afflicted Mrs. Newman, but without the advantage of prescription drugs supplied by Medicare. She was tempted to return to her apartment but didn't want these strangers to enter with her. True enough, they were policemen doing their duty, but they were still strangers to her and, therefore, would be viewed as intruders to Belle who remained very protective of their home.

Detective Peter McKay, a twenty-five-year no-nonsense veteran, had been asking the questions while his partner, John Carrey, took notes. Carrey was five years younger but had joined the force earlier and was two years closer to retirement. Mrs. Newman thought they could easily be actors on one of those police dramas she used to love to watch until the stories turned into science and technology lectures. She was waiting for one to play "good cop" while the other became more threatening, but since she was simply a witness and not a suspect, evidently there was no need to perform those roles, at least not yet. For the moment, she would cooperate, even provide advice if asked, as long as the interrogation remained civil.

"He was very upset with her. Screaming to get in the car." She shook her head in disapproval and then waved her hand toward the street curb in front of her apartment building.

"Did she seem frightened of him?" asked McKay.

"Lovely little girl. I'd let her hold Jezebel... Belle doesn't let just anyone hold her. Accused her of public defecation he did."

"I beg your pardon?"

"That man stepped in feces and had the nerve to accuse my Jezebel as if she were some common alley cat. Or a dog!"

The two detectives exchanged amused looks.

"You never answered Detective McKay's question," Carrey said. "Did his daughter seem frightened?"

"I'm not a mind reader," she snapped. Having demonstrated she would not tolerate rudeness or intimidation; she could now comfortably comply with any appropriate requests and provide useful assistance. "Although if Belle could talk, you'd have all the answers you'd ever need. Did you know that in ancient Egypt felines were worshipped for their magical powers? They were believed to have had psychic abilities and could predict the future."

Carrey put away his notebook. "Who would they tell and how?"

Mrs. Newman raised her eyes toward the heavens as if she were dealing with incompetents, or worse, nonbelievers. "You've obviously never raised a cat or experienced their personal connection with humans."

"Raised?" asked Carrey, not bothering to conceal his cynicism.

"Owned, if you prefer," Mrs. Newman responded,

matching the detective's scorn with condescension. If they wanted to prove they had the advantage in this relationship, her equilibrium had been tested by better. "Although cats are hardly capable of being owned. Very independent, you know." She hoped they had gotten the message that cats weren't the only ones capable of holding their own.

Carrey nodded. "So I've heard, although I'm more a dog lover. They're very loyal."

"Really?" she said. "Unexamined loyalty is hardly a virtue, especially when slavish behavior is demanded by those more insecure than their animals." She lowered her eyes to not embarrass the poor boy any further.

McKay handed her his card. "Mrs. Newman, if you think of anything that might help us, you can reach me at that number."

She took a step and positioned herself between the two detectives, surreptitiously searched the area, and then asked confidentially, "You think he did something to his own daughter?" She waited for a response and when she didn't get one, assumed the worst. "Shame, such a precious little girl. It's always the innocent ones who suffer."

The detectives proceeded to their car. Mrs. Newman stroked her cat and then suddenly seemed alarmed. She lowered her eyes and discovered cat droppings. She stared sternly at her cat, then looked around to make sure no one had noticed. She entered her building after giving a brief but innocent wave to the detectives as they drove off to their next appointment.

* * *

The school's security guard pointed toward the area where Ron had parked to drop off his daughter.

"I wish I had intervened or at least walked over to the car, see if that girl needed my help."

This time Detective Carrey conducted the interview while McKay took notes. "Did you notice if she had any bruises or if he made physical contact with her?"

The guard thought about it for a moment. "It's possible, but as I said, I was a distance from them. All I know is, he was very agitated, and he was taking it out on her. As I recall, she may have hurt her head but I'm not sure how."

"And you didn't go to her aid, offer assistance?"

The guard recoiled from the accusation.

"Of course I would have if she was injured and I sure as hell wouldn't have left the area."

The longer McKay studied him, the more uncomfortable he became, shifting back and forth and nervously tugging at his collar.

"Now that I think of it, maybe he was the one who hit his head on the car door." He directed his attention to McKay's silent partner. "Yes, that was it. Getting out of the car, he hit his forehead, and it made him really angry, blamed her. You could tell she wanted to get away."

Detective McKay handed him a card. The detectives left without shaking hands. If they hurried, they'd make it to Mr. Butler's workplace in time to interview his supervisor.

After introductions and a quick tour of the facilities, both detectives accompanied Sheldon Miller to his office.

"He was disappointed he didn't get the promotion. But that seemed natural." They entered the office. McKay looked at the desk, unorganized, folders scattered about. Doughnut boxes, food cartons, bags from fast-food restaurants littered the area. Newspapers were balled up or unfolded, mostly sports pages.

"I tried to explain to him that it wasn't anything personal. In fact, I thought he'd be better off without the additional responsibilities. Could spend more time at home." Miller looked away, uncomfortable.

"Is something wrong?" asked Detective McKay.

"I feel kinda guilty. I guess I made it seem he didn't get promoted because he had a kid to take care of and couldn't work when I needed him... It's strange, though."

"What is?" asked Carrey.

"That he got there late to pick her up. I mean, I let him off early 'cause he said they had something to do."

"What type of employee was he?" asked McKay. "Any problems? Attitude, attendance, working with others?"

"He was late sometimes. Had excuses about driving his daughter to school. But when he was here, he was fine. A bit argumentative at times, stubborn. But nothin' unusual. Truth be told, he was probably my best worker."

"Then why didn't you give him the promotion?" asked Carrey.

Miller shrugged. "Thought I was doing him a favor. Hate to think I pushed him over the edge."

"We'd like to take a look at his personnel file," said McKay. "That okay with you?"

"I'll have to check with the human resources administrator. Privacy laws and all."

"We are the law, Mr. Miller," said McKay with authority. "Since a child is missing, I suggest you cooperate, and that you do so quickly."

"I'll make sure you get everything you need."

"That would be in everyone's best interest," said McKay.

"Can I ask you something?"

McKay nodded.

"You think he's dangerous? I mean, should I let him come back to work? Wouldn't want to see anyone else hurt."

Carrey intervened. "There's no proof that anyone has been

hurt. You have any information that would lead us to believe otherwise?"

Miller rubbed his chin nervously. "No. None at all. Except these things usually don't turn out well, do they?"

"Mr. Miller," McKay said, displaying noticeable annoyance, "we'd like to see the personnel file now."

"Don't get me wrong. I'm hoping for the best. Naturally anyone would. Her being so young. But—"

Carrey cut him off. "Where's the human resources office?"

Miller rubbed his neck and pulled down his shirtsleeve. "I'll take you there."

Carrey motioned with his hand. "After you."

THIRTEEN

Ron lined up small train engines on a wooden track configured around a modified card table. When Jenny first went to school, he would rearrange the tracks every week or so, add a tunnel or two, place a bridge on one side and a depot on the other. He would bring her home and wait by her bedroom door for her reaction, which was always enthusiastic excitement. "Wow! That's cool!" Then she would rearrange the whole configuration until she was satisfied that it fit her personality and her idea of a perfect train station. He didn't mind that she destroyed the work that had taken him several hours to complete. He enjoyed watching her create her own masterpiece, even if it was completely implausible and would cause major train wrecks to occur in several strategic locations. After all, she was the conductor of her own locomotive company and could manage it any way she chose, even though it sometimes hurt his feelings, gave him a sense of inadequacy that he couldn't design a track that satisfied her personal aesthetics or travel expectations.

After she had annihilated his work, she'd step back to admire her dramatic alterations. Then she'd turn to him and wait for his approval.

"Brilliant, much better than anything I could have done," he'd always respond. And when she smiled, he'd add, "It's almost as beautiful as you."

She'd raise her eyebrows and dismiss his compliment with a look of disbelief, then rush toward him and give him a hug. "You really like it, Dada?"

"I love it," he would answer. "But I love you so much more."

Up until last year, she had called him Dada unless she was around her friends and then she would use a more sophisticated semi-adult voice in conveying the formal title "Dad." Until she was almost four, she tripled the word, "Da." It always brought music to his ears and a smile to his face. "DaDaDa... DaDaDa... DaDaDa," she'd call out, searching for him in the kitchen or bathroom or her tiny legs running out of control into his bedroom, serving as his personal alarm clock that would go off all hours of the day and night. Now that she was on the verge of becoming a teenager in two short years, "Dad" had permanently replaced "Dada," except on those occasions when he tickled her and she giggled hysterically, having no other recourse but to demand: "Dada, stop!" Although they both knew the demands weren't to be taken seriously. In fact, every plea was actually a dare to continue, to find new spots that would generate a higher-pitched reaction. He could almost hear those giggles now. Would give anything to hear them now. They had a way of escaping from her throat and leaping directly inside his heart where they would reverberate for hours.

He picked up one of the engines and studied it, trying to remember the name she had given it. All wooden train engines looked the same to him regardless of size or color. They all had pretty much identical faces carved in the front and painted ghost white. Most had the same frozen smiles, but the work engines displayed more serious expressions, and one or two even looked angry.

He saw his image in the dresser mirror. Unshaven and

exhausted, he initially didn't recognize himself and thought there was someone else in the room. But he knew he was alone and that thought terrified him more than any intruder could. He returned the engine to its track and looked across the room to Jennifer's bed, perfectly made with a variety of dolls propped up against two pillows. A yellow sweater had been tossed on the bedspread, probably from a last-minute change of wardrobe. He tried to remember if she had worn a sweater that morning. Maybe she decided she didn't need it. Maybe she was cold now and wished she had brought it with her. He hoped that was the only discomfort challenging her.

He folded the sweater across his arm, held it close. It smelled like her, clean with the scent of vanilla from the lotion she'd use every day to avoid dry skin. It was the same scent her mother used to love, but she had no way of knowing that. He had never told her. There was so much he had kept locked inside until she was old enough to understand. In truth, he simply couldn't tell her, couldn't risk talking about the past for fear he'd never face the future. That would change if he was given the chance. She had the right to know everything, and he was beginning to regret he had failed her, left her without the memories she was entitled to have. Her mother gave her life in order to bring her into this world and that gave his daughter the right to have the same pain and joy and loss and love that had been a part of his existence since that fateful moment when he lost a wife and gained a daughter.

He walked slowly toward her dresser, slid open the bottom drawer, and gently placed the sweater inside. It belonged in her closet, but he couldn't bear the thought of seeing all her clothes hanging neatly the way she loved to arrange them. He closed the drawer halfway and stopped to study a framed photo of Jennifer taken at her fifth birthday party with actors dressed as Barney and Winnie the Pooh.

He touched the glass, ran his finger over her smile, and used his shirtsleeve to dry the tear that had fallen on it.

FOURTEEN

Jennifer didn't know when the light would appear or how long it would remain. There was no reliable pattern, no rhyme or reason for darkness or light. Time was meaningless. Night was impossible to distinguish from day. Sleeping gave her no clue. She couldn't tell if she had slept for hours or minutes or, sometimes, at all. Her waking thoughts blended into dreams, then too often into nightmares. Even her hunger came and went so inconsistently that she couldn't trust her impulse to eat.

In the last two days the three girls had managed to talk a lot. At first, their discussions caused them to cry and be frightened, but eventually their conversations had a comforting effect. They tried not to talk about him or their condition, but shared stories about their families.

Selena was the youngest of six children. She had long, thick black hair that managed to shine even in these dim surroundings. Her family was in the country illegally and she worried that her brothers and sisters would be reluctant to go to the authorities, fearful that they would be arrested and then deported. Her parents didn't speak much English and had few friends. It would be unlikely that she could count on them to do anything but pray, and knowing her mother, she would cry while saying them.

He had abducted her from school when she decided to ignore the bus, which had often made her sick. She hated the smell and the constant jostling of her small body back and forth on old torn leather bench seats. The constant stopping and starting at red lights or to let off students was almost as annoying as the boys who sat behind her and pulled her hair. Except for Enzo, who didn't pull too hard and was really cute. So, at the last moment, she avoided the unpleasant ride and chose to walk home, taking what was supposed to be a shortcut. It turned out to be the longest journey of her young life.

Jennifer liked Selena a lot. She was shy and fragile but had such a wonderful smile. Perhaps it was so special because she was the only girl who had managed one, at least for the time Jennifer had been with them.

Mei Lin's brother studied medicine in college. Her sister was a high school honor student. Mei Lin, as the baby in the family, remained her parents' favorite. She defied them only when it came to hip-hop. She admitted to the girls that she was afraid her father would find and listen to her iPod and if she ever got out of this dungeon she would be punished until she was eighteen or older. Even though her father was born here, whenever their cultures or generations clashed, he would shake his head and walk away mumbling something about "Americans."

It didn't help that she had posters of Beyoncé, provocatively dressed, on her bedroom walls. Her father had ripped down the life-size poster of Prince wearing his classic purple velvet satin suit. Although she had to admit that a life-size poster of Prince "didn't exactly take up a lot of space." Then she looked at Jennifer and Selena, quickly evaluated the insulated walls, and announced, "Come to think of it, this place could use a poster here or there."

In fact, that might have been the day Selena smiled for the first and only time.

Mei Lin had been abducted at an amusement park. Her fourth-grade class had gone there as an award for selling the most baked goods for her school's fundraiser. She didn't want to go on the roller coasters, too dangerous. While she was waiting for her friends to ride, he approached her, offering a hamburger and a drink.

"My son ordered two and I don't want to throw it away," he said. "It would be a sin."

Ordinarily, she would have refused. *Don't take candy from strangers* and all that. But he seemed nice, and he mentioned his son and sin, which made him a father and religious and safe, or so she thought. It turned out that the Viper ride at Six Flags posed far less of a threat.

Anyway, she was starving and if she ate quickly, she wouldn't have to deal with her teacher wanting to know where she got the food. She took two quick bites and gulped down her drink, which had a bittersweet aftertaste. She didn't remember much after that, just a sensation of floating, dreaming.

Jennifer admired her hair; it was also long and jet-black but not as thick as Selena's. It looked like thin strains of silk delicately braided in the back. She was only nine, which made her the youngest in the group. Her eyes were so sad, like they were holding back tears and secrets and too many regrets for her someone her age. She had been here the longest, a month or more. Jennifer wanted to ask her what she had experienced, endured. But knowing what to expect didn't bring her comfort and she didn't want Mei Lin to relive anything that would cause those eyes to reveal how they began to look that way.

"Selena, toss me a roll of tissue?" said Jennifer.

"How come?" Selena asked.

"I'll show you."

Jennifer caught the roll. "How many dinners have we had since I've been here?"

"Three," answered Selena."

"I didn't eat one," said Mei Lin. "The meatloaf was nasty."

Jennifer tore off three sheets of toilet tissue and placed them underneath her cot. She tossed back the roll to Selena.

"What you do that for," asked Selena.

"We must find a way to keep track of time. We can count the meals we eat or the number of times we sleep."

"How about each time one of us takes a bath?" offered Selena.

"Anything that helps us to know how long we've been here," said Jennifer. "I'll tear one sheet for each day that I've been away from my dad. It's important."

"Why?" asked Mei Lin.

"'Cause we have to believe this is temporary. We'll count the days till we're back home. It's the only way to keep our hope up. He can't ever think he's made us accept this as our home because it's not and never will be."

"I won't let him control that," said Mei Lin.

"Me neither," Selena agreed.

"Good," said Jennifer.

They heard footsteps down the stairs followed by fumbling to unlock the door. He entered the room and proceeded straight to Jennifer.

"It's time for your bath," he said, then unchained her.

Based on what Selena and Mei Lin had told her, she should have expected this. Mei Lin had taken baths once a day until Selena arrived. After that, they alternated every other night. Now with Jennifer added to the equation, the schedule had changed again.

"I don't want a bath," she said, afraid to look at the other girls, not wanting them to be penalized for her confrontation.

"Hygiene's as necessary as water and air," he said. "That's not a matter for negotiation."

Jennifer felt sick. Her body trembled. What was he going to do to her? Was he going to undress her or watch her bathe? Or as he had for Selena and Mei Lin on other occasions, would he wait outside, keeping the key to the lock?

"Your water's getting cold," he warned. "Don't expect me to warm it for you. We don't waste God's resources in this house."

She wanted to stand, could sense his impatience, but the weight on her shoulders combined with the burden she carried in her heart, prevented her from rising from the cot.

He began to unbuckle his belt. Selena quickly stood as if her effort would encourage Jennifer to do the same. Mei Lin attempted to stand but could only manage to sit on the edge of her cot, her arms nervously folded around her chest, her gaze diverted to the floor.

Jennifer understood that this man had already accomplished the goal of terrorizing this young girl, who often balled herself up in a fetal position and cried herself to sleep. Or worse, she would stare vacantly into space for hours at a time. Selena still displayed some fight, if not outright defiance, but it was increasingly rare. Jennifer decided to avoid a battle with this man that would only result in defeat for herself as well as for the other girls. If she complied with his directives but did it her way after standing up to him, perhaps she'd gain a slight moral victory for them all. And as insignificant as that might be, it might make a difference in the long run.

Jennifer took a deep breath, refusing to cower in his presence. She stood and walked past his outstretched hand, waiting at the door for him to take her upstairs.

After they left, Selena took a roll of toilet tissues and tore off a number of sheets, placing them underneath her cot.

FIFTEEN

Ron had driven by the Culver City Police Department many times. He never paid much attention to it. It appeared rather small, a substation designed to handle minor arrests, a holding pen for those awaiting bail or a background check before being released on their own recognizance. It turned out to be a much larger facility than anticipated. The parking lot held dozens of police vehicles, several specially equipped vans, and an armor-plated truck used by either a bomb squad or SWAT team.

He waited inside in a common area that presented little privacy. Officers and detectives shared cubicles configured in such a way as to suggest seniority or rank. It smelled like a large storage room, musty, except this place didn't hold anyone's belongings, far from it. Ron wasn't sure why it reminded him of hospitals. Perhaps it was because he didn't feel comfortable in either place. People visited hospitals when they had no alternative. They needed help or they needed a cure. So they placed their hopes and too often their lives into the hands of others and prayed for a miracle. He wondered how many murderers and rapists and drug dealers had been marched through this place to be interrogated until they confessed to the crimes they committed or admitted to some that they hadn't.

Then he thought about the victims who came here seeking justice, forced to relive the ordeal by speaking to professionals who took notes dispassionately—the result of listening to one too many horrific stories of violence to act surprised or feel any genuine emotion. That was another thing police stations had in common with hospitals, whether dealing with detectives or surgeons: Necessity dictated a certain detachment, a maddening coldness. Your pain wasn't anything new to them and they couldn't afford to be moved by it.

His discomfort with his surroundings weren't helped by the fact that Ron shared a condition common to many African American men, passed down through generations, father to son, uncle to nephew, older brother to younger siblings—a mistrust of police, not limited to race but certainly heightened by it. Power, enhanced by a uniform, a gun, and a badge, tended to corrupt the nature of relationships. And if you were presumed guilty because of the color of your skin or viewed as dangerous by those with the responsibility to serve and protect, then any chance encounter, no matter how casual or innocent, could escalate to a physical confrontation with little provocation. A sudden unexpected move or a hand to the pocket to retrieve keys or reaching inside the glove compartment when asked for your registration was sufficient for an officer to feel threatened, endangered, and react accordingly with deadly force.

So now Ron sat powerless in a wooden chair across from Detective McKay seated behind his desk while the other detective, Carrey, stood by as if offering back-up protection, ready to pounce. The people he had been cautioned against all his life, advised to avoid at all costs, were the very people he needed most, the men who might save his only child.

"It's been four days that I've been dealing with your department and have gotten nowhere. Have you learned anything about my daughter?"

"Would you like some coffee, Mr. Butler?" asked Carrey.

Before he could answer no, McKay spoke. "Your neighbor said you and your daughter were having an argument the morning you took her to school."

"I was running late and—"

"The security guard at the school also said you appeared angry when you dropped her off," said Carrey, who didn't pursue the coffee offer. Ron now understood why one sat while the other roamed freely, hovering over the proceedings. It forced Ron to continually change focus, like a bystander watching a tennis match, turning from one player to the other, except this was no game and he was no bystander. Above all else, he feared he was quickly losing points with these two detectives, and ultimately the match.

"I don't understand... I came down here because you said you wanted to go over some things. I thought you might—"

"Mr. Butler, we're trying to get as much information as possible that would help us find your daughter."

"By asking me if Jenny and I were fighting?"

"Maybe she was afraid to come home."

"My daughter's never been afraid of me in her entire—"

"I never said she was afraid of you." McKay said "you" as if he had solicited a valuable piece of evidence that would lead to a confession. "I said she might be afraid of coming home."

"There's no one else at home but me. What else could you possibly mean?"

"Did you blame her for not getting your promotion?" asked Carrey.

"Blame her? What the hell are you talking about?"

"You left work early and yet you got to the school late. How is that?" McKay asked. Ron assumed this was a routine the partners had perfected over the years. Keep alternating the questions, tightening the vise, to keep a suspect off balance, splitting the attention between the two of them.

"I wanted to go to the store and buy her some video games. Then I had intended to go to the grocery to get some things to make her favorite dinner."

"Was it a special occasion?" Carrey took his turn.

"Yeah. I didn't get promoted, but I still had her and that was worth celebrating. Any more questions?"

"What games did you get her?" Carrey continued.

"None. My car broke down on the way to Fox Hills Mall and it took me an hour before I got it running."

"You call Triple A?" McKay moved away, making it more difficult for Ron to keep both of them in his vision without having to turn one way, then the other.

"I called them in the morning the first time the car broke down. That's the fourth time in the last two months. They don't come out after four calls unless I pay for it."

"We're going to need to take some information, check out your story." Carrey moved closer to him, blocking his view of McKay.

Ron stood angrily and noticed that the two detectives immediately took a defensive position which, as he had learned from previous experience, might not remain passive for long.

"Check out?" Ron found it difficult to breathe. "You're gonna waste time verifying that I have a broken-down car while my daughter's in danger, taken by God knows who?"

"We don't know that she's been taken by anyone, Mr. Butler. And we certainly don't know that she's in danger. Do you know that?" asked McKay.

Ron realized the implication of the question and didn't bother to hold back his contempt.

"I know my daughter's not home with me for the first time

since she was three days old. I know someone or something is keeping her from that home. And I know I want you to find out who or what the fuck it is!"

"That's good, Mr. Butler," McKay leaned against his desk. "Because we want to find out, too. And we will. With or without your cooperation. If you want to help, you need to sit down and answer our questions no matter how long that may take. The sooner you do that, the sooner we'll find her."

"Isn't it true that when a child is abducted, goes missing, if you locate them within the first seventy-two hours there's a chance you'll find them alive. But—"

"Actually, it's less than seventy-two hours," corrected Carrey.

Ron looked at the two detectives. He had never felt this helplessness, never needed help so desperately from the very people he had avoided so long, virtually all his life. Even as a young boy, he had observed instances where "To Serve and Protect" was a slogan that didn't always apply to him or his community. In fact, it often provided the police with the justification to inflict punishment on anyone who remotely appeared to threaten public safety. Being Black was enough of a threat, especially if you were with friends who looked like you.

Ron knew times had changed. At least, he wanted to believe that they had. This wasn't his father's or grandfather's L.A.P.D. Still, memories dictated future behavior and his memories of past mistreatment by the police hadn't faded. All that would change if these two detectives would use their skill to find his daughter, to safely return her to him. If that happened, he would sing the praises of the police for the rest of his life.

He slowly sat down, prepared to answer all questions these two men asked, no matter how much they stung. He just wanted this part to be over as quickly as possible so they could turn their attention to who took Jennifer.

He answered questions for the next two hours, refusing drink when his throat was dry or suggestions for a bathroom break when he needed to go or any other option that would delay this session. At the end, the detectives thanked him for his cooperation, and he left without shaking their hands.

SIXTEEN

SATURDAY APRIL 8TH

Her father kept his promise and rose early in the morning and prepared breakfast. To Rebecca's surprise he didn't read his *Wall Street Journal* or *New York Times* but talked about how much he was looking forward to proving everyone wrong. She watched him put on his knee and elbow pads. He did a few stretching exercises attempting to impress her and her mom who handed him his sunglasses that he wore as if going to his own movie premier. He crossed his arms in a defiant stance and like Tom Brady shouted, "Let's go!"

She appeared to be a tiny tugboat pulling a freighter without the benefit of the ocean's assistance. Rebecca yanked her father's arms, spun him around, and flung him forward like a rock on wheels ejected from a human slingshot.

Totally out of control with arms flailing wildly, Todd sped past other rollerbladers barely missing a dog, a baby in a stroller, an officer on a Segway, a juggler, and a young woman wearing only a T-shirt and a thong drawing penciled portraits for five dollars.

Rebecca raced after her father, gracefully avoiding the crowd on the bicycle pathway yards from Muscle Beach.

"Dad! Keep your arms tucked. You're gonna hit somebody!"

A teen zipped in front of him. Todd managed to avoid a collision with the boy by crashing into a trash can and diving into a mound of sand.

"My bad!" The teen apologized without stopping to help. Todd watched him skate toward a sausage stand.

Rebecca helped her twisted father to his feet.

"Yeah, you're bad. I'm bad. We're all bad. And some of us are evil." He brushed himself off and searched for blood or broken bones.

"He was trying to tell you he was sorry, Dad. My bad means my mistake or my fault."

Todd stood unsteady, slowly regaining his balance while he thought about his daughter's clarification. "I knew that," he replied sheepishly.

"You all right?"

"Do we have to come back tomorrow?"

She smiled and nodded yes.

"In that case, my ankle's broken and I threw out my back."

"Pizza and chicken wings should help." She pointed toward one of the eateries along Venice walkway. "Pepperoni on the pizza, Buffalo sauce on the chicken. And an extra-large orange soda."

"I don't know if I'll be able to carry both the food and drinks."

"If you have to make two trips, I'll understand."

He gave her a look of abject surrender. "You're starting to sound like your mother."

She touched her index finger to her tongue and then rubbed it on an imaginary chalkboard. He did the same in recognition that she scored a victory, and then pulled out his wallet and skated toward the pizza parlor.

Rebecca skated toward a water fountain, took a sip, and stared at the vast ocean glistening under the sun, sailboats gliding effortlessly along its smooth surface. This tranquil scene was as beautiful as the entire day had been. Rebecca couldn't remember the last time she had been alone with her father for this long. He really wasn't that bad a skater. After all, he could have been a lot worse. It was difficult enough maneuvering around the Venice Beach crowd without having to be distracted numerous times by the colorful and often exotic entertainers, bodybuilders, and half-naked cyclists. She had noticed more than a few nubile attractive skaters attempting to get his attention, but he was too busy trying to stand up. She couldn't blame them.

He was handsome, in great shape due to his morning workouts with his trainer. He had the right amount of distinguished gray at the sides of his hair that would be styled every ten days at his favorite Beverly Hills salon. He even looked cool with his elbow and knee pads and a bright red helmet. She loved it in those rare times that he would either take her to or pick her up from school. Her classmates were used to fancy cars and celebrity parents, but her girlfriends were still impressed with her dad. They thought he was a movie star or a famous model. They all had huge crushes that became obvious every time they would suggest a sleepover at her home. She wished they could see him now, standing in a long food line, in his Nike shorts and tie-dyed shirt that she had made him wear.

It would make him fit in, she told him. "I don't want to fit in," he said, then admired himself in the full-length mirror. "Well, maybe just this one time," he shrugged, and viewed how he looked side to side.

He waved at her just as an attractive blond skated up behind him, engaging him in a conversation Rebecca wished she was close enough to overhear. She figured this was going to take a while and headed to the skateboarding rink, a bowl-shaped area eight to ten feet deep. The recently redesigned park had an assortment of ramps and rails. She watched in astonishment as one death-defying feat was matched or surpassed by the next. She wondered if she could convince her dad to give it a shot. Maybe she'd be able to convince him after they ate, although, on second thought, that might not be a good idea for her dad or the surrounding skaters.

She admired the painted murals covering every inch of the large retaining walls that surrounded the park. Even the gang tags were artistically sprayed on and seemed to provide more of a welcome than a warning.

"Excuse me."

She turned around and saw a man holding a dog leash.

"Did you happen to see a small brown and white cocker spaniel?"

She shook her head, no.

"It's my daughter's dog. I was taking it for a walk when it broke away. Someone told me it ran this way... Look, I'll give you five dollars if you help me find it."

Rebecca searched the food line and saw her father was close to the order window and now busily chatting away with several people in line. Mr. Popularity.

She turned back toward the man who looked increasingly in need of help. "I have to wait for my father."

He handed her the dog leash. "If you go around the back, I'll go the other way. Between us, we should be able to get him before your father ever misses you."

She looked at her dad who had finally made it to the window. "What's its name?"

The man gave a grateful smile. "Freedom," he said.

She skated toward the left of the pavilion area.

The man observed Rebecca skating away, the back of her head, long wavy reddish-blond hair flowing behind her, shimmering underneath the bright sun. His attention gradually shifted to her small, tight waist, to the white shorts that gently clung to her body and then her legs, calves so firm, young, tender, well-shaped and extenuated by the lift caused by her skates. He rubbed his moist palm against his thigh as his pretty helper disappeared behind the first large mural, a depiction of a superhero riding a skateboard, rescuing a damsel in distress.

Freedom, what a clever and appropriate response, he thought to himself and then released a brief chuckle.

* * *

Todd skated cautiously, carrying a pizza box, drinks, and a bucket of chicken wings. Proud that he could balance all this by himself, he would make certain his daughter adequately conveyed his impressive skills to her mother. This day hadn't turned out to be as bad as he'd thought it would. After they ate, he would find that artist he almost ran over and get her to draw a portrait of Rebecca and himself, standing united on their skates.

He could hardly wait to get the drawing done and show it to his wife. He searched the area and was relieved to discover the artist hadn't left. Then he looked for his daughter, already picturing the way they would look in that portrait. Yes, that image would be worth the bumps, bruises, and sore muscles likely to last for at least a week. Maybe longer.

SEVENTEEN

"Rebecca Roth, daughter of prominent architect and civic leader, Todd Roth, was abducted this afternoon at Venice Beach."

Ron watched the television image of Todd Roth gradually replaced by a photo of Roth's daughter, Rebecca. A montage of photos followed: Rebecca playing outside in the yard, a current school I.D. of her wearing her class uniform and smiling, a portrait with her leaning against a grand piano looking off to the side, and the final image of her dressed as a ballerina, arms gracefully lifted over her head.

"Police Chief Anderson and F.B.I. representatives visited Mr. Roth and his wife, Elizabeth, at their Bel-Air home. Mayor Reynolds promised to use the full resources of the city to locate the twelve-year-old."

Publicity photos of Todd and Liz Roth attending various civic events filled the screen along with hotline numbers to call with information concerning the abduction.

The door buzzer sounded twice and then, after a beat, a third time. Ron rose from the couch, his attention remaining on the television.

"A news conference is scheduled at City Hall tomorrow, Sunday afternoon, at 2 P.M. where the family will make their first public statement. Anyone with any information regarding the possible whereabouts of Rebecca Roth should contact—"

He turned off the television with the remote and crossed to the intercom, pushing the access button. He didn't need to ask who wanted entry. He had been anxiously awaiting the visit ever since he received the call this morning. He opened the door and waited for the two detectives to exit the elevator and arrive at his apartment.

"We appreciate you seeing us," said McKay. Carrey stood behind, staring ahead, trying to see inside as much as possible.

"Something's wrong, isn't it? Whenever police come to your door, the news can't be good."

McKay replied, "We don't have any news to report. For police, that can be good, too."

Ron remained motionless, unaware that he was blocking access.

"Can we come in?" asked Carrey.

"Of course, I'm sorry, I just..." He stepped aside and the two detectives entered.

"Please forgive the way the place looks. I haven't had much time for—"

"There's no need to apologize," offered Carrey. "You should see my place."

The attempt at humor or empathy might have mattered in a different circumstance, but Ron wasn't in the mood for it at the moment. "Why did you want to see me, Detective Carrey?"

"You have an insurance policy on your daughter."

Ron felt his mouth drop open. If it were not for the momentary paralysis that had overcome his entire body, he knew he wouldn't have been able to prevent a string of expletives from escaping.

"Fifty thousand dollars," added McKay.

The paralysis started to ease as Ron's hand formed a tense fist that he pinned against the side of his leg.

"For the level of your income, it seems rather substantial," continued McKay.

Ron turned, took a few steps from the detectives, desperately needing to keep a safe distance away so that he couldn't snatch and squeeze their throats until they expelled apologies.

He took a deep breath, followed by another. He attempted to relax his shoulders and ease the tightening in his chest. "Why are you wasting time looking into how much I make and what type of insurance plans I have for my daughter when you should be doing your jobs and looking for her!"

"We know what our jobs are, Mr. Butler," said McKay. "And we know how to do them. Would you like to explain the policy? If not, we can end this now, but it'll only complicate matters."

Ron spoke slowly, deliberately. "It's a combination life insurance and college education fund. I took out a policy when she started first grade." He turned and faced them, more dejected than angry. "You gentlemen have a problem with a young Black girl going to college?"

"Mr. Butler, this isn't about race. We have a job to do. Unfortunately, that means asking some difficult questions," responded McKay.

"That girl taken from Venice Beach; what kind of questions are you asking her father? His daughter was taken this afternoon and you've already got helicopter searches, the feds, the mayor's office, and everybody else out looking for her. My child has been missing for almost a week and you're here tonight asking about her college fund. If this isn't about race or money or influence, then you tell me what the hell it's about!"

The two detectives remained quiet for several moments until Carrey broke the silence. "Do you mind if I took a look inside your daughter's room?"

"Why is that necessary?"

"Is there a reason why you might object to that, Mr. Butler?" asked McKay.

"There are a lot of reasons right now why I would object to whatever either one of you wanted to do, especially in her room. Unless you have a search warrant or a cause to arrest me, I want you out of my home."

"You sure you want to take this attitude with us, Mr. Butler?" asked McKay.

"Yeah, and I'm sure of one other thing. You tell the mayor and police chief, the F.B.I., and anybody else involved that I may not be politically connected, and the level of my income may not be *substantial,* but the most valuable thing in my life is my daughter. And I want her back home with me safe and unharmed where she belongs."

Ron marched to the door and opened it wide, waiting for the detectives to leave. As the two men exited, he stood at the doorway and said, "I pray to God that you're as competent as you are offensive." He was about to close the door when McKay spoke.

"If you think we're treating you like a suspect, we are."

Ironically, Ron's anger dissipated. He should have been furious but the honesty of McKay's accusation, despite its implications and possible consequences, was appreciated.

"You understandably don't like that and neither do I," continued McKay. "But unfortunately, when a child goes missing or there's a homicide involving a spouse, too many times the people closest to the victim are responsible. It adds to an already tragic situation, and it doesn't make me feel good about human nature, I'm sorry to say."

Ron instinctively opened the door wider.

"Now the sooner we can eliminate you as a potential suspect, the sooner we can devote all our energies to investigating other possibilities. I'm not happy that I may have offended you. It wasn't my intent. But so you know, your feelings are less important to me at the moment, than finding your daughter. That's the job we have. And that's the job we'll do, with or without your help." He turned away. "Have a good night."

McKay and Carrey proceeded down the hallway but stopped at Ron's command. "Wait."

The detectives turned around to face him.

"Please." He opened the door all the way. "Do your job the way you see fit." He stepped outside and motioned for the men to enter. "I'll cooperate in any way that you ask."

McKay nodded and he reentered the apartment along with Carrey.

"Jennifer's room is down the hall on the right. Mine is at the end to the left if you need to see that, as well."

Ron showed them the way. Carrey entered Jennifer's room while McKay continued down the hall, going into Ron's bedroom.

"Is it all right if I come in?" Ron asked Carrey.

Carrey nodded approval and walked around the room, inspecting the closet. "She's more organized than my wife, I can tell you that."

Ron smiled. "She has her own system. Blouses arranged together by solid colors, then stripes followed by plaids. Slacks and jeans are on the bottom rack. Jackets and sweaters on top."

"Organized by the same color scheme as the blouses," Carrey said.

"The space on the right is reserved for the school week. What she'll wear Monday through Friday."

"She plans ahead," said Carrey, impressed. "That's a good trait to have." Carrey moved to the dresser and looked at the several photos of Jennifer smiling with her father. He observed her tennis and soccer trophies and framed certificates for school achievements, including being on the honor roll. "An athlete and a scholar," commented Carrey. "Those are even better traits to have."

McKay entered the room. "I hope we didn't inconvenience you too much."

Ron looked at him and shook his head.

McKay walked to the train set perched on a custom table and grinned. "She liked trains?" he asked.

"Likes," Ron corrected. "She *likes* trains."

"So does my grandson. He's about her age." He took a step toward Ron. "After we find your daughter, maybe he can come over and they can play together."

Ron felt his eyes fill up with tears. "I'm sure she would like that," he said.

"We've taken up enough of your time," said Carrey and handed Ron a business card. "That's my direct line. When I'm not there it automatically transfers to my cell which I answer twenty-four seven. You have any questions, or you just need to talk, you give me a call."

"I appreciate that," commented Ron. "Let me walk you to the door."

"No need," said Carrey. "We're good at what we do. Some people think we're even more competent than we are offensive." He smiled, as did Ron, with a hint of embarrassment and regret. "You relax. We can find our way out."

Carrey left the room. McKay stayed behind for a moment, and then addressed Ron. "I wish I'd had your foresight and set up a college plan for my two daughters. By the time they were ready, I had to take out a second mortgage to pay for tuition. If I had known better, I could have retired five years ago."

"I'm glad you and your partner are still on the job, Detective McKay," said Ron. "I really am."

"He'll be happy to know that." He patted Ron on the shoulder. "So am I."

McKay left. Ron waited until he heard the front door close.

He walked to Jennifer's closet, looked inside, and straightened out one of her sweaters on the hanger. He slid open the closet door and observed the stranger in the mirror, which startled him. Could he have changed that much in just a few days? He touched the dark circles under his eyes and ran his hand over the five-day growth on his face and chin. Jennifer had sensitive skin, and he was careful never to put his cheek against hers unless he was clean-shaven.

He suddenly felt exhausted, finding it difficult to move. He sat on Jennifer's bed, resting his head on her pillow. He picked up a framed photo of her that was on her night table, cradled it, and then pressed it against his heart, hoping that the morning would give him a reason to shave and see the man his daughter loved.

EIGHTEEN

The new girl hadn't moved since he'd carried her in several hours ago and placed her on the remaining cot. The three girls had feared she might never wake up. Blood was caked on her right leg, streaking from her knee to the back of her calf and ending at her ankle, like a recent accident scattered across a narrow winding road. While it didn't appear to be a serious injury, it was still blood, enough to think the worst. When she arrived unconscious, she was wearing rollerblades, which he removed with some clumsiness. He searched inside the skates, apparently looking for a size. Frustrated, he tossed the skates to the floor. He measured her bare feet with his hands, placing his palm against the heel of her foot and then extending the fingers on his other hand beyond the tip of her big toe until he approximated the size which he wrote down on a small notepad.

While he was doing this, he never looked at any of them, acted as if they weren't in the room. His attention was focused solely on the skater. Before he left, he gently rearranged her hair and brushed it back from her face with his hand. Jennifer thought of all the times that her father had put her to bed, kissed her on the forehead or cheek, and stroked her hair, staying with her until she fell asleep. She resented that this man would enter her thoughts by reminding her of someone she loved so deeply. It repulsed her. She thought it fortunate that her stomach was empty.

"You think we should try and wake her?" asked Selena.

"We should let her sleep," replied Mei Lin.

Selena looked at Jennifer who, while she was among the three that had the least seniority, seemed to be the person the two girls had come to rely on and trust the most because of her age. "What do you think, Jenny?"

"Let's wait a while longer. Maybe an hour. She's probably drugged up quite a bit. No sense in waking her now."

Mei Lin asked, "What time do you think it is?"

Selena shrugged.

"I don't know," said Jennifer.

"You think it's day or night?" Mei Lin persisted.

"What difference does it make?" snapped Selena. "You got some place to go?"

Mei Lin became withdrawn and sat up on the cot, bringing her knees to her chest. She rocked back and forth, fidgeting with her clothes.

"Mei Lin is right to ask," said Jennifer. "We've got to be aware of things like that."

"We've got to change the formula for keeping time now," said Mei Lin.

"Why?" asked Jennifer.

"With the new girl, it won't be every three days before we take a bath, but four."

"Why don't we just count each bath as a day?" asked Selena, annoyed. "That way we won't have to count by threes or fours."

"Hey, you're the one keeping track of the baths, not me," Mei Lin reminded her.

"Fine," Selena huffed. "Let Jennifer do it her way, but sometimes I can't tell if he's giving us dinner or a lunch."

"What was the date he took you, Jenny?" asked Mei Lin.

"I think it was the April 4th. A Tuesday."

"We've slept four or five times since then," added Selena. "So, it's the eighth or ninth." She suddenly turned solemn, laid down on the cot.

"What's the matter?" asked Mei Lin.

"If it's the eighth," replied Selena, "it's my birthday. If not, then I missed it."

The girls remained quiet. Mei Lin bowed her head, a sudden sadness overtaking her. Jennifer noticed the change in mood and heard Selena crying quietly.

Jennifer stood up and walked toward Selena as far as the chain permitted. She cleared her throat and sang softly and slowly, "Happy birthday to you... Happy birthday to you..." She waited, and after a moment, Mei Lin walked toward Jennifer and joined in.

"Happy birthday, dear Selena." Selena sat up in the cot and watched her two friends serenade her. "Happy birthday to—"

"Where am I?" The unrecognized voice interrupted the singing.

The girls turned to discover the skater who was awake and standing.

She massaged her forehead; her legs were unsteady. "Who are you and what am I doing here?"

NINETEEN

SUNDAY APRIL 9TH

Police Chief Anderson stood next to Mayor Reynolds at the podium. Todd and Liz Roth stood behind them to the side. Liz wiped away tears with a handkerchief her husband had given her. "We've received no ransom demands but haven't ruled that out as a motive for the kidnapping," announced the chief as reporters wrote furiously. "We're working closely with state authorities as well as coordinating efforts with F.B.I. agents. Before I open this up for questions, Mayor Reynolds would like to say a few words."

Anderson moved back to join the couple. The mayor stepped up to the microphone and cameramen as local and national news networks jostled for position.

"Todd and Elizabeth Roth have been long-time contributors to this city and have been active in local and national phil-anthropic efforts. Whenever the city needed them, they responded. Now that they need the city, I promise them, we will not rest until—" The mayor stopped, his attention focused on the rear door that suddenly opened.

Ron walked down the middle aisle, through reporters and cameras toward the podium. Still unshaven, unkempt, clothes disheveled, he cradled an eight-by-ten framed photo of Jennifer that he had fallen asleep holding.

Mayor Reynolds nodded toward Security and tried to find a way back to his remarks. "As they have always been there for our fellow Los Angelinos, in this, their hour of need, we intend to stand with them, with our..."

The cameramen turned their equipment away from the mayor and directed attention to this strange intruder. Photographers snapped pictures; an explosion of flashbulbs assaulted an exhausted and disoriented stranger, who fought to make his way through the press corp.

The mayor gave a more anxious signal to security. Two guards jumped to close in on Ron and block his path. "We offer our resources... our friendship... our prayers."

"Does my daughter merit your prayers, Mayor?" shouted Ron.

Guards surrounded Ron, preventing him from moving forward. Photographers enclosed both the guards and Ron, taking numerous photos.

Ron tried to look over the surrounding crowd, pleading desperately to the members assembled, to the police chief, to the mayor, to the Roth family. Todd moved to the side to get a better view of the disturbance. It seemed as if Ron was speaking directly to him.

"Anybody here care about my daughter? She's missing, too."

He held up the photo, tried to place it in front of the competing news cameras. "Jennifer Butler... Jenny, eleven years old... Black... taken from—"

He pushed one of the guards aside to showcase the photo and was grabbed from behind by an officer while a second knocked the photo out of his hand. It crashed to the floor, bounced once, shattering the glass.

Ron broke away from the officer. "Stay away from me!"

Guards attempted to wrestle him to the ground, but he resisted violently.

The mayor placed his hands up in an appeal. "That's enough! Back off him!"

The guards released Ron and moved a few steps away, but continued to form a barrier around him, blocking him from reaching the podium.

Ron looked at the fallen photo, took a step toward it, and dropped to his knees. He slowly picked up the photo and removed the broken shards of glass jutting out from the frame. A piece cut him, causing him to bleed on the photo. The sight of blood on Jennifer's face terrified him and just as quickly enraged him. He jumped up, charging the guards, knocking down the first one who contacted him.

"See what you've done! Look at my daughter! Look at her!"

The mayor reluctantly gave the guards approval to remove the man. Security forcefully pinned him to the ground, forcing his hands behind his back, but could not easily cuff him. Eventually they gave up.

Pandemonium broke out among the news crew and photographers as Ron squirmed on the ground, screaming. "All I want is for somebody to find my daughter! For God's sake! Won't anyone help?"

He was lifted off the floor and taken into custody. Todd moved to him. The guards stopped for a moment. One cameraman managed to capture the image which would be broadcast nationally within the hour.

Ron looked straight into the camera and spoke calmly, so softly that a microphone barely recorded his words. "In this entire world, she's all I have." He smoothed out the photo which had been crumpled in the struggle and held it up in front of the camera operator, who zoomed in for a close-up of Jennifer, smiling.

While Todd studied the photo now exhibited on two large

monitors, Ron noticed a poster-board of Rebecca resting against an easel. It was the last image he saw before the guards carried him off.

Ron had been detained in a small lock-up within City Hall. Interviewed by the deputy manager to the mayor for over an hour in the presence of two police officers, he assumed he was going to jail. He had not asked for a lawyer and wondered if he had made a mistake. He probably would have, had it not been for the Roth family who evidently persuaded the mayor not to press charges.

He was released, given the photo of his daughter, and ordered to go home. He hadn't expected to find Todd and Liz Roth waiting for him. They were seated on a long, polished bench. When they saw him walk out of the holding area, they stood and approached him.

He spoke before they had a chance to. "I didn't mean any disrespect to you or your family."

"None was taken," said Todd.

"I appreciate you convincing the mayor not to press charges."

Todd gave a weak smile. "You don't need to thank me. Given the circumstances and an election less than six months away, I'm certain Mayor Reynolds wanted to avoid locking up a parent who only wanted justice for his missing child."

Ron lowered his eyes, stared for a moment at the floor. "Yes, I guess that would have been bad publicity." He raised his eyes until they made contact with Todd. "And I suppose we want to avoid that at all costs."

Both men stood in silence until Liz intervened and found a way to leave quietly and quickly. "I'll pray for both our daughters, Mr. Butler."

Ron nodded in appreciation. "Thank you, Mrs. Roth... So will I."

Liz and Todd Roth left, arm in arm. One of the officers who had remained with Ron in detention approached.

"Might be a good idea if you went home," he said, without any hint of hostility.

"Home? Yeah, I wanna go home." He looked at the blood-stained photo of Jennifer. "Trouble is I don't have one right now." He walked down the hallway, the sound of his shoes against the marble floors echoing in the chamber. He stepped outside and descended the stairs to the garage. A light mist felt cool against his face but provided no relief.

TWENTY

WEDNESDAY APRIL 12TH

He stood in line, holding children's clothing, dresses, underwear, socks, and pajamas. He didn't like the selection of shoes available. Too cheap-looking. He would go elsewhere to buy a pair of shoes for the new girl. The cashier's attention, along with several customers, was focused on a television monitor. He typically avoided looking up in stores, restaurants, banks, and other places likely to have surveillance cameras. It was increasingly difficult to avoid them, which is why he had used a variety of wigs and prosthetics to disguise his face and even shoes that added several inches to his six-foot frame.

"I don't blame that man, at all," said the cashier, who returned a credit card to one woman.

"I'd do the same thing for my daughter," the woman agreed. "I feel so bad for both families."

Having heard the conversation, he couldn't help but look at the overhead monitor. He hoped his expression hadn't betrayed him and was grateful that no one in line cared about him, their attention glued to the screen and the pictures of Rebecca and Jennifer.

"Beautiful girls," said the cashier. "I pray they're found and safely returned to their homes uninjured."

"Damn shame children can't be safe with these perverts roaming our street."

He flinched at the term "pervert" and wanted to snatch the woman by the back of the neck. How dare she lump him in with the deviants of society. He wanted desperately to know why the two girls shared the same screen. How could they be connected so soon? Had he made a mistake? He couldn't have.

The woman took her purchase, thanked the cashier, and left.

He wanted to leave, but it would look awkward, and he couldn't afford to draw attention to himself, not now. Plus, he wanted to learn more without being obvious. He placed the clothing near the register, not knowing if he should smile or look concerned. He settled on curious, inquisitive.

"What's happening?" He looked at the screen, feigning confusion, which, given his current state of mind, was actually not hard to do.

"Haven't you heard?" she asked. "It's been in the news all day. Front page of every newspaper."

He made a mental note to get the newspapers as soon as he left. Not at a store but at those metal and glass stands on most street corners where he could insert coins and grab as many as needed without relying on human contact.

She informed him in great detail about the African American man interrupting the news conference on behalf of his own daughter, who had been abducted from her school more than a week ago.

"Wow, that's amazing," he exclaimed. "Don't think I've ever heard anything like it. Have the police got any clues?"

"No but given that one of the girls is the daughter of a very powerful and *rich* friend of the mayor, governor, and everyone else worth knowing, I'm betting it won't take long before they find out something. If I was the person who took her, I'd be real nervous right now."

Well, thank the Lord you're not me, he thought. But it did provide a wrinkle in his plan, and he would have to keep a close eye on everything and adapt, if necessary. What the hell was a rich white girl doing at Venice Beach? Rich and white could be a definite problem for him. Maybe the woman was right, after all.

"I don't know what I'd do if someone took one of my daughters," he said, wanting to change the subject and appear anything but nervous.

"It's a sick world and it's getting more dangerous every day," said the cashier.

"I couldn't have said it any better."

"How many girls do you have?"

"Four... I'd like to have one more."

"You're unusual," she rang up the dresses. "Most men I know want sons." She folded the dresses and placed them in a large plastic garment bag. "In fact, most men don't do the shopping for their children."

"Civilization is born from the mother's womb. The future of our race depends on women who realize their own God-given power."

She stopped bagging clothes and looked at him. "Your wife's a very lucky woman."

He smiled, handed her cash. "I'd like to think so."

"Do you have a store credit card?"

"Don't believe in them."

"You can save twenty percent on your total order if you open an account today."

"Not worth it."

"It won't take but a minute."

He was certain of that. And he could use the savings. But he wouldn't leave a record of his activities that could be traced.

JEFF STETSON

Once he opened an account, he'd start getting solicitations from all types of stores and banks and firms waiting to punch in the data they'd collected on him and share it with the world. These companies know more about consumers' personal habits than the consumers did. And he couldn't afford to be in anyone's database.

When he first acquired Mei Lin, he had dressed up as a woman to shop for her. He struck a lovely image if he did say so himself. He wanted to fool the surveillance cameras that captured everything all the time. He wore a long blond wig and dark sunglasses and a loose-fitting dress, with matching flat shoes. He tried high heels for a second and twisted his ankle. His girls would stay away from such contraptions, nothing more than vanity traps that added to the filthy imaginations of adolescent minds as well as the rising cost of health care.

After a salesclerk had asked him about his right hand, he started wearing gloves, but that drew too much attention, especially when it was hot. When a woman had a deformity like his, people wanted to know how it happened. For a man, it's just a wound, some type of workplace accident or sporting mishap, the consequence of proving one's mettle. So now he shopped as himself and avoided cameras whenever possible.

Rebecca joining the family could be a problem. If he had known her background, he would have avoided her like the plague. Of the four girls, she was the only one without a wallet where he could have checked her identification. There was an advantage in taking girls directly from their schools. They carried backpacks with useful information, such as journals or notebooks or agendas with notations about friends or teachers. Obtaining knowledge about their classes and schoolwork provided him with personal insights, helpful in gaining their trust more quickly. The more you knew about their habits, attitudes, and secrets, the easier it was to manipulate them, gaining control of their still malleable minds. Diaries were like finding the key to the future, a virtual treasure trove of hidden desires. He had memorized entire passages of Mei Lin's most intimate thoughts and aspirations. It allowed him to exert power over her with just a stern stare, the expression she most feared from her strict father.

He observed the photo of Rebecca on the monitor. Why would a girl like her from a prominent family be at a park frequented by degenerates and tourists drawn to freak shows? He would need to be especially cautious. He was so close to his goal and couldn't afford to make a mistake now. He might have to move up the relocation date. They'd never find them in a place like New Mexico, where people respected privacy and where there was enough land to remain secluded, unbothered.

He would train the girls to farm, grow their own food, raise chickens and cattle, and maybe even ride horses. He knew they would love it there, thrive together without the interference of the outside world. He used his inheritance wisely and made the purchase three years ago. His father's untimely death was a life-saving gift. The death was neither untimely nor unplanned. It might have been unexpected to the miserable man who had forced his son to go fishing, knowing full well how much the boy hated worms and was terrified of the unsteady rocking of the small boat and what lay beneath the dark depths of the ocean.

But hatred can fuel anger which, if left to boil over, can—and did—lead to courage. He only hoped that his father hadn't drunk so much that he couldn't recognize it was his son who had held the hammer and struck once, twice, then one glorious final time. The body was never found, and the boy knew how to grieve in front of the police. God knows he had had enough practice over the sixteen years of his life. That act left him without a family, but he knew he would have one of his own making, the family his father would have despised.

Niggers and chinks and—what was the derogatory term he used for Mexicans? Wetbacks? Or some other equally offensive word. It didn't matter. That was a lifetime ago, better left in the past while serving as fuel for the future. He would prove his father wrong by mocking him every day that remained. If only hell had a telephone, he'd make one final collect call to that wretched soul and confess everything. And that would be worse than the fires of hell and more painful than anything his father had ever done to him and the friend he loved.

He looked at the palm of his right hand and remembered how it felt to have that hot iron pressed against the skin till he could smell his flesh burning. He studied the scars which he used to believe were the marks of the devil. But it had made him special. It made him know he could endure anything, even a vise crushing his bones and almost severing his fingers. The wounds eventually healed, but the burning, pain, hatred, revenge, those things would last forever.

"Did you need anything else?" the cashier asked. It was obvious she had been holding the two bags with all his purchases for some time.

"I'm sorry. I guess my mind wandered. Thinking of those girls and what their fathers must be going through." He took the bags and his change.

"Yes." The cashier nodded. "It's tragic."

"A nightmare," replied the man. "Have a nice day."

The cashier watched the man walk away from the counter and exit the store. She greeted the next customer, a woman who had been waiting in line.

"I couldn't help but listen to your conversation," said the customer. "Really an interesting man."

"Very unusual."

"You can say that again. Wish my husband was that sensitive."

"Don't we all." The two laughed as the cashier rang up the purchases.

TWENTY-ONE

"Do you think he's watching us now?" asked the new girl. "Because if he is, we can't let him see that we're afraid," she continued.

Jennifer was impressed with this girl. From the very beginning she seemed composed. Was there fear? Yes. But she wasn't overcome by the situation. No sense of panic. She thought she might have an ally; someone she could count on in the future. The two of them were the oldest and would have to keep the others strong and focused on how to escape when given the chance.

Her name was Rebecca Roth and like Jennifer had been lured away with the false plea for help. But in her case, she had been threatened with a gun pressed against her side and told he'd kill her and her father if she tried to get away. He held her hand tightly until they had reached a van parked on a side street, behind a Venice Beach café and bookstore. She climbed in the back and felt a cloth over her mouth and nose. She thought he was trying to suffocate her. Given that several fingernails were broken, she was sure she had put up a good fight but was eventually overpowered.

The girls had shared their stories and answered as many of her questions as they could. Yes, he took a girl with him and waited while she showered or bathed. They received three meals a day. Mostly microwave. Occasionally, a pizza—on rare nights, dessert. The food was always served on paper plates or in paper bowls or cups. No silverware, just plastic forks and spoons, never a knife of any kind. The portable cooler would be filled with plastic bottles of water and pouches of juices. He frowned upon sodas and sugar drinks in general but provided them infrequently.

No, they didn't know what he wanted or what he was planning. He spoke in riddles, hinting at some special or divine mission. He hadn't hurt them, but the threat was always there. They were expected to obey, not cause trouble. He wanted them to be a family and think of this place as home. Yes, he was definitely weird but kind in a strange way. He acted as if he cared for them, wanted to keep them safe.

"That's crazy," said Rebecca.

Everyone agreed. They told her of their desire to keep track of time and their various methods to accomplish that, the number of meals, how long they slept. Sometimes they took turns and estimated the hours asleep and then changed shifts. Jennifer showed her the hiding place for the torn tissues.

The lights could go on or off at any time from every few minutes to hours, perhaps a full day. Jennifer thought it was his method to keep them on edge, disoriented. They hadn't yet planned how to escape and didn't know when it was safe to speak, since he could listen to their conversations and monitor their behavior through the video cameras.

They speculated he had to leave to get food although he might have stockpiled frozen meals. On pizza night, they were sure he had to either pick it up or have it delivered since it was fresh and hot. They weren't sure if he had a job, but they didn't think so. The last thing they mentioned was bath night.

"Does he watch?" asked Rebecca.

"I'm not sure," answered Selena. Both Mei Lin and Jennifer remained quiet.

"Has he touched you?" Rebecca asked. None of the girls answered.

"If he tries to touch you, what are you gonna do?"

Jennifer thought about it. "Scream."

"It won't do any good," said Selena. "No one can hear you."

"How do you know?" asked Rebecca.

"I tried," answered Selena.

"We both did," said Mei Lin.

Selena moved toward Rebecca, stopping when she could go no further. "He..." Selena took a deep breath, tried again. "He... said he wouldn't hurt me if I stopped. I never tried, again."

Mei Lin cried quietly but stopped on Jennifer's voice. "He's going to make a mistake one day and when he does, we need to take advantage of it. Whatever else happens, one of us must escape and get help." She swallowed hard, straightened back her shoulders, and took a deep breath. "The one thing we can't lose is hope. My father always told me 'as long as you can see tomorrow, you can face today'."

The metal bolt slid back, and a lock was opened. The girls looked in the direction of the door that opened slowly. He walked into the room holding a bath towel and a robe. He inserted a key into the padlock and removed Rebecca's chains from around her waist.

"It's time for your bath," he said, his expression impassive. "Since you managed to work up quite a sweat at the beach, you should take it tonight. We'll get back on schedule tomorrow."

He took her by the hand, but she snatched it away, appearing as if she would refuse to leave with him. She looked at Selena, who shook her head and mouthed the word, "Don't."

Rebecca reluctantly walked with him, glanced at Jennifer

for a moment, then turned away. The girls watched the two of them leave.

After the door closed, was locked, and bolted, Jennifer bowed her head and quietly said, "Scream."

TWENTY-TWO
FRIDAY APRIL 14TH

Liz carefully placed everything in order. Todd stood at the doorway and watched his wife organizing their daughter's room. He knew she had to keep working, acting normally, preparing the room for Rebecca's return. If not, she would fall apart, and he would be the next to fall. He noticed the fresh flowers she had placed on Rebecca's dresser. He thought some of them may have come from the bouquet she had received at her school recital.

Liz partially pulled down the bedspread and methodically tucked it in one corner. She pulled the sheet over the bedspread, smoothing it out with her hand. She fluffed one pillow then the next, placing them side-by-side. She took the teddy bear and started to place it on one of the pillows, but suddenly stopped, studied it, held it close. He saw her shoulders slump and then tremble.

"We're going to get her back," said Todd.

She turned and discovered him slowly approaching.

He stopped in front of her. "I promise."

'It's been six days. You can't make a promise after six days."

She looked at the bear, straightened the blue ribbon around its neck. "I remember when she first found this in your storage room. I'll never forget the look on her face. Particularly when you told her it had been your favorite." She gently rubbed the bear's fur until the coloration matched and then placed it on the bed. "I've never pictured you having a favorite anything. I certainly never thought of you as sentimental. I always wondered of all the things you could've kept from your childhood, why you chose a stuffed teddy bear."

"I never went to bed without it. Somehow, I thought it might protect me. I had hoped it would protect her."

He knew he shouldn't have used the word "protect." It immediately affected his wife, brought tears to her eyes. He noticed her bite her lower lip which quivered slightly.

He gently touched his wife's shoulder. She didn't recoil or move away as she had done on so many previous occasions. She didn't move at all, as if his touch didn't matter, as if he no longer existed. He wondered what he could say that might make a difference, make the moment bearable, if not hopeful. They should be able to console each other. Comfort would be too much to expect, but didn't they share the same pain and wasn't "share" the operative word? Or would "pain" be the controlling factor in their lives, defining their future, assuming they deserved one together?

Todd needed her now more than ever, but not as much as she had needed him before the absence of their daughter revealed what was missing in their marriage. He felt guilty for so much but wasn't sure why, or to be more precise, wasn't certain why he had given so little of himself to his family that now represented the foundation for his regret.

When did he lose the capacity to touch or the desire to try? He loved his wife, adored their child, worked diligently to provide financial security, give them everything he never had. And yet he remained conspicuously distant, cold, despite every feeling to the contrary.

"When was the last time you held her? Told her you loved her?"

He looked away. This was not a discussion he could afford to have now.

She took a step closer to him. "I don't think I'll make it through another day if we lose her. But I really feel sorry for you. I don't know how you'll be able to face yourself, never knowing how special she was, never having loved her as much as she loved you." She reached to touch him, but stopped, the same way he had failed to touch his daughter so many times when she needed to be comforted most, held most.

"I will make it up to her," he said. "I'll make it up to you." He attempted to stroke her face, but she pulled back.

"It's too late for me," she replied, tears streaming down her cheeks. "I pray to God it's not too late for her." She observed the room, taking in every detail, then turned toward her husband. "You finally were forced to spend time with our daughter because she didn't give you any other choice, and you still managed not to be there when she needed you most."

He had been waiting for the accusation, the blame. When it came, it was not a surprise, but it still hurt more than he had imagined. And, yet the pain paled in comparison to what followed.

"I want a divorce."

He heard the words from a voice that had soothed him for years, even when those words were routine, unimportant, like "What do you want for dinner?" or "What time will you be home?" Home... a place made possible because of her.

"No matter the outcome. Whatever happens, whatever we discover about Rebecca, it's over between us." She walked out of the room. He sat on the side of the bed, his back toward the teddy bear.

Was it true that he had lost her? Was it possible that he would lose his daughter, his family, his entire world? He felt the tears but nothing else. He wanted to move, to keep walking, but where would he go? He knew it wouldn't do any good, but there was one place, the only place now, that mattered. And he was able to drive there in under thirty minutes.

The ocean breeze brought no comfort even though Todd had now tested it for several hours. He had experienced the sunset on Venice Pier forty-five minutes ago. He didn't remember how many times he had walked back and forth, travelling unknown miles past Santa Monica only to return to the spot where Rebecca had been taken. How could she vanish in the middle of so many? But that was the point, wasn't it? The Venice board-walk was filled with colorful distractions, fire-eaters, half-naked oil-slicked bodybuilders, jugglers, sword-swallowers, turban-wearing rollerbladers covered in tattoos, exotically dressed fortune-tellers, unlikely couples being serenaded by singers who couldn't sing or guitarists who couldn't play. There were artists who would sketch your portrait for a few dollars or for an illegal substance or a phone number that would lead to an illicit encounter. Thinking about them made him angry. If he hadn't been thinking of that artist, spending time looking for her, paying more attention to her than his daughter, maybe she wouldn't have been taken. But then if he had only been a father who attended his daughter's recital, none of this would have been necessary.

Yes, there was no shortage of distractions or places to disappear to, so how could he continue to expect that someone had witnessed something out of the ordinary in a place famous for being anything but ordinary? But that hadn't stopped him from asking anyone who would take the time to listen to study the missing person flyers he distributed. He wondered if the person or persons who had abducted his daughter might be here, mocking him, watching him from a distance, amused at his futile efforts. Maybe he or they took one of the flyers or removed one of the signs that had been posted throughout the area. Would they be so heartless as to hang it up in their apartment or home, make Rebecca look at it, giving her a false sense of hope that someone was looking for her but would never find her? As painful as that thought might be, he found relief in it. It would mean she was still alive. Only that belief gave him hope, which was the one commodity his fortune and fame couldn't guarantee.

And then he thought of the words that pierced through his heart. *I want a divorce.*

TWENTY-THREE

Ron didn't need to get up early to go to work since he hadn't slept much since his daughter's abduction. He had wiped off the shaving cream and tossed aside his razor, having no intention of making himself presentable to those people. Fuck 'em. Once he had arrived, he refused to make eye contact with his fellow employees. He knew they were staring at him, making comments as he pushed a cart containing a computer, a monitor, and a printer. He also knew that Miller had agreed to lend him the equipment because he was afraid of what might happen if he refused. But that hadn't stopped him from complaining.

"I don't understand why you can't do that here," his boss said while following him down the aisle. "You can work late if you want. It would have to be on your own time, though."

Ron stopped. "You said I could take it home. Can I borrow it or not?"

"I need you to sign for it," Miller replied nervously. "I don't want any trouble getting it back."

"Why would you have any trouble?"

"The best intentions sometimes go awry," Miller offered.

"William has the paperwork. Sign it before you leave. Here he comes now."

Miller hustled off quickly. William approached him with a paper to sign. Ron took the paper and signed it without reading it. He didn't care what he was agreeing to. He just wanted out of here.

"Under the circumstances, I think you're quite a guy to take company work home," William said. "Although I guess it might help you to take your mind off your personal situation."

Ron handed back the paper and pen to William. "I'm not doing company work. I need this to help me with my *personal situation.*"

"I fully understand," William said sympathetically. "And I just want to say on behalf of all of your fellow employees, nobody here believes for a single second that you did anything to harm your daughter."

Ron stared at him icily, then glanced around the room, causing his uncomfortable co-workers to retreat to their typing and programming.

"Anyone who's ever worked with you knows that would be unthinkable." William placed his hand on the cart. "Let me help you with that."

Ron calmly grabbed William's wrist. By the expression on William's face, the grip was powerful.

"Thanks for your help," said Ron. "I'll do the rest myself."

Ron let go of William's wrist and pushed the cart down the aisle and out of the office, leaving William to assess the damage to his hand.

TWENTY-FOUR

Detective McKay punched in some information on the computer screen and brought up a listing for pedophiles. In the box marked "List Desired Cities by Name or Zip Code," he typed in Los Angeles, hit the enter key, and struck the print button. He sat back and watched the inkjet spit out a list.

His partner approached and observed the pages being stacked. "What you got?" asked Carrey.

McKay held up several pages, single-spaced with names and addresses. "Child molesters released or paroled in the last six months."

"You don't think it's the father?"

"If it is, he's a better actor than Denzel Washington."

Carrey looked at McKay for a clue. "Which one is that?"

"You're kidding, right?"

Carrey shrugged and extended his arms, palms up, in a plea for understanding. "I don't go to the movies."

"Why not?"

"Too violent."

"Too expensive, you mean. Always were a cheapskate."

"Hey," said Carrey, "there's more than one way to assault a

person. I protect my wallet same as I protect myself." He took the stack of papers and skimmed through the first few pages. "This only for L.A.?"

McKay nodded yes. "That's why they call it the City of Angels."

"Let's hope every kid has one," replied Carrey. "I think you're right about Butler. That kid's room was filled with pictures of the two of them together, smiling like they were living the perfect life."

"Let's do our best to make it perfect for them again."

Carrey studied his partner. "Realistically, what do you think the chances are of that happening?"

McKay stopped working and looked away. "We both know the answer to that." He tossed aside some paperwork. "I think when this is over, I'm going to retire, spend more time with the grandkids."

"You say you're going to retire every time you get a case that rips out your heart."

"My heart can only be ripped out so many times before it quits on me, or I quit on it. Either way, it doesn't renew my faith in the goodness of man."

Carrey picked up a folder, opened it, and tossed it on the desk. A photo of Jennifer appeared to stare directly at McKay. "You want faith in goodness look no further than the tip of your nose. She was pretty."

"She *is* pretty," McKay corrected his partner.

"Butler got to you, huh?"

"He's a father. From the looks of it, a damn good one."

Carrey nodded in agreement. "Then let's get to work."

McKay punched a button on his computer and additional pages printed out of pedophiles in the area, some of whom were living and working closer than he imagined.

TWENTY-FIVE
MONDAY APRIL 17TH

He waited inside his car, parked across from the main exit, his heart racing in anticipation of the school bell that would ring at any moment. He wiped his moist hands against both thighs, which gave him a sudden burst of excitement, and then cautiously observed the parents waiting for their children. He had seen them so many times he could now match them with their daughters. He paid less attention to their sons, much less. Boys always appeared unformed and unusually soiled, caught in between growth spurts and in need of a bath. Nothing seemed to fit, mismatched body parts straining to find their purpose. No longer cute and years away from being fully developed, they displayed an awkwardness he found discomforting. Mechanical in their mannerisms, dishonest in their interactions, they were mere caricatures of future aspirations and hopes that typically belonged to their parents. Even their dreams were imposed upon them.

But the girls—the girls were another matter entirely. Their imperfections held promise. Every stage of their development made sense; whole beings made anew with each season. Where the boys evolved from one seemingly unrelated species to another, the girls had their own logical progressions, each unique and acceptable unto itself until corrupted by artificial interventions—inappropriate clothing and degenerate make-up, the scourge of modern commercialism and a society gone mad.

Sometimes he managed to sneak past the security gate to walk onto the unattended main practice field and watch their physical education drills. He enjoyed the track sessions, particularly the long-distance runners. Graceful, elegant, and free, they ran with an exuberance and determination that he envied. Dressed in their gray and green uniforms, they resembled an undisciplined army searching for an outlet for their boundless energy. Their gym shorts, made of lightweight nylon and cotton, were designed for comfort, elasticity, and most important, absorbing perspiration. He loved the way the material clung snugly to their bodies, conveying so much more than the changes taking place underneath the sheer material. And no matter how far or fast they ran, they always finished where they started. There was something exhilarating in that, hopeful and beautifully ironic. Freedom was illusionary, at best; in the end, there was no escape from your past and no real progress. That meant the future was his for the taking, predetermined—all he needed was to remain patient and eventually they would return to him, not at the finish line, but at the beginning of a new race that he was destined to win.

The bell rang on time, three minutes past three. The students rushed out of their classrooms and raced toward destinations that would lead home, a herd of cattle carrying backpacks and laughing unwittingly at their escape from safety to danger. He used to visit the local middle school, but he had lost interest, disgusted by how old the girls looked, influenced by music video sluts, no doubt. They wore tight torn jeans, blouses that revealed their growing maturity, and make-up that stole their innocence, robbing him of his pleasure. How could their parents allow mere sixth graders to dress that way? But then he'd observe some of their mothers and the answer was self-evident. Bored housewives concerned more with competing against their daughters than raising them. Some wore low-slung designer jeans, purchased faded and torn, in tribute to the memories of their youth, which they now attempted to relive through cosmetic surgery and their lookalike, trashy children. He despised them almost as much as he desired their offspring.

There was one girl whom he had initially considered, had thought about for a long time. She would have stood out from the crowd without the black motorcycle jacket, long blond hair teased like a fluffy unkempt cloud, flat canvas sneakers, and blue eyeshadow that gave her the appearance of a sad clown. Unusually tall for her age, she towered a full head above her classmates, always surrounded by a different group of friends competing to be close to her. He had spoken to her once, eliciting a warm smile from her that ironically diminished his sense of power. Her greeting had seemed forced, fake, as if she had grown accustomed to attention, even expected it, but didn't or couldn't appreciate it. He detested anything that wasn't genuine or real and would never tolerate indifference or dishonesty. He'd accept love, but in its absence would demand, actually prefer, fear. For despite the romantic ravings of poets, songwriters, and religious leaders, love was far less powerful. Ironically, if used properly, it could induce terror. Discover the thing someone loves, and you've discovered the tool for absolute control. Losing love is always more frightening than never finding it.

So after a brief but disappointing flirtation with the middle grades, he returned to the elementary schools where the laughter was authentic and the students were free of drugs and make-up and girls who dressed beyond their age. The poorer ones wore hand-me-downs or dresses made by their mothers from various scraps of discarded and discolored fabric, dyed unevenly. It gave them a precious appearance, contemporary children in antiquated costumes, with small, scuffed shoes and thick socks folded around slim, tender, and fragile ankles. They were perpetual bundles of energy, constantly in motion, unpretentious and unaware of how special they were or how beautiful they looked. They had been warned to avoid strangers countless times, by parents and teachers and silly cartoon brochures sponsored by tax dollars and distributed by fools who knew nothing of human behavior. A stranger disappeared the moment he educed a smile from a child and friendship began with that child's first laugh or an exchange of a stick of gum or a compliment made with conviction, or for those unaccustomed to positive reinforcement, any genuine attention at all.

Children didn't think like adults, didn't see danger around every corner. Their strength was their weakness—trust—and he would exploit it for all it was worth until the time came when he could restore it, but only for him. They would grow to trust him and him alone and they would accept his plan that would eventually become their plan. A future of bliss, a promise sealed in a secret pact, at least for now. In time, there would be no reason to hide, but that world didn't exist yet and needed to be created by those with shared vision.

He felt a rush, exhilaration at the thought that he had the power to make that happen. Then he saw her—the missing piece of the puzzle—the one he had studied for weeks and dreamt about for as long as he could remember. She would complete his mosaic and form the foundation upon which he would build his family. All his hard work and endless planning, the pain and suffering he had to endure, the time he'd spent in seclusion with his obsession—his glorious mission finally would be realized.

She ran to her mother, and they embraced. They laughed and crossed the street, walking past his car. "Be careful, Sakari," the mother warned as they avoided traffic. In that fateful caution, he now had a name and with it a key that would unlock the final step of his journey. Sakari.

He wrote down the name on the pad of paper he always kept with him. He would return Thursday, the day the mother arrived twenty minutes late to pick up her daughter who would wait patiently on the corner, as instructed. He turned the key in his ignition and allowed the engine to warm up. He carefully pulled out of his parking space, not wanting to hurt a small child or be cited for a traffic violation. His plan was too important to be foiled by something so mundane. Mistakes would be avoided at all costs, which was why he had spent so much time studying and learning from the mistakes of others. He would succeed where they had failed.

He stopped the car and allowed a group of students to cross in front of him. They didn't bother to travel a few feet to use the crosswalk. Inconvenience often resulted in risk-taking. He smiled at the notion that safety could be found at the corner, if only the journey could be completed without interruption. How unaware they were of what was staring at them from behind a tinted windshield. They were oblivious to everything but their own selfish needs which were defined by the moment, no matter how trivial.

They had made it across the street and were now pushing and shoving each other in front of a home undergoing reconstruction. Things were always changing on this block. Homeowners never satisfied, competing with their next-door neighbors for the best landscape or most elegant and impressive entryway with beveled-glass French windows that only exposed the shallow lives looking out in fear from behind gates or signs that warned: "Security provided by..."

Fools! Didn't they realize there was no such thing as security?

A horn blared behind him, signaling another impatient person in a hurry to go nowhere. He looked in his rearview mirror and saw a frustrated driver who kept motioning to move. There were times he wished he had become a serial killer rather than the savior of the world. This earth doesn't deserve him. In its current state, it could never appreciate him. But he would change that. He didn't have much time but if he hurried, he'd have had enough.

The horn blared again. This time, the face in his rearview mirror was screaming profanities, unconcerned about the children who were also in the S.U.V.

Some people had no decency and deserved the worst that could happen to them.

He stepped on the accelerator and sped off, not wanting to keep his girls waiting any longer. He could hardly wait to give them the presents he had purchased last week. They would truly begin to look like a family then.

TWENTY-SIX

It hadn't lasted long or maybe the boy no longer recognized time. It was his birthday and his mother had given him a little party that afternoon. The monster had helped with the decorations, balloons, banners in the front and backyards, even an inflatable bounce house for his fourth-grade classmates and neighborhood friends. The cake was his favorite, chocolate with strawberry icing. The monster was friendly with everyone. His friends told him he had a "cool dad."

It made the boy smile. Maybe it was the irony or perhaps it was what the boy had remembered from earlier times or most likely what he had wished for, so long. He opened his gifts, a football, a basketball, and a chess set that the monster said he'd help the boy learn. And a bunch of games that he probably wouldn't be able to play with his friends, who were usually not allowed to visit his home.

His mother had given him a watch. He wondered if she really knew how much he didn't want to know or remember about time. Everyone sang, "Happy Birthday." They gathered around him as he closed his eyes and made his wish. When he opened his

*eyes, he saw his father for a moment. He blew out the nine
candles on his cake, but the monster had returned.*

* * *

Todd woke up, startled. He had fallen asleep in a large armchair
in his den. Dr. Richard Stevens descended the stairs with a small
black leather bag and approached Todd, who had not yet recovered from the abrupt awakening. Stevens had tried retiring at least
three times, but he loved his work not only for his regular patients,
who were among the most powerful in the state, but also for those
who came to the free clinics that he sponsored and would personally provide services every Tuesday and Thursday. He knew
many of them came only so they could brag about having the
same doctor as those famous celebrities and sport figures.

"I gave Liz some sedatives. She should be asleep most of the
night. Wouldn't be a bad idea if I prescribed some for you, too.
Although it looks like you're about to pass out any minute."

"Just had a bad dream, that's all."

Concerned, the doctor held Todd's wrist and took his pulse.
"Your heart's racing."

"I nodded off. Guess you startled me when you came
downstairs."

"Just the same, I'd like you to stop by the office tomorrow.
First thing in the morning."

"I can't do that. I have to be here in case—"

"My office has these new devices called phones. If there's
any news, I'm sure you can have the call forwarded."

"Is Liz going to be all right?"

The doctor placed his bag on the floor and sat down in an
adjoining chair. "I imagine that depends on things neither one
of us can control, at least not for the moment." He took his time
in forming the next question. "Are you two getting along?

Forgive me for asking that so bluntly, especially given what you're facing. But—"

"Did she say something about us, about me?"

"No."

"You wouldn't be able to tell me if she had?"

"I'm a family doctor, not a priest. There are certain things I'm able to share with both of you. But right now, I think it's more important that you share your feelings with each other."

"I can't talk to her right now. I think being in the same room just complicates things." He hesitated, unsure if he should confide, reveal the extent of his troubled marriage. But he needed to talk to someone and who else did he have? "She told me she wanted a divorce. She's staying until we find out about Becky. Then she's leaving no matter what."

The doctor provided a sympathetic nod and collected his thoughts. "She's dealing with a traumatic situation the best way she can. Both of you are. What's said now, under the circumstances, shouldn't be taken as true or reliable. We say a lot of things we don't mean when we're afraid of what the future holds."

"I think we also say what we've been too afraid of saying, what we've been denying was true for too long. It's like a drunk revealing his feelings. Don't dismiss it just because he's lost control of what he says." Todd studied Dr. Stevens and noticed his discomfort. "You might as well get it off your chest. I know house calls aren't cheap, so I'd like my money's worth."

Dr. Stevens gave a weak smile. "Todd, a situation like this can be overwhelming to any of us... If you feel the urge to... if you should have a relapse—"

"I haven't had a drink in three years, Doctor. When Rebecca comes home, she'll find me sober... Hopefully, for the first time, she'll find a real father." Todd stood. "I'll be happy to walk you to the door."

"I know my way out. And I also know when I'm being asked to leave."

"I appreciate you coming over, Dr. Stevens. I really do. But there are no pills you can prescribe for this one."

Dr. Stevens stood and retrieved his bag. He touched Todd on the arm. "As quiet as it's kept, pills often mask the real problem."

"Then why do you doctors keep giving them?"

"It's not for the cure. It's for the hope that we'll find one. Sometimes, it's to see if our patients really want to get better." The doctor moved toward the door leading to the garden and the rear exit. "Don't forget to see me in the morning."

"Not until I find Rebecca. Know that she's safe."

"You let the police find Rebecca. Let me make sure she has a healthy father waiting for her when she returns... Deal?"

Todd didn't answer. Dr. Stevens shook his head in disappointment and left.

Todd crossed to the fireplace. Several logs were stacked together, and a small fire burned, filling the room with the scent of hickory. He looked at a framed photo of Rebecca on the mantel. She was dressed in a white summer dress, flowing chiffon. He turned on a large flat-screen television built into the wall, part of an elaborate entertainment system. He searched the list of recorded shows and selected one of his daughter's.

Todd's face became transfixed by the images of Rebecca participating in the school's dance recital. Graceful, beautiful, and full of confidence, she seemed to float in the air with each perfect movement.

She danced to "If I Could," performed by the school's choir. She knew it was his favorite song, the one he believed defined a father's responsibility. Todd listened to the lyrics, which sounded as if they were being sung by angels without a care in the world. The song was a reminder of the difficulties of growing up, the joy, the pain, the bruises a father hopes will heal, without ever leaving behind any permanent scars.

He smiled with pride at his daughter's accomplishment. He hadn't realized she was so gifted. He leaned forward in his chair, bent over in a sharp pain that attacked his senses as each lyric resulted in an incrimination of his failures. Why hadn't he shielded her from a world that would rob her of her innocence far too soon? Yes, he realized she had her own life and all he could do was watch her grow. But he wasn't prepared to let her go. Not now. Not at her age when she hadn't enough experience to understand the experience she's had.

He felt ill.

A reddish-yellow and blue light flickered from the fireplace, making the room disappear but not the pain.

His body shook.

The music ended.

The image of Rebecca on the monitor was now frozen in time as she stood center stage accepting the applause and adoration given enthusiastically by the overflowing audience in the auditorium.

Todd placed his hands over his mouth, not in fear that he would vomit a lifetime of regret, but in a failed effort to stifle the sobs that came and lasted all night.

TWENTY-SEVEN

Ron had established a makeshift work area on the dining room table, now covered with reams of printouts. Discarded notes were scattered on the floor extending to the kitchen and living room. His eyes burned from staring at the bright color monitor for four consecutive days and nights, ever since the equipment was loaned to him. The names and addresses that scrolled endlessly were little more than a fleeting blur. He didn't remember the last time he had slept, and it was clear he'd gone too long without proper hygiene, including a much-needed change of clothes.

The task before him was monumental. He had a better chance of finding the proverbial needle in the haystack or winning the lottery. Still, those things happened even if by mistake. As long as you keep trying, there's a chance. What else could he believe?

His door buzzer went off. He glanced at his watch: almost midnight. He wondered if the detectives had returned to search again. Who else would be ringing his bell at this late hour? If they had come back, he would allow them to search every inch of the apartment, if necessary, without complaint, as long as it forced them to aim their investigation in the right direction. But what if they hadn't come for that? What if this was the visit that every parent, dreaded—the announcement that would inalterably define their lives forever with the words, "I'm sorry to inform you..."

Another buzz caused him to rush to the door. "Hello," he spoke breathlessly into the intercom. He listened to the sound of wind hissing through the speaker and pushed the talk button again. "Hello."

He was about to walk away and return to his work, hoping it was probably just a drunk who pushed the wrong button. Then the visitor's greeting froze him in place. "Mr. Butler, this is Todd Roth. You were at my news conference the other day."

Ron rubbed his eyes. Of all the possibilities on the other end of this intercom, the last voice he would have expected to hear was the one belonging to Todd Roth.

"I apologize for coming so late, unannounced. I wonder if I—"

Ron pushed the button that unlocked the front entrance and opened the door. He straightened his shirt, then realized he wouldn't even be able to make himself presentable if he had an hour's warning, maybe more. He ran his hand through his hair and waited.

Todd opened the fire door and proceeded down the hallway dressed in a cashmere jacket, pants that were probably a blend of silk and linen, and shoes that would have paid Ron's rent for two months. While he looked tired and stressed, he still could have been on the cover of a men's fashion magazine.

He stopped in front of Ron, both men staring at each other in an awkward silence. Ron knew the man was already beginning to regret his visit. He could also tell that Todd was uncomfortable with the sight of the bedraggled human being standing at the doorway. He thought he should say something before Todd understandably ran off.

"How'd you find me?"

"The mayor's office. I asked security for your address."

"Pays to have friends in high places." The two men stood silently. Now neither one looked at the other, which made it a bit easier to move to the next stage. "Do you want to come in?"

Todd entered and Rod quickly closed the door. He didn't want to miss the opportunity to learn what generated the visit.

"Can I get you something to drink? A beer?"

"I don't drink... alcohol. Not anymore."

Ron knew that whenever someone said he didn't drink alcohol, and then paused before saying the magic word, "anymore," it could only mean the person had a past that continued to haunt the future. He studied Todd for a beat. For all this man's wealth, power, and connections, this unexpected guest seemed just as uncomfortable and vulnerable as the occupant. A week or two without your child will do that.

He motioned for Todd to take a seat. "Make yourself at home. It's not much of one at the moment, but it's the best I can do."

Todd sat down on the couch. Ron sat on the opposite end. Both men stared ahead like two nervous people on an awkward blind date. "The place isn't usually this disheveled. In fact, it never is. I guess I'm not exactly looking like Mr. *GQ* myself."

"Given the circumstances, you certainly don't have to explain anything to me."

"How are you holding up?" asked Ron, as if he was in any better position to answer the same question.

"Not too good. I'm afraid my wife isn't doing much better. Truth is, she's scared to death and maybe the only thing that gives her any strength is her anger at me."

"She blames you?"

"Not as much as I blame myself."

"Yeah," Ron nods. "I know the feeling." The men remained quiet for several moments.

"Did you receive any news?" asked Ron, not knowing if he wanted to know the answer.

"After nine days there's been no ransom demand so that means whoever took her..." He paused for a beat, cleared his throat. "Money wasn't the motive." It was now his turn to study Ron. "What about you? You hear anything?"

Ron shook his head no. "Well, as you can see"—he extended his arm and pointed to his surroundings—"ransom was never a consideration. And I don't know what's happening, but I am sure I don't have the same resources working to find my daughter as you have for yours." Ron realized the comment seemed harsh, but he didn't care. "I'm just trying to get the police to stop looking at me as the suspect and turn their attention where it needs to be."

"I'm sure they're just doing their jobs."

"Really?" replied Ron, with the first sign of anger. "And did they question you or your wife like you were the criminals? Did they ask why you had an education fund for your daughter?" He stood up and paced the area, agitated, frustrated, and confused. "Although I suppose you never had to worry about a college savings plan. Guess you would just write a check or maybe your well-connected friends would get her a full scholarship after you made a healthy donation to the university!"

Todd rose from the couch which caused Ron to stop pacing. The two men stood opposite each other, not so much in a fighting stance but more like two pieces on a chessboard waiting for a move, not certain who was entitled to go next.

"Mr. Butler, I didn't come here to fight with you. And I hope with all my heart that I get a chance to write that check for my daughter and that you're able to use your college fund on *your* daughter's behalf."

Ron returned to the couch, sitting closer to the middle. He looked down at the floor. "Why'd you come here? I know it wasn't 'cause you thought I could help you. So, why'd you'd come?

"I'm not sure. I just thought I needed to. It was something I had to do." He sat down next to Ron. "I needed someone to understand what I was going through, who better than you? I guess I also wanted to see how you were doing."

"If you find out, I'd appreciate you letting me know." More silence. "I thought you might have come here to punch me in the mouth for ruining your press conference. You have every right to be angry. If our positions were reversed, I think you'd still be in custody."

"But our positions aren't reversed, are they?"

Ron thought about it. How could their positions be the same? This man could have given his daughter anything in the world, things that Ron couldn't dream of giving Jennifer. And yet both daughters were now taken from them, and no matter the race or the bank accounts or the places where they lived or the people that they knew, in that one fact they were very much alike.

Todd noticed the computer equipment in the dining area and crossed to it. "Did I interrupt your work?" He picked up some of the printed material, looked at Ron curiously. "What's all this?"

"A list of child offenders within a twenty-mile radius of my daughter's school."

Todd turned page after page of the printout and then dropped it on the table. "There're hundreds of names," he said in disbelief.

"That's only a partial list. I ran out of printer paper before I could finish."

Todd slowly sat on one of the wooden chairs at the table, taking in the information. "How'd you get all this information on them?"

"Anyone can get it. Part of Megan's Law."

"And what are you going to do with it?"

"I'm going to do what any father would do. I'm going to do what the police should be doing. I'm going to do whatever I can to find my daughter. No matter how long it takes. No matter the consequences."

Todd stood and walked slowly toward the door. He opened it.

"Where are you going?"

"How long are you going to be up?"

"A few hours," said Ron.

"Then you're going to need more computer paper. I've got plenty at my office. Be back as soon as I can." He studied Ron for a beat. "If that's all right?"

Ron didn't know where this was going but he nodded approval and watched the father who, like himself, had a missing daughter, walk away.

TWENTY-EIGHT

There were hours spent in silence, where the girls didn't speak, wouldn't even look at each other. Whenever one of the girls cried, no matter how quietly, it would set off a chain reaction of misery that ended when they slept and began again when they awoke. They were never sure of when it was safe to speak above a whisper. Once one of the girls was taken for her time to bathe, it presented the perfect opportunity for everyone else to speak openly. They felt they had a few minutes after every lunch or dinner period to speak freely. They tried the best they could to communicate using signals but that wasn't effective. So, at one point, they simply decided to speak normally except for those occasions when they needed to talk about him or those special times when they were brave enough to talk about escape. Being rescued provided a topic that brought them the greatest hope until it didn't. Hope, as well as faith, had a limited shelf life with each passing day of captivity.

They needed to find things to do that would break the monotony, lift their spirits. It was important to never lose hope and, no matter what, they needed to stick together. Jennifer asked them to describe their favorite activities and after a bit of cajoling the girls willingly complied with the request.

"I love movies... Especially Disney," offered Selena.

"But we can't watch any. There's no television," said Mei Lin.

Rebecca jumped in. "We don't have to watch. We can talk about them."

Jennifer smiled. "Act them out. At least the parts we remember."

"And what we don't remember," said Rebecca, "we can make up. Each one of us playing a different character."

The girls smiled at the idea.

Yes, Jennifer would be able to count on this girl. Or so she hoped.

"*Toy Story* was great," stated Selena.

"I liked the mutant toys," added Mei Lin. "How they all ganged up on Sid."

"Keep that thought when we get to gang up on you know who," advised Jennifer. "In fact, let's call him Sid from now on."

Selena and Mei Lin nodded approval. Rebecca licked her index finger, marked an imaginary blackboard. Point made. Jennifer returned the favor by doing the same. Point appreciated.

Selena raised her hand. "I love the part when Woody and Buzz were flying toward the van."

"Uh, Buzz?" said Jennifer in her best Woody imitation. "We missed the truck!"

"We're not aiming for the truck!" shouted all the girls. They laughed but the mood changed quickly as the girls looked around and observed their surroundings, a prison without bars and, for the moment, without much hope.

"*Alice in Wonderland*!" exclaimed Mei Lin. "I watched the video eight straight times!"

"I wish we had some of that mushroom," said Selena.

"We could eat the side that makes us small," suggested Mei Lin, "and then sneak out of here.

Jennifer chimed in. "I say we eat the side that makes us big and kick butt!"

This false bravado allowed them to laugh again, although their nervousness remained evident. Their effort to renew their spirits was valiant, even if it wouldn't last long.

"*Bambi*'s my favorite of all time," said Rebecca.

"Except I hated what happened to Bambi's mother," Mei Lin reminded the group which forced them to think about the movie's ending. Worried expressions formed on the faces of all the girls.

"I liked the fact that the new *Little Mermaid* had a mermaid that looked like me," said Jennifer."

Mei Lin responded, "You don't look like a mermaid!" The girls laughed.

"I meant it was nice to finally see a character of color who was in charge." clarified Jennifer.

"Hey, don't I have a color," replied Rebecca.

Selena shrugged. "Yeah. But you're in all the movies."

"*The Lion King!*" Jennifer made another effort to change the mood. The girls smiled but once again reality sunk in.

"Simba's father died," said Selena. "I never realized Disney movies were that sick."

"My father's gonna find me," said a determined Jennifer. "I know he will."

"Mine, too," agreed Selena.

"Mine, too," added Mei Lin.

The girls turned to Rebecca, waited for her to agree, complete the commitment. Jennifer noticed the expression on her face, insecure, doubting. She thought Rebecca wanted to make it unanimous. But there was something preventing her from joining the declaration. "Mine, too," Rebecca finally said. But Jennifer recognized there was no conviction in the statement, no belief that she would be found by her father or perhaps anyone else. It made her reconsider whether the new girl could be counted on after all.

* * *

Lit candles surrounded his bed. Incense sticks burned, the smoke rising slowly, embracing his face as he watched the girls, amused.

The girls shared a look of concern, captured on the man's surveillance monitor in his bedroom. He had been watching all along, noticing the hesitation, the doubt on the faces of some of the girls, except for Jennifer. He could tell she was a leader. The girls responded to her, seemed to like her, depend on her.

She reminded him of the girl who had sat next to him in the second grade. Caramel skin that glistened in the sunlight, braided hair that she allowed him to touch, to see what it felt like. She could tell he was lonely, needed a friend. He'd looked into those vast brown eyes and discovered a retreat from all the bullies who had tormented him from his first day in school. And when she smiled, *when she smiled*, her ivory teeth looked like precious keys on a grand piano that would unlock the fears that waited for him at home. He would invite her to visit no matter the consequence. But even he had never considered the cost of such an innocent invitation.

He looked at his wall calendar. Thursday was circled in red although he didn't really need a reminder. He would be at the school at least fifteen minutes before the bell rang, like always.

TWENTY-NINE

TUESDAY APRIL 18TH

Todd drove his Mercedes 500 SLS AMG down Overland Avenue. Ron sat in the passenger seat.

"If you need any more paper or any other printing or computer support, you just need to call my office and they'll take care of it."

"You sure you wanna do this?"

"Do you have a choice? Then neither do I? Anyway, our efforts got some much-needed assistance. I hired a detective."

Ron appeared stunned at the information. "I didn't ask you to hire anyone," he replied angrily.

"What are you upset about? This isn't anything we can handle on our own."

"We?" He looked at Todd in amazement. "What's this 'we' shit? You can hire all the high-price detectives you want. That's not going to help me find my daughter."

"Why not?"

"Because they're working for you! Looking for your daughter! Not mine!"

Todd pulled the car to the side of the road, pulled inside a McDonald's parking lot and turned off the engine.

"Yes! They're looking for my daughter! I'll give them all the names on that list you compiled! They'll add more from every state if need be! But if in the process of searching they find your daughter, then—"

"If in the process!" Ron opened the door ready to exit. "You mean, if it's not too much of an inconvenience, on the way to saving the rich white guy's daughter, if we just happen to come across the other kid." He exited the vehicle, leaned over and glared at Todd. "You go ahead and spend your money. Deduct it as a business expense! If I happen to find your daughter while I'm looking for mine, I'll give you a call! Until then, go fuck yourself!" He slammed shut the door and stormed off.

Todd quickly exited the car, running after him. "Hey! Who the hell was it that came into my goddamn news conference?" He caught up with Ron who turned to confront him.

"You ought to be grateful! You got more coverage for the dollar!"

"So now you're just gonna run away?"

The two men stood face to face. Ron tried to regain control of his emotions and spoke calmly. "No... I'm gonna *walk* away."

As he walked away again, Todd waved his hand in an angry dismissal. "Fine," he said, calling after him. "Leave... Sacrifice your daughter to your ego." He turned and walked toward his car.

Ron whipped around and went after Todd. He grabbed him as he was opening the car door and spun him around. Both men cocked their fists ready to fly. They looked at each other, fists tightened, and then relaxed a bit. They dropped their hands to their sides. Ron released Todd as onlookers from the fast-food restaurant returned to their business. He took a step back, unsure of what to say, and sensing Todd felt even more awkward.

"You got your cell phone?" he asked.

Todd nodded.

"Give it to me."

"Why?"

Ron didn't answer, waited patiently. Todd reached inside his jacket, removed his phone.

"Open it to your address book."

Todd did so and handed the phone to Ron who scrolled through a series of phone numbers. "I expected to find the mayor, even the police chief. But the governor? The senator?" He handed the phone back. "We're not the same. Not by a mile. Our daughters are not the same. The police, the detectives, the damn F.B.I., won't see us as the same. You know why I released you just then? Why I stepped back to create a safe space? 'Cause anyone seeing us would have called the police and when they came, who do you think they'd point their guns at?"

The two men stare at each other, neither one having an answer to their situation. Todd finally broke the silence. "I'm not going to apologize for having money and influential friends. And I fully intend to utilize them and any other advantages my wealth and standing in this community brings. I don't know if I'll ever see my daughter alive again. But if I do, nothing will make me happier than for her to become friends with your daughter. If you're willing to allow that to happen. If it's even possible in this world for our girls to want it to happen."

They shifted their stance, embarrassed, like two boys who'd like to become friends but don't know how to admit it.

"My daughter likes trains," said Ron. "Actually, I'm the one who likes trains. I think she likes them because I do. In fact, I know she outgrew them at least five years ago, but didn't want to let me down because she knows how much I enjoy seeing her play with them. She allows me to build the station and organize the tracks, but I'm not very good at it, so she changes everything and makes it beautiful."

"My daughter likes to dance. I can't dance at all. I think she likes to dance because I can't." Todd chuckled uncomfortably.

"That and the fact her mother was a professional dancer until I came into her life and convinced her to marry me."

They both smiled.

"I think Becky, she hates it when I call her that. I think Rebecca would like your daughter."

"Jennifer loves to be called Jenny. She thinks Jennifer is too snooty. Don't think she'd be too thrilled with a 'Rebecca.' But I know she'd find Becky pretty cool."

Todd extended his hand.

Ron took it with a firm grip. They shook hands and nodded to each other, either a sign of approval, understanding or respect. Whatever it represented, it also meant that they were a team, at least for now.

"Let's find our daughters, Ron."

"And bring them home."

Ron entered the passenger side. Todd got behind the driver's seat and drove off.

THIRTY

The first three visits were uneventful. They received a polite "don't know anything," response from the person at the top of the list. The second person wasn't home. The third had moved three weeks earlier after the neighbors had discovered his previous crimes and threatened to kill him. They didn't expect things to change much with the next visit, but they were wrong.

Todd drove his Mercedes, while Ron reviewed the list and searched for the numbers on the side of the curb. "Number 1369 should be the large duplex," Ron said, pointing to a run-down L-shaped apartment complex on the outskirts of Culver City.

Todd found a parking space half a block away. They exited the car, approached the building, and stood together looking at the front entrance. Ron thought they were both thinking the same thing.

"You sure you want to continue this?" asked Todd.

"It's better than waiting at home and going crazy."

"What's the apartment number?"

"Six B."

"What do we say if he's home?" asked Todd. "Hi, we've come to see if you've kidnapped any young girls. Can you let us in to take a look around your lovely place?"

"Can we use your bathroom might work."

The two men made their way through a walkway that hadn't been cleaned in weeks. Weeds were the only signs of life benefiting from sprinklers spouting streams of water on a dead lawn.

They didn't need a security code to enter the building since the locks had been stripped away. Rather than use the buzzer, they decided to go directly to the apartment. Several lights in the hallway were broken or burned out. The numbering on the doors didn't proceed in any logical sequence.

"It's over here," announced Ron.

Todd knocked on the door several times.

"Try not to sound like the police," said Ron.

"And how do I manage that?"

"Don't sound arrogant."

Peter Winston opened the door wearing a dirty white undershirt and a pair of stained Dockers that would never make it on a commercial. Ron tried to peer inside and see as much as he could of the apartment. From the little he was able to observe, it was obvious the place was in disarray. The carpets were filthy, and it took less than a second for the odor emanating from the kitchen to attack his senses.

"Whatever you're selling, I don't need it." Winston studied Todd. His expression lit up with recognition. "You're that guy in the news," he said, flashing a crooked smile that revealed rotten teeth. "The one whose daughter was taken."

"Any reason you'd remember that?" Todd asked.

"I like kids," he said sarcastically.

The man attempted to close the door, but Ron placed his foot in the way. The man looked at him suspiciously.

"Are you Peter Winston?" asked Todd.

"Tell your colored friend to get his foot out of my doorway or I'll cut it off and feed it to my dog for his supper."

"Your dog's quiet," replied Ron.

"He's always quiet before he eats," answered Winston. "But he especially likes dark meat."

"A pedophile and a racist," replied Ron. "How imaginative."

Winston focused his attention on Ron. "I remember you. You looked heavier on T.V. Beggin' for help and sniveling like a bitch."

Todd touched Ron on his arm. "Let's go. This is a waste of time." He turned to leave but Ron didn't move.

"I don't know what you're so upset about," continued Winston. "These Black girls give it up pretty easily. Wherever she is, I'm sure she's enjoyin' it."

Ron charged Winston, knocking him backwards. They both fell into the living room knocking over a small table and shattering a cheap lamp. Todd rushed inside.

Ron choked Winston until pulled away by Todd. Still enraged, Ron had to be held back from getting to Winston who was rubbing his neck and laughing.

"You two comin' here is better than me winnin' the lottery." He rose from the floor and stared at both men, grinning like a man who had every reason to celebrate. "I can hardly wait to call my lawyer. Take a vacation to Mexico. They got beautiful beaches and really cute kids."

"You sick piece of shit," said Ron.

"If I'm sick, what does that make you two sorry motherfuckers? You come to my home. Why? You expect I've got your kid? Or you think all us ex-sex-offenders got some kinda hotline? Dial 1-800-Pedophile slash Child Abductor, and we can locate your molester of choice." He took a step closer to Ron. "You know how many communities I've been run out of? How many jobs I've lost since you vigilante types put together those computer hit-lists?"

"Are we supposed to care about that?" asked Ron.

"No. Just like I don't care about you or your two girls." He crossed to the door. "You got a lot of nerve comin' here. I made my mistake. Now I gotta pay all my life." He opened the door wide. "Hope you gentlemen do the same."

Ron and Todd exited the apartment. Winston slammed the door on them as they left.

The two men stood together in the hallway. "Well, that certainly went splendidly," commented Todd. "What the fuck was that about? You got any other ideas about what else we should do?"

Ron looked at his hands, sniffing them in disgust. "We should have brought some disinfectant."

"We'll pick up some rubber gloves before the next visit, just in case you want to choke somebody again."

They walked down the hallway toward the exit.

Ron suggested, "We should pick up an extra pair for you, just in case you get in the mood."

"We'll need more than gloves if you try some shit like that again. Honestly, Ron, what the hell were you thinking? What if he had a gun?"

"Then we should get one. I'm sure you got some that are bigger than his," answered Ron.

"Whatever we find out on these visits, we let the police know. We don't take anything into our own hands. And we certainly don't bring guns with us. That's only begging for trouble."

Ron gave him a look. "My rich friend, in case you haven't noticed, you never have to beg for trouble. It'll come, invited or not." Ron attempted to convince Todd, as well as himself, that whatever lay ahead they could handle. But he knew better and based on what he could surmise from his newfound partner's expression, the future challenges would bring all the danger and heartbreak they could withstand.

They left the building and would make five more visits before calling it a day.

THIRTY-ONE

Todd was exhausted from the day's nonproductive efforts. He wanted to be home in the unlikely chance he could find an hour or two of sleep. But this evening he sat at a conference table, across from James Harrison and two other private detectives who needed to meet with him. This wasn't a run-in-the-mill agency that made its money spying on unfaithful spouses, unless they were major celebrities who could afford the bill. Harrison had parlayed his twenty years with the L.A.P.D., ten with the F.B.I., and five with Homeland Security, into a well-connected, high-powered organization consisting of more than a dozen investigators, several of whom served in special ops in Iraq and Afghanistan. They had the talent, know-how, and ingenuity to solve problems quickly and discreetly. Their political connections allowed them immediate access to confidential information, which they utilized without regard to legal restrictions or ethical constraints.

"Do you have any idea how many sex offenders are listed on the state's computer system?" asked Harrison.

"One-hundred-twenty thousand," answered Todd.

"That's only a fraction of the number out there," continued Harrison. "Fifteen thousand haven't even bothered to register."

"There's another twenty-five percent who legally don't have to be included," added Brent Edwards, Harrison's partner. What he lacked in charm, he more than made up for in dogged perseverance and, if necessary, sheer ruthlessness. This firm believed serving its clients was a moral imperative.

"I'm aware of both the statistics and the magnitude of the task we've undertaken. Both Mr. Butler and I conducted the research before making the decision to proceed. And we're committed to it, now more than ever."

"Mr. Roth, you're the client, but I can tell you the best use of your time and ours does not rest with chasing down the whereabouts of the people on that list, who for pretty obvious reasons change addresses rather frequently." Harrison packed tobacco into a pipe but didn't light it.

"Mr. Harrison, I've got to do something. I've promised Mr. Butler that I—"

"I don't mean to be insensitive, but Mr. Butler is not your daughter, and helping him could get in the way of finding her."

"He also doesn't have your financial resources," suggested Edwards, "which means he doesn't face liability if someone he chokes in the future decides to sue." He leaned forward to underscore the point. "Even perverts have rights."

"And perverts usually have lawyers, assuming that's not a redundancy," quipped Harrison, to the amusement of his staff.

Todd refused to participate in the humor.

Harrison leaned sympathetically toward him. "Let us do our jobs, Mr. Roth. We'll find your daughter." He spoke as if issuing a warning. "But only if you allow us to focus our energies and talents where we can do the most good."

Todd stood. "I'll give you all the money you need to do your job, Mr. Harrison."

Harrison nodded appreciatively.

"But whatever else I decide to do to find my daughter, no matter how unconventional or inefficient, is my decision... Not yours."

He placed a business card on the table and slid it toward Harrison. "That's a private cell number. The line is dedicated solely for information on my daughter." He took his briefcase. "If you learn anything new, no matter how seemingly insignificant, you're to call me day or night."

Todd left Harrison's office and drove home in time for a late dinner, which Liz had waiting for him on his arrival. He wasn't sure if that had been planned. Most likely, she had expected to eat alone. And even though they sat at the same table, she managed to accomplish that. They ate without looking at each other, despite having to pass the vegetables or share the butter.

When he finally did look at her, something he used to find great joy in doing, he didn't recognize her. Even when she was exhausted, there was a vitality in the way she carried herself: an energy in her eyes and in the way she moved. Now, she appeared fragile and something that he would never have thought possible, defeated. And he could see, firsthand, her spirit increasingly vanishing each of the last ten days to coincide with Rebecca's disappearance.

They had nearly finished their meal when Liz broke the silence, finally recognizing his presence. "You're going to meet him, again?"

He stopped eating, but it was evident from his body language that he didn't want to have this discussion. Not with the stranger who sat across from him. "Yes." He tossed a cloth napkin on the table, and then proceeded to the living room, where he put on his leather jacket.

Liz left her place at the table and moved to the front door, blocking his exit. "This thing that you're doing, is it legal?" She waited for an answer. "Is it dangerous? Is it—"

"Crazy?" He retrieved his car keys from another coat. "Yes. It makes no sense at all. But I don't know what else to do. I just can't wait here with—"

"Me?"

They stared at each other with a sadness that still managed to convey hope.

"With the phone ringing and seeing how it affects you, and me, and yes. Yes. With you."

She turned away, giving him enough room to leave, but he moved closer to her.

"I see how you look at me. You blame me. I know you do. And you're right. I should have watched her. I should have taken her with me to get the food. Or I should have done what I always do. Found a reason not to be with her. If I hadn't taken her there, if I had broken my promise like I always had in the past, she'd be here. She'd be a—"

"Alive?" She lunged closer. Todd initially thought she would strike him. "Don't you say that! Don't you even think it! Our daughter's alive! You understand me? I don't care what the statistics say. If it's ten days or a hundred and ten days, she's alive."

He cast his gaze downward, unable to respond or look at her, until she grabbed his face with both hands, forcing him to make eye contact. "Rebecca's alive! You say that!" She removed her hands from his face. Her arms fell limply to her side.

He placed his index finger gently on her lips and spoke softly, reassuringly. "She's alive." He placed his hands on her shoulders and felt them tremble. He wanted to kiss her. And as inappropriate and untimely as it seemed, he wanted to make love to her. But all he could do was tell her what she wanted to hear. And what he needed to believe. "Rebecca's alive. I'll do everything in my power to find her. To bring her home."

"How, Todd? By running around with a man you don't even know. Using some computer list to track down criminals, who have absolutely nothing to do with her disappearance."

He stepped away from the foyer and back into the living room, needing to distance himself from her, but mostly desperate for a space to breathe. She denied the separation angrily confronting him.

"How is that going to bring our daughter home?"

He slammed his fist on an end table, knocking over the lamp, and shattering the light bulb. "I want her to know I'm searching for her! If she reads the paper or is somewhere to hear the news, I want her to know I haven't given up! Will never give up!"

He extended his arms to his wife, palms up, not in an attempt to hold her, but to search for the right words to explain his behavior and have her understand the depth of his determination. "If nothing else, I want the person who took her to know, there's no place on earth where it will be safe for him, if he harms my little girl." His voice broke on the words, *my little girl.*

Liz walked to the couch and slowly sank down. Todd placed the broken lamp on the table, and then picked up pieces of broken glass.

"I'll do that," she interrupted his work. "You go and do what you need to do, the way you need to do it."

He wanted to hear something other than the words that followed.

"Just go."

He watched her body gently rock back and forth as she closed her eyes in despair. He wanted to be there for her when she opened them but knew he was the last person on earth she wanted to see. He left quietly.

THIRTY-TWO

An overhead, dim light barely illuminated the area. Selena slept peacefully, while Mei Lin's sleep was far more restless. Jennifer and Rebecca sat quietly on their respective cots. Jennifer leaned her back against the wall and studied Rebecca, who had her knees pressed against her chest, rocking rhythmically back and forth, the way her mother often did when lost in thought or attempting to calm her nerves.

Despite Jennifer doing all she could to comfort her, the first couple of days were extremely difficult for Rebecca. Whenever Rebecca cried, she did so by turning her body away from everyone else and squeezing herself against the wall, stifling the sound, as if she didn't want to burden anyone with her troubles. But seeing the oldest girl in the group break down caused the others to cry, especially Mei Lin. Selena's speech pattern had begun to improve but it didn't take much for her to stagger her words, not quite at a stuttering pace, more akin to a young girl attempting to overcome shyness and fear. Having Rebecca solemn for several hours at a time also took its toll on Jennifer, who felt increasingly responsible for the welfare of the other girls.

Rebecca stopped rocking, and then extended her legs, alternately raising one and lowering the other. She stood and began a series of stretching exercises.

Impressed with her flexibility and needing to find a way to keep Rebecca as positive as possible, Jennifer said: "You're good." She shook her head in admiration. "I could never stretch that far."

"Sure you could. Just have to keep trying. You should see what my mother's yoga instructor can do with his body. It's pretty creepy." Rebecca extended her arms over her head, stood on her toes, lifted one leg, and bent it at the knee. She spun slowly, gracefully.

Jennifer applauded quietly.

Rebecca curtseyed several times, accepting adoration, as if receiving it from an auditorium full of enthusiastic fans. She gave one final grand curtsey, her head almost touching the floor.

Jennifer laughed. "Something tells me you like to dance, especially in front of a lot of people."

"It wouldn't matter if I was the only one in the room. There's really no other feeling like it. It's a freedom that's hard to explain. You think you can fly, reach heights you thought impossible."

Jennifer felt a tinge of envy, although it was outweighed by her respect for Rebecca's passion and talent.

"Sometimes I close my eyes and block out everything around me, and I listen to the music that's inside. My mom always said that every person has their own melody, a special song that belongs only to them."

Listening to Rebecca speak about her mother reminded Jennifer of the void, the continuing emptiness in her life. No matter how much her father loved her and had given her, he couldn't replace the missing part that always ached—the need to have a mom, to call out her name, and have her respond with a hug or with laughter that sounded like her own. How she longed to hear a woman's voice say the words her father had repeated every morning and night: *I love you, my daughter*.

"And when you hear that song and allow it to control the way you move," Rebecca shrugged, and released a youthful sigh. "I guess that's what you call magic."

Rebecca's love for her gift had almost allowed Jennifer to forget about the chains that entrapped them, as well as the conditions of their imprisonment. *Almost*.

"I'll always be grateful my mom signed me up for classes."

Jennifer thought about how grateful she would be simply to have her mom. "How long have you trained?"

Rebecca stood flatfooted, bent side to side, then returned to her cot, and sat. "She enrolled me in my first dance class as soon as I could walk. She used to be a dancer. That's how she met my father. He attended a ballet where she performed. She told me he ran out at intermission and bought two dozen roses, a box of chocolates, and reserved a private table at a French restaurant. He had a bottle of champagne waiting, along with a violinist, a piano player, and a singer, who serenaded them all night."

"How did he know she'd go out with him?"

"My dad's very persistent when he wants something." She began to rock back and forth, again. "Unfortunately, sometimes he loses interest when he gets it."

Jennifer observed the sadness in Rebecca's eyes and knew it had little to do with her confinement.

"What about your mom and dad?" asked Rebecca? "Are they still together?"

Jennifer thought it an odd question and wondered if it was asked because of her race, as if all Black children were raised in so-called *broken homes*. Then she realized her oversensitivity had little to do with any implication, real or perceived, but rather reflected her discomfort with the subject matter. "My mom died just after I was born."

"I'm sorry," said Rebecca. "You don't have to talk about it, if you don't want to."

"I don't mind. I like talking about her." That wasn't totally true, *needing* to talk differed significantly from *liking* to talk, but it could accomplish the same goal. "My dad doesn't talk about her much. I think he feels I can't handle it, but I know he's the one who still can't deal with it, after all this time."

"How do you know anything about her?"

"'Cause I know everything about my dad. And I know she must have been wonderful to have married someone like that." She hesitated.

"What?"

"I know where my dad keeps all her photographs, hidden in the back of his closet; two thick albums, including when she was younger than me. I saw pictures of her when she was in high school, and college, and all their marriage photos. I even found a shoebox filled with love letters. I know I shouldn't have read them, but once I started, I had to find out everything I could about her." Jennifer pressed her hands together, as if in prayer. "She had such beautiful penmanship. I tried to copy it. I think I came close, but then I changed it."

"Why?"

"Because I knew it made my father sad whenever he checked my homework or when I wrote him notes." She cleared her throat, and Rebecca stared at the floor. "Anyway, I needed to find out who I was. I guess I wanted to write my own signature, without it being like anyone else's." She looked at Rebecca, who finally had made eye contact. "Maybe in a way, that's like discovering my own song."

Rebecca nodded a sad agreement. "I don't think my dad and mom love each other anymore."

"Why do you say that?"

"It's just the way they act with each other. I used to blame it on my dad being away so much, always busy at work, involved in so many activities. But even if you're tired, you can still hold someone's hand, hug them, especially if you're married to them. Or..."

"Or what?"

"Or if they're your daughter," she answered, her voice fading.

Jennifer wanted to say something positive, to make Rebecca feel better. They needed each other. And Rebecca, more than the others, had to stay strong. Jennifer couldn't afford to deal with this on her own. She needed help, if she ever hoped to gain what Rebecca found when she danced, her freedom. "I can't imagine any father not loving their daughter. I don't think that's possible, especially with a daughter like you."

The two girls looked at each other, exchanging mutual admiration, perhaps forming a genuine friendship.

Rebecca nodded in appreciation.

"Will you teach me how to dance?"

"Here?"

"Well, this will have to do, until you can do a sleepover at my place."

Rebecca smiled. It was the first real smile Jennifer had seen from Rebecca since the day she arrived.

"Yeah, I'll teach you," Rebecca promised. "But I warn you, the stretching exercises are the hardest part."

"I guess I'll just have to find my melody as quick as possible."

"That works for the dance," advised Rebecca. "Not the torture of exercise."

"At least I won't have to face the pain alone."

"What do you mean?"

Jennifer pointed to Selena and Mei Lin, now awake and listening intently. "We're a team. We do things together."

Selena and Mei Lin nodded in agreement.

"When do we start?" asked Selena.

"Now's as good a time as any," answered Rebecca.

Selena, Mei Lin, and Jennifer jumped off their cots causing their chains to rattle against the floor.

Rebecca led the girls in stretching exercises, showing them proper positions, instructing them on a variety of techniques. She started with what she called, "morning exercises." The girls sat on the edge of their cots, their feet remaining flat on the floor.

"Okay, bend over and touch your feet with your hands."

The girls followed the instructions, correcting their posture based on Rebecca's advice. "You've got to arch your back." Rebecca evaluated their performance. "Hold for a count of ten."

The girls counted, releasing sighs of relief at the conclusion. "Great!"

The three trainees smiled proudly.

"Now repeat five times."

"Five!" exclaimed Selena.

"Five," confirmed Rebecca. "After that, we concentrate on the neck, then the back, then the hamstring."

The girls groaned.

"No way," said Mei Lin.

"I'm out, too," echoed Selena.

"Then we work on our balance," continued Rebecca, unaffected by the growing revolt. "I'll teach you how to do a wall slide."

"Is that a dance?" asked Jennifer.

"Nope," said a reenergized Rebecca. "You each stand with your back against the wall, feet shoulder-width apart." She demonstrated the position. "Slowly bend your knees, like this." She performed the exercise, while the other girls shook their heads in disapproval.

"I've got a bad back," Selena informed the group, to little sympathy.

"This will help," promised Rebecca. "Slide your back down

the wall for a count of five. Make sure your knees are bent at a forty-five-degree angle."

"Oh, now we have to learn geometry, too," Jennifer joked.

"If you bend more than that," warned Rebecca, "you could strain your knees."

"If I bend more than that," said Selena, "my back will break."

"Hold the position for five seconds, then slide up the wall until you're upright, knees straight. Then repeat the exercise—"

"Five times!" answered the group.

"I might make it ten," threatened Rebecca. The girls laughed, but stopped suddenly when they heard a thumping noise on the steps outside the door, a heavy object striking concrete every two or three seconds, until it stopped completely.

Jennifer recognized the sound of a metal bar moving against the width of the door, before a bolt dropped into place and a lock opened.

The door swung inward, but he didn't come in right away. The girls held their breath until he entered, back first, pulling an object.

When he was several feet inside, Jennifer noticed a portable cot, which he dragged across the floor and placed against the wall, next to Rebecca.

"You girls keep having fun," he said. "I'll be out of your way in a moment." He unfolded the cot, and then neatly lined it up so that it was even with Rebecca's.

He left without looking at the girls. The door closed. They heard the click of the lock and the bolt drop into place. The sound of metal scraped against the width of the door. The girls remained silent, staring at the empty cot.

THIRTY-THREE
WEDNESDAY APRIL 19TH

Ron sat at the computer early morning, printing out photos of sex offenders including summaries of their convictions. He couldn't remember when he stopped counting. There was a sick rhythm to each new photo being vomited from the printer that deadened his spirit; numbed him to the reality of why he was working this hard. Were there really this many? He watched Todd stacking missing children's flyers that had images of Rebecca and Jennifer.

"I'm including photos of the offenders on the list," Ron explained. "That way, if they're not home or they refuse to see us, we can wait outside and follow them if they appear suspicious."

Todd glanced at the photos. "*If* they appear suspicious? You see anybody in this group who doesn't look like they belong back in prison?"

"Actually, there are a few in there who look like they could be your friendly neighbor or even your trusted minister."

"Given the record of certain churches, that's hardly an endorsement."

"Guess that explains why I haven't exactly been a faithful parishioner."

"How'd you manage to access all this information?"

"As I said, most of its public record since Megan's Law. You can review it at any police department. Or get your own CD with names, photos, and zip codes. The best way is to access it directly from several data sites on the web. Justice Department updates their files regularly." He took a break and shared a soda with Todd.

"I've reprogrammed it to identify high-risk sex offenders released from prison within the last year. From everything I've read, they've got the highest rate of recidivism. I've further divided the categories by crimes and the type of victim profiles that match our daughters' disappearances." He handed a list to Todd. "These were all involved in kidnapping children younger than twelve."

"You and my wife should get together and compare notes. She's been collecting recent articles and books on pedophiles. Every other chapter, she breaks down and cries."

"I would never have thought I'd have to study something like this, not in a million years. The scary thing is, no matter how abnormal the behavior, it seems to affect otherwise normal, everyday people. I suppose it's like any other disease, it can strike anyone."

Todd finished his drink and organized a batch of posters. "How'd you get to learn so much about computers?"

"That's what I do for a living. If you can call it a living?"

"I take it you're not in love with your job."

"It almost pays the bills. Anyway, it's not the job, but the people I work for that are the problem. I was studying Engineering and Design in college. Wanted to be an architect like you... That all changed after Jenny was born."

"You've given up a lot for her?"

Ron turned off the computer. The printer spit out the last two sheets.

"She's given me more than I could ever hope to give her." He collated the material. "When she was a baby, she had the most incredible giggle. Hey, I guess all baby giggles sound the same. But for me, when I gently poked my finger into her belly, and I heard that noise jump out..." He laughed quietly, shaking his head in fond remembrance.

"I remember the first time she turned over on her back... The first time she crawled from one end of the living room, to the other... and when she took her first step... I know what those astronauts must feel when they conquer new worlds." He gave a bittersweet smile, and then it turned more solemn. "Yeah, raising her has cost me a lot, financially, personally, professionally. But I'd gladly pay any price to gain the one thing she taught me."

"Which was what?"

"That I was capable of unconditional love." He touched Todd's shoulder and nodded. "That's not a bad thing to learn, at any age."

"No," said Todd, sadly. "I imagine it's not."

"I never had much of a relationship with my father," said Ron. "I promised myself long before Jenny was born, that there'd never be a day without a hug or a night where I didn't tell her I loved her. That she was the most precious person in the world to me."

"I envy you."

"Me?" Ron laughed, dismissing the statement. "I can't even begin to imagine what I could have given my daughter if I had just one-tenth, one-hundredth of your resources."

"You gave her love... You can't put a price on that, trust me, I know."

"Here I am carrying on about Jennifer, and I know so little about your daughter."

"Sometimes, I feel the same way."

"What do you mean?"

"I know far less about my daughter than I should." Todd stacked a group of posters, tapping their edges against the table to even them out.

"I don't understand," said Ron.

"You're not alone. Neither does my wife." He began stacking a second group. "Rebecca certainly never understood." He looked at Ron. "I guess what I'm trying to say is, I didn't just lose my daughter last week. I lost her a long time ago." He studied the poster with the image of his daughter. "It makes me even more determined to get her back. No matter what."

He picked up a stack of posters, tucking them underneath his arm. "Ready to go when you are."

Ron grabbed a stack of flyers and the list of pedophiles containing their addresses and photos.

By ten o'clock they had tacked or taped more than a hundred posters and flyers onto trees, telephone poles and streetlamps starting on Lincoln Boulevard and ending on Washington at the Culver City line. They also, with the permission of the managers or owners, placed reward posters inside convenient stores, restaurants, and grocery markets.

They used the next two hours to make additional visits to those convicted felons on the list residing in the surrounding area.

By one in the afternoon, they were headed for number eleven on the list. He lived near Washington Boulevard, closer to Venice than the marina. Todd parked his Mercedes in a Chinese restaurant parking lot. They walked less than a hundred yards to the address.

"My wife's home, reading books about sex offenders," Todd said, "while we're making random visits to ex-convicts."

"Pedophiles."

"Who were convicted and paroled," replied Todd. "This place is just around the corner from a middle school on Coeur d'Alene Avenue. I thought registered pedophiles weren't supposed to be within two thousand feet of a school."

Ron looked at the list. "Gee. I guess Mr. Davis doesn't give a shit about the law. Who'd'a thunk it?"

"Suppose one of these pedophiles on the list took one of our daughters? We could be staring into his face and not know."

"But he'll know. And I'll recognize that," said Ron with conviction.

They entered an apartment building and walked toward the elevator.

"How can you be so sure?" asked Todd.

"Because if you took someone's daughter and had to look into her father's face, you couldn't conceal it either." Ron held up one of the flyers. "Especially when you hold this up and confront him with her picture." He pushed the button.

"These guys are sick. You think they're going to look guilty for you?"

"If you think this is a waste of time, I'll do it on my own. But I'm not staying home waiting for someone else to find Jenny."

The elevator door opened, and Detectives McKay and Carrey exited.

"Mr. Butler," said McKay who was clearly surprised to see him. "Do you mind telling me what you're doing here?"

Ron held up a stack of flyers. "Passing these out," he replied. "Would you like to take a few?"

The elevator door closed with both detectives blocking the entrance.

"And you just happened to select this building?" asked Carrey.

"Have to start somewhere."

McKay took one of the flyers, studied it briefly, and then

shared it with Carrey. McKay then focused his attention on Todd. "You're Todd Roth, I take it?"

He nodded.

"I'm Detective McKay and this is Detective Carrey."

Carrey just stared at Todd.

"I know what you two are doing here," McKay continued. "You two have become the talk of my police station. Cops are making bets which one of you murders someone first or gets murdered. Neither possibility is good for either one of you. You realize you're endangering yourselves and possibly your daughters, don't you?"

"Does that mean you don't suspect me anymore, Detective McKay?" asked Ron.

"I thought we had already made that clear, but to answer your question more directly, it means investigations are better handled by those in law enforcement. I want to find your daughter, Mr. Butler. When I do, she'll need a father that's still healthy and not in trouble with the law, which is what you could be facing if you lose control of your emotions."

"I haven't had control of my emotions since my daughter went missing. And, if it's appropriate, might I ask what you're doing here?"

"Our job," answered McKay. "Look, Mr. Butler, I can imagine what you're going through. I can even understand why you're doing this. I've been a cop a long time and very little surprises me." He glanced at Carrey. "And nothing surprises my partner. But the two of you working together? Now that's a first. One inexperienced crime victim working the streets for justice is a problem. Two is a disaster headed for a catastrophe. For the sake of your daughters, I hope you reconsider what you're doing and go home. The first time I say it, consider it advice. If I have to say it a second time, it'll be an order. There won't be a third time." He looked at Todd. "Nice meeting you."

The two detectives walked toward the front entrance and exited the building. Ron pushed the elevator button.

Todd looked at him. "You're not going listen to him?"

"I listened."

The elevator door opened. Before Ron could enter, he heard McKay's voice behind him.

"Good afternoon, gentlemen." Both men stepped back and watched the elevator door close. McKay approached the men while Carrey stayed behind smiling. "So nice to see you, again. Consider this your second warning. You can leave immediately or be escorted out."

The two men reluctantly walked toward the exit where Detective Carrey greeted them. "Enjoy the rest of your evening. And, oh, by the way, you can take Mr. Davis off your list."

Now Detective McKay smiled as Ron and Todd left under the watchful eyes of both detectives.

Ron and Todd didn't speak all the way to the car. Once inside, they continued the silence until Todd asked, "You had enough yet? This isn't getting us anywhere."

"Neither is waiting at home."

"At least you've got proof that the detectives assigned to your case are investigating every lead. That must mean something."

"The fact that they're visiting some of the folks on our list, doesn't mean we shouldn't. I'm not stopping."

Both men stared ahead, looking through the windshield. Ron turned and looked at Todd. "You got a gun?"

Todd gave him a look. "What? All rich white guys got to have a gun in their glove compartment?"

Ron shrugged. They stared ahead, again in silence, for several moments.

"It's in the glove compartment." Todd said quietly.

Ron opened the glove compartment and removed the gun,

held it for a second, felt the weight, then returned it to the glove compartment and snapped closed the lid.

"Don't you want it?" asked Todd.

"Never used one."

Todd gave him a look of disbelief.

"What? All Black guys got to know how to use guns?"

Todd shrugged. "My wife asked about you. Actually, she asked why I was working with you."

"Does she carry a gun, too?"

"Luckily for me, no."

Both men smiled but their moment was spoiled by a hard tapping on the passenger side window.

Two prostitutes stood together, leaning overlooking into the car, breasts overly exposed, in danger of being squeezed out of their tight, low-cut dresses.

Todd rolled down the window.

"Hi, sugar," said one of the women. "Y'all look like you could use a good party."

The second prostitute smiled at Ron and pressed her palms against her breasts. "You want some of this?"

Todd rolled up the window, started the engine and pulled off.

"Perverts!" yelled the woman, still holding her breasts. She joined her colleague and strolled down the street, preparing for the next proposition.

Todd turned toward Ron. "You want lunch?"

"No. Just drop me off at home. I feel I need to be there."

THIRTY-FOUR

Sunlight filtered through an open window into Jennifer's bedroom. Ron had worked for the past forty-five minutes, designing and redesigning various train stations and track layouts. Now he sat on the floor holding Jennifer's favorite train from *Thomas the Tank Engine*, a long bright blue diesel, with a shiny black trim. She told him it was the fastest and most powerful engine of the group. He tried to remember its name and guessed "Gordon," but there were so many similar-looking trains that he couldn't be certain. She used to complain there weren't any female engines. "Dada, how come women can't operate locomotives?" she asked, then added, "And where are the Black passengers? We ride all kinds of buses, so I know we must ride trains."

To correct the injustice, she took one of the female toy figures included in the set, painted it black, and made her the conductor. "If we can't engineer the trains, then we'll control them," she said, and named the conductor Harriet, after Harriet Tubman. He smiled at the thought of his little militant ending discrimination at the tender age of five or six or however old she was at the time. Her mother would have been so proud, he thought, and then he placed Gordon as the lead engine, pulling the longest chain of trains.

He stared at the train station—undoubtedly the best he had ever constructed. Even Jennifer would have approved. It consisted of an elaborate depot as the centerpiece, with stores and houses in the background. Trains would enter a long green tunnel, and then exit on the side of an extensive farming community that pictured a variety of live-off-the-land animals. He particularly liked the cows, sheep, and chicken, co-existing in idyllic harmony. Windmills were in strategically placed areas, efficiently generating electrical power, to say nothing about adding to the overall esthetics of his self-contained paradise. The bridge was a nice addition if he did say so himself. And then there was the loading area, providing trucks, caterpillar equipment, and machines capable of lifting heavy shipments of grain, fresh off the cargo ships, docked in the nearby seaport; not to mention logs that would be utilized to build new towns and cities.

Yes. He had created the perfect world. And in less than three seconds, he demolished it, using his arm as a huge wrecking ball that flung trains and wooden tracks across the room, as if a tornado unexpectedly had arrived, leaving total destruction in its wake. He studied the wreckage, trains piled on top of each other, tracks scattered everywhere, a collapsed bridge, broken windmills, roofs torn off their structures. And yet, in the middle of this devastation, this complete annihilation of his finest creation, one engine remained unscathed. Its smiling face pointed directly toward him, either mocking his efforts or giving him hope that it was still possible to survive, despite the odds. Jennifer had to be right. Gordon was, indeed, the fastest and most powerful engine of them all.

But it wasn't Gordon that he rescued from the rubble. He searched for the little blue engine, on which the entire series was based. He lifted wooden tracks off the trains until he found it. Thomas didn't look that special. In fact, it was rather small and unimpressive. But it caused him to smile and hum the tune, even though he couldn't recall the lyrics. Ron closed his eyes, and for a moment, could almost hear his daughter sing the *Thomas the Tank Engine* theme song.

It never really mattered what Jenny sang. It always filled the room, even when it was a quiet tune she sang to herself. Some nights he would stand outside her closed bedroom door and listen. When she was very young she'd talk to her stuffed animals, being protective of the smaller ones and telling the big ones they needed to be careful and not take advantage of their size. *Everyone is equal and should be respected*, she'd make them promise. She told them if they were good, she'd ask him to read them all a story at bedtime. And he would make sure to address everyone individually, which became a bit of a problem when her collection of stuffed toys began to take over the room.

What she loved most was when he sang her to sleep. She insisted this was just between the two of them, no one else could be included. Too special to share. Deep inside, he knew that she would have preferred her mother to share that moment. But he was the next best thing even if only a substitute.

He thought about the detectives. Todd was right. It did mean something that they were working on her behalf, and he didn't want to interfere or get in the way. But he wasn't prepared to stop searching, investigating. Even if he did it on his own.

He decided he would look up the lyrics to the *Thomas the Tank Engine* song and sing it to himself before he went to sleep. Maybe, just this once, he'd include her stuffed animals. He didn't think she'd mind.

THIRTY-FIVE

THURSDAY APRIL 20TH

He parked his car adjacent to the school and waited for the bell to ring. The students raced out like a stampede of wild bulls headed for the ring of death. Except their high-pitched squeals of laughter and silly grins suggested they had no idea where they were going. Leaving the safety of school and embracing the world with all its threats was enough to make them absolutely giddy.

When most of the students had left the area, he exited the car, carrying his dog leash. He surveyed the surroundings to make sure that the school crossing guards had completed their duties. And then he monitored the whereabouts of the security officer, who predictably drove his cart toward the athletic field. Given his previous behavior, the overweight cop would either take a nap under the gym's portable bleacher stands, grab a bite to eat in the cafeteria, or most likely, park behind the storage facilities containing sports equipment, so he could admire the girls running cross country, dressed in their skimpy shorts and tank tops.

Once comfortable that the coast was clear, he proceeded to

the area where he expected Sakari to be waiting for her mother who, based on her Thursday afternoon schedule, would be twenty minutes late or more.

He had looked up the origin of Sakari's name to confirm his initial impression. It was, as anticipated, Native American, and meant "sweet." *How appropriate*, he thought. Yet another sign that his plan was destined to succeed, be fulfilled the way he had envisioned. He immediately found her in her regular waiting area, leaning against the large tree across the street from the nurse's office, next to the main administration building.

The tree on the corner provided shade, and its location was ideally situated for an easy pick-up, providing convenient access for her mother or anybody else. Except this afternoon, it wouldn't be so easy for her. It would be impossible. When she realized her daughter wasn't there, she'd be hysterical, but had no one to blame but herself. If she had cared as much as a mother should, she would have arrived at school at least fifteen minutes before it let out. If he could make the effort, why not a parent? Because, he theorized, she probably cared more about her yoga class, Pilates exercises, or weekly massage. Maybe she was having an affair, and Thursday presented the only convenient opportunity to meet her lover. Although as a possible single mother, maybe she worked to support her family and had a child at a different school or day care center. If so, he was doing her a favor. He obviously could—and would—take better care of her daughter than she could.

Sakari was neatly dressed, not like some of these other girls who wore clothes inappropriate for their age, or in his opinion, any age. He gave her mother credit for that, although he didn't approve that she allowed this young girl to stuff those abominations in her ears to listen to music. He believed they weren't safe and could lead to permanent hearing damage. He would soon break Sakari of that dangerous habit.

He estimated Sakari was ten or eleven and, therefore, would

fit in perfectly with his family. She had striking features, but given her heritage, that was par for the course. Her long jet-black hair, carefully braided, reminded him of shimmering chains of pure silk. She had large dark eyes that, in keeping with her people's tragic history, reflected both dignity and defeat. Her jaw was rigid, as if sculpted by an artist skilled in combining beauty and strength. Her remaining features, however, were delicate, even fragile. Her mouth seemed too small for her face, but her nose would serve as a model for any accomplished plastic surgeon.

He approached her, showcasing a wave and friendly smile. She removed her headphones. He assumed the music she was listening to would not be missed. He had monitored the songs on Selena's iPod the night he had saved her and was shocked at the obscenities masquerading as lyrics. He had thought about deleting the songs, but took the more desirable route and burned, then tossed the scorched metal, including those unhealthy headphones, into the Pacific Ocean. Let the bottom-feeders listen to that filth.

"Hi, Sakari."

"How do you know my name?"

"I'm friends with your mother," he said, as if she should be aware of that fact. "Did you happen to see a small brown and white cocker spaniel? I tell you, that puppy has too much energy for me to keep up with."

She shook her head. "I love cocker spaniels. They're my favorite!"

"Well, I can promise you, this one is incredibly special."

"Why?" she asked, extremely interested.

"You'll have to discover that for yourself," he teased her, enjoying the look of excitement on her face. "You want to help me find her?"

She thought about it, checked her wristwatch, and then looked around the area. "Do I get a reward?"

"Absolutely," he assured her.

She flashed a wide smile, revealing a slight gap between her two front teeth.

He made a mental note that he would need to have that condition corrected, and then handed her the leash.

THIRTY-SIX

The four girls wore identical light blue dresses, white cotton ankle socks and patent leather black shoes, with thin straps across the instep. They looked like schoolgirls from an earlier era. They sat quietly on their cots, eating microwave dinners. Their attention was focused intently on their captor, seated in a chair positioned in the middle of the room.

"Do any of you know what the word 'prophesied' means?"

Selena tentatively raised her hand. He nodded approvingly and recognized her.

"Is it something from the Bible?"

He smiled, pleased with the effort. "Very good, Selena... That's very good."

Selena smiled proudly.

"It can come from the bible," he said, acting as teacher, preacher and friend. "But it doesn't have to. It just means that you can tell something about the future before it happens. You have to be very special to be able to do that."

Mei Lin listened, fascinated by the information. "Can I become special?"

Jennifer and Rebecca shared a concerned look.

"Yes, Mei Lin. When you're around a special person, you can become special, too a part of his magic. Share his gift, joined together in spirit and in flesh. A sacred union. A devoted family." He stood and walked in a gradually increasing circle, moving closer to one girl, and then moving away to become closer to the next, as if creating a mesmerizing trance consisting of fear and hopeful anticipation.

"I had expected to enlarge our family today. I was very close, but it was not meant to be. Eventually, when the time is right, we will accomplish that goal and complete our mission. Together, we will do that. I promise. Do you have any questions?"

"Are you going to let us go home one day?" asked Rebecca.

"Rebecca, you are home."

She stared at him, expressionless.

"Why are you doing this to us?" cried Jennifer. "We've never done anything to hurt you!"

"I'm not doing this out of pain," he said, displaying great conviction. "I'm doing this out of love. I'm doing this because the world needs us to set it right, to make it what God intended."

Jennifer shook her head in disgust. "You do whatever it is your warped mind tells you to do. But you leave God out of it. You understand me? Leave God out of it!" The outburst surprised Jennifer, as much, if not more, than it shocked everyone else.

The girls reacted nervously, not knowing what he would do in response to Jennifer's defiance. Mei Lin balled herself up underneath a blanket and trembled. Selena froze in her position, staring ahead, eyes wide open, as if the mere act of blinking would be cause enough for punishment.

Rebecca rose and stood by her cot, prepared to help her friend. And Jennifer didn't move an inch. But if her stare could burn, he would be incinerated in her fire.

To Jennifer's amazement, he smiled. It was brief, but clearly present... as was the danger in his eyes, a certain sickness that could spread quickly and contaminate anyone present. Those eyes made Jennifer back off and finally look away.

"In the not-too-distant future, you will learn never to question me," he said. "That lesson will be taught, and you will master it. Of that, I am as certain as I am convinced that night follows day."

But for Jennifer and her companions, night and day were now simply memories from another time, replaced by darkness and artificial light, controlled by a madman.

"And if you ever insult me again..." he said, his voice surprisingly calm, which ironically made it more frightening. "Well, I think you're a reasonably smart girl. I don't think I have to fill in the blanks for you. Do I, Jennifer?"

She shook her head.

"I didn't think so," he said, and then left, closing the door with more force than usual.

"Why did you say those things?" asked a frightened Mei Lin.

"Because I'm not afraid of him," Jennifer responded. "Well, I am, but I'm not going to let him know."

"But you're going to get us all in trouble," argued Mei Lin.

"Mei Lin's right," said Selena. "If he gets angry at you, he'll take it out on the rest of us."

"What do you think he's doing to us now?" asked Rebecca, coming to Jennifer's defense. "We're all in this together, and we need to find a way to fight back."

"He has us chained to the wall!" said Selena. "How do you expect us to do that?"

"What if something happens to him, and he's hurt, or he just decides to leave and not come back?" asked Jennifer.

"That would be good, wouldn't it?" said Mei Lin.

"Who would find us?" Jennifer said, reminding everyone of

their predicament. "We wouldn't have any food or anything to drink."

"Are you saying we should pray that nothing bad happens to him?" asked Selena. "'Cause that's a prayer that will never leave my lips."

"No," answered Jennifer. "I'm saying we have to find a way out. We have to plan for it."

The girls looked at each other, each one searching the other for an answer.

"I think our best chance," suggested Rebecca "is when he takes one of us upstairs for our bath. That person has to find a way to escape and get help for the rest of us."

Mei Lin and Selena didn't seem convinced but considered it.

"But he never lets us out of his sight," said Selena. "And he's bolted the front door from the inside. I've seen the locks."

"And the window in the bathroom is nailed shut," said Mei Lin. "I know, because I asked him to open it to let in some fresh air, and he told me he couldn't, and then let me try just to prove it."

"Maybe we could stuff the toilets and overflow the room with water," suggested Selena.

"I think he would let us drown," answered Rebecca. "Or stay wet until it dried on its own."

"How about we start a fire?" offered Mei Lin. "Someone would have to call the police."

"After we burn to death," replied Jennifer.

The girls lowered their heads in dejection.

"There's going to come a time when he lets his guard down," said Rebecca, temporarily getting them back on track.

"And that's when we strike," agreed Jennifer, providing grist for the mill.

"Is it wrong to pray for someone's death?" asked Selena.

"Probably," answered Jennifer. "But my dad said God is forgiving."

"That's good," said Selena.

"Does that mean God will forgive him?" asked Mei Lin.

"He's also just, so that would be a no," said Rebecca.

"That's even better," concluded Selena.

"I need another sheet of toilet paper so I can keep track," said Jennifer.

Selena tossed her a roll. Jennifer took a sheet, tore off a small piece, and added it to the pile underneath her mattress.

"How many days?" asked Mei Lin.

Jennifer had begun to tear each sheet in half, then in thirds. She separated each small piece of tissue in groups of five. She stopped counting and looked at Mei Lin. "Too many," answered Jennifer. "Too many."

The reality of that answer left the girls depressed. They stopped doing what they were doing and placed the sheets of paper to the side, dejected. The lights were suddenly dimmed, which didn't help the matter.

Jennifer grew increasingly concerned about her captor. He knew how to manipulate, how to grant compliments and rewards to gain favor. She wouldn't fall prey to that and knew Rebecca wouldn't either. But Selena and Mei Lin, because of age and the duration of their captivity, were both susceptible. She had to do something to uplift their spirits, ease the burden of their captivity. She started humming the *Thomas the Tank Engine* theme song, looking at the other girls to join her. After the first verse Rebecca joined, followed by Mei Lin. Their harmonization grew louder, filling the darkening room.

"Selena," said Jennifer. "You should join us." She waited for a response, and then once again called out her name. "Selena, what's wrong?"

"We're just fooling ourselves!" decried Selena. "Talking

about movies and singing stupid songs, like everything's all right... It's not all right! We're never getting out of here! Never!"

The outburst caused Mei Lin to cry, although she did her best to stifle the sound. Jennifer looked at Rebecca, but could hardly make out her features, in the darkness.

"You know you don't believe that," cautioned Jennifer. "You can't."

"Why can't I?" Selena asked, in desperation. "You know he's crazy, and sooner or later he's going to do something to us, something terrible."

Selena's words hovered over everyone in the room, threatening to crush whatever hope they had managed to cling to, thus far.

"Who's going to help us?" Selena asked. "You know so much, so you tell me. Who's going to help us?"

"We are," answered Jennifer, in a quiet, but committed voice. She rose from her cot, and while the chains constrained her movements, she walked as far as she could, and then knelt near the middle of the room. She bowed her head. "Our father, who art in Heaven..."

Rebecca walked as far as her chains would permit and knelt. "Hallowed be Thy name," she said.

Instinctively, Selena, and then Mei Lin, moved as close as possible to their two friends, and knelt. They extended their arms until they were able to touch their fingers. The four girls formed the spokes of a human wheel, not designed to travel forward physically, but united for the sole purpose of being spiritually uplifted. They bowed their heads and closed their eyes.

"Thy Kingdom come," all the girls prayed together. "Thy will be done. On earth as it is in Heaven. Give us this day, our daily bread. And forgive us our trespasses, as we forgive those who trespass against us. And lead us not into temptation, but deliver us from evil—"

The overhead fluorescent light buzzed to life, casting a yellowish glow on the girls and their meager surroundings.

The girls opened their eyes and looked at each other, less confident, but still hopeful.

"Amen," concluded Jennifer.

"Amen," agreed the remaining girls.

* * *

From the safety of his bedroom, the man watched the girls continue to hold hands. "Amen," he whispered. They were coming together faster than expected. He had thought the last girl might have been a mistake, given the prominence of her parents. It certainly created a higher risk, but great risks reap greater rewards. He turned off their monitor and would sleep well, tonight.

THIRTY-SEVEN

FRIDAY APRIL 21ST

Surrounded by adoring bridesmaids, a future bride studied herself in the full-length mirror, while a tailor took careful measurements.

"I don't want it too tight in here," the bride-to-be pointed just underneath her breasts. "But I want these babies to lift and separate enough, so the groom knows what he's getting and won't get cold feet."

"If he doesn't know by now," cracked the maid-of-honor, "he'll never know."

"You will look gorgeous," said the tailor. "He won't have any part of his body cold, once he sees you marching down the aisle, radiating warmth."

"Hot," she corrected him, to the delight of her friends. "Not warmth. I want to radiate hot! I want the sprinklers to go off just after he says, 'I do.'" She looked at the bridesmaids. "Or is he supposed to say, 'I will'?"

"As long as the sprinklers work," commented one of the bridesmaids, "he can just nod yes, and then take you on your honeymoon."

"And as long as somebody puts a diamond on my finger," replied the maid-of-honor, "I don't care if he says goodbye."

The women laughed. The tailor stuck another pin in the hem of the gown and called out to the owner to assist the man at the rear counter, who had been waiting patiently for the last five minutes.

The bridal shop owner approached him, offering a friendly greeting. "Good afternoon and welcome. May I be of assistance?"

"Yes, thank you," he said, keeping on his dark sunglasses and making sure he was not facing the surveillance camera. "I need four wedding gowns."

"I believe that's bigamy," the owner laughed.

He smiled politely. "Actually, the gowns are for the flower girls... My sister's wedding. She's written all the pertinent information." He handed her a slip of paper, which she studied.

"But these aren't typical dresses for flower girls," she said. "Does she really want wedding gowns for all of them?"

He nodded in the affirmative.

"And she wants hats with veils included for each girl?"

"What can I tell you?" He lightly touched her on the arm and confided with a wink. "She's been planning this for a long time."

"Will the girls be available for a fitting?"

"Actually, they don't live in the state. My sister asked me to take care of all the details."

"Well, aren't you the dedicated brother," she complimented him, smiling warmly.

"She's my only sister, and I'd do anything for her. And the girls are quite precious. I can personally attest to that."

"This is likely going to be a special order. When is your sister getting married?"

"Three weeks, but we'd like everything ready in ten days, if possible. I need to ship the gowns to the girls and make sure everything is perfect."

"I can expedite the order, assign an additional tailor, if necessary, but it would greatly increase the cost."

"Spare no expense. You only get married once." He paused, and then added, "Unless you're lucky," he chuckled.

The owner didn't find the humor in his joke. "Let me check my inventory and see what's available. There's coffee and tea behind the counter, feel free to help yourself."

He watched her proceed to the back room, and then he turned his attention toward the future bride, standing on a platform. The tailor unfolded the train, extending it several feet. The bride straightened her hat with the help of two of the bridesmaids, and smiled glowingly as the lace veil was lowered over her face.

The maid-of-honor elbowed one of the bridesmaids, speaking loudly enough for the bride to hear. "If she had taken my advice and kept her face covered, she might have gotten hitched long before now."

The bride lifted her veil to warn her. "It's not too late to have you replaced."

"Your fiancé told me I was irreplaceable."

"And when exactly did he tell you that lie?"

"Last night, when he whispered it in my ear."

The bride feigned getting off the platform, fists raised, as the other bridesmaids held her back. They all laughed.

"Don't worry about your fiancé wanting anyone else but you," the man in the dark sunglasses said. "You look absolutely stunning."

"Well, thank you," replied the bride. "But I'm not sure with those sunglasses you're that able to get a good look."

"I assure you my eyesight is better than it has ever been. I'm wearing these glasses to protect from a recent laser operation. But even a blind man could see how lovely you are.

The maid-of-honor raised her eyebrows and winked at the bride, giving her a mischievous grin. "You might want to check if your admirer is available for the wedding. Never know when an extra groomsman might come in handy. I know I could use a dance partner," she hinted.

The bride looked at him and smiled. "That was very sweet of you. And please don't pay any attention to her. She's off her medication, and you know how that can be."

"I can only imagine," he said, and then smiled.

Impressed and obviously interested, the maid-of-honor strolled toward him, as the rest of the women looked on knowingly." My name is Keela. And if this isn't too forward, and I don't care if it is, might I say that I adore your glasses. Makes you look mysterious."

"I rather like that notion," he said, exuding great charm.

She handed him a business card. "My home and cell numbers are on the back," she said. "When you're ready to reveal yourself"—she gave him a lascivious look—"give me a call, mystery man."

She sashayed back to the bride, who shook her head in disbelief and muttered, "You are so scandalous."

The owner returned and recorded the necessary information to complete the order. She required a fifty percent deposit, but he preferred to pay the full amount in cash, which resulted in a five percent discount. Once the transaction was finalized, he said his farewells to everyone and wished the bride much happiness.

"I look forward to revealing my real self, very soon," he said to Keela, who didn't conceal her pleasure. He held up her business card, waved it proudly, and smiled. When he left the store, he crumbled up the card and tossed it into the trash.

THIRTY-EIGHT

Todd's penthouse office, in the heart of Century City, wasn't listed on the directory in the lobby.

"I should have brought a box of tissues," said Ron, taking in the view of the world from the floor-to-ceiling windows.

"You've got a cold?"

"No. I get nose bleeds whenever I'm this close to high cotton."

Todd laughed. "I get mine each month when the lease is due."

Ron studied a scale mock-up of a proposed mall. "Not bad."

"Two years in the planning."

"You'll need another two to add restrooms after it opens."

"What are you talking about?"

"It's a beautiful design. But I wouldn't shop too long or drink too much Starbucks. Not if the plumbing plans are accurate."

Todd joined Ron and studied the model, demonstrating renewed interest. "You want to leave that computer job? Get back to design work?"

"Do I get a company car?"

Todd's secretary knocked on the door and entered. "Attorney Elkins is here."

"Did he bring those famous pastries this time?"

Michael Elkins peeked inside. "They were out of cheese Danish," he said. "And I'm afraid I ate the apple strudel on the way."

The secretary closed the door, and Elkins strolled in, hand extended. Todd shook hands, received a friendly pat on the back, and then introduced his attorney to Ron.

"Ron, I'd like you to meet Michael Elkins, my favorite attorney." He stepped aside to allow the men to shake hands. "Michael, Ron Butler."

Ron was impressed that the lawyer had to visit Todd instead of the other way around. Although he assumed the retainer was sufficient to demand that type of personal service.

"I'm only his favorite attorney because my brother-in-law owns the best deli and pastry shop in the city. I'm very pleased to meet you, Ron," Elkins said. His broad smile revealed perfectly capped teeth. "I wish it could be under different circumstances, but I'm sure the authorities are doing all they can to locate your daughter and bring her safely home to you."

Ron assumed Elkins made an excellent trial attorney. He could ingratiate himself very quickly with any jury. He displayed a charming demeanor, and his sincerity had probably been practiced thousands of times in front of a mirror. He certainly looked the part: distinguished, fit, a tan that didn't come from a salon, silver hair among the gray, old enough to convey wisdom gained through experience, but ten to fifteen years away from retirement or an appointment to a high-level judgeship.

Elkins wore Prada shoes. Ordinarily, Ron wouldn't be able to identify the designer, but in this case the name was embossed in gold, across the leather instep. His briefcase had the Louis Vuitton logo imprinted as part of the design. Actually, it *was* the design: an elegant "LV" duplicated dozens of times, as if a single "LV" would go unnoticed. The suit was probably Armani or someone else whose name ended in a vowel. His silk tie and linen shirt, with monogramed French cuffs, were undoubtedly custom-made by an Italian tailor, who coordinated the complete outfit. Ron assumed his closet was organized by the week or maybe the entire month, a different outfit for each day.

Todd invited everyone to take a seat around the conference table. Elkins sat at the head, and then immediately assumed control of the proceedings. "I thought it wise that we all met before your activities go too much further." He removed a leather portfolio that contained a pad of writing paper.

"Activities?" said a perplexed Ron.

"Believe me, I understand the pressure you're under, Ron." He took the cap off his fountain pen.

"He's not alone in this, Michael," Todd intervened. "The pressure's shared."

"Let me be blunt." Elkins moved his pad of paper to the side. "Besides the fact that what you're doing is dangerous, it places my client, Mr. Roth..."

Ron noticed it had become formal very quickly. He also detected he'd been excluded from any notion that the attorney was there to safeguard his rights.

"In a very precarious position, legally and financially." He studied Ron, as if closing in on a hostile witness. "I don't mean to pry, but would you mind indicating your annual income, and could you include your total net worth? An approximation would be fine."

Ron stared at Todd, who appeared to share both his anger and his embarrassment.

"He might not mind, Michael," said Todd, in a tone that reassumed command. "But I do."

"Todd," said Elkins, but was prevented from going any further by Todd, who dismissed him with a wave of his hand.

"No. Stop right there. I asked Ron to come here because I was led to believe you might provide legal advice, to both of us."

"And I'm doing precisely that," Elkins insisted. "You're both vulnerable to lawsuits and possible criminal activity, but only one of you has deep pockets that would invite future litigants to seek redress through the courts." He directed his comments to Ron. "Since Mr. Roth is my client, I'm obligated to protect his interests, whether it pleases him or not. I would be negligent in my duties if I did anything less."

"Please don't talk about me as if I'm not here," commented an increasingly frustrated Todd.

"I'm quite aware that you're present, Todd," stated Elkins, showing a degree of annoyance, if not, arrogance. "I'm simply addressing Mr. Butler, so that there's no mistaking the seriousness of your actions and the precarious position you could potentially find yourselves in. For example..."

Elkins flipped a page of his pad, put on his glasses, and reviewed notes he had written prior to the meeting. "There's Mr. Peter Winston, who has filed a complaint alleging that Mr. Butler assaulted him in your presence and with your assistance or implied consent. I believe he's claiming he was choked to within an inch of his life and is currently suffering severe neck pain, along with the inability to sleep, due to reoccurring traumatic nightmares stemming from the incident."

Ron shook his head. "A pedophile is having a traumatic nightmare and wants to sue me?" he said, incredulously.

"Actually, he wishes to sue you both. And guess who his attorneys will go after."

"The man was a bigot that directed racially incendiary insults to Ron about his daughter," said Todd. "What did you expect him do?"

"Did it ever occur to you that he might have intentionally provoked Mr. Butler, in order to elicit that reaction?"

"He didn't strike me as that clever," responded Todd.

"He didn't strike anyone. Mr. Butler did," Elkins replied, exasperated. "Todd, who do you think you're dealing with? These are people who are experts at manipulation and deception. And you arrive with a dollar sign painted on your forehead, and then you act surprised when they want to take it from you."

"Fine. You've made your point. It won't happen again."

"That doesn't resolve the issue." Elkins returned to his written notes. "I've spoken to the authorities coordinating both investigations, and they are unanimous in their view that your intervention only complicates their efforts." He lowered his glasses, balancing them on the tip of his nose, and then he peered over them. "And I have to be frank. They feel, as do I, that by continuing these reckless pursuits, you may be unwittingly endangering your daughters." He leaned back in his chair. "Honestly, Todd and Ron..."

It had turned informal again, but Ron was in no mood to be casual or friendly.

"What in God's name do you hope to accomplish by visiting every pedophile in Southern California?"

Ron clenched the side of the table. He wanted to scream or take Elkins by the shoulders and shake him until he understood. But he feared Elkins might be right, and he was ill-equipped to challenge this man on the legalities confronting him, or for that matter, the logic and persuasiveness behind his admonition.

Todd pushed his seat back, ready to leave. "You've more than adequately discharged your responsibilities. We've been duly informed of the possible consequences of our actions." He leaned forward, speaking in a more accommodating tone. "Michael, you've known me for a long time."

Elkins nodded in agreement. "I've been your attorney since before you designed and built your first high-rise."

"And in all those years, have you ever known me to give up

doing something that I believed in strongly, simply because of the risks involved or the negative opinions of others?"

Elkins removed his glasses, placed them on the table, and spoke not as an attorney, but as a concerned friend.

"This isn't about getting approved for a building permit from a hostile city council or negotiating a politically complex deal for a multi-million-dollar mall. This is about what's best for your daughter." He turned his attention to Ron. "And yours, as well." Elkins returned his focus to his client, conveying a renewed urgency. "Does Liz approve of your conduct?"

Todd slammed the palm of his hand against the table. "Damn it, Michael, don't bring Elizabeth into this!" He lowered the volume and sat back. "You're my lawyer, not hers."

"But I'm a friend to both of you. And now I'm speaking as a friend, not as your lawyer." He leaned over and touched Todd on the arm. "Talk this over with your wife. Please."

Todd rubbed his chin and appeared lost in thought. Ron sensed Elkins had scored a major point with the jury and was about to rest his case without calling any more witnesses.

"Did she call you?" Todd asked, suggesting more disappointment than anger. "Did she put you up to this?"

Elkins didn't answer.

Todd nodded. "If you don't have anything else to add, I think that concludes our meeting."

"I've got one more piece of business to discuss before I leave," he announced, and then assumed his lawyer's demeanor, arranging his legal pad so he could write comfortably. "I'm reluctant to tell you this, but I'm obligated to. I've had numerous inquiries about obtaining the rights to your stories."

"What do you mean by *rights*?" asked Ron.

"Book and film rights. I've got three major New York publishers offering significant advances and several high-profile Hollywood producers anxiously competing against one another to make a deal."

"A deal?" Ron said, not hiding his disgust. "Don't they want to know how the story ends?"

"They're more interested in what talent they can attach. Right now, they're going after Will Smith and Tom Cruise."

"I was hoping for someone taller," said Todd, also not withholding his disdain. "But he's a great choice," he added, as an afterthought.

"What, Denzel's not available?" asked Ron.

"I take it I should tell them you're not interested," said Elkins, writing a note as if he needed a reminder, although it was probably a legal necessity to record his client's response, to confirm he had exercised "due diligence" in carrying out his responsibilities.

"That's a polite way of telling them," Todd said.

"I have a more impolite response, if you'd like to record it," said Ron.

Elkins put the cap on his Mont Blanc fountain pen, folded his portfolio, and placed it inside his attaché case. "I believe I can adequately convey your sentiment. I need to advise you; they may find a way to tell the story without your approval."

"How can they do that?" asked Ron.

"Through other sources: police, private investigators, news reporters. If necessary, they can claim it was 'loosely based on' or 'inspired by.' There is a myriad of legal ways they can get around you." He closed and locked his case. "You two have certainly provided ample material to various news outlets that would allow them to assert the story is in the public domain."

"Which brings up something else," said Todd. "I need your advice on another matter."

"Seeing as how you haven't taken any of my previous advice," replied Elkins, "I'd be only too happy to see my counsel rejected, again."

Ron felt a surge of satisfaction in seeing a high-powered attorney, pout.

"Do you think I should increase the public reward?"

Elkins didn't have to think long about the answer. "It's only likely to create a surge in the number of useless calls to the tip line and tie up your investigators even further."

"I was thinking that it might place more pressure on whoever took Rebecca."

"I'm not sure that's wise," responded Elkins. "Based on my conversations with the police chief, forcing the hand of whoever took Rebecca could lead him to panic, and that's the last thing we need for him to do. Just allow the police to handle this. They know what they're doing."

Ron felt as if he should leave the room. Somehow his daughter was no longer part of the equation, and he certainly wasn't privy to personal updates from the police chief. And yet, the attorney's advice directly affected him, since he had tied his wagon and his daughter's fate to Todd. He wondered if the man's high profile had turned into a liability rather than an asset. Was Ron jeopardizing Jennifer's life by teaming up with a man capable of drawing great attention to his plight? And would that increased attention frighten his daughter's captor and cause him to... Ron wanted to remove that thought from his mind, but he knew it would linger like a terrifying shadow. Was the shadow due to the danger lurking behind, or was it caused by his foolish missteps?

The thing that scared him most was the knowledge that he had no choice but to continue down the path he had started. No, actually the thing that terrorized him most was the chance that Jennifer's captor had done the unthinkable—that no amount of pressure or attention would make a difference, because he had already committed murder and discarded the body. He knew it made little sense, other than to conform to a father's desperate wish, but he believed Jennifer was alive. He couldn't explain it rationally, other than to say there had always been a special connection between them, as if her umbilical cord had been severed from his wife and reattached to his heart or, at least his spirit.

They shared more than a father—daughter bond. "Mind-meld" they joked, when they had the same thought or said the same thing, at the same time. He would get up in the middle of the night and go to her room, because, somehow, he knew she had kicked off the blanket and was shivering. Or he could always find a favorite toy she had misplaced, by putting himself in her shoes and speculating on her previous actions. Then there were the times when she was coming down with a cold, and he could tell long before the first sneeze. Or if she had an argument with a friend in class, he sensed it before the school bell rang, and he would ask her about it on the way home.

It always amazed her that he knew that much about her. She wondered if he had a secret hotline in the school's counseling office or if he had managed to electronically monitor her brain. "How do you do that, Dada?" she would ask. And he would smile without answering because he didn't know either. Surely, with that strength of a connection, he would know if it was broken completely, disconnected forever. He wanted to believe that. He needed to believe that. He did believe that.

THIRTY-NINE

Liz sat at her dining room table, staring at the stack of books in front of her. Her husband entered the room and placed his hand on her shoulder. He studied a variety of titles ranging from psychological profiles of pedophiles and sex offenders to crime statistics.

"You think you should continue to do this? Haven't you read enough?"

"While you're out playing amateur detective, I thought I should do my part."

He thumbed through one of the books, and then placed it back with the others. "You called Michael Elkins to ask me to stop?"

"You've always listened to him," she said. "You're a rational, logical man, not prone to act on mere emotion, which is why you wouldn't have listened to me." She stood up, moving to the other side of the table. He knew it wasn't to retrieve any books. She simply wanted to get away from him and the touch of his hand.

"You know what I discovered in my reading?" she asked. "I guess I already knew it, but I never had been forced to think about it before. Every day that passes increases the likelihood that the crime won't be solved that it won't be a missing person's case any longer, but a probable homicide. The books didn't agree on much, but they all agreed on that one fact."

"Don't do this to yourself."

She leaned back in the chair and spoke, displaying little if any emotion. "Although there are these rare miracle stories about girls being found years, even decades, after they went missing. You remember that girl from Utah, and that poor child in Northern California?" She swallowed hard. "They were kept prisoners, living in deplorable conditions. But they were alive. And, incredibly, they were reunited with their families." She stood and faced her husband.

"I had terrible thoughts, Todd, shameful thoughts. I considered that it might be better for this to end quickly, rather than have Rebecca live a tortured life for so long. My God, do you think was I wrong?" she asked, pleading for an answer. "Is that a dreadful thing for a mother to think? Do you believe Rebecca will be punished because I didn't have enough faith or strength?"

"Please stop this, Elizabeth!"

"So, it's Elizabeth now," she said, a combination of regret and fear evident in her voice. "That's not good." She pushed a second stack of books closer to the first. "It's Liz when you want to keep it light. But Elizabeth when you know you've lost the argument or find that I'm too close to a truth you'd rather not deal with."

She crossed to the French doors overlooking the backyard pool. He followed her, but remained a respectful distance away.

"I almost see Rebecca licking her finger and chalking one up for Mom, congratulating me on finally winning." She turned to face him. She smiled, and he wanted to believe it was genuine, and that it was for him.

"Although that's something she reserved for you. She

enjoyed that little accounting system, keeping track of the total points scored. I think you both did."

Todd took advantage of the moment to move closer. "I don't even remember how that started." He now stood next to her. "Or for that matter, when."

They both gazed outside at the pool, a bright green shimmering surface that looked like iridescent ice or something bright and colorful that had fallen from the sky and landed in the perfect place.

"Ron Butler was telling me the things he remembered about his daughter. I was watching his face as he recalled the memories. In the middle of all that pain was the joy of reliving those moments. The way she giggled. The first time she crawled. The way her voice sounded when she spoke her first words. The way she moved when she took her first few steps."

They had turned away from the pool and were facing each other.

"He told me he hugged her every day. Told her he loved her every night."

"What did you tell him about your relationship with Rebecca?"

He was the one who wanted to move away now, but he remained motionless.

"That I lost her a long time ago."

He studied the expression on his wife's face but couldn't tell if what she felt for him was admiration or pity, maybe a little of both.

"You must like him a lot... to be that honest."

"I want another chance, Liz." His voice broke, slightly. "With you and with Becky."

"For our daughter's sake, I hope you have that chance with her. I really do."

He lowered his gaze, disappointed that she hadn't included herself in a future with him.

"I was wrong to have those thoughts," she said. "Whatever she's going through, her life is more valuable than anything some madman steals from her. I just want her home. No matter how long it takes. I just want her back home."

She opened the French doors, allowing fresh air to enter. She took a step outside, and then turned toward him.

"You should invite Mr. Butler for dinner this week."

"You think that's a good idea?"

"Why should you be the only one to have the chance to be honest with him?" She closed the doors and walked away.

FORTY

SUNDAY APRIL 23RD

Ron took the scenic route. He needed the extra time to think about what was happening in his life. He wondered if it made sense to continue a seemingly hopeless search—one that, in the opinion of the detectives and Attorney Elkins, might only serve to endanger his child. He wasn't sure if he should continue to work with Todd Roth. Was it really all that productive to join forces or was he being used? But that, on the surface, appeared ridiculous. The man had all the resources in the world. He needed Todd far more than Todd needed him. Then again, maybe the *need* had nothing to do with resources or even finding their daughters. Perhaps it allowed them to remain sane until they discovered the truth, assuming they ever did.

But what if they never found their daughters? Or one did, but the other didn't. Would they forever be joined together by their shared experience, or would they walk away after it was over?

He drove up North Beverly Drive and marveled at the homes. The street was wider than most highways. He guessed the city of Beverly Hills didn't want all those luxury cars, parked on the side of the road, to be accidentally sideswiped by his lowly Volvo. He didn't begrudge the rich. He'd gladly be one of them, if he could. *But did they really need all this?* Mansions, exotic cars, and every extravagance imaginable.

It was understandable that the children of the rich should share in that exuberance. But should they have that great an advantage over children less fortunate? Should their public schools be so much more superior, along with their parks, and public services, and even the quality of their food at the local convenience store? Were the lives here more valuable than those in a less-desirable zip code, requiring extra safety and security provided by the police and fire department? He suspected those maids and other servants, who rose early each morning and took the bus to tend to these families, paid a higher portion of their meager paychecks in taxes than the corporate executives who lived in these communities. They were unable to take advantage of the write-offs and loopholes in the tax code or call their lawyers and accountants to maximize assets and minimize liabilities.

He turned right at Sunset. The recently refurbished Beverly Hills Hotel was about a hundred yards to the left. Some months ago, he'd needed to use the restroom and had pulled into the driveway. He drove past a series of new Ferrari and Maserati sport cars, showcased in front of the hotel.

A valet appeared, amused at his beat-up Volvo. Ron tossed him the keys, acting as if he was a well-known jetsetter who commanded the valet's respect. "I'll only be a minute. Don't scratch the car," Ron said, expressing a degree of seriousness that gave the attendant reason to pause.

After being directed to the restroom, he opened the door and discovered a suite that had more space than the living conditions experienced by some families of four. There were several private stalls that had thick polished mahogany doors. The Italian marble floors were free of any scuffs. The tinted mirrors, that wrapped around two walls, didn't have a single smudge. The basins were spotless, without a trace of water splashed anywhere. An attendant stood by to help turn the golden faucets on and off. If you wore a tie, he would hold it over your shoulder to ensure it didn't get wet. A pyramid of carefully folded, tightly wound white cotton hand-cloths, kept warm under a well-positioned heat lamp, replaced ordinary paper towels.

The attendant unfolded a cloth for each occupant, and then patiently waited for it to be returned, to be promptly tossed in the conveniently placed wicker baskets. The hand lotion, a creamy, soothing mixture, with a hint of vanilla and cinnamon, was in abundant supply. If the room had a flat-screen television and leather armchair, Ron would have seriously contemplated leasing a space. But then he realized the attendant expected to be tipped for services, and he would have to choose between having permanently soiled hands or consistently empty wallets —Better to visit, but only when absolutely necessary.

He drove past UCLA and considered the plans Jennifer had made to enroll at the university. He had taken her to the campus several times, to attend concerts and art festivals. She fell in love with the place on her first visit and wanted to know if she could live in the dormitory. He answered, "When you turn thirty."

She thought that might be a bit old for a college student. He countered that it would work out fine, if she received her master's, doctorate, and law or medical degrees. "That would pretty much coincide with your thirtieth birthday," he explained.

Her *thirtieth* birthday. *God, please allow that to happen.*

He arrived in Bel-Air and followed Todd's directions. He drove through a gated area and maneuvered his vehicle around a series of winding roads. Each home appeared larger than the next, as if the builders or owners were competing with one another. And, of course, they were. Each landscape could have been mistaken for individual parks; except they were much better maintained with no shortage of space. Each lot had to be an acre or more. The land was undoubtedly needed for the comfort of the main house, guest house, servant quarters, tennis court, Olympic-sized pool, garage, and additional carport. Tempted to turn around, he thought about returning to his two-bedroom, twelve-hundred-square-foot apartment. It had been enough for Jennifer and himself to have a wonderful life, and now that she was no longer there, it had more room than he would ever need or be able to endure.

He reached the address, pulled up to the entry phone, dialed the access code, and waited as the massive wrought-iron gate separated in two and pushed back, welcoming him to the estate with a friendly wave. As he drove through, he watched in his rearview mirror as the gates slowly came together, closing behind him in a more sinister manner, like an oversized trap catching a slow-moving object. He was reminded of all those bad horror movies that locked you inside, preventing your escape, until you solved the puzzle or battled the monster or became the last man or woman standing, bloodied but victorious.

He parked his Volvo in between a Porsche and a Jaguar and behind a Cadillac Escalade, which caused him to think about the cost of gasoline, a problem that probably never occurred to the Roth family. He figured the Mercedes must have been in the garage next to an exotic classic model, driven on special occasions and displayed at vintage auto shows. As he walked past the automobiles, he recalled his experience at the Beverly Hills Hotel. He could hardly wait to check out the restrooms. By the time he wound his way around the garden leading to the front entrance, Todd greeted him at the door. They shook hands.

They entered the home. Ron was struck by the elegance of the foyer and spiral staircase leading to the second floor. The ceiling was twenty feet high, probably more. The floors were Italian marble, and the walls were covered with original paintings inside ornate frames, each of which were more expensive than his monthly rent. They moved into the living room, which made the foyer look like the lobby of a cheap, flea-bitten motel.

"Did you have any problems finding the place?" he asked.

"No. Your directions were perfect."

"You have a beautiful home," he said, and then immediately felt like an idiot. He might as well have complimented Michelangelo for using colorful paints.

"It's a lot less beautiful than it was two weeks ago," he said, relieving Ron's guilt for stating the obvious and substituting it with a different level of awkwardness.

"Let's hope that it will be more beautiful than ever, as quickly as possible."

Liz appeared in a robe as Todd tried to greet her with a slight hug which she immediately rejected.

"Ron, this is my wife, Elizabeth. Liz, this is Ron Butler who I—"

"I know who he is." She looked at him and asked with a polite sadness. "How are you holding up?"

Todd took an awkward step back and looked like an uncomfortable guest.

"Not very well," Ron replied. "But it helps to have your husband as support."

Her eyes closed briefly, as if she had removed herself from the room. "He speaks very highly of you."

"And I probably don't have to ask, but how are you doing?"

"Outside of the occasional hysterical outbursts, the fits of crying that are temporarily interrupted by Valium, and my constant reliance on sleeping pills, I'm actually not doing very well, at all." She looked at her husband, without emotion. "Todd, why don't you take your guest to your den? Dinner should be served in the next hour. Mr. Butler, I'm afraid I won't be joining you."

"Please, call me Ron."

"I'm glad we finally got to meet," she said before turning to walk down the foyer where she stopped and turned back toward Ron. She hesitated, then finally spoke. "I hope... I hope they find your daughter." She left before he could respond.

Todd led him down a hallway that served as an art gallery, with various sculptures showcased on individual marble stands or contained inside smoked-glass display cases showered with the proper amount of ambient light. Ron joined Todd in his den.

"I'm sorry about my wife."

"No need to apologize. I totally understand what she's going through."

"It's not just the situation with Rebecca. Her abduction has raised a lot of issues we should have dealt with long ago."

"Maybe I should leave. We can do this at a better time."

"Better time might not come."

The two men sat in silence for a time, then discussed sports, and politics, and the weather, and everything they could think of, that would keep them from discussing the only thing that mattered. Eventually, they turned to that subject, too, thanks to Ron noticing a leatherbound album, with a gold-embossed family crest on the cover.

Todd turned the album around so Ron could get a good view and flipped through the first few pages, starting with baby pictures. It didn't take long for Todd to angle the album closer to himself and turn the pages more slowly, appearing to savor each new photo. It forced Ron to move from his chair and position himself next to Todd on the couch, so they could share the images.

The way Todd responded, smiling proudly, and attempting to explain the origin of each photo, Ron had the distinct impression that they were both admiring the contents of the album for the first time. At the very least, Todd hadn't viewed these pictures in quite a while, and he was enjoying the opportunity immensely. He covered Rebecca's pre-school period, moved to kindergarten and first-grade class pictures, and concluded her school experience with photos from her most recent school recital.

Ron studied a photo of Rebecca holding a bouquet of roses and thought it odd she wasn't smiling. On the contrary, she appeared distraught.

"She was the star of the show," Todd said.

"You must've been very proud."

"I wasn't there," he said, and then continued turning pages, but to Ron, the mood had changed dramatically. Todd went through the rest of the album mechanically, showcasing summer and winter vacations, exhibiting no enthusiasm or personal reaction. To Ron's surprise, many photos didn't include Todd, not on vacation nor at amusement parks or state fairs. When Todd reached the final page, he stared at it for a moment. It was a beautiful photo of Rebecca ice-skating, frozen in the middle of what appeared to be a rapid spin. It reminded Ron of those concluding moments of a routine captured forever at the Olympics, where style points mattered, and gold medals were at stake.

Todd closed the album and placed his hand on the cover, as if about to take an oath on the bible, swearing to tell the truth, the whole truth, and nothing but the truth—*so help you, God.*

Ron responded to the awkward silence by pulling out a stack of photos from his wallet, covering essentially the same timeline, from Jennifer's birth to her posing in front of her train set, to her accomplishments in sports. Virtually all the photos included his smiling face, posed next to hers. He took special pride in pointing to a recent team photo of her dressed in a soccer uniform.

"She won the MVP, setting school records for goals scored."

"Congratulations."

"She's actually a better tennis player," Ron added with a huge grin. He then pulled out a photo, from another compartment in his wallet, and showed it to Todd. It was of Jennifer dressed in a tennis outfit, holding a large championship trophy.

"She has a beautiful smile," acknowledged Todd.

"She inherited that from my wife."

Todd nodded. "Tell me about her mother." He paused for an uncomfortable moment. "How did she die?"

Ron diverted his focus to the floor, then shifted his view to the certificates and awards on the wall behind Todd's desk. He rubbed his chin and cleared his throat. He finally mustered enough courage to look at Todd and respond to his question.

"She couldn't take any radiation or chemotherapy because of the pregnancy. After Jenny was born, the cancer had advanced, spread throughout most of her body. It was a miracle Jenny survived."

"How much longer did your wife live?"

"A few hours. She got a chance to hold our daughter, just before she passed. Jenny insists she remembers being held by her mom. I know that seems impossible, but she says it with such conviction, there are times I believe her. She describes the hospital room in great detail, which I guess doesn't take much imagination. Even if you've never been in one, you couldn't go wrong identifying a bright white antiseptic space."

"It's amazing what children remember, in their own way," replied Todd. "There are reputable theories that contend we remember the pain of being born but we suppress it." He shrugged. "Maybe we wind up suppressing a lot more pain as adults. We just don't do as good a job." Todd took a sip of coffee.

"Here I am revealing personal details about me and my family," said Ron, "and I don't know anything about you."

"I'm like you. I've lost my daughter. Except, as I've told you before, I lost her a long time ago... That gives me even more of a reason to want her back."

"What do you mean you lost her a long time ago?" Ron studied Todd with growing interest. He was obviously struggling with emotions that went far deeper than dealing with a missing child. Ron was about to ask the question in a different way when Liz entered, now dressed for dinner.

"Mr. Butler... Ron... I'm sorry for the way I acted. There's no excuse for treating you as if you were the problem."

"Mrs. Roth—"

"Liz."

"Liz, if you'd rather be alone, I—"

"Alone is the last thing I need to be and the one thing I'm accustomed to. I haven't had a visitor for quite some time, and I won't give up the opportunity to join you for dinner which is now ready."

Todd looked both relieved and regretful that the opportunity to answer Ron's question had passed.

Dinner was fit for a king, a true banquet displayed in a way that would make any gourmet magazine envious. But for all the delicacies available, very little food was consumed. Ron used his fork to move vegetables around his plate, in a failed attempt to act comfortable.

Liz and her husband barely spoke to each other, although they did try to keep him if not entertained, at least, not feeling alone. But their best effort failed to conceal the tension between them, and their comments were followed by extensive periods of silence. And to Ron, nothing was worse than sitting around a table full of food with people who didn't eat and couldn't or wouldn't speak. Or at least, they couldn't speak intelligently or comfortably about what was truly on their minds. He had a sense that Liz was going to cry or scream at any moment, and he did whatever he could to avoid saying anything that would push her over the edge.

It was true that the two men, in an effort to eliminate discomfort, could exchange photos of their children. In a strange way, it allowed them to maintain normalcy in their lives —to function as if it was just another day. Two fathers sharing bragging rights, with unstated competition designed to declare: "My daughter is prettier and more talented than your daughter." *And if you don't believe it, just wait till she proves it again.*

But that was all a part of a grand deception, because neither man really knew if their children would be given another chance to compete or if there would be any additional photos to add to Todd's album or place inside Ron's wallet. Which was precisely why they couldn't play the same game with Liz. As a mother, she would recognize it for what it was: mere posturing, an effort to hide the fear, the reality that those girls, whose achievements generated so much pride, might never return home. The daughters that they loved so dearly and completely, would never again know the depth of that love.

It was only natural that the one person who had no tolerance for deceit or false blustering would, after a few cursory comments, call an end to their charade.

"Well, it was a good effort but a bad idea," remarked Liz.

"The food's delicious," commented Ron. It's just that—"

"I had hoped being together would bring us some comfort," Liz interrupted him. "Instead, we're a continual reminder of our predicament." She placed her cloth napkin on the table and stood stoically. "I hope you'll excuse me. I'm not feeling terribly well." Surprisingly, she leaned over and kissed Ron on the cheek. "We should do this again at a happier time." She left the room.

Todd seemed embarrassed as he put down his silverware. "I'm sorry. I guess she's not ready for dinner guests."

"Especially this one," replied Ron.

"She respects you a lot. It's just—"

Ron raised his hand to stop him. "You don't need to offer

any excuses or apologies. Like your wife said, good effort, bad idea." He stood. "I'd better go. We've got a long day tomorrow."

"I'll walk you to the door."

"You sure you don't want to call me a cab? Assuming they pick up Black people in Bel-Air."

"I thought you drove here."

"I did. But it's a long way to travel from here to your foyer," Ron commented, appearing serious. "And then I have to hitch a ride from the front entrance, through the garden walkway, all the way to your carport."

Todd smiled. "You should see the home next door. Makes this place look like a guest house."

Ron looked around, as if inspecting the home. "Well, it's not bad for a fixer-upper. I'll say a prayer for you. Maybe you can trade up in a year or two."

Both men looked at each other. Todd nodded. "Thanks for the effort at humor. I could use it."

Ron shrugged. "You think I'm joking?"

Todd shook his head and released a weak chuckle.

Ron realized that humor was another way to construct a false sense of normal, to fool the heart into thinking that if you just tough it out, grin and bear it, it will be better in the morning. Except the morning brings the sun and with it enough light to reveal the truth... It's not any better, far from it.

Todd placed his arm around Ron's shoulder. "I'll take that long walk with you to your car. I could use the exercise."

They made it to the front door and stepped outside.

"So, what are we going to do next?"

"I don't know," answered Ron. "Guess we stick with the plan."

They walked past the garden and reached Ron's vehicle.

"Long as we can see today, we can face tomorrow," said Todd.

"It's as long as we can see tomorrow, we can face today," corrected Ron, who opened his car door.

"Well, then," said Todd. "See you tomorrow."

Before Ron could enter his car, Todd's cell phone rang. He held up his hand for Ron to wait, and then quickly answered the call.

"Yes?"

Ron watched Todd's expression change from mild interest to deep concern.

"Where?" he asked. "Did they give you any other information?"

Ron felt tightness in his stomach, while his heart raced rapidly.

"Ron's with me. We'll meet you there." He disconnected the call and looked at Ron.

"What?" Ron asked, increasingly alarmed.

"They found a child's body."

At that piece of news, Ron confronted the reality that it wasn't only the morning sun that revealed the truth, but the dark shadows of night as well. He hadn't realized that he was now sitting on the ground. Is this the moment that he has dreaded for these past nineteen days? Has it come to this? His daughter would be returned, but not the way he had hoped. The way he had prayed. And what if it wasn't Jenny but Rebecca? Would his own relief compromise his compassion for a grieving father? He finally looked at Todd and realized he needed to ask, "Where?"

"A side road in Malibu. You okay?"

He shook his head. "What if it's..." Ron couldn't finish the statement. He stared off into the dark. He looked up to Todd hoping that he might have an answer to his unfinished question. Todd extended his hand. "Let's go," he said.

Ron took his hand and was helped upright.

The men climbed into Todd's Porsche and drove off.

FORTY-ONE

Todd drove along Pacific Coast Highway past the Big Rock Area. Ron pointed to the police activity, and Todd pulled behind several emergency vehicles. Ron exited the car before it had come to a complete stop. Todd followed behind, but both were prevented from moving beyond the area cordoned off by the police. The demarcation of the crime scene, highlighted with yellow tape, created a barrier of more than twenty yards.

Ron inched as close as possible, but stopped when he noticed a white sheet over what appeared to be a child's body. He spotted the coroner's van backing up to within a few yards of the paramedics, who were milling around. They unloaded a gurney from the back of the van, rolling it toward the remains.

Ron's heart sank. His knees weakened, and he looked for a place to lean against, settling on a signpost.

"You all right?" asked Todd.

Ron stared ahead, his focus shifted from the vast ocean in the background to the small lump underneath a sheet that rippled with the wind, resembling a wave breaking against the tide of life and death. A police photographer snapped pictures of the scene, the flashbulbs ricocheting off the water's surface like fallen stars sacrificing their last rays of light.

Private investigator Harrison left the officer in charge and approached Todd.

"Do you know?" asked Todd before Harrison could extend his hand in greeting.

"The body's too decomposed," replied Harrison, who turned his attention to Ron. "Is this Mr. Butler?"

Todd nodded. Harrison extended his hand. Ron shook it.

"James Harrison," he introduced himself. "Mr. Roth retained my agency to assist in locating his daughter."

"Is there any way we can see the body?" asked Ron.

"I'm afraid not."

One of Harrison's assistants approached and whispered information into his ear. Ron's gaze was glued on Harrison's face, searching for any clue, whether an expression of relief or dread.

Harrison released a deep sigh. "Just got word that it's a boy."

Ron turned his attention to the gurney carrying the boy's remains. Two attendants lifted the stretcher and slid it into the van that swallowed it whole, like a hungry beast accustomed to being fed, but never fully satisfied.

The back doors of the van closed, and death was successfully hidden from view, but not from the imaginations of the police, who despite their experience, appeared deeply affected. A few walked aimlessly, while others stood with their heads lowered. One young officer was comforted by an older detective, who offered him a handkerchief.

"Thank God, it was a false alarm," said Harrison, without any awareness of his own emotional detachment The statement, however, did not go unnoticed by Ron.

The coroner's van snaked its way through the barriers past spectators who had gathered near the scene, snapping photos with their cell phone cameras. Ron assumed the pictures would appear on Facebook or YouTube, within the hour.

Harrison placed his hand on Todd's shoulder and patted it twice. "Don't give up hope," he said, and then walked away.

Ron thought of the boy underneath the sheet making his way to some cold slab, where he would rest with a tag on his toe and a temporary John Doe I.D. that, in all probability, would list the cause of death as a homicide. He wondered if the boy's parents or brothers or sisters or friends or classmates had benefited from the sincere guidance, "Don't give up hope."

Todd entered the driver's side of his Porsche, racing the engine. Ron stepped over the yellow tape and approached the car. He climbed inside but didn't acknowledge Todd.

Todd lowered his head as if offering a brief prayer.

"If it had been my daughter..." Ron stared ahead through the windshield, then turned and faced Todd. "Would she have been a false alarm?"

"He didn't mean—"

Ron raised his hand to stop him and shook his head regretfully. "The sad thing is, I was relieved, too. Almost said, 'Thank God,' before he did." He looked away, tapping the dashboard with his fingers. "Imagine that. Thanking God that it was someone else's child."

Ron sensed that Todd didn't want to continue this conversation, and based on Todd's next question, his speculation was confirmed.

"I could use some coffee. You interested?"

Ron shook his head. "Let's just head back to your place so I can get my car. Might be a good idea if we took tomorrow off and got a fresh start Tuesday morning. With any luck, we can finish the Culver City list in a day or two and start on Santa Monica no later than Thursday."

Todd hesitated, appeared to want to say more, but didn't. He drove the car past the police vehicles. Ron glanced outside the window to the spot where he first saw the remains, discovering a chalk outline depicting the position of the boy's body. He remained fixated on the scene that gradually became a series of blurred red police lights in the distance, as the car merged into traffic and sped away.

FORTY-TWO

MONDAY APRIL 24TH

He sat in his customary seat, offering his lecture, as the four girls ate their meals.

"As Noah selected two of each species on a mission to create a new world, I have chosen each of you. With me, you will create a rainbow brighter than any other. By now, your loved ones have accepted their loss. Soon, you will accept the family you've found in each other. I will be your partner, more than father, brother, husband, or friend." He stood, walked slowly in a circle, extending his arms as if to embrace the girls as a group. "Do you understand why you've been selected?"

"My father doesn't want me to curse," said Jennifer. "But you stay away from us, you crazy shit!" Jennifer threw her plate of food at him, striking him on the leg. Rebecca did the same, followed by Mei Lin and Selena. They looked at each other, empowered for the first time.

He stood motionless and gave no reaction. After what appeared to be an eternity to Jennifer, he walked toward the sink and grabbed a paper towel. "Before I bring you any more food, you will each eat every crumb off this floor. If you repeat this defiance ever again, the only sustenance you'll share will be the vermin I'll set lose upon you."

He walked toward Jennifer, who failed to conceal her fear. He placed his hand on her head, stroked her hair. She closed her eyes. Her body trembled. Feeling light-headed, queasy, and convinced the room was spinning, she held onto the side of the cot, gripping it with all her might.

"Look at me, Jennifer," he said, sternly.

She opened her eyes and stared at him, mustering as much defiance as she could.

"My father believed your people to be savages." He leaned over until they were face to face, inches from one another. "Please don't prove him right." He handed her the paper towel. "Wipe your garbage off my pants."

"Wipe it yourself!" she snapped, looking at Rebecca for confidence, but finding an expression of alarm and growing concern.

He removed his belt, wrapped it once around his fist, and extended his arm in the air. She flinched, preparing herself to be struck. But he turned away and walked toward Rebecca.

"Since you obviously don't care about your own safety, perhaps your attitude will change when you see your friends harmed, because of your behavior." He raised his arm ready to strike Rebecca.

"No!" Jennifer screamed. "Please stop!"

He smiled, lowered his arm, and turned to face Jennifer.

"I'll do what you ask," Jennifer said. "Just don't hurt anyone."

He walked toward her, the belt now dangling in his hand, the tip of the metal buckle scraping against the floor, as he approached.

For a moment, she was reminded of the day when they met, when he carried a leash and pleaded for her to help him find a dog that never existed.

He stood in front of her, like a statue of a conquering dictator. She wiped the food off his pant leg with the towel.

"Very good," he said. "Now since you started this food rebellion, you have the honor of being the first to eat what you discarded. You can start with the food on that paper towel."

She looked at him, despondent, and then searched for some sign from the other girls, but all she saw were their tears, which now matched her own. She held the towel, brought it closer to her mouth, and began licking the food off the paper.

He addressed the remaining three girls. "You may begin to locate your food from where you tossed it. I will remain until all of it is eaten. Every single morsel."

He returned to his chair, as if it were a throne. He watched them pick up the scraps of food and eat it.

Selena scraped macaroni and cheese off the floor and took a mouthful. She gagged, coming precariously close to vomiting.

"I warn you, that if you should get sick," he said, absent an ounce of compassion, "you will need to digest the product of your illness, as well."

Jennifer noticed the harsh, condemning stare that Selena concentrated toward her.

She felt a sudden surge of guilt. This was her fault, and now everyone had to pay for her outburst.

He held his belt to the side, occasionally swinging it back and forth, dragging it across the floor, as if he was headmaster of a circus, handling a whip that kept the animals in check.

Jennifer thought she would rather be beaten by him, than see another judgmental expression directed her way, from one of the girls.

FORTY-THREE

Ron brought roses, six yellow, three white, three red and a single orchid, her favorite, and placed them at Nikki's gravesite. He used to do this on every major holiday and special occasion, Thanksgiving, Christmas, their anniversary on June 21st, her birthday on August 17th, the birth of their daughter, which also marked the date of his wife's death, November 1st.

She had once joked that if she were first to go, he was to find a suitable spot with shade, not too much, enough to let in a bit of sun that would remind her of his smile—the way it brought her warmth and lit up the room. On a hill, if available, overlooking something grand that would remind her of their marriage. She added it should be steep enough to cause great difficulty to anyone wearing high heels just in case he had found a replacement and had the nerve to bring "the heifer" with him on his visits. He told her she had a "sick" sense of humor, and she immediately replied, "Who's joking?"

And then they made love.

He wasn't certain, but he believed with a high degree of confidence that Jennifer was conceived that night. Several months into the pregnancy, ironically during a check-up to ensure the baby's health, the doctors discovered the lump—actually, more than one. She'd thought it was simply her body adjusting to the realities of motherhood.

"This child won't go hungry," she laughed, and then gave a seductive glance at Ron, "and neither will you."

She refused chemo and wouldn't consider terminating the pregnancy, not after all she had gone through to finally reach that state of bliss. She'd handle it after the birth, as soon as she knew their baby was safe, healthy. By that time, the cancer had rapidly metastasized. There were complications in the delivery room, and the extended labor had drained her of the little energy that remained. But not before she had accomplished her goal. Their child was born kicking and screaming, full of life. She asked to hold their baby. For a moment, Ron thought she would recover. Her eyes gleamed with the luminous glow that had been so much a part of her personality. The color came back to her face, and she smiled, as if it was the first day of the rest of her life when, in fact, it had become her last.

"Let's call her Jennifer." She looked at Ron for his opinion, and he nodded agreement. The slight movement of his head caused the initial tears to fall. He turned away for a moment, not wanting her to see his grief. He secretly wiped away the moisture on his cheeks.

She looked at the newborn. "You like that name? Do you, Jennifer?"

Her gaze swept over everyone in the room, her doctor, nurse, an attendant, and then she locked eyes with her husband. "We did a good job," she said, her voice barely audible. "We made a beautiful little girl." Her final image was saved for their child. "You are my beautiful, precious Jennifer... My Jenny." She closed her eyes, never to reopen them.

The nurse took Jennifer, who cried at the separation—screamed would be a more accurate description, a terrifying wail that lasted throughout the night. Ron feared it signaled a serious health problem, some undiagnosed ailment that was causing her inconsolable pain. He demanded the doctors do something to help his daughter. And then he collapsed into the chair next to his wife's body and held her lifeless hand until the morning, when two male nurses arrived to take her away.

All that remained for Ron was to honor the wish she had made months earlier, which at the time seemed like such an irrelevant joke. He found the perfect spot for her resting place. Now, he had come to visit, this time to ask her to return the favor, to deliver their child, once again, and bring her home safe and healthy.

It was sunset when he arrived. He wanted to be alone with her, and so he waited for an elderly woman to say her prayers at her husband's site. He knew it was her husband because they had spoken several times over the course of the last three or four years. He couldn't remember her name, probably never knew it. Those who visit their loved ones in places like these usually don't ask too many personal details of each other. They just nod, give their condolences, and move on. If anything, they introduce the ones buried, perhaps for the benefit of those underground, so that they'd know a little about their perpetual neighbors.

The woman left without ever acknowledging his presence. That happened a lot, as well. Grief and memories of their loss overwhelm the senses. People experiencing it, don't have time to be polite, nor do they take offence at any perceived slights.

Once she had gone and was a safe distance away, he spoke to his wife. "I did everything you could have ever wanted me to do for our little girl," he said, "and it wasn't enough." He observed the view from the vantage point of the hillside, the way she would, if she could. "Help me, Nikki. If there is a God, then surely, you're with Him. I know you'd want her with you, but not now. She's got so much life left to live. Finish school, learn how to drive a car, experience all that the world has to offer." He spoke quietly to her, calmly, as if she was lying next to him in their bed, and they were having a conversation about their daughter's future.

"She has the right to fall in love, hold her children and watch them grow old. Something you were denied. That can't happen to our child, not after the sacrifice you made. Please, Nikki, with all my heart, I'm begging you, if your spirit is alive in her as it is in me, protect her and lead her home."

He knew he should pray, but he wasn't sure he could absolutely believe in those words, and if there was, indeed, a higher power, it would recognize his insincerity and punish him for it. Like most everyone else, he wanted to think that there was more than simply this life. But if Jennifer came back to him, this life would be enough. If immortality was possible and heaven is not, then he would live on in the works and good deeds of his child, as she would with hers. That was all the faith he needed. Not in an afterlife or in a deity, but in the lives of those he loved and who loved him. And if God existed, as he still hoped, then his soul would be in good hands, either way.

He went to one knee, unprepared to go to both, and gently touched the ground above his wife's decaying body, drawing strength, and hoping to return it. Their touch had shared that magic so many times before, why not now? Being here reminded him of how much he missed her, as if he ever needed a reminder. But now their daughter was also gone, and the resulting emptiness was too much to bear alone. He came to this gravesite seeking comfort, which in some mysterious and marvelous way, is why anyone visits, to be reconnected with the sacredness of everlasting love. The poets say it conquers all. He just needed one victory, and if being here brought it to him, he would stay as long as it took.

He heard a noise in the distance and discovered workers digging a grave in preparation for a new arrival. It was as if their shovels were opening a hole in his already damaged heart. He felt sick. It was foolish, of course. What did he expect? Did he think gravesites simply appeared when called upon? Someone had to do the work. And new graves were created as needed, probably every day. But the reality of death, as a near future possibility, stung him. He feared that this could be a fateful premonition, rather than a simple coincidence. Was his wife preparing him? Was God?

No, he would not stay any longer. The questions he had would need to be answered somewhere else, anywhere else, but not here. Whatever power he needed, he would find in himself, and the people sworn to help. Death wouldn't rob him again, steal his Nikki, and then take Jennifer, too. That cruelty he'd prevent. He didn't know how. He didn't know when. He just knew that he would, even if it meant exchanging his own life for the chance to live in the memory of his daughter.

He slid his hand across the width of the gravesite, leaving behind a path that held his fingerprints. He decided he would take the orchid with him and keep it alive and blooming as long as possible. He walked away ignoring the sounds of workers preparing for the morning's events, choosing instead to stare ahead into the oncoming night and whatever darkness it would bring.

FORTY-FOUR
TUESDAY APRIL 25TH

Ron turned on the radio and found his favorite channel. He took the last piece of pizza that remained in the box on his dining room table. "You want to split?"

"No thanks. I had more than my share," replied Todd. He crossed out several more names from the list. Their last visit had been with a man with the last name of "Lawless," which they both found appropriate. He'd met them at the door, impeccably dressed. Before Ron could show him the flyer he invited them inside with the greeting, "I was expecting you? I've been following your exploits. I must say, I admire your efforts, as futile as they may be. And let me save you some time. I don't have either girl. Don't want any girl under the age of thirty-five. And she would have to show two forms of identification just to be on the safe side."

Meeting Lawless forced them to rethink their efforts. Lawless had been a teacher, which made sense since you rob banks because that's where the money is, and you teach school because that's where the children are. He had been a young teacher, a three-time Teacher of the Year, who slept with a fifteen-year-old who said she was eighteen and looked twenty-one. "Things are not always what they seem," he said as they were leaving.

Now they were no longer sure of the profiles on their list. They hadn't studied what makes a child abductor or one who engages in child molestation. Were they the same type of people who would kidnap adults? Were they more likely to sexually abuse or kill? Were they usually white, single, twenty-to-thirty range, abused as a child, arrested previously, a dropout from high school? Were there differences between those who abducted boys versus girls? And how long did they keep them before letting them go or doing away with their bodies? They read the same type of books Todd's wife had purchased to come up with answers but the more they read, the more questions they had.

The only question that had been answered was the one they didn't want to believe: "What's the chance that an abducted child will be found alive after being missing more seventy-two hours?" Slim to none. That reality caused both men to speculate on different reasons why children might be taken. Maybe it was someone who really loved children but didn't have any of their own. Although that typically included lonely women who kidnapped babies or stole infants from a hospital nursery. That didn't apply to Jennifer or Rebecca but still, it was possible that their daughters were safe, well taken care of by a disturbed person who meant no harm.

Ron read about children who had been reunited with their parents years, even decades, after they went missing. He had reached the insane point where increasingly the only sliver of hope was that Jenny would be alive, captured by someone who wouldn't physically hurt her. Someone who would allow for the possibility that he would one day see her again. Hold her again. That belief created a scenario less debilitating than the alternative, that she was part of an international trafficking organization or enslaved by a demented sexual pervert who will take her life after savaging her innocence.

Todd had grown tired and frustrated at devising various profiles and debating with Ron which type was most likely to be the one they were looking for. He concluded it was time to consider a different strategy. "I think those two detectives are right," he admitted. "We don't know what we're doing. Maybe we could meet with them, ask them the best way to proceed. They're the professionals with all the experience. We don't know the difference between an abductor or a molester or if they're the same thing. We're spinning our wheels and wasting time on what we should be doing. What do you think?"

"You know what I think? I think you want to talk about everything except the one thing you should talk about. You never talk much about your daughter. Other than she dances. That's all I know about her. All I really know about you is that you don't dance. And you don't drink alcohol."

"Anymore," corrected Todd.

"What did you mean when you said you lost her a long time ago?"

"Did I say that?"

"At least twice."

"I think you must have misunderstood."

"Did I misunderstand when you said we're capable of blocking out pain?"

Todd gave a bittersweet smile and shook his head. "No," he admitted. "No, you didn't misunderstand me, then."

The announcer on the radio turned to hard news, covering wars, legislative budget battles, election coverage, and then: "Seventeen days after the abduction of twelve-year-old Rebecca Todd, her father, famed architect Todd Roth, today announced a one-hundred-thousand-dollar reward for any information leading to—" Todd turned off the radio.

"I take it you didn't follow your attorney's advice," said Ron, barely concealing his disdain.

"I meant to tell you," Todd said, in the form of a weak apology.

"You don't owe me any explanation. You did what you had to do. What your money allowed you to do. You don't need my approval." He didn't sound convincing. "That kind of money ought to generate a lot of tips. Should keep the police plenty busy running down leads."

Ron picked up a stack of missing child posters displaying the faces of Jennifer and Rebecca, side-by-side. "Guess you might want to have new posters made up," he said.

"These are the posters we agreed to have printed. These are the ones we'll continue to use," responded Todd

"Look, if I acted like I resented you offering the reward, I do. I resent anything that might shift resources away from finding Jenny... But I don't blame you. I'd do it myself if I could. Unfortunately, I'm not you."

"If I could be you, I'd trade all the wealth and privilege I have."

"And why would you do a crazy thing like that?"

"Because I'd be in every important picture with my daughter and we'd both be smiling." Todd stood up, retrieved his coat and car keys. "I'll see you in the morning."

Ron heard the door close and decided not to eat the last slice.

FORTY-FIVE

For the first time in over thirty-nine months and eleven days, Todd entered a liquor store. He left five minutes later with a bottle that didn't remain in his bag very long. He got behind the wheel of his car and placed the key in the ignition but didn't start the engine. He unscrewed the cap and could smell the bourbon before he tasted it. He had expected the first swallow to burn or at least sting, punishing him for staying away so long. But like a best friend who he hadn't spoken to in years because of a falling out, it was just like old times, better in fact. It made him want to forget the reason for the banishment; it made him regret he hadn't made up sooner, hadn't welcomed it back into his life much earlier. He continued tasting, until his hand finally stopped shaking.

By the time he reached home, his hand was still steady, but his legs were not. He had savored every drop, and when he reached the bottom, when the bottle had run out of anesthetics and excuses, he remembered why he had stayed away for so long. He entered the living room leaving the lights off and proceeded to the kitchen. He leaned against the wall, took a deep breath, braced himself for whatever journey lay ahead, and took several unstable steps.

He sat directly underneath a small chandelier hanging over the dining room table and picked up one of the child molestation books with his right hand, while holding onto the empty bottle with his left. Or perhaps it held onto him. He took both with him into his daughter's room, sat in her favorite chair, and read until he fell asleep.

The boy lay in bed, his face partially covered by his teddy bear. He tried to block out the noises, but on those rare occasions when he succeeded, the silence had frightened him even more. Although he came to understand that the silence never lasted very long. He peered from behind the stuffed animal and spotted the doorknob, moving slowly side to side, just above the wooden chair blocking easy access. The doorknob turned more violently. The door pushed against the chair to no avail. Then it stopped. The doorknob remained still, and the boy's heart stopped racing. There was no more pressure against the chair. Perhaps this time it would offer the protection it had failed to provide so many times before and the silence would bring comfort, if not security.

He pulled the blanket over his head and his right arm surrounded the teddy bear, gripping it in a mutually protective embrace. As the moments of quiet continued, the boy eventually relaxed his grip around the stuffed animal. The bear shook a little. The boy couldn't stop trembling and then he started crying. Maybe it was from relief, or more likely he knew that more than tears would follow.

The door crashed open, splintering the wooden chair and scattering pieces across the floor. This time, the boy didn't hide underneath the blanket or behind the bear. This time, the boy stared ahead into the bright light in the hallway, framing the silhouette of the monster that tried to conceal itself as a man. As usual, it was stooped over, holding a bottle. It moved forward but not before closing the door. The light disappeared along with the boy's hope. He closed his eyes and listened to the unsteady steps across the floor. One... Two... Three... Generally, it took no more than eight or nine, but sometimes the boy couldn't tell because the monster would stumble to one side or the other or drag its feet. One time it fell and remained on the floor for a minute or two, before it dragged itself to the bed and climbed next to him. He had cried out in the past, screamed his mother's name. She never heard him or perhaps she couldn't come because the monster had already visited her and warned her not to move or tell anyone. The same warning the monster had given him the last time he had tried, more than a year ago. Or was it two?

Six... Seven... Eight. And then, no more steps. Just feeble groping, muted groans, and the stench of dead dreams.

Despite his past failures, he wanted to scream for his mother, but he knew she wouldn't come. He wanted to scream for help but had learned it would be forever outside his reach. Perhaps if he screamed loudly enough, the past would be heard sometime and someplace in the future, where they had learned to protect the children from the monsters, who attacked them at their most vulnerable, when they found themselves most in need of help. Despite the odds against him, he considered making one last effort.

How far did his scream have to travel before someone would save him? Could it find its way beyond his barricaded door to the room where his mother slept? Would it reach the home of a neighbor willing to intercede? Or be heard by the guard who drove the patrol car past his protected residence late each night, providing security to those who feared invasion from strangers?

Exactly how loud would this boy's scream need to be? Loud enough for God to finally answer prayers, that had been previously ignored or deemed too inconsequential or too late. What type of scream could he conjure up from his young lifetime of pain, and shame, and remorse? Might it sound too horrific or *unbearable for a compassionate human being to comprehend let alone resolve?*

How many screams had already betrayed him, caused him to suffer more than he would have, had he simply agreed to remain silent or kept still or allowed himself to die inside while being repeatedly violated? After all this time, and everything that he had gone through, why attempt another scream? Why now? Did he hope that it would be recognized for what it was—terror inflicted upon the innocent by a monster who whispered the word, "son"?

He balled up his tiny hands into determined uncompromising fists, opened his mouth as wide as possible, and released a scream so powerful that it thrust itself into a place where the child became a man, and the man became free from the past that had haunted him. The future had finally heard his screams and screamed back with a thunderous roar, which had restored dreams previously shattered and innocence that had been forsaken. Light had finally destroyed the silhouette that had given cover to the monster pretending to be a man, revealing a father who had given him life, only to drain it from him, one tortuous night at a time. He screamed again, not for salvation, but forgiveness, and found neither.

Todd awoke from the nightmare he had been living most of his life. His mouth stretched open, locked by a familiar terror that had revisited him not in the room of his youth, but that of his daughter's. His throat was dry, his body damp from a fever that raged within. The tears burned but did not cleanse; no amount of fire could accomplish that. But now, at last, he would face the source of the pain, replaced by a greater loss than his own innocence stripped from him as a child.

His father.

How could that be possible from a man supposed to protect him?

His father!

Why has he refused to confront the monster for so long? Did he in some bizarre fashion blame himself, take the guilt that should have been his father's, and transfer it to himself?

His throbbing heart raced like a frightened animal unable to escape, trapped by self-imposed limitations and terrorized by the unexpected. He managed to close his mouth, but not the wound threatening to rip him apart. He discovered his shirt soaked with perspiration, and then felt his face drenched in tears flowing from some untapped well filled with sparkling images of grief, unrelenting nightmares, and soundless agony.

"No!" he cried. "No!" He pounded the night table, knocking the empty bottle of alcohol to the floor. "No! No! Goddamn you! No! You fucking bastard!" *It wasn't my fault! It was yours! All yours!*

Shouts turned into whispers, whispers into whimpering, whimpering into silence, until he felt nothing and could cry no more. He stared at Rebecca's empty bed and saw the teddy bear. He moved toward it, without realizing he had left the chair. Once he reached it, he was incapable of touching it. He tried once. Then again. Then a third time, before rushing to the bathroom where he sank to his knees grabbing the sides of the toilet and vomited a lifetime of suppressed pain and distorted denials. He knelt in a twisted perverse position, wrenching the last bit of booze from his system, and when there was nothing left but misery, he tried desperately to expel the sick child his father had created. His body convulsed, turning against itself; lungs attacking ribs; memories assaulting the senses; pain rising from inside a tortured soul, maneuvering through veins, and arteries, and heartache, to deliver a crushing truth that drove his face to the floor, jamming reality through his brain.

His lips quivered, forming the words, "My father."

"Todd!" His wife rushed into the bathroom, half dressed and disoriented from prescription pills that failed to bring her sleep or ease her depression. "Todd! What is it? My God, tell me!"

"The bastard!" he sobbed. "The bastard!"

She cradled him, rocked him gently, like a mother with a sick newborn. His body shook violently, as if he were a recovering addict in the last throes of the drug that he would either conquer or be consumed by.

"My father!" he shouted. "It was always my father and I concealed it. Did nothing all these years!" He desperately looked at his wife. "But no more. I swear to God, no more."

He escaped from an embrace desperately needed on so many other nights, but not this one, and ran from the bathroom to the outside world slipping on the wet lawn. The garage door remotely opened allowing him to race his car out of his driveway, kicking up gravel and dirt.

FORTY-SIX

Selena and Mei Lin were asleep. Jennifer stared into the darkness. Except for the fact that she couldn't see the other girls, darkness was preferable to the light, which only served to intensify her growing sense of despair. The light caused her to see padded walls, drab surroundings, and a lack of privacy when she needed personal time. Most of all, it allowed her to see the chains. Not only her own, but the others as well. They signaled no escape, reminding her every moment that she was nothing more than a prisoner. Whereas the darkness also meant he would leave them alone, at least he had thus far. He came when the light was on, bringing his own form of darkness. The type she truly feared.

While unkind to think this way, she was relieved there were other girls. She wasn't proud to admit that; in fact, she should be ashamed that she wanted others to share her fate. It was selfish, mean-spirited, and above all else, wrong. But without them, she doubted she could have survived this long. But exactly how long had that been? It was too dark to count the pieces of tissue.

She called out in a hushed tone, not wanting to wake up Selena or Mei Lin, and not wanting him to listen.

"Becky?" she said. "Are you awake?"

"Yes."

"How many dinners have we had since you got here?"

"Seventeen, I think."

That meant Jennifer had been held against her will for at least twenty-one days. She remained silent for a minute, maybe two. "Becky?"

"Yeah?"

"Tell me, again, how you feel when you're dancing."

Jennifer waited for a response, and just when she thought Rebecca wouldn't answer her request, the silence broke.

"Free," Rebecca said, causing Jennifer to smile. "Like I'm flying... Like anything is possible."

* * *

He watched the grainy infrared images on one of the two monitors in his room. The other wasn't set up with night vision technology and remained useless in the dark. He turned up the sound and listened to Rebecca over a tiny speaker attached to a nightstand near his bed.

"You feel you're part of the music. That it waits for each step you take. Each movement you make. Until there's no difference between you and the melody."

He moved his face closer to the lit candles that surrounded the room. He bathed himself in the warmth they provided. The blue and yellow flames flickered off the monitor, and he envisioned Rebecca dancing before him, generating vibrant colors and a vitality that excited him to a point where he knew he would not sleep for many hours.

"I think it must be like being with God," Rebecca said.

He smiled.

"Will you teach me one day?" asked Jennifer.

"I have been teaching you."

"I mean outside, when we get back home," clarified Jennifer. "Not here."

The smile was erased from his face, and he stared ahead, expressionless.

"Yes," answered Rebecca. "Yes, I'll be happy to do that."

"As long as you can see tomorrow," Jennifer said.

"You can face today," Rebecca completed the sentiment.

He considered the expression, nodded approvingly, and then lowered the volume on the speaker until it was off.

FORTY-SEVEN

Todd's Mercedes sped by a freeway sign that read Chatsworth. He hadn't visited his childhood home, really visited, in ten years. He'd drop by during Christmas for Rebecca's sake. Give gifts but leave before they are opened. And he had always managed to avoid Thanksgiving. That was one holiday that was off-limits in that home. With the benefit of minimal traffic, Todd had made it to his destination in less than fifty minutes. He pulled into the driveway, parked hurriedly, leaving the car partially on the front lawn. He raced across the gravel pathway and met his mother standing at the doorway, wearing an apron and a look of genuine concern.

"Todd, Elizabeth called... She's worried to death. Is it about Rebecca?"

He rushed past her without any greeting. "Where's Dad?"

Mrs. Roth closed the door and followed behind her son. "Todd, what's gotten into you? You're acting like a madman. You're frightening me."

"I need to see him! Where is he?"

"In the den, but—"

He pushed her aside and raced down the hallway.

"Todd!" screamed his mother. "Todd! Your father's not well!"

That was something he didn't need to be told. He found Frank Roth seated in a chair near the window staring out on the backyard. A desk light barely illuminated the room, casting a weak shadow of his father, as if he didn't deserve a full image of himself. Todd stood by the door, the anger and rage dissipated the moment he walked in and discovered his father seated in his favorite overstuffed leather chair that squeaked, like a broken toy, whenever it swiveled. The room looked so much smaller, as did the man whose name he now softly called out.

"Dad?" he said. "Dad, it's me. Todd."

Mr. Roth turned to face his son, who now saw how fragile this man had become with age and the distance of time. He had a gaunt, hollow-eyed stare. The ravages of Alzheimer's had taken its toll, far more quickly than expected. The disease changed the contours of his father's face, made it appear like a well-worn map that led nowhere. Todd entered the room and turned on a floor lamp. Despite the extra light, it was a room filled with dark memories made familiar by the musky scent of his father. It made him appreciate why he had stayed away so long.

"Dad, how are you feeling?" He waited for a response, but wondered if his father realized he was no longer alone. "Don't you recognize me? It's Todd." He thought he saw a glimpse of recognition, a glimmer of a smile. Perhaps his father's condition wasn't as bad as he imagined. That hope surrendered to the reality of Mr. Roth's first words.

"You lose your baseball glove again?"

Todd forced himself to hold back tears. He had vowed that he would never again shed them for this man, but the room suddenly became blurry, and he feared he'd violate that promise. He studied the surrounding area, observed the photos of his father posing with dignitaries, being honored at major civic and political events. He observed the certificates and awards that covered one full wall and parts of two others.

"Don't expect me to buy another."

Todd moved to the desk. He picked up a mahogany-framed photo of himself as a child with his father standing next to him, smiling proudly. His dad's arm was around his shoulders. He couldn't remember when the photo was first taken. He wasn't sure he had ever seen it before, although he must have. He couldn't have been much older than five or six, and he was certain of only one thing. Like all the photos of him that he did remember, he didn't look happy in this one, either. He placed the photo back down on the desk.

"I haven't lost my glove, Dad."

"I'll take you to a game this weekend."

Todd bowed his head for a moment, unable to answer.

"You've got to do well in school, though." Frank turned to his son. "That shouldn't be too much of a problem for you. Smart as a whip, you are. Got my genes and your mother's good looks." He smiled, showcasing teeth in a state of slow decay.

Todd slid a chair next to his father and sat. He leaned close, spoke in a gentle, but firm voice. "I need you to help me." He touched his father's hand. "Can you do that?

"You ask your mother?"

His grip on his father's hand tightened, although both men seemed unaware of it. "Tell me, Dad. It's very important." He swallowed hard, tried to determine if his father understood what he was saying. "I know what you did... to me... when I was a child. When I couldn't protect myself." He searched for a signal that his words were getting through. "I remember it all. I always have. I just want to know, why?" He waited for an answer that would either liberate him from his father or trap them inside their own personal hell. "Why did you? How could you do that to me?"

Mr. Roth ignored the question and turned back to the

window, where he continued to stare out, an expression so vacant that it didn't appear human or capable of achieving understanding or insight of any magnitude.

Todd grabbed his father by the shoulders, not roughly, just enough to gain his full and complete attention.

"Dad, I need to know." He shook him, as if trying to awaken a child from a deep sleep. And then, without realizing it, the anger that he had suppressed for a lifetime assumed control, or rather exhibited a lack of it. "Answer me!" He shook him violently. "You son-of-a-bitch! How the fuck could you do that to your own son!"

Todd raised his fist ready to smash his father. His hand froze in midair, and then trembled. The muscles in his arm tensed, and then twitched, working against its own impulse. Defeated by instincts that either betrayed him or reaffirmed his ultimate goodness, he lowered his hand to his side, and buried his head in his father's chest to conceal the tears that were now flowing freely.

Mr. Roth slowly raised his hand and placed it gently on his son's head, comforting him. "It's all right, Toddy."

He hadn't heard his father call him that in forty years.

"Everything is going to be all right. Tell your mommy to make you some warm milk and let her know I said you could have some cookies. Go on now. Do as your daddy says."

The phrase, "do as your daddy says," struck him more powerfully than any sledgehammer ever could have. Those five simple words had always preceded the violations, the terror, and the unending nightmares. Todd raised his head and looked into his father's vacant eyes hoping to find a clue that might heal them both, but he found nothing, and as requested, he left the room intending never to return. But first he needed one more resolution. He went into the kitchen that once had been a hiding place of warm cooked pies and aromas of his favorite food that provided a brief sanctuary from the room of his waking nightmares.

Mrs. Roth slapped her son's face. "How could you ask him that?"

"You knew?" Todd asked, not wanting her to admit it, but when she avoided him by turning away, her shoulders slumping ever so slightly, he had the answer he had feared. "Did you know?"

His mother's upper body quivered.

"Goddamn it! Did you—"

"Yes!" she screamed, before he could complete the question.

Now it was his turn to slump, and he did so convinced he might fall and never get up.

"Yes, I knew," she admitted, or more likely confessed.

"And you did nothing?" His voice broke, but not as much as his spirit.

"What was I supposed to do?" she pleaded. "He's my husband... He's your father... Todd, it was a lifetime ago. He was another man, with a terrible sickness. You saw him. You see what's happened to him. He's paying for his sins now, isn't that enough?"

"And what about me? Do you know how long I've suffered? Do you have any idea what it's meant to carry that vile secret all my life? Not being able to tell anyone? Wondering what I did to have him do that to me? Do you realize I was afraid to touch my own daughter? Terrified that I might be like him, or she would know that I was damaged, and I'd have to confess why I was." He waited for her to answer any of his questions or to say anything at all, but the only response came from the sound of glass crashing, and furniture being smashed to the floor. He rushed to the den followed by his mother. They reached the doorway. He attempted to hold back his mother from looking inside. She managed to push him away, but stopped suddenly, placing her hand over her mouth in desperation. He entered the room and saw the chair on its side, which from the look of it, had been used to shatter the window frame. Shards of glass were scattered throughout the room. Traces of fresh blood stained the carpet.

"Call his doctor," he directed his mother. "I'll go get him."

Todd rushed out of the den, exiting the home through the kitchen. He raced past the pool area, its greenish-blue surface glistening under the moonlight. He cut across a narrow alley and slipped through a redwood fence, which led to the rose garden behind his father's den. Mr. Roth had taken great pleasure in the variety of roses and colorful flowers that somehow managed to bloom year-round. He enjoyed creating new hybrids until he found the most unusual colors, and then he experimented with size, and sturdiness, and fragrance, a virtual potpourri in the making.

But it was obvious the garden hadn't been tended to in months. The scent of dead and dying roses was overpowering. Hedges were uneven, bushes and shrubs had grown wild, thick with branches that jutted out in odd places. Rambling vines twisted around clusters of floribunda roses in a confused spider web pattern, their spreading tentacles threatening to entrap any intruder. Bougainvillea shrouded a small retaining wall, as if concealing some great mystery or helping to beautify a dreadful stack of cracked cement blocks. Todd had difficulty making his way through the thicket, slipping several times on the moist undergrowth.

"Dad!" he called out. "Dad! Nobody's going to hurt you!" He wasn't sure he could keep that promise, but he made it anyway.

Todd stood motionless. The moon hid behind a chain of clouds, casting an eerie Gothic shadow over the garden and surrounding landscape. In the distance, behind tall rows of barren rose bushes that stood like a frozen honor guard, he heard a sorrowful whimpering, as if the grief-stricken garden was mourning its own demise.

He moved carefully toward his father, hiding behind hibiscus bushes overtaken by weeds strangling whatever remaining life existed among the wilted plants, barely supported by decaying roots. He had pressed himself against a tree, blending in with the decomposing environment that provided him shelter from the light, but not the cold.

"Can you tell me why?" he asked his father, to no response. "I just need to know how you could do that to your own son. How you could do that to anyone." Wanting an answer and prepared to demand it, Todd was greeted only with the bitter-sweet scent of dying, but once lovely, flagrant flowers. He tasted the aftermath of his tears mingled with sweat, and vomit, and evening dew, dense with smoke from burning leaves. He was tempted to shove his father's face into the thorns that surrounded him, slice flesh and bone until his bloodied corpse rotted in darkness, and dirt, and the destiny that awaited the dishonorable. He wanted to strangle him with his hands, squeeze the life out, one gasping breath at a time, destroying the pitiful thing that cowered a few feet away. And then, the monster spoke.

"I love you, Son... I love you."

Hate and forgiveness gripped Todd between a vise, crushing him from opposing sides. Conflicting emotions engaged in fierce battle for his sanity with nothing less than his soul at risk.

"I never meant to hurt you," said the weak voice, coming from just outside a shadow that once represented indescribable fear.

The vise relaxed, perhaps because it had accomplished its goal, forced life, or the desire for it, out of his body, leaving him with a profound emptiness that had space for despair, but no room for his father's voice. Other words followed, spoken in a tongue foreign to the human spirit, unrecognized by a son betrayed too often and too deliberately.

Mr. Roth reached out his hands, cut and bleeding from the damage done by roses protected by thorns, a similar safeguard never provided for his child. His son covered those hands with his own, and then gently touched his father's shoulder. "You better go back inside. It's getting cold."

He walked away from the pathetic figure that was once a man, but never a father. He left behind broken and sacred memories of his childhood and replaced them with love for his daughter that he feared he would never hold again. That possibility now caused him greater terror than the childhood he had managed to endure. He looked at his hands and discovered they were stained with his father's blood. His mouth opened slightly seeking fresh air but resulted in the release of a single word: "Rebecca."

Todd walked by his mother without acknowledging her presence, which under the circumstances, was a kindness she did not deserve. He wanted to go home, but the confrontation with his past had weakened him, and the after-effects of the alcohol had robbed him of whatever strength he had left. The unexpected downpour made it unwise for him to travel given his exhaustion and emotional state. His mother suggested he spend the night.

"You can stay in your old room," she offered.

But he could tell by her body language and the tone of her voice that she had hoped he'd decline. He knew she wanted him out of the house as soon as possible, but as had been her custom, wasn't honest enough to tell him. He wanted to leave as well, but he knew he couldn't. If he did, the nightmares would continue to follow him again. No. He had faced his father, what was left of him. Now he had to face the demon and slay it once and for all.

He stopped in front of the bedroom that had been his prison

as a child. It was time to defy the monster. To destroy the grip it had on his life. He was determined not to allow it to imprison him anymore as an adult. He walked in and knew that any monsters from the past had long since ceased to exist, except in his dreams. He stood in the middle of the room, shocked at how small it had become. The walls were painted a bright blue, but no matter how cheerful the décor, the room would always have a certain gloominess for him. In a sense, it reeked of a greater level of decay than the garden he had just left. Perhaps the monster had died, but its ghost had remained, waiting for his return.

Well, here I am, he thought. *Take your best shot.*

He looked at the bed that occupied the same space that he remembered from his childhood, pressed against the wall opposite the door with its headboard to the left of the window that had promised escape, but never delivered it. He stared at the bed, with equal parts dread and bewilderment. He knew he shouldn't fear it, but he did. The thing that should bring a person rest, comfort, even safety, has stolen his youth, his dreams, and so much more. What would it take, tonight? What, if anything, did he have left to give?

He sat on the edge and looked at the door. There would be no need for a chair propped up against it tonight, no makeshift barrier to keep evil at bay. Whatever had been haunting him was already in the room, lingering, waiting for the chance to do permanent harm. He slowly leaned back, rested his head against a pillow, closed his eyes, and beckoned the monster's ghost to do battle one last time, so it could be vanquished forever.

Shadows engulfed a small child, lying awake in his bed. A large teddy bear concealed the boy's face. The rattling of the doorknob was not unexpected, nor was the boy's subsequent response. He pulled the blanket up beneath his chin and held it tightly. As always, he moved his stuffed animal to the side and placed it face down so that it wouldn't have to be a witness to what would inevitably happen, despite the chair propped underneath the doorknob.

The door burst open with such violence that it shattered the wooden legs of the chair that had done its best to give the boy a reasonable chance of protection. As the footsteps made their unsteady way toward the boy, he pulled the blanket a little higher, until it served as his burial shroud, and then he brought the teddy bear to his chest.

The monster stumbled forward, taking one last sip of a bottle now empty and as useless as the child's whimpering plea. "Don't, Daddy... Please don't." Mr. Roth sat on the bed next to his five-year-old son and placed the bottle on a small night table. He removed the blanket from the child, without resistance.

"Put the bear away, Son... Todd, do what your daddy says."

Todd placed the bear to the side, between himself and his father.

"No, Daddy... Please... No, Daddy." Except this time, the words remained in the boy's throat, to be swallowed and then suffocated by the knowledge of previous violations.

Tears fell from this small child's face. Mr. Roth pushed the bear to the floor, and Todd wondered if he had seen tears on his father's face as well. Yes, he had.

Todd opened his eyes, and the nightmare was replaced by a vision of his father standing in the darkness, holding a blanket, and staring at his son. Mr. Roth slowly approached and placed the blanket over his son's legs, then pulled it up to cover Todd's chest. He patted it once to stay in place, and then left.

Todd stared at the door that his father had left open. Would he be returning to check on his son? If so, there was no need to be concerned. This time, he would be able to protect himself and given that his father's condition was too weak and feeble to do any more harm, the monster would no longer need either one.

Todd held onto the blanket and either through his will or the natural unevenness of the room's structure, the door gradually closed on this chapter of his life.

Where the next chapter would open, he could only hope.

In the morning Todd sat at the kitchen table. Mrs. Roth brought him some juice and a freshly baked muffin. "Are you going to say goodbye to your father?"

"Would it matter?"

"You shouldn't blame yourself for what happened," she said, her hand shook slightly, while she poured coffee into a cup. "You were just a child." Coffee spilled onto the saucer. "It wasn't your fault."

He looked at her in disbelief, briefly contemplating whether to choke her or cry. He turned away before he could make the choice and chose, instead, to laugh, and then ignore her as he spoke.

"I never dreamed as a child," he said.

His mother used a cloth to absorb the spilled coffee.

"I always thought that was weird, but now I realize it was because I wouldn't allow him to be there. If I couldn't stop him while I was awake, I sure as hell could stop him while I was asleep. My nightmares he could have. They belonged to him. But dreams? All the pure and decent things that belongs to a child that makes him believe in the future. They were mine, even if I couldn't have them."

She gently wiped away any residue of coffee on the side of the cup.

"He stole that from me, the ability to feel safe at night, to have the right to dream." He grabbed her hand to prevent her from cleaning the mess. He confronted her with a harsh, dangerous glare. "You both did."

He studied what he thought was fear on her face, but realized it was shame. He let go of her wrist. "God forgive you... because I never will." He left, bumping into the table on his way out, causing the coffee cup to tip over.

Mrs. Roth sat down and watched the coffee spill onto the floor, where her gaze remained until she closed her eyes and cried.

FORTY-EIGHT

Liz washed Rebecca's clothes, which had been in the laundry basket since she went missing, and then placed them in the dryer, adding two sheets of fabric softener. When they were done, she folded them carefully. Despite going through the wash, a pair of white socks was still soiled. She removed them from the pile and sprayed on detergent that claimed to be effective at removing stains. Liz rubbed the socks together, gently at first, and then more vigorously, with an urgency that frightened her. She did this for a long time, until her fingers ached, and her hands became raw from the constant friction.

She tossed the socks aside and leaned over the dryer, her head lowered either in fatigue or defeat. Her chest heaved, struggling not to cry. She struck the top of the machine with the palm of her hand, struck it again and again, until she had created a noticeable dent in the metal. She took one of Rebecca's blouses and refolded it neatly.

Liz held it to her chest, turned around, pressed her back against the washing machine, and slowly slid to the floor.

She looked at the blouse and discovered a trace of blood, which had trickled down her hand, which had suffered a cut, either from the friction or from striking the dryer. Attempting to remove the stain, she ran her finger over the bloody droplet, but only managed to smear it to a wider area. Lifting the blouse, she buried her face into the fabric and wept uncontrollably until she heard a car pull into the driveway in anticipation of the moment she both feared and desired.

She'd had a warning call from her mother-in-law, advising her that Todd was on his way home, but that he probably *would not be himself*. Elizabeth had hoped that much would be true.

"You two have been through so much," her mother-in-law said sympathetically. "We all have. I know it will be all right. It must be." She hung up before Liz could respond, which had saved them both from any unpleasantries.

* * *

Todd had driven, not paying attention to the traffic or how fast he was travelling, or the time required to arrive home. It was a miracle that he hadn't caused an accident, but then, hadn't he just been involved in one, an emotional wreck that had taken its toll on everyone he had ever loved? And like too many victims, he felt responsible, and guilty, and heartbroken. He used his remote to open the gate leading to his driveway. He wished he had been able to control steel fences this easily when he was a child. Perhaps then, his father might never have been able to enter his room and Todd, years later, wouldn't have felt compelled to construct impenetrable walls that kept his daughter outside his reach.

He parked the car and wondered if subconsciously, because of his childhood trauma, he had been inspired to become an architect. Was he destined to design magnificent structures built to withstand natural disasters, all the while providing a false sense of security to those who inhabited them? He contemplated that question, and then opened his front door unsure of what he would need to confront next.

He entered through the foyer and made his way into the living room. He took a few steps and stopped when he saw her. As drained as he felt, the sight of his wife buoyed him, bringing him a sense of relief. It caused him to cast aside all questions regarding the walls he had built, both physical and emotional.

When he was close to her, he tried to speak, but she spoke first.

"Is it true?" she shuddered. "Did he really do that to you?" The word "that" was filled with such disgust and disdain, that it forced Todd to relive the revulsion.

He looked at her, his eyes filled with tears, which caused Liz to place her fingertips over her lips and mutter, "My God. Why couldn't you tell me?"

For the moment, God was someone who Todd had great difficulty believing in, let alone dealing with.

She touched his face, but then withdrew her hand. He understood that human touch, contact of any kind, would overwhelm them both. "I couldn't tell you. It was more than shame. I was terrified by what you'd think of me. I knew you wouldn't blame me as a child. Only I could do that. But all my adult life, I lied to you, to Becky, to everyone. To myself. There were times I denied it. Repressed it so deep that I couldn't believe it really happened. If it had, I'd never had become so successful, respected. I'd never had someone like you love me. How could I?"

"When I saw you on the bathroom floor, whimpering like a frightened, no... *terrified* child. Calling out your father's name with such contempt, such hatred, I knew it couldn't be anything else." She took a deep breath, massaged her hand the way she always did when dealing with adversity, trying to bring clarity or sanity to a situation that had difficulty accepting either.

"I think I've always known, or at least suspected. Seeing you wake up in the middle of the night, panic-stricken. Tossing and turning. Sometimes crying like a small child who had nowhere to turn, no escape." She moved a bit closer to him. "Is that why you couldn't touch your own daughter? Is that why you didn't want more children?"

The questions caused him to close his eyes in a futile effort to hide. If he couldn't disappear, then the rest of the world would have to, even if only for a few seconds. He opened his eyes and realized how much she mattered and always had. "With everything inside me, I wanted to hold her... To toss her in the air, knowing I would never let her fall. To hug her. To be there. I just never could." His throat felt dry, restricting his ability to speak, as if his body was trying to save himself from words that once spoken, would change him forever.

"Even though I did everything to block out my father from my memory, to forget it ever happened, I was afraid I would be like him. I was afraid she'd become like me... unable to touch because that's what she learned from me."

"You could have told me. You should have told me. I could have helped. I wanted to help, all this time."

Now it was his turn to step closer to his wife. They were mere inches from one another. He could feel her breath on his face. The scent of her perfume filled his lungs. He wanted to reach out, touch her. He wasn't holding back this time because of any emotional deficiency on his part. Rather, it was out of respect for what he knew were her wishes, to be left alone.

She wanted a divorce, that's what she had told him. But could Dr. Stevens be right? That he couldn't, and shouldn't, trust or believe decisions made under conditions like the ones they were facing?

"I'm sorry," she said.

Those two simple words paralyzed him. If they had been uttered by his father, would that have been enough to forgive him? He was unsure what they meant, coming from his wife.

Was she sorry about what happened to him as a child or for what he had become as an adult? Did she regret the ending of their marriage or was she offering an apology to remain together? Was she remorseful because she finally understood his inability to be the father Rebecca needed or was it an expression of pity that he had failed so miserably at the attempt?

He didn't know, and when she walked away and left the room, he feared he never would. The only certainty he had was that those two words, "I'm sorry," would haunt him all the way to his grave and beyond.

FORTY-NINE

WEDNESDAY APRIL 26TH

It started as a simple drizzle, turned into a light, but steady rain, and then the floodgates opened. Ron's windshield wipers needed to be replaced a year ago, but since it never rains in Southern California, why incur the expense? The answer: for nights like this. He pulled his Volvo to the side of the road, a safe distance from what little traffic existed, and unbuckled his seatbelt. He flashed his emergency lights and turned on the defrost allowing him to see the magnitude of the downpour, and nothing else, until lightning lit up the sky. The thunder that followed caused him to jump, barely missing hitting his head against the roof. His ribs were not so fortunate, striking the steering wheel, which caused the horn to blare. Given the racket going on outside, it went unnoticed. Unprepared for the ferocity of the storm, he decided to stay in the car, the roof of which sounded like it was being attacked by a shower of nails.

He had traveled to Mother's Beach in Marina del Rey, because that's where he used to take Jennifer each weekend when she was young and could fit easily into the black plastic bucket seats attached to the swing-set for small children. There were a series of four or five chairs lined up in a row. Parents, usually mothers (hence the name), would push those seats from behind, propelling them high enough to produce the most amazing laughter and childish expressions of wonderment. When Jennifer turned four or five, she joined the older kids on the slides or hid in the king's castle or kept watch on the pirate ship or raced her newly acquired friends to the water's edge, and beyond. Once she was brave enough, which was much sooner than her father anticipated or agreed to, Jennifer graduated to the *real* swings. Occasionally, she was forced to ask for an initial push or a boost to get her to the highest point possible. That's when he would forget about snapping photos and position himself to break her fall, which he was certain would happen at any moment, but never did. She'd thrust her legs forward, generating significant torque in her body. That effort was sufficient to propel her high enough to hang upside-down, feet pointed toward the sky, and head inches from scraping against the sand, although her ponytails left behind quite a trail.

"Not so high, Jenny," he'd warn her, to no avail.

She'd only kick harder and hang lower, while his heart remained trapped inside his throat.

"Hold on tight, baby!" he'd *encourage* her, which was a father's term for "ordered" or a quick way of saying, "If you don't stop, you're going to give me a stroke."

He was even more frantic, worried to death when the training wheels came off. Come to think of it, he ran alongside her bicycle even when they were attached. After all, she could just as easily fall off a four-wheeler as a two-wheeler. Well, technically it was a three-wheeler in the back with one in the front, but danger is danger, and a child is a child, and you could never be too safe... *Safe...* How he wished for those times when safety meant slowing down or holding on tight or wearing a helmet and elbow pads or simply letting go of the back of the seat so your child could make it on her own.

He'd thought, had hoped, that going to the beach would

bring him comfort. He could almost see her on the swings, hear her laughter. He used to catch her on the backswing, hold the seat-bucket high in the air, as she clapped her hands in excitement. They counted together, "One, two, threeeeeee, which she would always pronounce as "Weeeeeeee," and he would let go with a shove. The memory caused him to smile, but not for long.

The lightning struck again, even brighter than the last time. He braced himself for the thunder, but his attention had shifted to the flash of white peeking between the passenger seat and the console. He slid his hand down the narrow crevice, grabbed onto an envelope with two fingers, and slowly lifted it up and out. At first, he thought it might be a bill that had fallen between the cracks, in more ways than one. *Just what he needed.* He pushed the overhead courtesy light button and immediately recognized Jennifer's handwriting.

To My Dad, it read. The rain never let up, but he didn't care about the world outside the confines of his automobile, nor for that matter, had he noticed what was happening inside and how much his hand shook. He came close to rolling down the window. He needed air desperately, but he needed to safeguard the envelope from the rain even more.

He ran his index finger across the edge, and then tried to gently unseal the envelope without tearing the paper. Like a child receiving his first gift-wrapped present, he wanted to rip it open as quickly as possible and discover what was inside. But he didn't want to damage anything about this last communication from his daughter. He hesitated before trying to unseal it, again. He thought about how she had searched for it, after he dropped her off at school. Remembered how he had been impatient and yelled at her, wanting to get to work for the promotion he had been denied. He should have opened it then and there, to let her know what she had given him, whatever it might be, always would be more important than a promotion, a job, or anything else.

But he didn't.

And now with a desire heightened by fear and intensified by the need to read her words as a poor substitute for hearing her voice, he lifted the middle of the seal and slowly pulled it open.

He removed the card from the envelope. Small hearts were scattered on the cover. When he opened it, a gigantic heart popped out, as if on a spring, pulsating back and forth. The words *I LOVE YOU*, were handwritten underneath in large block letters. He had difficulty reading the message that followed, letters blurred together, and ink-stained words merged. He looked out the front windshield, rain droplets steadily attacked the glass, streaming down like a rapid waterfall.

He ran his fingers over his eyes to clear them of tears but had managed only to release a reservoir of grief that had been barricaded by time and the necessity to carry on. He held the card nearer the courtesy light and as the words came into focus, he heard nothing, except the voice of his daughter.

You have been officially promoted to the best dad, ever! A job you will have for the rest of my life! His heart ached, his hand shook, and his head felt like it would explode. He willed himself to read the rest of the message. *Your biggest fan and your only daughter, I am so proud of you—love forever, Jenny.*

He saw a heart drawn in red, surrounded by X's and O's for kisses and hugs that he would now give anything in this world to receive—to feel his daughter's embrace, and be able to return it.

He lowered the card, held it briefly, slipped it into its envelope, and placed it inside the glove compartment. He turned off the engine, removed the key, left on the emergency lights, and exited the car into the storm.

In a dark haze, he walked down the street, and then aimlessly onto a sidewalk. He wasn't aware that he had started jogging, slowly at first, unsteadily to be sure. Soaked in a matter of seconds, he stepped off the curb and into deep puddles, which flooded his shoes and socks. He jogged faster, the rain attacking all his senses except the ones that mattered, the ones he needed to drown, to numb, by any means necessary. He picked up his pace, arms and legs pumped harder. Rain competed with tears, obstructing his view of what lay ahead. Suddenly, he broke out in a full sprint, either racing to a place that would change his life for the better or running from some evil thing that would destroy it, once and for all.

Breathing heavily, gasping for air, his mouth opened to release pleas for help, but instead swallowed rain, and desperation, and for the first time since Jennifer's disappearance, a sense of hopelessness. He screamed, not words, or anything else that could be comprehended by the human ear. No, these were sounds that could be understood only by the human heart, those who had experienced the pain of losing a child, of having the future ripped away in an instant to be mercilessly assaulted by memories that used to contain joy, and laughter, and love.

You have been officially promoted to the best dad, ever!

His body, now out of control, his arms flayed against the wind and cold. He attempted to scream once more, but was driven to his knees, incapable of moving forward, and stunned by the silence that inexorable terror creates.

A job you will have for the rest of my life!

He managed a whisper that he believed the world could hear if they understood the true meaning of love.

"Jennifer."

FIFTY

THURSDAY APRIL 27

Todd drove his Mercedes for more than fifteen minutes without saying a word to Ron.

"You okay? You're unusually quiet," said Ron.

"Just tired. You haven't had a lot to say, either."

"I dance with the one who brung me. In this case, the one who's driving. I'm just along for the ride."

Todd remained silent.

Ron inspected him more closely. "You look awful."

"Thanks."

"That wasn't a compliment."

Todd studied Ron. "Compared to the way you look; I'll take it as one."

"You had a rough night?"

"Rough doesn't do it justice. How 'bout yours? You get any sleep?"

"The rain kept me up."

"All night?" asked Todd.

"And into the morning." Ron avoided the suspicious glance Todd tossed his way by studying the list and comparing it to the street address. "I think this is it." He pointed to a small home that looked like an oversized garage, subdivided into two tiny one-bedroom apartments.

Todd pulled into a parking space across the street from the property and turned off the engine. He focused his attention on the duplex. "I don't see any lights on inside."

"Maybe he's conserving for the benefit of the environment," quipped Ron.

"A socially conscious pedophile. How heartwarming." Todd looked at a photo printed out from the database. "He's even smiling in his mug shot."

Ron tapped Todd on the shoulder. "He's not smiling now." He pointed toward the duplex.

Todd stared through his window, and saw a man leaving the building, headed down Centinela Avenue. He had a set of keys in his hand and appeared headed toward a parked car.

"That's him," said Ron.

They exited the car and crossed the street. Todd moved quickly after the man who used his remote to unlock his sedan, the lights flashed, coinciding with a short beep.

"Mr. Lungren?" Todd called out. "Are you Theodore Lungren?"

The man nervously walked away from the car, ignoring Todd's overtures. His pace increased. Todd and Ron closed the distance between them. The man looked over his shoulder and noticed Todd holding a sheet of paper with his mug shot.

"We'd like to ask you a few questions," Todd said, perhaps with a bit too much force and harsh tone of authority.

Lungren broke out into a full sprint, racing down the avenue and cutting through an alleyway. Todd and Ron chased after him, avoiding garbage cans and other objects that Lungren tossed in their path.

Lungren raced around a corner, headed toward Culver Boulevard with the two men in hot pursuit. Patrons along the avenue were pushed aside. Lungren knocked over an elderly man. Ron stopped to help the man, but Todd continued the chase.

Lungren crossed a busy intersection, dodging traffic to get to the other side of Culver. Todd nearly missed being struck by an S.U.V. Its driver swore a few choice words. Several drivers slammed on their brakes. A Toyota rammed into the back of a Ford Sedan. That rear-end collision was followed by another.

Lungren cut across a lawn, avoiding sprinklers. He slipped and fell, sliding on a grassy area and into a group of tall hedges. He regained footing and managed to cross the avenue divide. Todd charged him, tackling Lungren to the ground less than two hundred feet from the Culver City police station. Lungren kicked Todd in the face, knocking him backwards. He attempted to drive his knee into Todd's stomach, but Todd grabbed Lungren's leg, twisting him back to the ground. Lungren tried to get up and spin away, but Todd pounced on him, striking the prone man relentlessly, rapidly pounding fists to the face and head.

Ron arrived and tried to take Todd off the defenseless Lungren, but was pushed aside as Todd, totally out of control, continued the beating.

"Todd! Stop it! You're gonna kill him!" screamed Ron but Todd wouldn't relent. Ron charged Todd, tackled him to the ground, pinning him there as police from the neighboring station intervened.

Ron and Todd were kept in a detention room, grilled by two policemen who were taking down their accounts of the fight.

"Everyone here already knows your story," said one of the cops. "And we're sympathetic. But you can't go around beating up people you suspect of being involved in your daughter's disappearance."

The second officer spoke more to the point. "In addition to

possible criminal charges, you've opened yourself up to one hell of a civil suit."

"He ran," said Todd. "Innocent people don't run."

"They do when they're being chased," continued the second officer.

The more sympathetic officer intervened. "I suppose if we don't try to put his ass back in jail for some type of violation, we can convince him not to press charges against the two of you."

"I don't know if that's a good idea." Everyone turned to see Detective McKay at the doorway. He walked in with Carrey and gave a signal to the officers. "Mind if we have a few minutes alone?"

The two policemen left the room. McKay slowly pulled back a chair and rested his foot on it, leaning toward the two men, seated together, like two schoolchildren in serious trouble with an irate principal.

"So, are both of you finished playing the Lone Ranger?" asked an obviously miffed McKay.

Carrey intervened, none too pleased. "My partner and I have given you a lot of space hoping you'd come to your senses and let us do our job. But you're putting yourselves in physical and legal jeopardy and, what's worse, you've placed your daughters right in the middle of it."

"Jennifer's been gone for twenty-three days!" responded Ron angrily. "Twenty-three! Every damn day, every fucking night, I wait for a call, a message from her or you or the bastard that took her. I can't sleep. I can't eat. I can't even pray anymore because I've run out of things to beg for, and I can't afford to say what I really think about God. I don't even know if my daughter is still alive! And instead of you two being out on the streets looking for her, you're in here with us!"

"And why is that?" asked Carrey, his hands on his hips in frustration. "Because you two are involved at playing cop or vigilante and all you're really doing is getting in the way of our investigation." He took a step away and then moved closer. "Every moment we have to spend cleaning up your mess is precious time that keeps us away from finding your daughter."

McKay addressed Todd. "In a way, maybe I can understand Mr. Butler's actions. We didn't exactly get off to the best start. But you?" McKay studied Todd in disbelief. "You've got the mayor's office looking over our shoulders at everything we do, the damn F.B.I.'s running around like chickens with their heads cut off and a half-a-dozen private investigators are scaring the bejesus out of everybody." He released an exaggerated sigh. "I mean, what the hell is it you hope to accomplish, other than having some pervert out there put a bullet through your head and getting away with it?"

Todd diverted his eyes, gazed at the floor.

McKay removed his foot off the chair and took a step back, taking better aim at both men. "You two didn't take my advice. Now, let me make it an official warning... Stay away from this."

"Would you stay away if it was your daughter?" asked Todd.

McKay looked away, frustrated. He sat down at the table and tried a softer method. "I don't know what I'd do," he admitted. "Maybe I'd do everything that the two of you are doing. But I'd be wrong. And it's a mistake my daughter might have to live with... or die from."

"You need to listen to Detective McKay," said Carrey. "He has your best interests at heart. We both do. Through some miracle, you might just happen to stumble onto something and wind up making the sickos who have your daughters even more nervous and frightened than they already are. You want to help, gentlemen? Go home and pray."

"I don't have a home anymore!" shouted Ron. "And if I have to depend on you to find my daughter, I'd never have a home again. I know how you think. I know how you treat someone whose been gone as long as Jenny. You assume the worst, which is another way of saying they don't exist for you. They're not a priority."

"I'm not going to lie to you," said Carrey. "With each day that goes by, the chances to find your girls decrease. You've done your homework, so you know what we're dealing with. But don't you think for a second that we're not working with every fiber of our being to bring your daughter home. Both of your daughters."

"We know you're doing your best," replied Todd. "You said you weren't going to lie to us. If you're truly going to be honest, this isn't the only case you're working on. You've probably got dozens. We've got one. The two of us are out there every twenty-four hours looking for leads, researching profiles to understand what type of person would do something like this."

"You want to know what type of person would do this?" asked McKay. "A person who doesn't give a fuck about your feelings or research or theories you've got or the goddamn law!" He slammed his palm against the desk and took several moments to calm down. "You know what else? He doesn't want to get caught and if you keep flaying around, you're gonna make him nervous and desperate and a nervous and desperate criminal is a dangerous one."

"We're just trying to find our daughters," replied Todd. "Everything you've told us, everything we've read, says we're running out of time."

Carry nodded his head and said, "Which is why we can't spend it dealing with you getting in trouble. We've got a team working on finding Rebecca and another one searching for Jennifer. We're doing all we can to bring them home."

"What if the same person or persons have them both?" asked Ron.

Both detectives gave each other a look. "We haven't ruled that out but it's highly unlikely," responded McKay.

"But it's possible," said Ron.

"Anything's possible," said McKay. "But it would be extremely rare. Kidnapping one child and keeping them hidden is difficult and risky enough. And certainly, to take two children within a week of each other, Mr. Butler, it doesn't happen one in a million times."

"Look," said Carrey. "We promise we'll keep you informed as often as we can. If you've got any ideas or theories or profiles or anything else your research has turned up, we want you to share it with us. But I'm pleading with you, let us follow up on whatever you have. For your safety, as well as your daughters." He moved to the door and opened it, waiting for them to leave. "Let us do our jobs before you drive my partner to take an early retirement."

Ron and Todd remained seated at the table in silence.

McKay took out his handcuffs and extended them. "Or I can lock you up for a few days. It's entirely up to you."

Ron and Todd looked at each other. They understood there was nothing left to say, and it was time to leave.

* * *

Carrey closed the door and looked at a skeptical McKay. "You think we got through to them?"

Carrey shrugged. "Doesn't matter if we did. They're gonna do what they need to do. Can't say I blame 'em." He massaged his forehead. "Can't say I'd do different if I was in their shoes. Who the hell knows? Maybe they'll do some crazy shit and wind up causing the perp to do something stupid that brings him to our attention."

"That's what I'm afraid of. With all this publicity they're generating, the last thing we need is a nervous pervert who's worrying he's close to getting caught. What's the latest on the condition of the flake they beat up?"

"Badly bruised and scared shitless," answered Carrey. "He

said he ran because he'd heard they were looking to kill everyone on their list."

McKay thought about it. "Maybe we should pay him another visit at his home. Tell him we're there to offer protection. It'll give us an excuse to check out the place."

"You think he could be involved?"

"Don't know. But I think we'd better find out who took those kids before their parents really do start using that list to permanently eliminate all suspects and they wind up serving twenty-five to life."

"What's the chance the same perp took both kids?" asked Carrey.

McKay rubbed his forehead and looked at his partner. "You got any Excedrin?"

Carrey shook his head. "You emptied the bottle an hour ago."

McKay opened the door. "Let's go."

"Where to?"

"First to Lungren. Then the next seven on our list."

FIFTY-ONE

Todd and Ron exited the station and proceeded across Culver Boulevard to retrieve the car.

"You want to tell me what that was all about?" asked Ron. "You looked like you were trying to murder the guy."

"I saw something in his face."

"You think he's involved?"

"No."

"Then what did you see?"

"My father."

Ron stopped dead in his tracks. Todd continued walking. After a few seconds, Ron caught up. Both men walked quickly until Ron placed his hand on Todd's shoulder, halting his progress.

"We need to talk," Ron said. "Now."

Todd nodded agreement.

They located the car and drove to a public park in Washington Square. Children from the nearby elementary school played dodge ball, while their teachers supervised.

The two men walked across the baseball field and sat on one of the wooden benches adjacent to the picnic area. Ron waited for Todd to explain his behavior. It took a while, but he remained patient.

"You remember telling me about your daughter, thinking she could recall everything about her birth?"

Ron nodded. "And you told me—"

"Young children, perhaps even infants, have the capacity to recall events, but they block out things they find too painful."

"I remember," said Ron.

"Well, if you ever need to study someone who's suppressed painful memories, you need look no further than the person sitting next to you."

"And why would you make such a good example?"

"I didn't dream as a child. I used to think that was odd, but I made up for that lost time as an adult. In one of my recurring nightmares, this huge man wore a flannel black and red checkerboard shirt. He looked like a deranged woodsman with a shaggy beard and arms shaped like a lumberjack. He wielded an ax, with a long wooden handle and a shiny steel blade sharp enough to cut through bone, which I was convinced it would do the moment he swung it in my direction."

"And did he?"

Todd shook his head. "No. Not even once. But he would always prevent me from reaching my father, who I could see in the distance, yelling at me to hurry up. I begged my dad to help, but he just stood there waiting for me to join him. No matter how hard I tried, I couldn't get around this man."

"A father's supposed to protect his child from the boogey-man." Ron commented.

"Not if he's become one," Todd responded, in a hushed voice. "All this time, the person who I thought was trying to hurt me, by keeping me away from my father, was actually trying to save me from him."

"Why would he be saving you?'

"For the same reason you and I are looking for our daughters."

He didn't understand until Todd completed the answer.

"To save them from a pedophile, a child molester of the worst kind, the ones who lives in your home."

Ron allowed the implication of the statement to sink in. "Jesus," he muttered.

"Yes, I called out to Jesus, too. Probably screamed his name as loudly as a child could, but he never answered." He shrugged. "Although maybe he showed up as that lumberjack, and I didn't want to recognize him."

One of the dodgeballs rolled toward Ron. He picked it up and tossed it back to a young boy, who instantly used the opportunity to hurl a rocket, hitting a schoolmate in the back of his head. The victim flashed a toothless grin, retrieved the ball, and chased the little culprit until he had gotten revenge which, in turn, had renewed the unending cycle of reprisal all over again.

There was a long period of silence between the two men. Ron searched for the right words but couldn't find them. Luckily, Todd spoke first.

"I think the reason I really came to see you that first time was that I wanted to know how you managed to be so close to your daughter."

Ron observed the students line up and head back to the school, paying particular attention to an African American girl who resembled a younger Jennifer. It served as a constant reminder that everywhere he turned, he would find something or someone that forced him to think about her. He would never free himself from the journey he now found himself on, and he wondered, based on what had just been revealed, if Todd had freed himself from one crisis, only to face a far more difficult test.

"I wanted to be around someone who was everything I wasn't," continued Todd.

"Why? What could you possibly learn from me?"

"If she came back, if I was allowed a second chance with her, I wanted to know how to be a father, a good one."

Ron massaged his eyes and forehead.

"Didn't expect to be invited to a confessional today, did you?"

"I asked for it."

"The sons continue to pay for the sins of their fathers... I just never knew how much." Todd nervously tapped his fingers against his thigh, and then stopped. "Can I ask you a personal question?"

"You mean, as opposed to all the other questions we've been asking each other?"

"You ever think of getting remarried? You come close with anybody else?"

Ron scratched his neck just underneath his shirt collar, but that wasn't the only discomfort he was experiencing. Dating wasn't a subject that came easily to him, even when his daughter insisted it was time to *stop fooling around and get serious with someone.* He stopped fidgeting and finally answered the question. "It's not easy to compete with Jennifer. She's priority one, and it takes a special woman to accept that."

"Maybe they're not competing with Jennifer. Maybe it's her mother they can't compete with."

Ron knew that was a contest that no one could or would ever win. "I take it subtlety isn't one of your strongest assets."

"Wait till you get to know me better. My insensitivity grows on people."

"Thanks for the warning."

A family of four spread out a picnic cloth on the largest table in the area and arranged food taken from a wicker basket. The father placed a Styrofoam cooler on the ground and removed bottles of soda and packets of juice. He held up two drinks, offering them to Todd and Ron, who thanked him, but declined.

The sight of a family enjoying themselves provided Ron with yet another example of the heartache that could be found lurking around the next corner. Everywhere he turned, he would find something or someone...

"If you don't want to talk about it, I can wait five minutes." Todd focused attention on his wristwatch. "Four-minutes-fifty-nine, four-minutes-fifty-eight, four—"

"I went to visit her the other day."

Todd stopped looking at his watch, appearing confused.

"The gravesite," Ron explained. "I brought her favorite flowers. And I asked her, begged her really, to help me bring Jennifer back home. I think my exact word was 'deliver' as if she could give birth again, return an eleven-year-old to her natural place." He shook his head in disbelief and released a deep sigh. "That's crazy, isn't it?"

"I don't think it's crazy at all."

"You don't?" He laughed.

"I think it would be crazy not to believe in a higher power, whether it's in the heavens or buried in the ground."

"When I was talking to her, I didn't imagine her remains in a coffin, the decay that's occurred in the past decade. I saw her face, the radiance in her eyes. I don't think I could have called on her spirit without that image."

A homeless man approached the family, and the mother gave him a piece of chicken and two packets of juice. He placed the drinks in his backpack, sat underneath a tree, and ate the food. That was something Jennifer would do, Ron thought. Give away her last dollar if she thought someone needed it more.

Everywhere he turned... Something or someone... He would never free himself.

"How did you meet your wife?" asked Todd.

"I had just come to L.A. from back east. Didn't even have my apartment furnished. I was invited to this party in Long Beach. I had no idea where that was. When I got there, I walked through the living room, sidestepping the crowd on the dance floor. I made my way to the kitchen to get a drink, and I saw this woman rinsing a glass at the sink, with her back turned toward me. She wore tight jeans and a red and white striped tube top. She turned and we were face to face. It was like being tasered by a stun gun, but without the pain. Although when she smiled it was more like a stunning gun that hit me between the eyes because that's what she was, absolutely stunning."

Todd laughed.

"Yeah, she laughed, too, when I told her about the stunning gun thing. 'Creative but corny,' she called it. She wanted to know how many times I had used that line in the past and if it had ever worked."

"And what did you tell her?"

"The truth. I had never used it before, and after meeting her I knew I would never have to use it again, not on anyone else."

Todd smiled, but Ron noticed that it was bittersweet, a melancholy moment that had an undercurrent of great disappointment and more than a little pain.

"Todd." Ron said his name to bring him back from a place that he didn't need to be. "There was something about that moment. I know it sounds like a Hollywood movie, but as soon as our eyes connected, I believed I had met the woman of my dreams, the one I would one day marry. We started dating that night and never looked back. I made myself a promise that I would never do anything to jeopardize our marriage. I would never lose her. I hadn't realized that my promise didn't mean anything, that I had no control over it, no matter how hard I tried." He shook his head. "No. I really don't think much about getting remarried."

Ron felt awkward for revealing so much and sensed that Todd was equally uncomfortable.

"I guess confessionals run both ways," Ron said. "Given our circumstances, I apologize for burdening you with—"

"Actually, you lifted my burden," Todd interjected. "Or maybe you made me realize that I was carrying one, and it was time to put down the load. We're a lot alike, Ron."

Ron chuckled. "I agree, wholeheartedly. Our lives are exactly interchangeable. We're two peas in a pod, except our pods live in completely different neighborhoods, which might as well be different worlds."

"You think our incomes or race make us different?"

"Are you serious?" Ron scoffed. "I don't think you needed to barge in on my news conference. You remember? You had the one with the mayor, F.B.I., police chief, and the national media. And I had the one with..." He paused as if to think about it. "Oh, that's right, I didn't have one. The most I had was a meeting with two detectives who treated me like a suspect, because I had the audacity to set up a college fund for my daughter."

"Our daughters are gone," responded Todd.

"You think I need to be reminded of that?"

"No. But maybe you need to recognize that we feel the same pain, and the same fear, and the same rage. And the size of our respective bank accounts or the color of our skin or the zip codes that identify where we reside, can't change what we feel as fathers." He turned away and spoke quietly. "Or for that matter, what we've experienced as husbands."

Ron leaned closer to Todd, as if he didn't want anyone else to overhear their conversation and, yet his voice rose steadily as he spoke. "If we weren't both facing the same tragedy, you think we'd be sitting here talking like old friends? You think you'd have any reason to spend time with me or that we would expend a single second sharing our most intimate thoughts, and hopes, and fears? You really think that?"

"No. I don't think that," admitted Todd. "And I don't care. What matters now is that we *are* sitting together. That we're trying in our own way to support each other, to help find our daughters, to provide comfort at a time when we need it most. I fell in love with my wife the moment I saw her. She wasn't in the kitchen, rinsing a glass. She was on stage dancing, and every time she leaped, so did my heart. But it wouldn't have mattered where I first saw her. I know the reaction would have been exactly the same. And my wife didn't die, but I lost her, too. And maybe I can win her back. Maybe I won't. Maybe I'll find my daughter or spend the rest of my life searching. But whatever does or does not happen, we're in the same boat. And if it sinks, we both drown."

Ron wasn't convinced. "I have a feeling your life preservers are a bit better equipped than mine."

"Being kept afloat isn't the best way to live."

"It is, if it's the only way," responded Ron. "And right now, I'll settle for treading water, if it keeps Jennifer alive."

"When you need help," Todd said, "it doesn't matter which life preserver you use. It's just important that someone is willing to share it."

"I'll keep that in mind next time I take my annual luxury cruise." Ron regretted the response as soon as he had uttered it, but he made no effort to take it back. Instead, he stood, ready to leave. "We should head back to the car. Finish what we need to do."

"Aren't we going to work with the detectives?"

"Yeah. Soon as they work with us." Ron walked away, but not before giving the homeless man his last dollar.

Todd rose from the bench and stood motionless for a few seconds. He shook his head in disappointment and then left the park.

FIFTY-TWO

Todd stared at the ceiling. He tried to fall asleep, but he kept reliving the confrontation he'd had with his parents, as well as his conversation with Ron at the park. He gently nudged his wife, who had her back to him.

"Liz, are you asleep?" She didn't respond. He leaned over and kissed her cheek. He lightly touched her hair and left the room, unaware that she had opened her eyes.

He went into the kitchen to make something to eat, but then decided against it. No food could satisfy the type of hunger that gnawed at his insides. He moved to the family room and played an older recording of Rebecca dancing on stage. She was younger, maybe seven or eight, but he was still in awe at how graceful she appeared, so confident, self-assured, each movement precise. A young male, a teen, joined her on stage, took her hand, and they danced together.

She fearlessly leaped into the air, into the boy's waiting arms. He caught her, raised her over his head, and then let her down carefully. Rebecca twirled across the stage, spinning in tight circles. Todd thought that if scientists or dance teachers ever needed the perfect ballerina, his daughter would fit the bill.

She returned to her young partner to complete the routine. He bowed, and then held her hand. She curtsied, acknowledging the adoration of the audience. She was given a beautiful bouquet of roses. The boy slowly exited, allowing her to have the stage to herself. Rebecca owned it, appearing in total command, displaying radiance underneath klieg lights that paled in comparison. Todd watched her smile, bright, and proud, and full of life. He felt enormous delight in her accomplishments, as well as great heartache in his loss. He sat on the couch, prepared to view a second recording.

"I was watching that two nights ago."

He looked up and discovered Liz at the doorway. She approached him, a sad smile appeared, and then quickly disappeared. "What made you want to see her dance? Does it help you think of her under different circumstances?"

"I wasn't watching to think about her. I wanted to think about you." He studied her to see if there was any reaction to his response. But she had gotten good at concealing her true feelings. As an expert in the practice, he should know.

"She moved like you, graceful and elegant, full of life and confidence. I know she's just a child, but I always imagined that you danced exactly the way she did, when you were her age."

"I was never that good."

"That's because you never had the advantage that she had. You were never taught by someone as gifted as you."

Liz sat down on the couch next to her husband. "What's brought all this on?"

"Ron Butler talked about when he first met his wife. About the magic of that moment, and how he knew she was the one." He looked at her. "And I told him about how you and I met. How I felt the same way."

"He must have been bored to tears."

"Oh, there were tears all right, but not from boredom, and they weren't shed by him."

She brought her palms together.

He touched her hand and regained her attention. "I'm sorry, Elizabeth. I'd give anything in this world to change it all; the way I treated you and Rebecca."

"I'm sorry, too," she said.

There were those two words again. But this time there was no mistaking what she meant when she said them.

"I'm sorry that I allowed it to go on so long. She deserved better from you, from both of us."

She moistened her lips, and he would have given anything for one kiss, like the ones they used to share, passionate, and real, and long-lasting.

"For the past year, maybe more," she said, "I avoided looking into your eyes, because I couldn't face the truth that I no longer saw myself in them. Now, I'm afraid I can no longer look in your eyes because I see our daughter. You look so much like her, and I can't bear that anymore. Not when I know I may never be able to hold her again. And I can't use you as a substitute. I won't do that to you or her."

She took his hand and held it tightly with her two hands. "You accused me of blaming you for her abduction. I don't feel that. I never meant to accuse you of that. But you are guilty of losing her, of losing me." She let go of his hand. "I can forgive you for what's happened to us. In time, maybe we can even find a way to make our marriage work. But what you did to her..."

She spoke with an intensity that forced him to close his eyes for a moment, her words were overwhelming because they were true and delivered without pettiness or vindictiveness.

"Todd, she adored you so much. And she didn't need it returned the same way. She just needed to know that she mattered and that you loved her. And damn it, with all your talent, and creativity, and success, you couldn't manage to accomplish that."

She stood up, ready to leave, but not before she finished what she had to say. "If you couldn't do that with her, as wonderful and perfect as she is, then in God's name, will you ever be able to demonstrate that, to anyone?"

He watched her leave, and then walked toward the entertainment center and turned off the recording. He no longer needed it to see his daughter.

FIFTY-THREE
FRIDAY APRIL 28TH

Rebecca wanted the nightmare to end, but the water and steam served as proof that she was fully awake, sitting in a tub filled with bath bubbles. She closed her eyes and prayed that they would lift her up, floating to a safe place where she could be reunited with her family. She knew the bubbles had no such power and soon would offer no more shelter. But miracles were still possible, weren't they?

When she felt a washcloth against her back, she shivered.

"Are you cold?" he asked.

She opened her eyes and looked straight at her captor. "Please leave," she said in a voice that comingled a nervous plea, with a more resolute command.

A slight smile appeared on his face, and then disappeared as quickly as the washcloth, which he dipped into the water, submerging it several times, before returning it to her back, gently removing the soap from her skin.

She knew that no matter how often or how hard he scrubbed, she would not feel clean tonight. Nor would she find refuge from the dangers that would visit her while she slept, where the nightmares would duplicate and magnify her terrifying reality. As reprehensible and unforgiveable as his actions had been, he'd committed an even greater evil. He had violated her sleep and stolen her dreams.

She was committed to finding a way to recapture them no matter the consequence. That was her sole goal and to achieve it she knew what she had to do. It required planning and waiting for the precise moment and the proper circumstance. It might necessitate coordination, eliciting help or assistance or some type of support from the girls. But they were ready. She believed in them and knew that they believed in her. She'd have to find a way when she wasn't chained. When he was preoccupied. When he was more vulnerable than they were. She would spend every waking moment preparing herself to seize the moment. The goal one day, one hour, one minute, would be in her grasp. She only had to reach out and take it. Freedom!

She escaped the confines of her bathtub to return to the imprisonment of her room. But this time, with faith renewed and a plan to share with her friends, who listened intently.

FIFTY-FOUR

Todd and Ron ate breakfast at a local café on Washington Boulevard in Marina del Rey. This was the tenth day since they had started their fruitless quest and today had three more names on the list who resided in Venice. Once that was completed, they would travel to neighboring Santa Monica to continue their visits.

"What if he's not a pedophile?" asked Ron. "Suppose my daughter or yours was taken to be part of some cult? Or sold into a child pornography-slash-sex trafficking ring? Or were victims of a random act of violence?"

"Thanks for not bringing up your various theories to my wife at dinner last week." Todd poured two sugars into his coffee. "She was beginning to like you."

"Granted, it sounds crazy, but I've been going over the possibilities, no matter how unlikely. I even came up with the notion that she might have started walking home and fell through a trap. Or got in an accident and has amnesia. And she's been wandering the streets lost."

"You forgot the one about it all being a bad dream, and you or I are about to wake up, and everything will be all right." Todd took a quick sip of coffee. "That's occurred to me, maybe a dozen times or more, every night since she went missing, to be exact. But then I wake up, and the nightmare is real. And trust me I'm something of an expert on nightmares."

Todd sampled his breakfast, a forkful of scrambled eggs, a small piece of ham, a bite of his English muffin, and then set the plate aside. "What really brought all this on beside the normal fears and doubts that have become a part of our daily lives?"

Ron spread a dab of grape jam on his toast but didn't taste it. "I took a walk through a pretty bad section of Venice last night. I saw this girl working on the streets. She wasn't much bigger or probably much older than Jenny. Her pimp wasn't far away, lurking in the background like some evil force destroying everything innocent."

"The evil's always been out there," said Todd. "The only difference is we're looking for it now, that's all."

"But not before it found our daughters."

Todd took another sip of coffee and glanced outside the storefront window. "No... Not before that."

"That little girl I saw working the street is somebody's daughter," said Ron. "I didn't know what I could do to help. Didn't even know if I wanted to. My wife used to tell me we're one big, interconnected piece of humanity. What happens to one happens to all. And until we care about the least of us, nobody's safe."

"I think a lot of people find Jesus in prison," added Todd. "The rest of us care about humanity when we're close to losing our own."

Their waitress approached and filled Todd's coffee cup. Ron placed his cup upside-down. "Can I get you some more juice?" she asked.

"No thank you," replied Ron.

"None for me," said Todd.

"Let me know if you need anything else."

"Just the bill," requested Todd.

The waitress promptly removed a small green pad from her apron and tore off the bill, placing it in the middle of the table along with two peppermint candies. She left, but not before giving both men a noticeable inspection.

Ron had grown accustomed to stares whenever he and Todd were together and even when he was on his own. The media had covered their exploits extensively, and it was difficult to appear in public without having someone take their picture or offer their sympathies and prayers. He always thanked them for their expressions of concern and well-wishes, but the encounters were frequently awkward, particularly when confronted by someone extending "condolences for your loss."

At first, he reacted angrily, wanting to scream that Jennifer was still alive. His overreaction was later tempered with a brief, but insincere, "Thank you," to be eventually replaced by a simple nod of appreciation. He would find an excuse to leave, to avoid continuing the conversation. But getting away from the public's reaction wasn't so easily accomplished, as he was immediately reminded once he left the café and was inside Todd's car.

A popular radio shock-jock that went by the single name "Russ," was in the middle of one of his infamous rants. The subject that caused his listeners to flood the phone lines just happened to be Ron and Todd.

"You want me to turn that off?" asked Todd.

"What's the point? Might as well listen to what the masses are saying about us." He shrugged and muttered derisively, "Can only increase interest in the movie."

"I say those guys who are trying to find their daughters by tracking down everyone on the state's sex offender list, ought to be given medals, instead of being hassled by police," said the radio host, in a voice that conveyed authority and genuine conviction. Although it was the same inflection, he used whether dealing with social or political issues, sporting events, celebrity gossip, race-baiting, or hawking commercial products ranging from gold coins to back pain relief.

"Call in and let me know what you think... This is Russ, what's your fuss?"

"Hey, Russ, love your show," said the first male caller.

"Join me and my mother," said the host. "Talk to me."

"I absolutely agree with you. But instead of medals, I'd give 'em guns to blow away all those scumbags."

"When you're right, you're right. Let's take another call. This is Rusty, and I'm so Trusty. Talk to me."

"I think if people had any guts, they'd all get a copy of that list and start makin' visits in the middle of the night," said the next caller. "Sooner we rid ourselves of these animals, the sooner our kids can feel safe."

"Take control 'cause you're so bold," barked Russ. "Caller number three, you're on my line, so don't waste my time. Talk to me."

There was silence for several seconds. "Caller three, are you there? If not, we—"

"I think those fathers are placing innocent people in jeopardy," interrupted the voice that had kept the four girls terrorized.

"Oh, really?" responded the host, reflecting unhidden disdain. "Well, what planet are you from? You card-carrying member of the no-guts-no glory club."

The voice continued to speak deliberately and emotionlessly. "Vigilante efforts and promises of large financial rewards can only create a prejudiced frenzy, likely to generate an unfortunate backlash. The victims of such ignorance are always the children." The call disconnected before receiving a response.

Todd glanced at Ron, his eyebrows raised, expressing amazement at the caller's views.

"Everyone's got a toilet seat," said Ron, "with an opinion to match."

The radio host made a long guttural noise, which evidently represented his disagreement with the preceding opinion. "Oh, I just had me a caller that used fancy psychobabble, a gifted graduate from the university-for-the-highly-insane. I'm Russ, call me if you must. Talk to me!"

Ron switched to an F.M. station, and they listened to music for the rest of the trip.

* * *

The candles were lit in the man's bedroom. He kept his focus on the two monitors as the girls hadn't awoken yet from a longer than usual sleep, aided by sleeping pills he had crushed and added to their meals last night. He had wasted his time and patience on a phone call to an ignorant and rude radio host. He realized he was a voice in the wilderness. As such, there was no point in trying to convince ignorant sheep who followed the dictates of whatever ideas or assumptions were popular at any given moment. He wondered if he should wake up the girls but decided against it. *Let the little angels rest.*

FIFTY-FIVE

After he had phoned in his comments, he knew something had to be done, something dramatic that would end this ceaseless chatter and eliminate the pressure generated by all the media attention. The reward had grown to well over one hundred thousand dollars, closer to two, and that amount of money would be too tempting to ignore. He expected a fair number of crank calls to the hotline that would throw authorities off track, keeping them busy chasing false leads. And those bogus tips could only aid him. But eventually, someone might stumble onto a piece of information that would lead back to him. He had been careful, done everything right, but that didn't matter. He couldn't afford any mistakes, including allowing the population of overzealous reward-seekers to grow exponentially.

He picked up the newspaper and read about Butler and Roth's escapades. *If you want to solve the problem, you must study it. And the answer will reveal itself.* That was what he had always believed, and his belief had sustained him through the difficult times. He reviewed the police interventions, the lawsuits, the people harassed, although he couldn't muster much sympathy for beleaguered pedophiles. They deserved whatever misfortune befell them. And then it came to him, as he was convinced it would—an inspired solution brought about by his disgust of these contemptible miscreants.

Misfortune.

Yes! That was the key. Their misfortune would be his opportunity, compensation for eliminating a despicable creature and thereby resolving his dilemma. He imagined that's what was meant by the saying, *killing two birds with one stone*. In this case, *killing* was the operative word. He returned to the news article, reading more carefully the section on lawsuits stemming from Roth and Butler's interventions. Who was that person that Rebecca's father attacked? When he found what he was looking for, he smiled.

He went downstairs and notified Mei Lin, "It's time for your bath." She left with him, as the remaining girls watched helplessly.

When she entered the bathroom and began to undress, he stopped her. "That won't be necessary," he said. "Please extend your left arm, like this." He demonstrated the position with his own arm, and she complied.

He held her arm with his left hand, and then she saw the knife, long, sharp, the metal shining underneath the heat lamp. Terrified, she pulled away, but his grip was firm. "Be still," he said, harshly. "If you keep moving, you're only going to make this worse."

She stopped struggling, as he expected she would. She was the youngest and had been with him the longest. They had developed a relationship and, as a result, she had begun to trust him, fully complying with his wishes. Still, he needed to reinforce that trust and test her loyalty. "Have the other girls been saying bad things about me?"

She shook her head.

"Are you being truthful?"

She nodded yes.

"You know what happens to little girls who lie?"

She made no response.

"Have they spoken about escaping? I don't want to have to ask you more than once."

She told him what she knew about exercising to stay in shape and remaining strong for when the day came. Rebecca and Jennifer were the main ones to devise plots, but Selena had also agreed.

He patted her on the head, thanked her, and placed the blade against her forearm. "This will only hurt a little, and then it will be over." He gave her a sincere smile. "I promise."

After he cut her, he soaked up the blood with a warm white cloth as he ignored her protests. He bandaged the wound and returned her to the basement where he watched her collapse onto her cot and cry. He studied the concerned expressions on the other girls and reassured them with his only words as he left. "She'll be fine."

It took him less than twenty minutes to find the Hollywood police station. He would have used the public library, but that would have required a card. And he had judiciously avoided leaving behind any record that would include him in a database. Anyway, there was something stimulating about entering the lion's den in search of his prey. Some would consider his actions risky, even reckless. He preferred to see them for what they were—daring.

He wasn't exactly enthused to be in a room of deviants being questioned or booked by the police. Yet, he had to admit, he found an odd enjoyment in watching police actively engaged in performing their tasks. Gangbangers, and pimps, and drug dealers, were being processed through the system. He assumed they would be released back into the streets far too soon, only to repeat their transgressions against society.

He approached the officer on duty filling out paperwork at the main desk.

"Excuse me, officer. I'm interested in inspecting your sex offenders list that you maintain under Megan's Law."

"Second floor, room 211," the officer pointed toward the stairway, still busy filling out forms. "You'll need to sign in to use the computer."

He had brought his fake I.D. so that didn't present a problem. "Thank you, sir." *No reason not to be polite.* He had made it to the bottom step when the officer's voice forced him to abruptly stop.

"Hey!"

He could feel his heart thumping a rapid warning signal against his chest. He feared if he turned around to face the officer, the sudden appearance of sweat and nervousness would give him away. *Was it time to run?*

"You might want to check out the hotline," the officer continued.

He turned around, displayed a genuine smile, and noticed the officer was still engaged in his work.

"Justice Department keeps an updated registry," the officer informed him.

"I'll do that," he said, hiding the relief. "Thank you very much for your assistance."

He proceeded up the steps and immediately knew he would leave as quickly as possible. He no longer felt threatened, but the stench of this place would make anyone uneasy. He assumed there must have been a room nearby designed to disinfect the degenerates, apparently without much success. The corridor smelled like vomit and piss, with diseased blood thrown in for good measure. Maybe they had a torture room. He assumed all the urban police stations had at least one.

He waited for less than five minutes to use the one available computer which was already booted up and signed in at the California Department of Justice website. He opened a small pack containing a wet wipe and used the moist towelette to thoroughly wipe the keyboard. Once he felt it was safe to touch, he took out his notepad and checked the name he had recorded from the newspaper article. He scrolled through the screen, increasingly fascinated by the sheer number of names and the details regarding their crimes and convictions.

He previously had read about pedophiles—the sick and broken minds that saw the innocent as a depository for their perversion. He despised them, would torture their bodies ending in castration, guaranteeing they'd never perform their wickedness again. These disgusting subhuman sex addicts could never be healed or cured of their disease. They had to be destroyed or confined in an escape-proof hellhole, where they'd suffer indefinitely for sins against the children. The really evil ones imprisoned their victims for months, sometimes years, taking control of their minds, and their spirits, and whatever remained of their souls.

They were driven by selfishness and disgusting sexual urgings. And they caused only pain, grief, and heartache. When they were caught, they paraded their accomplishments before any media whore willing to give them a national showcase. Experts would feebly explain their actions by applying outdated analysis and offering psychological descriptions that scientifically dignified deviant behavior, caused by an equally unforgiving childhood upbringing.

There would be no place for these miscreants in his world. The children he saved would never know such treachery or evil. They would be protected, nurtured by him. They, and they alone, would understand him, see him for what he was, their salvation. There would be no secrets, dark or otherwise, among them. He knew the outside world would never comprehend his love, his sacrifice. They would mistake him for those he condemned. But these girls would tell his story, revel in it one day. And they would not be alone.

The children from their sacred union would be proof that Eden was still possible, but only for the chosen few, the ones who had the courage to defy custom, and man-made laws, and artificial definitions of morality and marriage. He was free of those restrictions and would see to it that they, too, would never feel confined by the impositions of others. He would break the invisible chains of bondage that had crippled the thinking of so many, distorted nature, and abandoned true, unbridled, untarnished, emotion.

He slowed down the scroll, stopping it on the felon for whom he had been searching. Theodore F. Lungren—convicted of multiple sex crimes, always on children under the age of thirteen. His last arrest, on kidnapping, had been plea-bargained to lesser included offences. Those convictions were overturned on appeal, based on inappropriate conduct from the prosecutor's office. He thought about the irony; a system penalizes law enforcement for its shortcomings but allows these perverts to remain free to prey on the helpless. Well, he would soon rectify that.

Rebecca and Jennifer's fathers, in their ambition to destroy his world, had provided the solution to all remaining impending problems. He wrote down Lungren's address in his notepad. As a precaution, he used another wet wipe to clean the keyboard, removing any fingerprints he may have left behind. After all, wasn't he led to believe that cleanliness was next to godliness? He chuckled at his sense of humor. He glanced at his watch. It would take him no longer than an hour to implement his plan if he left now. Which he did.

* * *

As soon as he had returned home, he served the girls lunch and, as a special treat, provided them with freshly made banana pudding purchased at a specialty market. He felt it only right to celebrate the brilliance of his plan by sharing a nice dessert. He threw away the paper plates and placed leftover pudding in a plastic container which he put in the refrigerator, after sampling it twice. Delicious, he thought. *The girls must have loved it.*

He put on a pair of thin latex gloves and removed various objects from his bedroom closet: one of Rebecca's rollerblades; a white cloth he had used to wipe off the blood on her wounded leg; clothing worn by the girls when they were first taken; a watch, bracelets, and earrings; Selena's cell phone; a backpack; school I.D.s; and a few books. He placed their belongings in a duffle bag, and then zipped it closed.

He proceeded to the bathroom, opened the cabinet underneath the sink, and removed a plastic bag containing the cloth stained with Mei Lin's blood. He stared at it for a moment, regretting that he had been forced to cut her. But one day, she would understand it was necessary and forgive him. Since he had been forced to hurt her, due to circumstances beyond his control, he took full advantage of the moment by challenging her loyalty. It served as a useful side benefit of a bad situation. Rather than thinking he needed a sample of her blood, now she would believe the punishment was for not answering his questions truthfully, the first time she had the chance to do so. He was confident that lesson would pay dividends in the future.

After a quick shower and shave, he put on a suit, knotted his tie, and selected a short black wig to wear. He studied himself in the mirror and decided to add a pair of glasses to his look. It made him appear more official, but less dangerous. He stood full frame in front of the mirror and practiced flipping open his wallet to display his police shield. It certainly appeared legitimate, but he thought the badge would look even more impressive attached to his belt. That way, once he opened his jacket to show his credentials, he'd be able to reveal the gun inside his shoulder holster. *Nice touch.* Flashing the badge and gun, guaranteed that if he was denied access with the former, he would gain it with the latter.

As he inspected himself in the mirror one last time, he couldn't help but think about the stressful events of the past few weeks and conclude that, all in all, everything was turning out for the best.

FIFTY-SIX

SATURDAY APRIL 29TH

Police tape cordoned off the crime scene at Lungren's apartment. Detectives Carrey and McKay arrived just before midnight, two hours after the body was reported. They recognized the smell of death as soon as they entered the apartment. The stench had filled the hallway leading to the apartment and based on their previous experience, they estimated that the victim had been deceased for at least twenty-four hours. That estimate, according to the medical examiner, was spot on, give or take no more than half a day.

Lungren's discolored bloated body lay in a bathtub filled with rancid water. Someone from the crime lab took a series of photographs. Each flash bulb bounced off the bathwater and made the tiny self-contained room look like a much larger grisly murder scene. All that was missing were a few palm trees and this could have been at the ocean. The people working in the room certainly could have used the fresh breeze.

McKay pointed to an electrical cord plugged into a socket extending from the bathroom vanity to the tub. "Was that the method of death?" McKay asked one of the men handling forensics.

"It deep-fried him, no doubt," he answered.

When the call had come into the station, McKay personally asked for the assignment, fearing that one of the fathers had finally crossed the line. But for now, that didn't appear to be the case.

McKay tapped the photographer on the shoulder. "Take a picture of that." He pointed to an envelope with the printed words, "God forgive me," taped to the mirror.

The photographer focused the lens of his camera on the envelope and snapped three shots. "Make sure every inch of that mirror is dusted for fingerprints," ordered McKay. "Let's see what the folks at the lab can recover from the tape and envelope."

"You want to read what's inside?" asked a rookie officer who appeared as if he could lose his breakfast, lunch, and future dinners at any moment.

McKay looked at Lungren's body. "He won't be writing another note anytime soon. I can wait."

A lab technician whispered something in Carrey's ear. Carrey turned to McKay. "Better take a look at what they found in the bedroom closet."

The technician let the detectives into Lungren's bedroom where some evidence had already been collected and bagged.

"We found a small girl's rollerblade," said an officer. "We also recovered jewelry, watches, earrings, all belonging to young girls. There was also a towel and a washcloth found hidden underneath the bed in a plastic bag, both articles appear to contain blood stains."

"Any identifying markings on any of the clothes?" asked McKay.

"The sweater had the name 'Jennifer Butler' on the inside label. A gold bracelet had the inscription, 'To Rebecca with love, Mom & Dad.'"

"Son-of-a-bitch," said McKay, disappointed and saddened.

He walked around in a small circle. "Let's not give out any details to the media until we notify the parents."

"The chief will want to know about Roth's daughter ASAP," said Carrey. "The mayor, too."

"We tell the parents first. Fuck the mayor."

The rookie entered the room, color having almost returned to his cheeks. "Okay if the coroner's office removes the body?" he asked McKay.

"Drop another appliance in his bath water first," said McKay. "Electrocute his ass a second time on behalf of the state."

The young officer looked confused and nervous, unsure what to do.

McKay shook his head and sighed. Carrey smiled along with the other more experienced officers.

"Detective Carrey," said McKay, "Please inform the rookie that I was only kidding."

Carrey turned toward the officer and addressed him in an official manner. "Detective McKay was only kidding."

The rookie appeared relieved and nodded in appreciation.

FIFTY-SEVEN

SUNDAY APRIL 30TH

Ron arrived early in the morning at the Culver City police station, followed a few minutes later by Todd and his wife. They were all asked to be seated in the conference room and wait for Detectives McKay and Carrey who would join them momentarily.

Ron and Todd spoke very little and avoided looking at each other. Liz made a half-hearted attempt at a greeting that Ron acknowledged with a brief embrace. Her cheeks were puffy, her eyes glazed over, as if heavily sedated by drugs or traumatized by an awful accident that she had either witnessed or endured. She had the appearance of a battered woman, struck repeatedly by the reality of what she had gone through, as well as what she was about to confront.

Ron studied the interior of the room. The walls were painted a drab light yellow or perhaps they had been gray before being discolored with time. The floor looked like it hadn't been washed or waxed, ever. At best, it was swept every other week by an employee who didn't care about his or her janitorial evaluations. One of the two large florescent lights needed to be replaced. Fortunately, there were no windows to shed sunlight on the dismal surroundings. Unfortunately, the absence of windows prevented anything resembling fresh air entering. The entire room smelled like a closet full of old clothes that needed to be dry-cleaned.

Ron read a sign posted on the door: "*Conversations may be monitored and/or recorded.*" He paid close attention to every detail of the table and chairs in front of him, to avoid a conversation with the other two people in the room. They, in return, cooperated by alternately staring at the floor or occasionally at the door that finally opened.

A somber McKay and Carrey entered and sat together at the conference table, as if they needed each other's mutual support. Detective Carrey spoke first, but could only manage two words, "I'm sorry," before he was cut off by Liz, who broke down sobbing. In the small confines of the room, her anguish was amplified, ricocheting off the walls and threatening to release the torment steadily building up in Ron. Todd put his arm around her shoulders, in a failed attempt to comfort her. If anything, the human contact made her more emotional.

"Mrs. Roth," said McKay. "Would you like us to request medical attention?"

She shook her head.

"We have a grief counselor available, if that would help."

She regained control of her emotions, but her upper body still trembled. Ron slid a box of Kleenex toward her, although not before he removed a few tissues for himself.

"Thank you," she said, her voice was hoarse from the screams she had emitted at her home, after being initially informed of the news. "That won't be necessary, nor is it possible for anyone to ease my grief. I just want this to be over. I want to know what happened to my daughter. I'm sure Mr. Butler feels the same."

Ron nodded in agreement.

"I would appreciate it if you were totally honest with us,"

said Todd, "and provide all the information you have." He looked away for a moment, and then spoke without addressing anyone. "If you're trying to spare our feelings"—he now looked at both detectives—"holding back the truth will only cause us more pain."

"Mr. Roth, that's not our intent, nor would it ever be our goal," said McKay. "The only details we have, at the moment, are contained in his confession."

Ron finally spoke. "Are you certain he was the one? I've been told people sometimes confess to crimes they never committed. They just seek attention. Isn't that possible?"

McKay looked at his partner, who accepted the responsibility of conveying the facts.

"Not in this case. We collected articles found in his home," Carrey said. "Jewelry, clothing, cell phones, schoolbooks and I.D.s." He focused his attention on Liz Roth and spoke softly, with compassion. "We found one skate that we believe belonged to Rebecca."

Liz's shoulders slumped, as she sunk lower into her chair. If not for the support of the table in front of her, she might have disappeared altogether. Ron thought her expression turned more tormented if that was possible.

"We need to ask you to identify the evidence," continued Carrey.

Ron flinched at the notion that articles belonging to his daughter would be referred to as, "evidence." He wondered if that's what Jennifer would have been considered if they had asked him to identify her body.

"I know this is extremely difficult," Carrey said, "but it would help us a great deal if you could do that today."

"Help?" asked Liz. "You mean, help you to close the case," she said with some degree of resentment.

"Help us bring closure to all involved," responded McKay, sympathetically.

"We're running tests on a blood-stained towel," added Carrey. "If it doesn't match the suspect's D.N.A., we'll need permission to review your daughters' medical records. If we can take a sample of your D.N.A. that would also be—"

"Helpful." Liz completed the sentence, but the bitterness was replaced with resignation, a sense of hopelessness.

Todd placed his hand on top of his wife's wrist. "My wife and I will give you whatever you need."

"As will I," said Ron.

"We appreciate anything that you can do," said Carrey.

"I was told there were other children involved," said Ron.

"It would appear so," responded McKay.

"In addition to your daughters," said Carrey, "he abducted two other girls. A ten-year-old, Selena Santiago, taken from her school in Cerritos about a week before Jennifer was taken. A month before he took Selena, he kidnapped Mei Lin Furakawa, the youngest of the group, while on a school trip at Six Flags Mountain. She turned nine while in captivity."

"I don't understand," said Ron. "You just found out about these missing girls?"

McKay responded. "The girls were abducted in various areas of the state. It's my understanding that the parents of Selena Santiago may have waited to report her missing for fear the family might be deported. They're undocumented."

"So, let me get this straight," responded Ron. "They disappeared. Just vanished. You didn't know about it. I never saw a news report or read an article about them. By any chance, were they less important and newsworthy because one was Hispanic and the other Asian? And if I hadn't busted into Todd's news conference, would no one have known about Jenny, too?"

"Mr. Butler," McKay said firmly. "I understand your emotional state, but any missing child is given our full attention and maximum effort. This tragic situation and the attention given to it, had nothing to do with race."

"You know, whenever I hear someone say a situation had nothing to do with race, I know it had everything to do with race. And while I didn't want to believe it, or accept it, Jenny was just another..." He stopped himself from saying it. "Just another unimportant lost girl."

No one spoke for several moments until Todd broke the silence. "Ron, I hope you know how much I care about you and our mutual loss. But this isn't the time or place. We both need to know what happened and how it happened."

Ron stood and walked away from the table. "I know what happened. Our daughters were taken and terrorized and murdered and I wish I had never stopped you from beating that evil piece of shit to death." Ron banged his fist against the wall with such force that it shook the room.

"Are you going to be all right, Mr. Butler?" asked McKay.

"No." He sat in a corner chair. "I apologize for my outburst and don't wish to delay this any longer." He turned to McKay. "Did he indicate what he did with their bodies?"

The question made Ron feel light-headed.

McKay hesitated to answer, rubbing his mouth, as if that would elicit the words that needed to be said, but no one wanted to hear. Carrey relieved him of the task.

"In the letter he left behind," said Carrey, "he confessed to mutilating them, and then disposing of the remains."

Liz released an anguished sound that was muffled by pain. She bent over, her body moving back and forth attempting to relinquish whatever it was that now had control of her body.

Ron tried to take a deep breath, but his lungs were already filled with a sorrow that pressed against his chest with an internal force that resembled the final stages of a heart attack. But more than his heart was at risk. His very sanity was in peril. Every emotional impulse was being tested. Images of his daughter bombarded his mind; her body viciously torn apart, disassembled like she was a piece of her favorite train station.

He doubted if he could survive any additional details, and yet, he knew he could not exist without knowing what happened to his only child.

"Where?" asked Ron, his voice barely audible. "Do you have any idea where the remains are?" His voice cracked on the word *remains*.

"Ocean," responded McKay, who lowered his voice and his head. "Landfills. It's also possible that he incinerated at least two of the girls. We don't know which ones."

Ron bent over in pain, emitting a sound impossible to define, other than to say that no human being should ever have to experience it. He stood wanting to escape both the room and the anguish, but his legs quickly failed him. He pressed his weakened body against the wall for support. McKay rushed to his side and eased him back into the chair.

"I think it advisable if we all took a break," said Carrey. "Maybe inspect the articles in ten or fifteen minutes."

"No," said Ron. "I want to do it now. I don't think any of us can survive this any longer."

Carrey focused his attention on Liz. "Are you ready to continue, Mrs. Roth?"

She answered by standing and grabbing her purse from the table. Todd stood and held his wife's hand.

"It's down the hall," said Carrey. "We'll show you the way."

"Before we go," interrupted Todd. "I need to know. Do you think my confrontation with him brought this on? Please be honest."

Ron was also interested in the answer.

"There's no evidence of that," said McKay. "To the contrary, it would appear he murdered the girls well before your visit. If anything, that may have been the reason he took off running once he saw you."

Carrey chimed in. "He may have thought you had somehow discovered evidence implicating him in the abductions. We think he took his life because he figured it was just a matter of time before we arrested him. And given the nature of his crimes, prison would be the last place he wanted to be. Under the circumstances, suicide would be preferable to the punishment doled out by inmates rendering their unique form of justice to child molesters."

Todd nodded and spoke softly. "I'm ready."

Carrey opened the door and held it for Liz and her husband. McKay touched Ron on his shoulder. "Are you gonna be all right?"

Ron stood face to face with the detective. "No," he said, and then exited the room, followed by McKay.

The office they entered was longer than the conference room, but much narrower. The walls were just as colorless. The objects on the two folding tables appeared to give the room a special vitality, despite the irony that the items belonged to children no longer alive. The tables held a variety of articles contained in individual plastic bags that were each numbered and catalogued. Had it been another setting, Ron would have thought it was some hastily conceived garage sale of mismatched items that no one wanted. But there was one item he saw that he would have paid any price to own—Jennifer's brown sweater, her favorite and the one she wore instead of the yellow one she had discarded on her bed. *She had worn a sweater after all.*

Ron and Todd shared one moment: a brief look at each other that needed no further communication. Together, they had completed a journey that had brought them to this tragic ending. For Ron, it also marked the beginning of a life without his daughter.

The detectives remained a respectful distance away, as they watched these two families identify the belongings of their children, young girls who would never put on those clothes or carry their schoolbooks or wear their jewelry, again.

Ron touched Jennifer's sweater. Tears filled his eyes. He pointed to a watch. His voice and legs unsteady, he looked at McKay. "That's hers. The watch and the sweater belonged to Jenny."

Ron took the bag containing the sweater and sat down, clutching his daughter's clothing. His body rocked slowly, a mournful movement, going back and forth, back and forth, until the motion released a steady stream of tears.

Todd held the bag containing the single skate. He looked at the detectives and nodded yes.

Liz slowly approached the table, as if a member of a funeral possession, radiating a quiet dignity combined with a profound sorrow. She reached for a gold bracelet, but stopped before she could touch them.

"Is it all right if I pick that up?" she asked Carrey, who nodded approval.

She extended her hand, came close to the object, but couldn't complete the movement. Her hand hovered over the bracelet as if it was transferring some magical power to her, Rebecca's spirit emanating from a precious metal, the alchemy generated by a daughter's love and a mother's loss.

Ron observed her and thought he saw a brief smile, a recognition of something special. Perhaps it had been a present that she had given to Rebecca, or a family heirloom handed down for generations, from mother to daughter. Maybe her reaction had nothing to do with it being a gift. Perhaps it was simply enough to be in the presence of the last thing her daughter had worn on that fateful day. Whatever the reason, the bittersweet moment was gradually replaced by the most horrendous expression of pain he had ever seen or could continue to bear to watch.

Finally, she embraced the small bag. With trembling hand, she lifted it, held it to the light, and inspected it, as if seeing her newborn for the first time. Her fingers closed around the packet, and then clutched it with urgent desperation.

"Oh my God... Rebecca! Rebecca! Oh God no! Not my baby! Not my baby!"

Todd attempted to hold her, but she broke away and rushed to the corner of the room, where she fell to her knees, lowering her head over a wastebasket. Her body convulsed, but there was nothing to expel. No matter how hard she tried. She coughed violently but could not rid herself of the grief trapped inside her throat.

Todd went to her, but she raised her hand to stop him. She became perfectly still—the calm before the next storm that would be more powerful than its predecessor.

Ron walked slowly toward her and stopped a few feet away. He extended his hand. She looked at him and took it. He helped her to her feet. She mouthed the words, "Thank you." And then she wept in his arms, as he did in hers.

The detectives made the sign of the cross, bowed their heads, and prayed.

After taking D.N.A. samples, the detectives joined the two families in the parking lot. McKay spoke with Todd and his wife, while Carrey walked with Ron.

"I'm so sorry, Mr. Butler," said Carrey. "If I can do anything—"

Ron shook his head in resignation and spoke quietly. "I didn't mean to make your job more difficult than it had to be. I'd like you to know that."

"All I can tell you is I wish this had turned out differently," Carrey said. "As a father of two children, I really do. But at least that monster will never be able to hurt another child."

"There is one favor I'd ask of you. I'd like a copy of his confession if that's possible."

"I'm not sure that's a good idea. You may want to think about that for a day or two."

"You have any idea how much thinking I've done in the last few weeks? I'd like a copy of the confession of the man who murdered my daughter."

Carrey considered the request for a moment, gave a reluctant nod. "I'll get that for you before you leave."

"Thank you."

"I'll be right back." Carrey returned inside the station.

McKay approached Ron and offered his condolences, and then left.

Todd waited until McKay was gone, then approached Ron. The two men faced each other in silence, searching for the right words to say. Ron finally spoke.

"They were together. Jenny and Rebecca. They were together all this time."

"I hope they had a chance to become friends," said Todd, his voice breaking on the word *friends*.

"I'm sorry for your loss," said Ron.

"And I for yours." Todd hesitated. "That job offer still stands, if you're interested."

Ron gave a weak smile. "Under the circumstances, we both know that would be a bad idea. I don't think it would be healthy for either one of us to see each other again. At least not for a while."

Todd extended his hand. Ron started to reach for it, then pulled back. He knew he couldn't afford human touch right now. It would be too much. He didn't need to fall apart, not out here, yards away from his daughter's belongings.

Todd withdrew his hand. "Take care of yourself, Ron."

"I'll do the best I can," Ron responded.

Todd walked away a few steps but stopped when Ron called out to him. "Todd."

Todd turned around and faced him.

"I hope you get rid of all those nightmares."

Todd nodded. "Unfortunately, they've been replaced by something far worse... reality."

Ron watched Todd and his wife enter their car and drive off. He waited in the parking lot, until Detective Carrey brought him a copy of the confession stuffed inside an envelope. Ron felt as if he was holding the murder weapon. In a sense, it proved more unsettling than the actual instrument of destruction. What he held was personal, more intimate than that. It contained the thoughts and the handwriting of the man who'd tormented Jennifer and three other children, forcing them to endure a living hell, robbing them of their innocence in an effort to take their souls, before he eventually took their lives.

Perhaps the detective was right. It was a mistake to ask for the letter. But it was a mistake he would now live with. He entered his car and drove home.

FIFTY-EIGHT

Ron had thought about calling her but even considering their history, he felt it necessary to travel to Sherman Oaks and give his mother-in-law the news in person. After Nikki's death, her mother felt there was no way for him to raise Jenny alone. She'd insisted that her granddaughter be raised by her. "That's what my daughter would have wanted," she said repeatedly until he finally refused to talk to her.

Their relationship was never good, but she had grown more supportive once Jenny started school. After all, she was a straight-A student so Florence Carrington had to grudgingly admit that he must have been doing something right. Nikki was her only child and considered a miracle baby since the doctors had told her she'd never be able to conceive. He had no doubt that she had been a great mother and raised Nikki to be the woman she became. But that didn't mean he was going to turn over his baby to be raised by her grandmother. That might have been a custom within his community, but not for him.

Would it have been easier if he had? No doubt. But easy seldom is the right choice and it hardly ever reflects true and lasting love. As he pulled into her driveway, he knew easy wasn't about to rear its ugly head.

As it turned out, he didn't have to tell her about her grand-daughter. He knew that immediately once she opened the door sobbing. It was already a worldwide news story. Four girls kidnapped by a child molester, murdered, possibly dismembered. God knows how they suffered, were tortured, and abused.

They sat on the couch. He held her, wanting to bring her comfort but he realized whatever strength and compassion he thought existed had been emptied out long before he made the trip to her home.

"How did it happen?" she asked. "How did you let it happen?"

There was no need to respond. He knew she didn't expect him to answer. She would never forgive him for excluding her from the role she insisted she should have. It didn't matter how good a father he was. To her, he had denied her granddaughter the chance to be raised by a woman. If he had had a son, that would be one thing. A boy needs a man to guide him in this world. But a daughter? A girl? *Ain't no role a man can play on his own, turning a baby girl into a righteous woman. Simply not natural.* Or so it went in the gospel of Florence Carrington.

"Did she suffer?"

Of course, she suffered, he thought. Then answered, "No."

"The bastard robbed us, Ron. May his soul burn in hell for eternal damnation."

Anger, rage, and calls for damnation wouldn't ease the pain. It simply redirected it to a place less intense. If that worked for his mother-in-law, he'd be more than happy to try it in the future.

She stood and offered him some tea, which he graciously accepted. He watched her cross into the kitchen. It was the first time he had a decent look at her. At nearly seventy years old she still displayed a remarkable grace, even an elegance that she certainly had passed on to her daughter. And he had to admit, Jennifer was also a beneficiary. But she also appeared fragile, as if she could snap at the first strong wind.

She returned carrying a silver platter holding enamel teacups that looked as delicate as she did. She placed the set onto a coffee table but didn't hand him the tea. In fact, she ignored it and focused her attention on him. He was reminded of Nikki's eyes that could drill through a person to find the truth, or console, or simply make a lasting connection. Whatever tension or conflicts or disappointments that existed between them had to remain in second place to the undeniable fact that they she was family. The only one he now had.

"I'm sorry," she said.

He wondered if there was something wrong with the tea.

"I shouldn't have said what I said to you. I don't blame you. I never have. I should have been there for you. I could have helped. You needed a new car and I—"

He held her hand. "You know, I never would have accepted money from you. I know you doubted if I could have been the provider you expected your daughter to have. We had difficult times. But Nikki never needed anything that was important to have. I did my best to make sure Jennifer felt the same. We were happy for as long as we were together. And I always knew, no matter our differences, when push came to shove, we could always count on you."

"And Mama." He had seldom called her that and he could tell it affected her, deeply. "Push has done some serious shoving, and I don't know what I have left to give to push back. But whatever it is, I'm going to dedicate my life to my baby's memory and let the world know what they have lost."

They drank three cups of tea and cried in between each serving. When he finally left, she told him she loved him, and they cried once more, but not for the last time.

FIFTY-NINE

Rebecca stood motionless in the middle of the room, wearing a wedding gown, her face partially covered by a silk embroidered veil. He gently lifted the veil and observed her with admiration. "You're beautiful." He turned to include the remaining three girls, all of whom were wearing identical gowns.

"Isn't she beautiful?"

None of the girls reacted.

"As are you all. Beautiful in every way. I'm very pleased, and I hope you are as well, because this means the future begins now, the next chapter of our lives, together." He clapped his hands. "Everyone get back into your regular clothes and be extra careful when removing your gowns. You don't want to ruin our special day when each of you should look perfect."

Mei Lin and Selena began to remove their gowns. Jennifer made eye contact with Rebecca and appeared to give her a signal.

Rebecca stepped toward him and smiled politely. "I would like to dance for you, if that meets with your approval."

He placed his hands together and nodded in appreciation. "That would be lovely. I'm deeply honored."

Selena and Mei Lin gave each other a confused look and remained in their gowns. Jennifer concealed a slight smile.

"Please sit, make yourself comfortable, and I'll perform for everyone," announced Rebecca.

He moved his chair to the center of the room. "Your wish is my command." He sat, as if he were king, about to be entertained by one of his subjects. "Don't you need music?"

"I dance to the music inside me."

She did a few stretching exercises, giving Jennifer a determined look. She placed her arms above her head and began a routine, but stumbled badly, constrained by the chain around her waist.

He jumped up from the chair. "Here, let me help you before you hurt yourself." He removed a set of keys from his pocket and grabbed the lock.

While he was preoccupied, Rebecca gave Jennifer another quick glance and winked. Jennifer acknowledged the signal by using her index finger to touch her tongue, and then chalked up a winning point on an imaginary board.

He removed the chain from around Rebecca's waist, casting it aside. "That should be better," he said, and then retook his seat.

Rebecca positioned herself in a basic ballet stance, an arabesque. She carefully balanced her body, extended one leg behind her and to the right. Her shoulders were perfectly aligned, facing the direction of her body. The movements of her arms were graceful, elegant, and varied in relationship to the position of her grounded foot. She displayed several forms of glissades, gliding one foot across the floor, and then leaping into the air, the other foot following suit.

Selena and Kia watched dejectedly. Jennifer's fingers tensed, forming small fists.

Rebecca flawlessly performed an allegro step by extending her legs and attacking air. She executed a petite cabriole, the working leg thrust into the air at a forty-five-degree angle. The underneath leg followed and beat against the first leg, sending it higher. She landed on the underneath leg. This was followed exquisitely by a grande cabriole, executed at ninety-degrees, which created more power, enabling her to reach greater heights.

Rebecca's movements became more intense, spinning a series of pirouettes at a dizzying rate.

"Dazzling," he said, and applauded approvingly.

She spun again and again in wider circles, engulfing more of the room, gaining momentum and speed. He had to twist and turn his body to keep track of this amazing display of talent.

Her gown appeared to float, suspended in air, twirling around, and having a mesmerizing effect. Rebecca closed the circle, moving within three feet of him. Then, from nowhere, with the full force of her foot, a high kick smashed into his face, knocking him to the floor, where he groveled in pain. Blood immediately gushed from his nose. Rebecca made a mad dash for the door. He lunged for her leg. His fingertips contacted her foot, tripping her, but she managed to regain her balance. The lunge brought him closer to Jennifer, who took her chain and quickly wrapped it around his neck.

Rebecca reached for the door and looked back.

"Get out!" screamed Jennifer. "Hurry!"

Mei Lin and Selena tried to help Jennifer, but she was just outside their reach. Rebecca slid open the heavy door, pushed back the wine rack, and raced up the steps.

Gasping for breath, he clawed at the chains around his neck. Jennifer used all her strength to restrain him, but she was no match for his power and growing desperation. He swung wildly, arms flaying behind him. His elbows struck her in the mouth and both cheeks. He rose in a crouch, flung his body backwards, driving his head into Jennifer's face, knocking her unconscious. He removed the chain from around his neck, coughing violently. Like a wounded animal, he rushed unsteadily to the door, and then ran up the steps.

* * *

Rebecca had made it to the living room struggling to open the front door, but it required a key to unlock it from inside. Terrified, adrenaline pumping and breathing heavily, she tried to open windows, but they were bolted shut, as she had been warned by Mei Lin.

She ran to the kitchen and tried to open a side window over the sink. She managed to pry it open, halfway. She picked up a chair, smashing it against the glass. He rushed through the living room and saw her in the kitchen. She climbed onto the sink, attempting to fit through the opening. He dived at her grabbing her foot, but she kicked him hard in the mouth and escaped his grasp.

Unable to fit through the window, he unlocked the rear door and chased after her.

"Help!" Rebecca screamed. "Help me!" She lifted her gown and ran, but it was dark, and she was on a treacherous hillside still saturated from last week's downpour. Steep cliffs and jagged rocks were to her left. In front of her lay a thicket of bushes and wild brush. She plunged ahead, branches slashing her face and arms, shredding the sleeves of her gown. She slipped and fell several times, sliding dangerously close to the edge.

Her white gown glistened as she cut through the woods. She turned to see his deadly expression. It was frightening and almost made her stop in terror. It was the first time she had seen his face showing any sign of him being deranged. He ran down a side path and she feared she would be cut off before achieving her escape.

Exhausted, crying, with her chest heaving so forcefully she

feared her body would explode, Rebecca ran for her life. In the distance, city lights burned through the blackness like bright dots attacking the night in a hectic video game. A cloud-covered moon provided a gray mist, but little if any guidance. Lost with no place to go, she ran aimlessly to her right, her hands periodically raised, protecting her face. She pushed back branches, snapping off the more brittle ones. Her arms were extended outward, like a blind girl feeling her way ahead.

She reached a point where the only escape available was to descend to a steep cavern below. She took a deep breath, closed her eyes, and readied herself for the task. Before she could jump, he snatched her from behind, pressed his arm against her throat, and covered her mouth with his hand, preventing her scream from being heard.

She closed her eyes, convinced he was about to kill her and set her free, at last.

SIXTY

Detective McKay studied a file, and then tossed it onto a stack of other folders piled high on his desk. He drank his fourth cup of coffee and gently rubbed his chin. A half-eaten carton of shrimp fried rice remained open on his desk.

His partner approached carrying a duffle bag, ready to go home. "Aren't you gonna call it a night?"

"Not yet."

Carrey pulled up a chair and sat across from McKay.

"You read Lungren's file?" McKay asked.

"Pretty sick, huh?"

McKay nodded, but it was clear something was troubling him.

"Hard to believe someone could be that deranged or evil, to do what he did to four little girls, and then dismember the bodies."

"Yeah," agreed McKay. "Real hard to believe."

Carrey studied his partner. "What you thinkin'?"

McKay shrugged. "Too much, as usual." He leaned back into his chair. "We get the lab reports on the apartment, yet?"

"You want me to check?"

"Go home… I'll do it. No sense both of us winding up getting divorced."

"My wife will never leave me." Carrey rose from the chair, gathered his bag. "Where else would she find a specimen of a man as handsome and charming as me?"

"She could start with Craigslist," suggested McKay.

"Try to get some rest, 'cause your sense of humor is definitely tired." Carrey headed out, but then stopped and observed his partner, lost in thought. "You got your doubts, don't you?"

McKay looked at him, took a deep breath. "He didn't own a car. How you gonna kidnap four girls from all over town, without a car?"

"But he did run when he saw the parents," said Carrey. "You think that's just a coincidence?"

"No," answered McKay. "I think it's just a convenience."

Carrey thought about it, placed his bag on a nearby desk. "I'll see if those lab reports are ready."

"Light a fire under their asses. Make 'em earn their overtime."

Carrey picked up a phone and dialed an extension. McKay opened another file, placed both feet on the edge of the desk and started reading.

It would be a long night.

SIXTY-ONE
MONDAY MAY 1ST

Ron vacuumed the carpet in Jennifer's room. He polished the dresser and changed the sheets on the bed. He fluffed the pillows and placed some of her favorite stuffed animals against the headboard. A wallet-sized framed photo of himself, with his cheek pressed against a smiling Jennifer's face, rested on the night table. He removed the photo from the frame, placing it inside his shirt pocket.

He walked slowly toward the door and took one last look at the room. His finger touched the light switch, paused for a moment, and then left it alone. He closed the door behind him, retrieved his car keys, and exited the apartment to find Mrs. Newman standing at the top of the stairs of the apartment building. As always, Belle was with her, held like an infant against her bosom. Ron walked past her.

"You should wear a coat. It's supposed to be very cold tonight."

He responded without looking at her, "Won't need one where I'm going." He stopped and turned to look at Belle. He took a step toward her, studied the cat in a way that unsettled Mrs. Newman. He extended his hand, gently rubbed Belle underneath the chin, the way his daughter had done on so many occasions. His eyes filled with tears, and he smiled briefly, before turning away and walking to his car, parked in front of the building.

Mrs. Newman shrugged and stroked Belle in the back of the right ear.

He entered the car, looked straight ahead through the windshield, and observed the neighborhood that appeared different to him: much smaller, far less attractive, in many respects a foreign world that appeared cold and empty. Without his daughter, he no longer wanted to be a part of it. He inserted the key into the ignition. He sat behind the wheel of his Volvo, attempting to start his car. It sputtered several times, and then died.

He remained motionless for a few seconds, and then popped open the trunk. He exited the car, showing no emotion.

"Would you like me to call Auto Club?" Mrs. Newman asked.

He ignored her and walked to the rear of the Volvo. He removed a tire iron, gently closed the trunk, and calmly proceeded to the front of the car. He stared at the hood and muttered something toward Mrs. Newman. He raised the tire iron over his head, and then attacked the car methodically. He swung deliberately, robotically, moving from side to side until the entire front of the car was demolished.

Mrs. Newman hurriedly sought shelter behind the entry door, where she remained peering through a small windowpane, shielding Belle from the violent onslaught.

Ron continued around the vehicle, smashing the side and rear windows, exploding glass and discharging shards, which pierced his arms, chest, and barely missed his face. Splotches of blood stained his shirt and pant legs. Increasingly enraged, the swings grew wild, more desperate. The sound of iron striking steel and glass echoed throughout the neighborhood. In less than a minute, he had demolished the trunk. In less than two, he had annihilated the top, and ruined the door on the driver's side.

Ron raised the tire iron with both hands, ready to strike the passenger door when it creaked open. He lowered the tire iron, stared at the door, fascinated by how easily it had opened. He closed it, and then tested whether it would open again. It did, effortlessly, to his utter amazement. He opened it one last time, then slammed it shut, causing the glove compartment to crash open. Jennifer's card eased out and rested on the lid.

He reached through the windowless opening and retrieved the card. He dropped the tire iron to the ground, held the card, and finally noticed his blood from the many cuts of glass. He removed the photo from his shirt pocket and studied the two of them together—his daughter displaying the smile that had always warmed his heart. He looked at his face pressed against hers, eyes partially crossed, one of his many "Dada, you're weird" poses. She insisted he frame it and put it on her night table so it would be the last thing she saw each night before she went to sleep, and the first thing that greeted her each morning. He tried to remember how long it had been there or how old she was when it was taken.

He removed the card, placed the photo inside, and then inserted the card back into the envelope. He walked past the heap of damaged metal and broken glass and headed toward the entrance of the building. Mrs. Newman avoided the elevator and scurried up the steps before Ron managed to open the door. Belle, uncharacteristically, jumped out of her arms, leaping the stairs two at a time, beating her owner to their apartment. Ron stopped at the top of the steps, held the front door open. It was his daughter, not his car, that had prevented him from taking his own life. Jenny had saved him.

SIXTY-TWO

He had left Rebecca unchained. "Move around if you like," he said. "The only freedom you'll ever have is the one I offer you." He looked at Selena and Mei Lin. "If anyone tries to escape again, you will all be severely punished." He walked to the door and slid it open.

"Aren't you going to help Jennifer?" Rebecca asked. "She needs a doctor."

He faced her. "The only cure she needs is to accept me, totally, completely, and unconditionally. If she doesn't do that, no doctor on this earth will be able to help her or anyone else in this room." He left. The door closed, sounding like thunder, echoing throughout their dungeon, and shattering their nerves, as well as their spirits.

Mei Lin cried uncontrollably. "See what you've done!" she managed to say, despite the tears and her body trembling. "You've made him angry and we're all going to be punished."

"He's been punishing us every day. Can't you see that?" asked Selena, coming to Rebecca's defense. "Jennifer and Rebecca were right. The only chance we've got is for one of us to escape and bring back help."

"What help?" asked Mei Lin. "The kind of help we got for Jennifer?" She pounded her cot with her fists, furiously punching the thin mattress, striking metal until her hands bled. "I don't care what you say! No one's going to help us! Not you! Not Jennifer! No one! I hate this place! I hate it!" She collapsed face down onto the cot, her tormented cries muffled by the mattress.

Rebecca moved to the sink, ran water over a towel. She sat next to Jennifer, still unconscious, and lifted her shoulders until she could cradle the top half of her body onto her lap. She gently dabbed Jennifer's forehead and face with the damp cloth. She studied the injuries, one eye swollen shut, large purple bruises on her cheek and neck, her lip cut, still bleeding.

She observed her own hands and arms, scratched, cut, her gown bloodied, torn, and caked with mud. She touched her face and winced in pain. She could feel the damage inflicted by the low hanging branches and bushes that whiplashed against her skin. She was grateful there were no mirrors, although looking at her friend, she hardly needed one.

"Is she going to be okay?" asked Selena.

"I don't know," answered Rebecca, softly, attempting not to cry.

"Are you?" Selena said.

Rebecca didn't respond. She leaned closer to Jennifer and whispered, "I'm sorry, Jenny. I'm so sorry."

She touched Jennifer's right hand. To her surprise, Jennifer's fingers closed around Rebecca's hand, an increasingly firm grip.

Rebecca spoke so quietly that no one, other than Jennifer, could hear her words. "I'm not giving up," she said. "I'm not."

Jennifer's lips moved, a slight tremble, making a courageous effort to speak. She mouthed the words: "Neither am I."

Rebecca's tears streamed down her cheeks as she stroked Jennifer's hair and closed her eyes.

SIXTY-THREE

Ron sat defeated on the couch, holding the card with both hands, afraid to let it go. For the moment, it was the only thing keeping him together. For the past three weeks, six days, and three-hundred and fifteen-minutes, he had missed everything about her; picking her up after school each afternoon and listening to her stories about what she had learned and which boy had worked on her last nerve; making her dinners and snacks before bedtime; helping her with her homework, although she usually had to explain the new math; sitting with her on the couch and watching her favorite television shows.

Most of all, he missed their quiet time, just after her bath and before she went to bed, when they sat together on the couch and listened to music or read or played a board game until her eyelids drooped. He'd gently flick her earlobe, something she used to do to him the first three years of her life, and then he'd notify her, "Time to have great dreams." She'd insist she wasn't tired even though her eyes could barely remain open. In the middle of her protestations, she'd fall asleep. He would carry her to her room, put her to bed, and cover her with a blanket filled with cartoon characters.

"Dad, I'm too old for that thing," she complained, and yet never found a suitable substitute, no matter where they shopped or how long they searched.

But when he combined all the things that contributed to missing her, they paled in comparison to the void now experienced in every fiber of his body. If ever he doubted that pain could ache and grief could burn more powerfully than the night he lost his wife, that uncertainty had been permanently erased the moment he stepped into the evidence room at the police station and held Jennifer's sweater. In reality, he had lost Nikki again, although this time part of him had been taken with her. He didn't know how large a part. But he knew he would soon find out.

He noticed Lungren's confession. The handwritten letter rested on the coffee table in front of him. He picked up the sheet and read it for the hundredth time. It made him ill, destroying him a little with each new reading. The apology was the most difficult part to accept because it detailed the abuse, outlined the brutality, the conditions of her last few days on earth, and how she was murdered. Slaughtered like an animal and then discarded like garbage.

He placed his daughter's card next to the letter written by her murderer. Two extremes were now side-by-side—one a message of hope and love, the other a confession of despair and hate. He studied both signatures, first his daughter's name and then Lungren's. The contrast couldn't have been more revealing. A love of life written in crayon and emphasized by a drawing of a heart, versus the emptiness of death written in black ink and signed by a madman who... He thought his heart stopped and then raced. He picked up the confession and studied it more closely. He was confused, then puzzled, then curious, and then he rushed to the dining room and retrieved the list of pedophiles he had compiled. He skimmed it until he found Lungren's name. He circled it and then turned on the computer, waiting impatiently for it to boot up.

"Come on!" He hit the top of the monitor then slapped the side of the computer as if that would speed up the process. Once ready, he grabbed the keyboard and quickly typed the web address for the Justice Department's registry of sex offenders. He used his bookmark to go directly to convicted pedophiles residing in Culver City. He scrolled down the screen, took a shortcut by going to last names starting with "M," and then scrolled up a few listings to Lungren.

He leaned back in his chair and stared at the screen. He used both hands to massage his face and then looked at the name again. He compared it to the signature on the confession and then slammed both palms against the table.

"Yes!" he shouted.

He rushed to the telephone and called Todd.

* * *

The phone rang in Todd's living room, but he ignored it. He carried two suitcases and lined them up against the wall in the foyer. He watched Liz put on her coat.

"I don't want you to do this," he said.

"I want a memorial service for her. I'll help plan that with you if you'd like."

"There's no reason for you to go. I'll rent a place somewhere and you can stay here. This is your home."

"This is where I live. I sleep at night and wake up in the morning and my clothes are in the closet but, *home?* The person that made this a home and made us a family, she's no longer here. So, no Todd, home is the last term I'd used to describe this place."

"Don't leave, Elizabeth."

The phone stopped ringing.

"There's that name, again," she said. "Not Liz. But the one that lets me know I'm right." She walked to the door but didn't open it. "I don't know how long I need to be away from you. I just know that I do. I want to be able to look at you and see my husband. See the man who helped me give birth to a precious little girl. Until I can see that, it's best for both of us if we stay apart."

She opened the door. "Help me out to the car, will ya?"

He picked up the suitcases and carried them to her car. He placed them into the trunk. Liz opened the driver's side door.

He could hear the phone ringing again.

"You should get that," said Liz.

"It's probably your mother to see if you've left yet. I'm sure she can hardly wait for you to move back in."

"Mothers are like that," she said, her expression filled with sadness. "It's hard to let go of your only child." She kissed him on the cheek and entered her car, starting the engine. She rolled down the window. "I'll call you in a few days to make arrangements for Rebecca."

"I love you," he said.

She nodded and then drove off.

The house phone stopped ringing. He walked toward his front door but stopped when his cell phone rang, the line devoted exclusively to information regarding his daughter. He took out the phone from his pocket and looked at the text message.

Call Ron... Urgent!

SIXTY-FOUR

He slowly paced the floor, his face swollen and his nose slightly discolored.

"I never wanted any of this to happen," he said. "It was all supposed to be beautiful. It still can be. I want you to trust me. I want to be able to trust you."

He stopped pacing and moved slowly toward Rebecca. He sat next to her on the cot.

"What you did was very dangerous, not only for yourself but everyone involved. What do you think would have happened if you had managed to get away? I would have had no choice but to deal with your betrayal in the harshest terms. Don't you care about your sisters?"

Rebecca looked at him. "I just want you to help Jenny. You hurt her?"

He walked over to Jennifer and sat next to her. Her right eye was swollen shut. He touched her on the shoulder. "I was no older than Mei Lin. My best friend in the whole world was Black. She had the most beautiful smile. You remind me of her."

He reached to touch her cheek, but she withdrew from him.

"I wanted to run away with her. Until my father came home

one day and saw us holding hands." He extended his right hand and turned it over showing her his palm, scared and disfigured.

"This was the hand that touched her. The hand my father whipped then placed in scorching water. To clean the infection, he said. And then he took me out to the garage to his woodshop. My father was a very talented craftsman who taught me a great deal about carpentry and how to build beautiful things. He made me place my hand inside a vise, told me to count the number of times the handle made a complete turn. I made it to three before I started crying. When I counted five, I was screaming. I passed out before I made it to six. When I awoke, he was by my side, demanding that I bandage the wound by myself. I learned many valuable lessons from him. The most important was that I had the ability to heal. But I had to find a way to do it myself, discover my own power and eliminate those who would cause me any more pain."

He walked around the room, extending his damaged hand, displaying it to each girl. "What was once ugly, I made beautiful. I think it's really a mark from God. To separate me from those who would destroy themselves. It protects me from those who have the invisible scars of hate and ugliness... You see? I told you I was special."

He stopped in front of Rebecca. "How long do you think it will be before you're healthy enough to dance for me again?"

He waited for a response. She didn't give him one.

"It doesn't matter, you too, will find a way to heal yourself," he said, then turned to address Jennifer. "I have all the time in the world."

He left the room and locked the door. Jennifer rose from her cot and lifted it. She raised the other corner and then tossed the mattress to the side, angry and afraid. The tissues were gone. He controlled their time, after all.

SIXTY-FIVE

Todd never went back inside his house but drove directly to Ron's apartment. He avoided the elevator and raced up the stairs. Ron was halfway down the corridor to greet him, waving the confession.

"I thought we weren't going to see each other?" Todd said.

"Never mind that, hurry up inside. I've got something important to show you."

They entered the apartment and he shoved the confession at Todd before the door was closed. "Read that."

"If that's the confession, I don't want any part of it."

"Just take a look at the signature, not the whole thing."

Todd reluctantly took the letter and glanced at it. "Okay, he signed it. We already knew that."

"Take a closer look."

Todd studied it, and then handed it back to Ron. "It's still his signature. You wanted me to come all the way out here to show me that?"

"He didn't do it."

"What are you talking about?"

"Lungren didn't do it. Just take another look," Ron pleaded, extending the confession to Todd.

"Get that thing outta my face!" Todd walked away, aggravated, frustrated, then took a deep breath and turned to face Ron. He spoke calmly, sympathetically. "Ron, they're gone." He moved closer. "Your daughter. Mine. They're gone. As hard as that is to accept, we have to." He looked at Ron and shook his head. "You were right about us not seeing each other. It was a mistake coming here."

He walked past Ron and headed for the door.

"He didn't do it, Todd. I'm certain of it."

Todd spun around. "How the hell can you be so sure?

Ron held up the letter. "It's here... in his confession. He confessed all right, but not to killing our daughters." He stood by Todd's side and pointed out Lungren's signature. "He misspelled his last name."

"He was about to electrocute himself," responded Todd. "He was probably on drugs before he did it. And you want to analyze his penmanship checking for spelling errors?"

"His name is spelled L-U-N-G-R-E-N. He spelled it L-I. He underlined three letters. One small line under the L and I. Another line under the next to last letter in his name, E."

"Lie?" Todd stepped away, considering it. "He wrote the thing quickly, half out of his mind. This is nothing but a—"

"His middle name was Francis," Ron interrupted. "Theodore F. Lungren... He substituted the letter "A" for his middle initial. A lie. His confession was—"

"A lie," now Todd interrupted. He took the confession from Ron, studied it more closely. "Have you told this to anyone else?"

"I will as soon as I can catch a ride to the Culver City police station."

Todd tossed him the car keys. "You drive. I'm too excited."

* * *

It took them less than ten minutes to arrive at Detective Carrey's office and about thirty seconds for Ron to explain his theory to both partners.

Carrey studied the signature with McKay looking over his shoulder. Ron and Todd waited for a response, but the detectives didn't show a clue as to what they were thinking.

Carrey handed the confession back to Ron. "Nice work," he said calmly. "I'm glad you talked me into giving you a copy."

"You're not surprised?"

"Better direct that question to Detective McKay. He had doubts all along."

Ron looked at McKay, waiting for a response.

"Oh... I'm surprised," McKay said. "I'm surprised I missed this. I surely did."

"But you knew?"

McKay moved around to the front of the desk and leaned against it. "I think it's time that we worked together instead of doing our own separate investigations... You two agree?"

"Completely," answered Todd.

"Good... Why don't you give those private dicks you hired a call." McKay handed Todd the phone.

An hour later, McKay and Carrey sat at the head of the table in the conference room. Ron and Todd sat together on one side. Harrison sat alone, across from them.

McKay chaired the meeting. "We had the lab technicians go over every inch of Lungren's apartment. No unusual hair or fiber on any of his clothes, carpets, nothing. If he was anywhere near those girls, something from them would have been detected. The jewelry and clothes and everything else had to be planted."

"So, we're back to square one?" commented Harrison.

"Not hardly," said McKay. "We know that at least four girls have been abducted by the same person or persons. And that those girls, in all probability, are still alive."

"Why do you believe that?" asked Todd.

"To be honest, I can't be absolutely sure. But Lungren wouldn't have been murdered and then set up if the girls were dead. There'd be no reason for it. Whoever murdered Lungren wanted us to stop looking for him *and* the girls." McKay picked up the confession. "Lungren wasn't the only one who left us a clue. This confession contains information about who we're dealing with. Only the signature is false."

"We got a guy who has at least four girls who he didn't have ten weeks ago," said Carrey. "He's had to buy clothes, food. Change his customary habits. Maybe even be seen in public with one or more of them. We know what it is we're looking for. Now we just need to determine who it is we're looking for and find him."

"I'll notify the other parents," said McKay.

"Should we give them false hope? I'd love to tell my wife, but she couldn't take it if we're wrong."

"They have a right to know there's still a chance, no matter how small," replied McKay. "But we're going to need them to keep this secret for as long as possible. I want whoever is responsible for this to think he got away with it. It gives us the element of surprise and buys us some time. Everyone on the same page?"

They all nodded in agreement.

"Nobody does anything without first clearing it with either me or Detective Carrey." He looked at Ron and Todd then shifted focus to Harrison. "Have I made myself perfectly clear?"

"As clear as Scotch tape," said Harrison.

"Good. Because the first person who violates that rule gets tossed in jail for obstruction. Any questions?"

Ron raised his hand. McKay recognized him with a nod.

"What happens to the second person?"

McKay released a sigh, shook his head in resignation, and focused attention on his partner. "You know what I'm going to do after we find these girls and bring them safely back home?"

Carrey nodded. "Fill out your retirement papers but then never turn them in."

McKay shrugged. "Probably," he said, and then smiled.

SIXTY-SIX
TUESDAY MAY 2ND

He prepared a tray with several paper plates of food. He decided to add fruit, wanting the girls to get their daily dosage. He placed two apples on a cutting board and started slicing. He hummed a tune that was playing on the radio. The music was interrupted by a news bulletin.

K-CAL news has just reported that Theodore Lungren, the man suspected of taking his own life after confessing to the killings of four kidnapped girls, may have been murdered after being forced to write a false confession. Police believe the four girls are still alive and are being held against their will. More on this stunning development coming up on the noon midday report.

He stabbed the knife into the cutting board and turned off the radio. He paced the kitchen, and then stopped to open the refrigerator. He closed it and opened it several times as if he needed the comfort of the cool air. He slammed it shut.

Impossible! He couldn't believe what he had just heard. The news report indicated the girls might be alive, that the confession was a fake! How could that be? He had conceived the perfect plan and yet, somehow, he had failed to achieve the desired goal. To the contrary, he had unwittingly provided valuable information to the authorities. Now they knew the four girls were linked together and if they had learned that, how long would it be before they discovered who took them?

He slammed his hand onto the kitchen counter and turned on the sink faucet. He ran cold water over his hands, and then poured it onto his face. *Think clearly!* He wondered what other mistakes he had made. Did he leave any incriminating evidence at Lungren's apartment? How could the police be so sure it was a setup? He had plotted every detail, left nothing out. And to compound the failure, Rebecca had almost escaped. How could he be tricked by a mere girl? He had been careless, too kind, too trusting. That would have to change.

He ripped off a paper towel and dried his face. This must be happening for a reason, he reassured himself. After all his accomplishments and given his meticulous planning that took years, it was inconceivable that he'd be denied victory at this stage of the contest. He placed his hands on the edge of the counter and pressed hard. His muscles tensed throughout his body, and then he relaxed. It had come to him, as it had on so many occasions in the past. Yes. This had to be for a purpose. It was time to take the girls away. He'd burn down this place and leave no trace that he was ever here.

He would delay finding the fifth girl. He could start his family without her, for now. When he finally selected her, the others would help with her indoctrination—ease her transition from the other world to his, *to theirs.*

There was little time to waste. They would leave within the week, two at the most. He could hardly wait to tell them. But maybe it was too soon to let them know. If one of them had been so bold as to attempt an escape, what would all four do, given the chance? No, it was safer to incapacitate them. He would need enough sedatives sufficient to insure they would present no problems for the duration of the trip. If he traveled without a major stop, other than for gas and a quick bathroom break, he could leave before daybreak and be there by nightfall—849 miles to Santa Fe, twelve to fourteen hours by car, assuming he stayed within the speed limit. And of course, he would. No sense breaking the law and tempting fate.

He would start packing immediately, taking only the bare necessities. Whatever else he needed he had already obtained for his other home, the place where he would start a new life for himself and his precious family. He would feed the girls later. There were more pressing concerns that demanded his attention. He ate a slice of the apple he had cut. No sense allowing good food to go to waste. It was a sin.

He traveled to the drug store and had his prescriptions filled, using his father's medical benefits. The man had been far more useful in death, than he ever had been in life.

God bless his tortured soul.

"Yes," he told the pharmacist. "His father was having great difficulty resting in peace and needed the sleeping pills."

He waited for the prescription to be filled by flipping through a few gossip magazines. He chuckled to himself and thought about what he had said about his father *having great difficulty resting in peace.* Even in times of enormous turmoil, he had not lost his sense of humor and keen wit.

SIXTY-SEVEN

McKay slammed his palm against the top of his desk. "How the fuck did they find that out this soon?"

"We'll never know for sure. But my bet is on Harrison," answered Carrey. "Never did trust private dicks. Probably sold the info for a pretty penny." He released a deep sigh. "There goes what little advantage we had. I'll call the fathers. Make sure they know." Carrey pulled out his phone book. "You think this will scare him into doing something?"

"We don't have a whole lot of time to find out." McKay put on his jacket. "Well, since the cat's out of the bag. Let's turn it into a lion. The media likes to use us. It's time they returned the favor and got the public to help."

Carrey nodded agreement and made the first call to Ron who had just heard the news report and had already called Todd, who hadn't.

* * *

Todd pulled his Mercedes into his in-laws' driveway. He jumped out of the car and raced across the lawn. Liz rushed out of the home before he made it to the front door.

Liz ran into her husband's arms. "Is it true? Oh my God, Todd, is it true?"

"We don't know that for sure. But the police think so. They didn't want the media involved. Now that they know, we need as much exposure as possible and hope that the public can provide information. We shouldn't raise expectations until we know it's real. And there's no proof for that, not yet. I don't want you to go through this again, Liz. Hoping beyond hope."

"She's still alive, Todd. I don't know why I'm so certain. Call it a mother's intuition... All those girls are still alive. They must be. We wouldn't be given this second chance only for it to be taken away. No God would be that cruel."

Liz's mother appeared at the front door, followed by her father who placed his arm around his wife's waist. She looked at her daughter for a signal. Liz smiled and nodded yes. Her mother broke out in joyous laughter and tears of relief. She rushed to her daughter.

"Is it possible?" she asked Liz. "Oh, Lord, is it really possible?"

"Yes, Mother! Yes! We have to believe that it is."

The two women embraced, jumping up and down in excitement. Liz's father joined them, holding his daughter, while his wife threw her arms around Todd and cried.

SIXTY-EIGHT

Detective Carrey interviewed the department store cashier, who had called his office regarding the "missing girls." They started the interview on the main floor in the children's clothing section but moved to the manager's office after being interrupted several times by customers requiring assistance.

"Most men don't shop for their daughters, so he stood out," she said. "I hope I'm not wasting your time, but when I saw pictures of those girls on the news last night. It just broke my heart. I started going over things in my mind, wondering if I had seen anything unusual. My husband told me I had an overly active imagination, and what were the chances someone like that would shop here." She made a sucking sound, dismissing her husband's comments. "I told him he had to shop somewhere, so why not with me?"

"We rely on the public, people just like you," Carrey reassured her. "The smallest piece of information often helps us solve a case."

"Really?" she asked, impressed, and a bit excited. "Well, I believe in doing my part as a responsible citizen. I've never missed a vote, not even in the off-year elections. You never know when your vote is the deciding factor in a tight race."

He opened a notebook and removed a pen from his shirt. "What was it about his behavior that caused you to be suspicious?"

"It's difficult to explain," she shrugged. "At first, I liked him, thought he was terrific. But the more I thought about it, the more it struck me that there was something odd about him. Not an oddball per se, but different. If you catch my drift."

"How so?"

"Just the way he talked. He said something about society or mankind, no it was civilization. That's what he said: 'Civilization coming from the womb.' That the future of the race depended on women," she smiled. "Not that I would disagree with his sentiment, mind you, but no man I've ever known would say anything like that. Certainly not the one I married. You can bet your paycheck and double your monthly income, believe you me."

Carrey sighed, and then turned a page of his notebook.

"He had, I'm not sure how to describe it exactly, a weirdness factor. Look, my husband might be right. I mean, what's weird to one person is marriage material to another. My husband calls me weird, and you know what I tell him?" She waited for the detective to respond, but he didn't. "I tell him, 'I'm *unique*, which is why you've stayed with me twenty years.'" She crossed her arms. "You're a detective. You tell me. You think someone would stay with a person that long if they were really weird?"

"You remember what he looked like?" he asked, ignoring the question.

"I see so many people on my shift. Plus, it was three or four weeks ago. I don't know." She glanced upward, as if counting the ceiling tiles. "I remember he wasn't wearing a wedding ring. I thought that was strange for a guy who respected women so much." She closed her eyes, and then lightly struck her head with her palm in an effort to shake free her memory. Carrey shook his head and smiled.

She opened her eyes. "He was handsome, tall, maybe six-two or more. Fairly sure he was blond, kind of a dirty blond now that I think of it. Although that might have been his roots showing through."

"You think he dyed his hair?"

"I don't know why I said that. But it must have occurred to me back then. Funny how things keep popping back in my mind. My husband would tell you it's because I've got a lot of room up here." She pointed to her head. "He should talk," she said as an aside. "Like I told the officer I spoke to on the phone, he was pretty normal looking, probably late twenties which was another thing that stood out. That's kinda young to have that many children, although these days kids are havin' kids. Then people have the nerve to wonder why the country's in such a mess."

"Did he use a credit card?" he asked, attempting to keep her on track.

She snapped her fingers. "That reminds me, he paid cash for everything. I tried to get him to apply for a store card." She leaned close and spoke confidentially. "We get a kickback for each new application, assuming it's approved. With FICA scores being what they are, that's not as easy as you might think. Although I'm not implying anything," she quickly added, and then reassumed her original position. "I told him he could save an extra twenty percent, and since he was buying a lot of clothes, that could be a real savings, but he wouldn't hear of it. I could give you an application to fill out if you like. Only take a minute to process."

She looked around to see if any of the managers were listening. "Kick in an extra five percent on every purchase you make today, except for the clearance items. Those are the ones with the red stickers."

"No thanks."

"Between you and me, I wouldn't buy the clearance stuff either. There's a reason we couldn't sell it after the first two markdowns. You know what I'm sayin'?"

"Anything else?"

She thought about the question and shook her head, and then, after a moment, remembered something. "Oh, wait. I don't know if this is important, but his wife was either expecting another child or maybe he said he wanted another one... Another girl. Yes, I remember, he wanted another girl."

Carrey wrote down the information, putting an asterisk next to her final statement.

An hour later, he met his partner at the bridal shop, where they interviewed the owner. She told both detectives, "In all my years in the bridal business, I've never had to order one, let alone four wedding gowns, with hats and veils for children. Never."

The surveillance system was useless, since the recordings were taped over each other every forty-eight hours, unless needed to document missing inventory or a store break-in. There was no credit card transaction. "He paid the total bill upfront in cash and picked up the gowns a little more than a week later," explained the owner.

"Could you describe him?" McKay asked.

"He was wearing these wide wrap-around sunglasses, very dark lenses. Really couldn't make out much of his face."

"He never took off his glasses in the store?" asked Carrey.

"He told the bride he had recent laser surgery and needed them for protection. My sister had the same problem. Filed a major lawsuit but settled out-of-court."

The detectives thanked her for her time, but before they left, she asked: "If it turns out he's the one who took those girls and you capture him, am I eligible for any of that reward money?"

"That's not up to us, ma'am," answered McKay.

"Well, I'll say a prayer," she said. "For the children," she added, unconvincingly.

From the bridal shop the detectives travelled to Palisades Elementary School and met with Private Investigator Harrison, in the administration building. His office had received a call from the mother of one of the students. He alerted the lead detectives, since the school counselor, Ann Frazier, was coordinating the meeting and required the police to be involved.

Mrs. Lydia Sanchez sat nervously, holding the hand of her daughter, Sakari.

"I found the money in my daughter's backpack, around two weeks ago," said Mrs. Sanchez. "Two five-dollar bills. Some man wanted her to help him find his dog, and then all of a sudden, he didn't, but gave her the money anyway."

"I asked for it," Sakari, said proudly.

Mrs. Sanchez gave her a warning look.

"Well, Mama, he promised me a reward if I helped," she responded defensively. "Wasn't my fault, it didn't happen."

"Sakari," said Harrison, "tell the detectives what you told me about why the man changed his mind about you finding his dog?"

She shrugged. "He said I was pretty. Thought all Native Americans had beautiful hair. When I told him I wasn't Native American, he seemed like he didn't want me to help anymore. I hope he found his dog."

The detectives exchanged a look.

"Was I wrong to ask for the money?"

"No, Sakari," answered Carrey. "You weren't wrong."

"Then, Mama, can I have the ten bucks back?"

Everyone laughed, except Sakari, who didn't understand the joke.

McKay touched her on the shoulder. "Sakari, if I get someone to help you draw a picture, do you think you could describe what the man looked like?"

She nodded yes. "Can I draw, too? I'm pretty good, especially with crayons."

"I'm sure you are," smiled McKay. "And maybe you'll be able to help the artist, if that's okay with your mom." He focused his attention on her mother. "Mrs. Sanchez, I'm going to ask a sketch artist to sit with your daughter. Do I have your permission to do that?"

"This man..." Mrs. Sanchez said, and then hesitated. "Does he hurt children?" She looked at Sakari, concern evident by her worried expression. "I don't want my daughter involved, if she has to see this man again."

"All she has to do is describe what he looked like," answered McKay. "I promise your daughter will never have contact with him again. But what she tells us might help make sure he never hurts any child again."

Mrs. Sanchez considered it. She looked at Sakari's counselor for help. Frazier nodded encouragement.

"Sakari, would you like to play a game?" asked McKay. "See if a friend of mine can draw all the faces that you tell him to?"

Sakari looked at her mother for approval. She nodded agreement, which caused Sakari to flash a huge smile. "Do I get more money?"

Counselor Frazier laughed along with the detectives and Harrison. Even Mrs. Sanchez eventually smiled.

SIXTY-NINE

Wednesday May 3rd Stanley Carter waited for the elevator, a daily newspaper tucked underneath his arm, pressed tightly against his ribs. He held a thick briefcase in one hand and a fresh cup of cappuccino in the other. It was the one luxury that he treated himself to every morning. His wife thought of it as an addiction but given the range of possible compulsions that he could indulge in, Starbucks was a godsend.

He took a sip, got cream on his upper lip, and licked it off. It probably looked unprofessional, but he had long ago stopped caring about impressing anyone, at least since that young intern had worked in his office. She was from Kansas and had traveled to L.A., like a million other beautiful women, seeking stardom. A few found their way to the casting couch. They may have been the lucky ones. Ah, the tragic lore of Hollywood and lessons yet learned. The intern loved children, which was why she applied for a temporary position in his office. She also had been adopted, a major plus during the interview.

But, alas, she lasted less than a month. The adoption business had its rewards, paid in joyful tears for each and every successful placement. Unfortunately, the line of children waiting to be claimed was filled with rejected boys and girls whose tears were far more frequent and a great deal less pleasant. In just under four weeks, Miss-Kansas-intern-wannabe-starlet, having become an unwilling expert in the ecstasy of raised expectations and the agony of rejection, resigned.

The elevator creaked open, one of three elevators in the building that took forever. A UPS delivery man, in a hurry to make his next drop-off, rammed his cart into Carter's arm causing a sharp pain and a loss of a six-dollar cup of coffee, sans tax and tip. *Hope he does a better job driving his truck.* After the prerequisite apologies and heartfelt cursing, Carter made it safely to the twelfth floor, which given the state of disrepair of those steel traps providing limited transportation, was never a sure thing.

Once inside the agency, he shared perfunctory greetings with staff on his way to his office. After he opened the door to the executive suite, he saw the smiling face of his secretary, Trina Castle, who loved to tell him that "a man's home was his castle." He wasn't sure what she meant by that, but her continuing play on words had stopped being funny after the hundredth hearing.

"Morning, Trina."

"Good morning, Mr. Carter," she returned the greeting, and then announced, "Got some warm doughnuts waiting to be devoured."

"Glazed?"

"Honey and chocolate covered."

"Trina, if I wasn't happily married with two children—"

"You'd probably be sunning yourself on some beach in Mazatlan."

"Cabo San Lucas," he corrected her. "But one Mexican beach is as good as another."

"If you don't mind dodging machine-gun fire."

He smiled. If her typing and organizational skills were as sharp as her rapid retorts, she'd be *his* boss.

"Where's your coffee? Don't tell me Starbucks went on strike."

"Not strike, *struck*, as on my elbow, courtesy of our delivery man."

"Oh, he's cute."

"And married," he pointed out.

"The best ones are."

"With regard to where my coffee is at the moment, I would offer an educated guess and say my shoes, the lobby, entrance to elevator two, and given our crack custodial staff's work habits, the coffee will find its way onto a mop in I'd estimate..." He looked at his wristwatch. "Eight hours."

He entered his office and tried to find a spot for his briefcase. Out of necessity, he settled on the floor. He leaned it against one of the stacks of files that appeared like wallpaper around the overcrowded room. This was a state agency, after all, and given recent budget cuts to children's services, he was fortunate to have a desk. Although given its cluttered arrangement, it could hardly be considered functional. This was where he would remain ten hours a day, five days a week, not counting the paperwork he brought home for weekend study. The moment he entered this inner sanctum, he was reminded of his unbearable workload, the fact that resources were extremely limited, rare would be a more accurate description, and that he had no space to adequately service the needs of the public.

And he *loved* every minute of it.

Had loved it for over twenty years and God willing, and the creek don't rise, another twenty. He had forgotten the total number of children he had placed, but the memory of those faces would live with him forever, the smiles, laughter, cries of joy, a new family formed in front of his eyes every week or so.

He recalled it all like it was yesterday. *Who says public service can't make you rich?*

Not all the stories turned out well, of course. There were mistakes made in judgment, homes that turned out to be anything but. And then there were more than enough examples of abused children whose emotional problems were too great, even for the most compassionate and committed adults. But he couldn't think of a better job, and if there was one, he wouldn't have taken it.

He removed his jacket, slung it over the back of his chair, and tossed his newspaper on his computer keyboard. Trina entered carrying a cup of freshly brewed coffee, which was public employee code for "instant." She looked for a space on his desk that wasn't taken but couldn't find one.

"I think you're just going to have to hold this, either that or work a lot faster."

He removed a set of folders and cleared some room on his desk. She put down the Styrofoam cup.

"Thanks," he said. "But I keep telling you, that's not in your job description."

"I don't mind. Sooner you get your caffeine fix, sooner I can relax."

"You say that now. First time you don't get your merit raise —bam! I'm written up on charges of sex discrimination and harassment."

"I'd make your coffee even if you were a woman." She gave him a wink. "Might not put as much sugar in it."

"You're in a particularly good mood."

"It helps knowing those little girls might still be alive. The reward's now over two hundred thousand dollars. That should shake up things."

"Those who help children only for money are the ones we really need to be protected from."

"Those girls could use all the help they can find, no matter what the motive. You see the profile on the guy they think took those kids?"

He shook his head.

"Creepy," she shivered. "Wants to set up his own United Nations."

"What are you talking about?"

She took his newspaper, unfolded it, and pointed to the cover page.

Carter read the article with increasing interest.

"You mind if I take an early lunch?"

Too engaged by the article, he didn't answer.

"And a vacation in Spain, on your credit card?"

"Sure. Go ahead," he mumbled. His attention remained focused on the paper.

She blew him a kiss that went unnoticed, and then she left the office.

Distressed, he put down the paper and considered the implications of the news article. He took a quick sip of coffee which, by his reaction, he found distasteful. He looked around the office at the hundreds of files, closer to thousands.

Where to begin?

He opened one of four large metal filing cabinets and began a search that became more frantic with time.

SEVENTY

Todd had gone stir-crazy pacing the floors at home while waiting for news about Rebecca. It didn't help that in addition to his daughter, his wife was also no longer there. He knew the place was large, but without the presence of those he loved, it had become a massive void. Every footstep he took resounded throughout the empty corridors, a constant reminder of him being alone. He decided to go to work where he would be surrounded by familiar faces and have a reasonable chance to be productive. As soon as he entered his office, he was met by his secretary.

"Mr. Roth," she said anxiously, "I've been trying to reach you for the last hour."

"I'm sorry, Andrea, I left home in a hurry and forgot to take my cell. Is there a problem? You look troubled."

"Someone called Mr. Harrison's office this morning... Left a message that he might know who has your daughter and the other girls, as well."

"What makes Harrison think that's not another one of the five thousand crank calls he gets every day?"

"The man who called heads an adoption agency in Los

335

Angeles. He said he remembered someone who fit the profile that appeared in the paper."

"Did he say who he thought it was?"

"He didn't want to accuse the person until he investigated the matter further but expected to have additional information by the end of the day."

"Did this man leave a number?"

"Only a name. Stanley Carter."

"Could you call all the adoption agencies in L.A. and see if—"

She handed him a slip of paper that contained a phone number and address. "I already did a Google search. He's in charge of the state agency handling all adoptions in Southern California. From the information on his website, he's held the position for many years."

Todd stared at the number, bit down on his lip.

"Oh, dear God, Mr. Roth, I hope this doesn't turn out to be another wild goose search."

He nodded. The thought had occurred to him as well. "Could you get Ron Butler on the line for me and patch a conference call for the two of us to Mr. Carter's office."

"Right away, sir." She grabbed the phone and dialed.

He entered his private suite and sat down. He drummed his fingers on the desk and stared at a framed photo of Rebecca and Liz on his desk. He leaned back, closed his eyes, and waited for a call that might restore his life.

SEVENTY-ONE

It was easy to get lost in these hills. Carter had already taken
several wrong turns which led to dead ends. He finally found
the correct street sign and drove on a narrow dirt road, leading
to the address he had written down on his notepad. He had
made a mistake driving his personal car. An S.U.V. wasn't
ideally built for roads carved out of a mountainside. He nearly
collided with several trash cans and barely avoided sideswiping
a mailbox. He assumed the house at the end of Canterbury
Avenue, without any clear identifying numbers on the curb or
over the front door, was the one he had been searching for.

He parked the vehicle as close to the curb as possible,
checked his notes, and then tossed the pad onto the dashboard.
He observed the residence while remaining inside the comfort
and safety of his car. Well, if the man lived here, he had selected
the most isolated home in the area. The word "remote" didn't
give the location justice. He wondered if he should just knock
on the man's door and come up with an excuse. He was lost and
needed directions. That would give him an idea how the man
interacted, if he could see anything odd in the house.

This was dumb, he realized. What were the chances this

guy had kidnapped those girls? One in a million. Simply because he wanted to adopt multi-racial kids didn't make him suspicious. It was commendable. He wished more people were that open-minded and caring. Still, he'd never forgive himself if it turned out this was the place that had the girls and he never checked it for himself. He thought about notifying the police, but they probably were inundated with calls and regular crime-fighting. That's why he contacted the private investigator whose number was listed on the reward flyer. He was out for lunch, but his secretary assured him that she'd give him the message. She suggested he call back later but the longer he waited the more convinced he was that he should just check it out for himself. Anyway, if there was anything to it, he was certain the investigator would be in contact with the proper authorities.

Carter had always been a model citizen. Done the right thing for the right reason. If there was someone who needed help crossing the street, he'd be the one to lend a hand. Need assistance with groceries? He'd be there. He couldn't remember the number of down-and-out families he had given a few bucks to. At the same time, he didn't want to be sued for defamation for accusing an innocent man of such heinous crimes. And if he wanted to be honest with himself, which he always was, he did know about the reward money. No reason to share it if he was the one to take the risk.

He exited his car and confirmed just how secluded the house happened to be. Sitting on top of the hillside and situated at the end of a long winding road, you weren't likely to get here by mistake. If you bothered to make the trip, it had to be on purpose. And you really had to have a good reason to be here.

If it snowed in Southern California, the occupant at this address would be held captive for weeks. On the positive side, however, Carter thought it had to have a killer view. On the other hand, one powerful mudslide would send this structure cascading over the cliff, crashing into the canyon, which had to be at least a mile below the famous Hollywood sign. He didn't want to think about the consequences of a major earthquake. As wonderful as this view might be, he'd just as soon keep his home in the valley, firmly constructed on a flat parcel of land. That way, he was reasonably certain his bedroom wouldn't slip or slide into regions unknown.

The pathway on the side of the house provided little room to maneuver, due in large part to the wild growth of bushes and overlapping tree branches, in desperate need of trimming. He doubted this area would meet compliance with the city's fire code. He attempted to peer through a small window, but a large piece of furniture, perhaps the back of a bookcase, blocked his view. Carter made his way around the side of the home, surprised to find that there was much more land in the rear than he had expected. Granted, it wasn't exactly suited for a family barbecue, but if you enjoyed living on top of a forest with steep declines, you could do worse.

Carter began to appreciate the tranquility and natural beauty of the backyard, enhanced by the sights of the city, far in the distance. It merged nature with urban life in a way that made modern technology compatible with God.

He removed a shovel from a crate and leaned it against the house. He placed the wooded box upside-down and stepped on it, but still had to stand on his tiptoes to look through a window. Again, his view was blocked, this time by thick curtains. He wondered why anyone with this amount of privacy would need to keep curtains drawn and windows blocked. It's not like any deer in the area would be guilty of being a peeping Tom.

He almost fell off the crate. *The last thing I need is to break a leg*, he thought. Which caused him to reconsider the whole trip. The possible reward was tempting but he wasn't cut out for detective work, especially regarding finding someone sick enough to abduct children. What the hell was he thinking? Doing the right thing. And the money, that's what. A lot of it.

Why shouldn't he be the hero? Solve the case. Have his picture and name on the front page of every newspaper in the city. Probably interviewed on national cable news. Still, maybe he shouldn't have come alone and alerted the police instead, to be on the safe side. It wouldn't affect him receiving the full reward money, so far as he knew. All two hundred thousand of it, which he was more than willing to share with some of his needy families. He also was prepared to use some of the reward to fund necessary resources in his office and the department as a whole. That's what true humanitarians do. Not too late to make the call. He retrieved his cell phone from his pocket.

"Can I help you?"

The voice caused him to lose his balance again and drop the phone. He stepped down from the crate, more embarrassed than nervous.

"I'm sorry." He fumbled with his jacket and sheepishly addressed the man who had discovered him. "My car seems to have stalled out. Guess it couldn't take the extreme change in altitude. To complicate matters, my cell phone's unable to get a signal this high up."

The man picked up Carter's phone but didn't return it. "And you thought your phone service would function better in my backyard?"

"I wanted to see if someone was home. I knocked on the front door, but there was no answer."

"Really?" he said, suspiciously. "I must not have heard it, which is unusual, since I have a tendency to hear the slightest noise."

"That must present a problem for you each morning," Carter said, smiling. "I imagine the birds must drive you crazy." He regretted using the term, "crazy," but based on the man's strange demeanor, he feared it was an accurate description.

"I can assure you, there are other annoyances that bother me far more."

"You have a beautiful place, from what I can tell." Carter said. "The location is gorgeous, very private."

"It more than meets my needs. Would you like me to take a look at your car? I'm quite good at fixing things."

"Don't trouble yourself. If you could be so kind as to return my phone and I'll attempt to call road service again or if you could try with your home phone, I would be extremely grateful."

His stare unsettled Carter.

"You don't remember me?"

Carter shrugged, unconvincingly. "Not really, should I?"

"I thought our meeting was memorable, perhaps I was mistaken. It *was* a long time ago. Five years, three months and one week, to be exact."

Carter found the specificity of the date to be alarming. What type of person would recall a meeting in such detail, particularly when it was held so long ago? He played along and went through the motions, inspecting the man more closely. "You do look familiar, but I honestly don't recall. I see so many people in my line of work."

"I'm sure that's true."

"I handle adoptions."

"That's wonderful. I once thought about adopting." He looked around, and then returned his attention to Carter. "Is that what brought you here, your work?"

"Uh, no, I was actually looking for some property in the area and got lost."

"People get lost a lot in these hills. But they usually don't get all the way up here unless they intended to."

Carter felt increasingly uneasy, realizing it was a serious mistake to make this visit. He thought about running back to the car, but decided to continue the ruse, no matter how weak or ineffective.

"You mentioned you had once considered adopting. Maybe

that's how we met." Carter took the game to the next level. "Wait," he said, and feigned searching his memory. "Randolph?" Carter blurted out, and then pointed at the man. "Gary Randolph?"

Randolph smiled. "How nice of you to remember. I'm flattered."

"This is quite a coincidence."

"I don't believe in them," Randolph said in a deadly tone. "All things happen for a purpose. Don't you agree?"

Carter took a step away, but Randolph casually blocked him.

"For example, I was initially disappointed, quite crushed when you were unable to find proper placements for me. I was so looking forward to adopting children who needed love."

"I apologize if I—"

Randolph held up his hand, "No need for that."

"Trans-racial adoptions are difficult," said Carter, "particularly when you request children from so many diverse backgrounds."

"I was able to rectify the matter on my own. As it turned out, your rejection was a blessing in disguise."

"I'm pleased to hear everything turned out for the best," said Carter, who could no longer maintain the pretense that he wasn't nervous. "Look, I've taken up enough of your time. I don't want to trouble you any further." He walked away from Randolph and headed toward the side of the house but continued speaking. "I'll just turn the car around. I should be able to jump start it without too much difficulty."

"Need a push?"

Carter turned around to respond, but never had the chance. Randolph smashed him flush in the face with the shovel. He dropped to the ground, groaning in severe pain. Randolph aimed the tip of the blade at Carter's neck and drove it into his throat. He studied Carter as he lay dying, struggling for breath, groaning until it gradually stopped, replaced by blood gushing from Carter's opened wound, a deep cut that had severed an artery.

* * *

Randolph searched Carter's pockets for car keys. After finding them, he located the S.U.V. and drove it inside his garage. The vehicle was large enough to hold Carter, as well as a small Vesper motor scooter. He would dispose of the car containing the dead body and use the scooter to ride back home. It was neither safe nor speedy enough for use on the freeways, but it was more than adequate for the major streets. It would also provide him with a convenient excuse to use a helmet and shaded faceguard, concealing his features.

He removed Carter's personal items but left the registration in the glove compartment. Randolph found the note containing directions to his home on the dash. He'd burn it tonight along with other articles belonging to the recently deceased. If he could have added Carter's body to his fireplace, he would have done so, gladly. Randolph had killed again. Not a member of the family but ironically, someone who had denied him one. So, it was equally justified and certainly as necessary. Now that he had a moment to consider what he had done, the act gave him as much of a thrill as he had experienced as a frightened teen. Although being older, the fear no longer existed, and it allowed him to appreciate the deed with greater pleasure. *Youth might be wasted on the young, but murder has a practical use at any age.*

It took more than an hour to clean up Carter's blood in the backyard and about the same amount of time to disinfect the car. Randolph made certain to remove any evidence that he had ever been inside. He would wait until nightfall before abandoning the vehicle. He still believed that if he studied any problem, the solution would reveal itself. The answer to this current dilemma, however, would need to come quickly, requiring him to rethink and reevaluate his previous plans. He had no doubt that this perceived setback would create more rewarding possibilities. The only thing demanded from him was that he maintained his faith, believing in the ultimate righteousness of his cause.

When it rains it pours, he thought. But since water is the source of all life, who was he to question the mysterious ways of a higher power? What hero in myth or reality, hadn't been challenged on his sacred quest? None. As a result, he would remain patient, accepting whatever obstacles were placed in his path. They could only make him stronger, more worthy of receiving the fruits of his labor.

In the interim, he fed the girls their dinner, bathed Selena and Mei Lin, and resumed his normal chores, as if nothing unusual or untoward had occurred.

SEVENTY-TWO
THURSDAY MAY 4TH

Ron, Todd, and Harrison sat huddled together in McKay's office, looking despondent.

"Where'd they find the body?" asked Todd.

McKay answered. "Trunk of his car. Two teenaged boys got pulled over for joyriding. Said they found the car with the windows down and the keys in the ignition. When the officer opened the trunk one of the kids fainted. The other one's probably still screamin'." He removed a cap from a bottle of water and took a swig. "Mr. Harrison, you want to fill me in again on the details?

"My office received his call a little before eleven o'clock yesterday morning," Harrison looked at Todd. "My secretary took the message and suggested that he remain in his office until he heard back from me. When I couldn't reach him to enquire about the details, I immediately relayed the info I had to Mr. Roth. This Mr. Carter told my secretary that he had a crazy idea about the case but didn't want to accuse an innocent person."

Carrey stepped inside the office leaving little room for

anyone else. "Looks like his idea wasn't so crazy after all." he said. "And the person in question wasn't so innocent."

"Now what?" asked Ron.

"We've asked for permission to review all adoption records in Carter's possession," answered McKay. "Placements. Rejections. People on the waiting list. We're also going to need to examine their office's employment records. Maybe the person worked there or applied for a job."

"What happened to the composite sketch you were working on?" asked Todd.

McKay slid a drawer open, removed an artist's pad, and then tossed it on the desk.

Todd studied it and commented, "That looks like Leonardo DiCaprio."

McKay nodded agreement. "Sakari saw *Titanic* twelve times," he shrugged. "If that's not enough to make you permanently seasick, I don't know what is." He flipped the notepad cover over the sketch. "That's the only face she remembers, which is a lot like the poster hanging on her bedroom wall."

"Do we know where Carter may have gone after work? Did he have any meetings with anyone?" asked Harrison.

Carrey shook his head. "Just got off the phone with his secretary"—he took a quick glance at his notes—"a Trina Castle. She's pretty shaken up. Has worked for him for over ten years. She said he left while she was on her break and had no idea where he went. Wasn't like him to leave the office. Usually ate lunch at his desk. And when he never came back, she thought it odd, but he sometimes makes wellness visits, wants to see how the new adoptees were doing."

"Wasn't the car found in Compton?" asked Ron. "Wouldn't that mean he traveled there to investigate the person he suspected?"

"He could have been murdered anywhere," said McKay. "The person who did it could have driven the car a hundred miles in any direction, leaving it in an area where he knew somebody would take it, destroying any useful evidence inside."

"Wouldn't he have to find a way back to wherever he lived? Wherever he's kept the girls?" asked Todd.

McKay answered. "We're checking public transportation, taxis, buses, Uber pick-ups. We can't rule out an accomplice or some innocent bystander who offered a ride. There are thousands of ways he could have traveled back and forth without being noticed, especially in that area late at night. We're lucky some gang member or drug dealer didn't take the car. We never would have found it or probably Carter's body."

"The best thing we've got going for us now is reviewing those office files," said Carrey.

"Don't you mean the only thing we've got?" asked Ron.

Carrey shrugged. "Sometimes the only thing we've got, just so happens to be the best thing. And on that optimistic note, Detective McKay and I will get back to work."

SEVENTY-THREE

Ron sat in the passenger seat of Todd's car. "I'm not sitting in here all day waiting to hear something," said Ron.

"You remember the name of Carter's secretary?"

Ron thought about it. "Detective Carrey said it was Trina Castle."

"Well, then, we better be on our way to offer our condolences."

"Don't we need directions to the adoption agency?"

Todd patted his jacket pocket. "Got it right here."

"Sometimes you amaze me."

Todd smiled. "I know." He stepped on the accelerator and sped off.

A supervisor comforted a distraught Trina who was in Carter's private office. Todd and Ron stood by waiting patiently. She recognized them and asked the supervisor to leave.

"We're sorry to barge in on you at this time of grief. I'm—"

"I know who you are, Mr. Roth." She looked at Ron. "And you too, Mr. Butler. I've been reading all about you and your daughters. I gave Mr. Carter the newspaper yesterday morning. If I hadn't, he might still be alive today."

"Why do you say that?" asked Ron.

"I told him all about the news article and how the person had taken four girls from different racial or ethnic backgrounds. Said it was a regular United Nations. He got real interested, ignored everything else I was saying. He stayed glued on the story."

"Did he say anything to you that might help us?" asked Todd.

"He didn't even tell me where he was going."

"Do you think we might look at his files?" asked Ron, ignoring the look Todd gave him. "Not all of them, just the ones you might consider important."

"I can't do that. Privacy laws," she said. "I told a detective that, but he said he would have the appropriate court orders to have access to everything and he and his partner would be here within the hour."

Ron asked, "You remember the detective's name?"

"I wrote it down 'cause I'm not sure I can remember anything today." She searched the office but couldn't find the paper. "Oh, I think it was McDonald. I try and associate names and I was planning to have a Big Mac for lunch."

"Could the name have been Detective McKay," asked Todd.

Trina thought about it. "That was it. You know him?"

"We work together," replied Ron while avoiding Todd's look. "Since he's bringing the court orders, you think it'll be all right to grant us access? It'll save everyone time."

"I think that would be okay as long as you're working together."

"We've been working extremely close," said Todd, now avoiding Ron's stare. "Where should we start?"

"I wouldn't know where to begin. Mr. Carter had his own

system of filing, and he pretty much remembered every child he had placed as well as those he couldn't. He remembered those most of all."

Both men look at each other, expressing their disappointment.

"What about the people who were refused adoptions?" asked Ron. "Especially any single men who wanted to adopt more than one child, from different races."

"Those he kept more private than the actual placements. Confidentiality laws have gotten increasingly strict over the years." She looked at his desk and became emotional.

"Are you all right?" asked Ron.

She held back tears and pointed to his desk. "That's the newspaper I gave him. It's still opened to the article about your daughters."

"Do you mind if we took that with us?" asked Ron. "Maybe there's something in it that will give us a clue."

"Since it's the last thing he held, I'd really like to keep it. Maybe his wife or children would want it. But I can make you a copy if you like."

"That would be great," said Todd.

Ron watched Trina as she took the newspaper, folded it to fit the copier, and then opened the lid. She stopped to remove a sheet of paper and he noticed her discomfort. She held it tight against her body. She'd lost all color in her face.

"Is everything all right?" asked Ron.

She walked unsteadily to Carter's desk, sat down, pressing the sheet against her chest.

"Is there something we can do?" asked Todd.

"I think I know where he went." She placed the paper face down on the desk. "That was in his copier. Technically I can't show it to you."

"If that's truly where he went, the name on that sheet might be the person who murdered him, the same person who might have our daughters," said Todd.

"Mr. Carter was a good man," she said. "A decent man. He wouldn't want me to break any laws." She turned the sheet of paper face up and positioned it on the desk so that it could be easily read. "So please don't ask me to betray any confidences." She left the office and turned at the doorway to address them. "He also spent his entire life helping children in need. I need to use the restroom. If you're not here when I get back, I'll understand. I hope you find your daughters. I'll be praying that you do." She left the executive suite.

Ron picked up the paper and stared at it. His hand shook noticeably. His expression changed. Deadly. Committed. He spoke as if the words would be forever cemented in stone. "Gary Randolph." He looked at Todd, reluctant to believe it was possible that he had named the man who could have their daughters. He felt his heart race then pound against his chest. Would he be reunited with Jennifer one month to the day she was taken from him? He looked at Todd. "You think this could be the guy?"

"Only one way to find out."

Ron wrote down the information from the paper. He handed the address and name to Todd, then continued writing on a second note paper.

"What are you doing?" asked Todd.

"I'm leaving her a note to give McKay the information and let him know we're on our way there just in case we need them." He placed the note on her desk.

"That's a good idea. I'll call Harrison with the details and ask him to meet us."

"Let's get there before anyone else does and make sure if our daughters are there, our faces are the first ones they see."

SEVENTY-FOUR

Gary Randolph had time to think, and panic was influencing every move. How had they discovered Lungren wasn't the murderer? He had perfected his plan and yet it failed! How was that possible? And now that fucking bureaucrat, Carter! A damn fool who denied him the chance to make a more perfect world. Not denied... He reconsidered. Delayed. Yes, all this was an inconvenient delay. But no more. It was time to make it right, like it was supposed to be. He'd check on the girls and tell them the good news, after all. Why wait?

He wasn't doing this for himself. It was for the girls. For his father, to condemn him for all of eternity. To heal the world. Surely that would be clear to anyone of good will. It was time to begin his final journey, the one he had dreamed of from the moment his hand was disfigured but his soul saved. He looked at that hand, touched it to feel its power, to embrace its destiny. And then he heard a car driving up the hill.

"Not again," he promised himself. "Not again," he whispered.

* * *

Todd maneuvered his Mercedes through the narrow roads of Hollywood Hills until he located Gary Randolph's address. He parked directly across from the house leaving the car on a dirt pathway that led to a trail through a heavily wooded area. "I should have brought my mountain climbing equipment," he said.

"We've climbed enough mountains," responded Ron. "I've got a feeling we've already reached the top of this one."

Ron grabbed a missing person's flyer and reached for the door handle. Todd touched his arm to prevent him from leaving. "Harrison wanted us to wait until he got here with the authorities."

"Sounds like a good plan... for you." Ron opened the passenger door. "I'm going in now. If you're joining me, bring your gun." He exited the car.

Todd opened his glove compartment, removed his gun, but then returned it inside and left to join Ron.

"Thought you were going to wait for Harrison," Ron said, walking toward the house.

"Like you told me: 'Gotta dance with who brung you.'"

"You bring the gun?"

"Like I told you before, nothing good will come from that. We'll play it smart and leave it to the police to back us up."

"You lived in Bel-Air too long."

The two men approached the front door. "You drove," said Ron, "so technically, you 'brung' me."

"Guess that means I should do the honors and ring the bell." Todd pushed the doorbell.

Ron didn't hear anything. "Step aside, let an expert try." He took control and knocked on the door, three times.

Todd shot him a glance. "I could have done that."

Ron knew the two of them were keeping it light to offset the fear and urgency that was overbearing. If he took his blood pressure right now, he no doubt would be rushed to emergency.

Noticing the perspiration on Todd's brow—Mr. Calm, Cool, and Collected who never seemed to sweat even while walking the streets under the hottest conditions—Ron realized that he wasn't the only one whose heart rate required medical attention.

They heard a fumbling at the door, tinkering with several locks, a noise that resembled a heavy bolt slipping into place. Ron broke out in a sweat, and it had nothing to do with the temperature.

"Can I help you, gentlemen?" Randolph asked pleasantly.

Ron thought the man standing in front of him would be the last person selected in a lineup of possible pedophiles. He doubted, for that matter, that Randolph would be accused of so much as petty theft. Collegiate handsome, physically fit, he looked more like a candidate for a starring role in a romantic comedy than a kidnapping suspect. But then again, if you were looking for a child molester, wouldn't you cast against type? He thought about the police sketch based on Sakari's description. Maybe *Titanic* wasn't the only thing on her mind.

Ron showed Randolph the flyer with photos of Rebecca and Jennifer. "Did you happen to see either one of these girls?"

He gave the flyer a cursory glance. "Every night," he answered.

Ron and Todd exchanged a concerned look.

"It's impossible not to see them," Randolph explained. "They're on television every hour and in the newspaper every day." He studied Ron, and then shifted his attention to Todd. "My God," he exclaimed. "Aren't you their parents?"

"I'm Todd Roth. This is Ron Butler."

"A pleasure," he replied. "I'm Gary Randolph. I've been following your plight along with half the country, it would seem. I can't imagine what you're going through." He shook his head, spoke sympathetically. "To have your children taken then, horror of all horrors, to be notified of their deaths only to discover they might still be alive." He released an exasperated sigh. "I could never survive such torture, having my emotions whiplashed like that."

The men remained silent for a beat, and then surprisingly Randolph opened the door wider. "Please come in," he said. "You must be exhausted given all the travel you've been doing."

Ron rubbed his chin. He certainly didn't expect this, and based on the look Todd gave him, the sentiment was shared.

"Thank you, Mr. Randolph," said Todd, who entered first, followed by Ron.

Randolph closed the door. "I prefer Gary. Every time I hear 'Mr. Randolph' I assume someone's addressing my father," he smiled warmly.

Ron noticed the number of locks on the door and immediately felt queasy. Something about this door reeked of imprisonment. He had the distinct impression that the locks weren't meant to keep anyone out but rather to ensure someone couldn't escape.

"You have quite a few locks," Ron commented. "Some of them are highly specialized." He pointed to an unusual bolt and floor lock.

"Well, as you can undoubtedly appreciate, it's an unsafe world," said Randolph. "I've had several break-ins. Not having next-door neighbors provides the luxury of privacy, but being so isolated also has its disadvantages." He quickly changed the subject. "I want you to know, I've prayed for your daughters virtually every night."

"That's very kind of you," said Todd.

"Not at all," Randolph responded. "I was deeply touched by your predicament. I love children and the thought that they could be in danger, well, let me just say I would kill anyone who harmed those I loved." He studied the two men. "I assume you feel the same way."

Randolph ushered the two men into the living room.

Ron's uneasiness grew. This was a strange man. But was he the man who took his daughter? "Do you have any?" he asked.

"Any what?"

"Children."

Randolph chuckled and then nodded that he understood. "Afraid not. I tried adopting once, but the bureaucracy discouraged single parents from doing so. Considering there are so many children out there who need love, their policy would seem to be quite counterproductive. But who am I to judge? Would you like to sit down, make yourself comfortable?"

Comfort would be the last thing Ron felt. "No thank you," he said.

"I was an only child. Perhaps I'm compensating by wanting a large family one day, maybe five or six boys. I don't think I would know what to do with so many girls. One daughter would be more than I could handle."

Ron wondered, once again, if the man standing in front of him who was so accommodating and willingly inviting strangers into his home, could be capable of the crimes he was suspected of committing. *He could... if he's a very good actor or a psychopath.*

"Can I bring you something to drink?"

Todd shook his head.

Ron took a few steps away from Randolph and noticed a stack of cardboard boxes and three suitcases lined up against the wall in the hallway. Two of the boxes were half-filled with kitchen utensils, dishes, and glasses wrapped in newspaper.

"Did we interrupt your packing?"

"Actually, I'm storing a few things before I take an extended vacation."

"If you don't mind me asking, where are you going?" asked Todd.

"Europe. Always wanted to visit Paris and Rome. Who

knows? Maybe that's where I'll meet the woman of my dreams, settle down, and raise a family."

"Of five or six boys," said Ron, a tinge of disbelief apparent in his comment.

"Maybe even more," Randolph said, smiling. "Speaking of places to visit, what brings you all the way out here? This is quite a distance from where your daughters were taken. If I recall correctly, wasn't that Santa Monica or somewhere else on the Westside?"

"There was a report that children... young girls... were seen in this general vicinity," replied Todd.

"Really?" He appeared surprised. "I hadn't heard."

"We wonder if you've noticed anything suspicious," said Todd.

"This is a very quiet area. I'm an artist who stays home all the time. I'm sure I would have noticed anything out of the ordinary. Among my other talents, I'm quite observant." He shrugged. "Some might even suggest, nosey."

Todd walked around the room. "Lovely place. I'm an architect. I appreciate unique homes."

"My father left it to me. To be more precise, I inherited his money and invested wisely. Although I'm proud to say I've made many improvements to the overall design. I'm a bit of an amateur carpenter and all-around handyman. Would you like me to give you a tour?"

"If it wouldn't be too much trouble," Todd replied.

"Not at all. Let me just make sure I don't have anything indecent in my bedroom. As a single man I'm subject to late-night entertainment of an adult nature." He placed his hands palms up, and shrugged. "Please don't report me to the police," he laughed. "I'll be right back. Make yourself at home." He rushed into the bedroom. Ron and Todd exchanged looks.

"He's weird, but if that were a crime we'd need a lot more prisons," said Todd, speaking quietly. "What do you think?"

"He did say that he tried to adopt. I doubt someone who just murdered the head of an adoption agency would volunteer that information." Ron looked at the front door. "But the locks on that door don't look quite normal to me."

Todd shrugged. "Some people like elaborate security systems, others depend on locks and bolts. I better go check on him."

"Todd," Ron stopped him. "Be careful. This doesn't feel right. Psychopaths get away with shit because they're psychopaths."

"I know," said Todd. "But we won't be alone for long and there's two of us and only one of him."

"In that case I better go with you."

They proceeded down the hallway and Todd knocked on the side of the bedroom door. "All right to enter?"

Randolph tossed a blanket over the monitors. "Yes, please."

Todd entered, followed by Ron, who observed lit candles surrounding the room. "You must like candles a lot," he commented. "I assume it cuts down on the heating bill."

"There's an energy I receive from them, a spirit that warms the air. No pun intended." Randolph picked up a metal container filled with incense sticks. "I add incense from India to the mix. Purifies the senses and aids meditation. I'd be happy to burn some for you. The fragrance is out of this world, so soothing."

"Maybe some other time," said Ron.

"This room has a great deal of character," said Todd. "The woodworking is from a different era. Such craftsmanship is rare to find. It's quite magnificent."

"That's so kind of you to say," said Randolph. "But I'm afraid I must plead guilty as charged."

The way he said "guilty" sent a chill down Ron's spine. Was this guy playing with them? If so, he was certainly enjoying himself. It's hard to believe that a person who had kidnapped four girls and was now in a room with two of their fathers could be this calm. Not exhibiting a bead of sweat. But maybe that's the point. That's precisely the type of person who could kidnap girls and get away with it.

"I designed most of what you see. I'm particularly proud of the crown moldings. All the detail was carved by hand. Took me six months for each corner." He looked up at the ceiling. "You should experience the room at night when it's quiet and the candles are lit reflecting off the walls. Combine that with the aroma of the incense, smoke slowly drifting to the ceiling, carrying such an innocent and fresh fragrance. Well, let me just say, there are only one or two things in life that bring me more pleasure, and I'm prohibited by law to reveal to you what they are." He smiled and studied the two men. "Are you sure you don't want to experience the incense. You can take some home with you if you like. Consider it my contribution to your cause. Perhaps it'll bring you luck."

Ron believed continuing to deal with this weirdo was a colossal waste of time. He gave Todd a signal to leave but then noticed a blanket over what appeared to be a television. He stared at it the odd site.

"I see you've noticed my computer monitor that I've been meaning to have repaired," said Randolph. "I have it covered because it annoys me to see anything broken. These things don't last for long. Whatever happened to made in America?"

Ron gave Todd another look but this time he wasn't certain it was time to leave.

"You've been very hospitable but I'm sure we've taken enough of your time," Todd said.

"There's so much more to see. But I understand you have far more pressing things on your mind. Please, don't give up hope. Miracles do happen."

"We believe that's possible, too." Todd stepped outside the bedroom.

"Could I use your restroom?" Ron asked. "I'll only be a moment."

"Of course," Randolph replied. "It's straight down the hall to the right." The first sign of sweat formed on his brow.

"Are you all right?" asked Todd.

"Indeed, I just don't have many guests, that's all. Want to make sure I'm accommodating, being a good host." He smiled. Todd didn't.

Ron stood in the middle of the bathroom. Stared at the tub. Something came over him. A dread, a sickness. He inhaled the room and sensed what he thought was the presence of his daughter. He always believed he could tell if she had been someplace, any place. He'd told Todd that, who didn't really seem to believe him. Maybe Ron just wanted it to be true. A father's instinct would always allow him to protect his child. But he was convinced that people can sense when their loved ones are in trouble. He'd read countless stories when a mother woke up in the middle of the night, aware that something awful had happened to her son or daughter or husband. Was he experiencing that in this room? He needed more time here. How much, he didn't know. But he wasn't ready to leave this room, or this home.

"Your friend is taking a long time," said Randolph. "He is your friend, I assume."

"He is. We've become quite close."

"I can only imagine. Such a tragedy either brings you close or tears you apart. I'm grateful, this unfortunate circumstance has given you a—"

Ron approached.

"Well, hello there, I was thinking of checking on you, to make sure you were fine."

"I'm fine, thank you."

"Well, I can't tell you how much I enjoyed meeting you both. Let me show you out."

Ron and Todd walked with him toward the front door.

Randolph opened the door.

The men prepared themselves to leave.

"We really appreciate your hospitality," said Todd. "I hope our being here wasn't too terrible an inconvenience."

"My goodness! Not at all. I enjoyed your company." He extended his hand. Todd reluctantly shook it.

He then extended his hand to Ron, who took it and suddenly felt a surge of evil. As Randolph shook his hand, and said, "I hope you can remain positive during this difficult time. Remember, as long as you can see tomorrow you can face today."

Todd stood with his back pressed against the wall, his fists tightened. Ron tightened the grip on Randolph.

"That's odd," he commented. "I don't recall ever saying that before... It's a lovely expression though, don't you agree?" Randolph smiled.

Ron let go of his hand, took a step closer to him. "Where's my daughter?"

Randolph's smile disappeared. "How would I know?"

"I'm going to ask you one more time. What have you done with my daughter?"

"I don't like your tone. I think it best if you leave, immediately." He pushed Ron out of the way, but Ron drove his shoulder into him, knocking him further into the living room.

Ron turned toward Todd. "Search the house!"

Todd ran down the hallway, frantically opening and closing doors, searching desperately for any sign of their daughters.

Randolph took advantage of Ron's distraction and charged him, pinning him face-first against the wall. He drove his fist into Ron's kidney, then pummeled him on the back of his head, smashing his face into the doorway.

Todd kicked open the door to the bathroom, opened the medicine cabinet, swept his hand against the shelves, flinging all the contents onto the floor. He rushed out of the room into a second bedroom converted to a den. "Rebecca! Becky! Can you hear me?"

Ron spun around and drove his knee into Randolph's midsection. Randolph doubled over in pain but managed to drive his head into Ron's chin. Ron blocked a punch and countered with a right cross, followed by a chop to Randolph's throat.

Todd opened a closet door, discovered it was a wine cellar. He galloped down the concrete steps. He looked around, headed back up the steps. "Rebecca! Rebecca!"

He made it back to the top of the steps when he heard, "Daddy! Daddy!" He stopped at the stairs, stared in disbelief, and then turned, jumping down the steps two at a time. He crashed into the wine rack. Discovered it was fake. He looked for a switch, tried moving the case. After several futile efforts, he tore away the façade and managed to slide open the barrier. He discovered a reinforced door that had a metal bar across its width and a steel pole bolted to the floor pressed against the frame.

Randolph ran into his bedroom, quickly searching his closet. Ron raced into the room and dove into Randolph only to be head-butted, driving him backwards onto the bed. Randolph jumped on Ron, hit him twice. Attempting a third punch, Ron managed to flip Randolph over, crashing him into the wall and knocking over several lit candles. Ron went after him, a man possessed. He struck him in the midsection, threw a series of punches to the ribcage.

The bed skirt caught fire, then in rapid succession, the sheets, blanket, pillows, and mattress. The flames spread quickly throughout the room, jumping from one curtain to the next. The crown moldings that Randolph had been so proud of moments earlier were now melting under intense heat; the whole room had become nothing more than a tinderbox ready to explode.

Randolph ran to the door but was tackled again, this time tumbling back into the living room. Ron let him up only to spin him into the wall. Randolph turned to be confronted with one, two, three punches to the face and a final pulverizing shot to the solar plexus that drove him to knees. He threw one more devastating punch to the side of the head, knocking Randolph unconscious.

Downstairs, Todd banged his hands against the door. "Becky! Jenny! Are you in there?"

He heard his daughter's voice through the thick door. "Daddy! It's Rebecca!"

He kicked at the pole to dislodge it then slid the metal bar until he could open the door. He raced in. The dungeon was directly underneath Randolph's bedroom. Smoke seeped through the ceiling and walls. The girls coughed. He saw Selena and Mei Lin chained.

"Daddy!" Rebecca screamed, crying uncontrollably. He focused his eyes in the dimly lit room and finally saw her. He rushed to her, lifting her into his arms. He noticed her face bruised and scratched. He kissed her.

Ron rushed in, stopped in his tracks when he observed the room. Saw his daughter standing, also chained, face swollen and beaten. He started crying and rushed to her.

"I knew you would find me," Jennifer cried out. "I knew it."

He tried to remove the chain around her waist but realized it was locked and attached to the wall. He pulled at the chain attempting to dislodge it from its anchor.

Todd did the same, but it was useless. Smoke began to fill the room. He shouted at Ron. "Get the gun from my car."

Ron didn't want to leave Jennifer but had no choice. He raced up the stairs and rushed out of the house toward Todd's car.

Todd directed the girls to take their blankets and soak them in the sink. He helped put the blankets over Rebecca's shoulders to protect her from the heat. Then they helped do the same for the other girls. He told them to keep the blankets over their face, so they wouldn't breathe the smoke or get it in their eyes.

Ron ran back down the stairs and gave the gun to Todd. He told the girls to cover their ears and pulled Rebecca away from the wall. He aimed the gun at the chain and fired two shots. He then did the same for Jennifer and Mei Lin. He was about to free Selena when the door slammed shut. Ron charged the door, smashing his shoulder against it, but too late. Randolph had locked it and trapped everyone inside.

Randolph ran back up the stairs. The dream of his family was gone. He felt like a beast that could destroy anything in his way. His rage caused him to claw at his skin, a madman punishing himself for his failures. He should have left a week ago! Now it was too late. He heard his father laughing from the grave. He could hear the screams of the girls below. They reminded him of his own screams when his father punished him, disfiguring his tiny hand.

Todd freed Mei Lin. All the girls huddled together, using their blankets to form a tent over their heads to keep out the smoke, to no avail.

"How do we get out?" asked Ron.

"There must be windows!" Todd ripped away the padding from the wall. Ron worked on the other side of the room, ferociously clawing away at the mats and insulation. His eyes burned; his throat became raw from swallowing smoke. The room became an inferno. Ron gasped for breath. He tore down another section of padding and ripped away yards of insulation.

"There!" he said, pointing to a window about six feet from the floor.

Todd and Ron grabbed all the bed cots and piled them on

top of each other. Ron jumped on top and tried to open the window. It was either locked or stuck. "Give me the gun!"

"I thought you didn't know how to shoot!" Todd said.

"Don't need to shoot! Give me the damn gun!"

Todd handed him the weapon.

Ron turned his face away from the window, sheltered his head with one arm, and used the butt of the gun to break the glass. He shattered the glass around the frame. The last time he struck the glass the gun flew out. He took a blanket, wrapped it around the wooden pane and pulled it, leveraging both feet against the wall. He used all his strength and his full body weight. He fell to the floor pulling the entire frame, now providing enough space to exit.

"Get the girls lined up!" Ron ordered.

Todd ushered the girls in a line. He helped Mei Lin to the top of the makeshift platform. Ron lifted her up to the window and pushed her outside the opening. Selena went next. Selena and Mei Lin, once outside, helped pull out Rebecca, and then all three girls helped Jennifer, grabbing her chain, and towing it like they were on the opposing side of a tug-of-rope battle.

The ceiling could collapse at any moment. Ron yelled at the girls. "Move far away from the house! Stand outside! Jennifer! Rebecca! Help the other girls!"

Ron turned to Todd and extended his hand. "Come on!"

"You go first!"

"Don't argue with me. You always pay the check. This one's on me! Move it!"

Ron interlocked his fingers from both hands, holding them palm up and gave Todd a boost up. As Todd struggled to crawl through, Ron shoved him from behind. Todd knelt outside, extended his hand through the opening, and grabbed onto Ron who climbed up and squeezed himself out of the frame with Todd's assistance. He helped an exhausted Ron to his feet. They both ran toward the front of the house to join the girls.

Ron made it to the front first then held back Todd from moving any further.

Randolph had his arm around Rebecca's neck. He held Todd's gun and pointed it at her head.

"Let her go!" Todd demanded.

"When I'm safely away, you can have your daughter back. If you try to follow me, I'll kill her. Give her the keys to your car."

Ron wondered why Randolph hadn't escaped using his own vehicle but then saw the garage fully engulfed in flames.

"Leave her alone!" shouted Jennifer.

"Do you want to take her place?" Randolph asked. "Or perhaps you'd like to come with us?"

Ron heard sirens and fire engines in the distance.

Randolph became more desperate. "All I wanted was to create a perfect world! And you stole my dream!"

He looked pathetic, his face bloodied, swollen, bruised from the physical assault.

"You ruined it, all," he whimpered. He now looked like a heartbroken petulant child whose toys were taken away. "Give her the keys!" Randolph shouted.

Todd removed the keys from his pocket. He extended them out toward Rebecca who reached for them but just as she was about to take them, Jennifer snatched them away, breathing heavily, obviously nervous.

"Honey, what are you doing?" asked Ron, increasingly concerned.

"If you don't give me those keys, I'll take them off your dead body!" Randolph pointed the gun toward Jennifer.

"Jenny? Give him the keys!" ordered her father.

She closed her eyes and sang quietly. "He's the one... He's the one... He's the really useful engine—"

Rebecca joined Jennifer. "That we adore."

Ron wondered if the pressure had finally overwhelmed the

girls, traumatized them so they were incapable of making reasoned decisions. He looked at Randolph who appeared confused.

Jennifer opened her eyes and looked at Rebecca. She displayed a nervous smile and then said, "Uh, Rebecca? We missed the truck."

All the girls shouted, "We're not aiming for the truck!"

Jennifer tossed the keys high in the air, and as they started to descend, Randolph instinctively raised his hand to catch the keys. Rebecca broke away, diving to the ground. With Randolph's attention focused on the keys, Ron and Todd charged him. Randolph tried to shoot but they knocked him to the ground. He struck his head against the concrete and collapsed unconscious.

Rebecca ran to her father and Jennifer jumped into Ron's arms as the fire trucks arrived.

"Daddy! I knew you'd come! I knew you would save me!" said Jennifer.

Ron smiled but then noticed Randolph slowly rising, still groggy. He had managed to get to one knee.

Ron touched Jennifer on the cheek. "Excuse me a sec, sweetheart." He walked over to Randolph and kicked him very hard in the middle of his face, breaking his nose and knocking him out. He stood over the body. "That's for hurting my daughter, you sick piece of shit." He returned to Jennifer.

"Dad, you swore."

"Technically, shit isn't a swear word. It's a biological function."

Jennifer raised her eyebrows in doubt. "You sure?"

"Positive."

She looked at Randolph's prone body. "I suppose I can let it slide this once."

"Guess what I did last week," asked Ron.

"What?"

"I fixed the car door."

"Holy shit," she replied excitedly. "That's great, Dad."

He gave her a warning look. "One week punishment."

"But, Dad," she protested, "it's a biological function."

"And another week for arguing. No T.V."

"Do I get credit for time served?"

He smiled and then held out his arms. She rushed to him, and they embraced.

* * *

Harrison arrived with McKay and Carrey. Harrison cuffed Randolph and kept him under guard. McKay gave Ron a look that suggested he wasn't too pleased. Ron shrugged. McKay shook his head and grinned.

Todd hugged Rebecca. If he hugged her any harder, he might break her. "I love you," he said, with a combination of desperation and relief. "You hear me? I love you and I'm never going let you out of my sight again."

"Daddy?" Rebecca said, trying to breathe. "I just got out of one hostage situation. Do I have to be in another?"

He held her at arm's length and studied her. She placed her finger on her tongue and chalked it up on an imaginary board. Todd placed his finger on the tip of his tongue and returned the favor.

Mei Lin and Selena joined Jennifer and Rebecca. The four girls stood together and held hands, Jennifer on one end, Rebecca on the other.

Both fathers approached the detectives. They shook hands. "I want both of you to make me a promise," said McKay. "If God forbid, you should ever get in trouble again, please let the police handle it."

Ron and Todd agreed.

"We'd like you to make us a promise, too," said Ron.

McKay took a deep breath. "Okay, what is it?"

"Don't retire!" Rod and Todd shouted.

The detectives laughed. "You just wasted a promise," said Carrey. "My partner's never gonna retire. You both take care. I'm glad to report that sometimes the good people win. Go be with your daughters."

Todd and Ron held their daughters' hands, now joining together with Mei Lin and Selena. The girls watched the house that had been their personal hell engulfed in flames and burn to the ground despite the heroic efforts of the fire fighters attempting to save it.

EPILOGUE

SATURDAY MAY 13TH

"You think your dad will let you sleep over tonight?" asked Rebecca.

"I don't know," replied Jennifer. "He's not too cool with me being out of his sight."

"I know what you mean," said Rebecca, who'd completed showing Jennifer her favorite dolls. "My parents follow me to the bathroom, and then wait outside. It's embarrassing."

"I thought we got rid of the chains," said Jennifer.

Rebecca touched her tongue with her index finger and ran it across an imaginary chalkboard. Jennifer did the same.

"You like trains?"

"You mean, like riding on them?"

"No," Jennifer said, smiling. "I've got a great collection. You should come over and we can design a track, a whole train station."

"Cool, but my dad and mom will probably want to be the conductors."

They laughed.

"Well, I see you two are getting along," said Todd, who'd entered his daughter's room, followed closely behind by Ron.

"Dad, is it all right if Jennifer sleeps over tonight?"

Todd turned to Ron. "Is that okay with you?"

Jennifer gave her dad a desperate plea-filled look, then followed it up with a hopeful smile, eyebrows raised, face full of optimistic wonderment.

"You've still got some catching up to do with your studies."

"Mr. Butler," interjected Rebecca. "We can study together all this weekend."

"Yeah, Dad," Jennifer chimed in. "Rebecca's really good at Math."

"And Jennifer can help me with History," remarked Rebecca.

"And Geography," boasted Jennifer. "And Science," she added, which caused Rebecca to give her friend a "don't push it," look.

"I've never heard my daughter so enthusiastic about studying," said Ron.

"Mine, either. Guess we can't stand in the way of education."

Everyone turned toward the sound of metal scraping against the marble floors outside Rebecca's room. Liz skated inside, balancing herself by holding onto either side of the doorway. She wore a tight bright yellow pair of shorts, a Stanford T-shirt, argyle knee-high socks, and a purple Lakers visor.

"You girls ready to go?" asked Liz.

"We were born ready," answered Rebecca.

Todd looked at his wife, giving her an expression that suggested both admiration and alarm. "You're coming, too?"

"You think I'd let you and Ron have all the fun?"

"But you're coming with us, dressed like that?"

"Dad," said Rebecca. "We're going to Venice Beach. Duuuuh!"

"So maybe your mother ought to wear a tiny yellow bikini and I can skate behind her." He smiled lasciviously.

"Mr. Roth," said Jennifer. "There are children present."

"In case she falls," Todd clarified his position. "I can be right there to catch her."

"What's wrong with what I'm wearing?" asked Liz. "You object to my alma mater?" She pointed to her college T-shirt, and then to her visor. "Or my favorite team's logo?"

"I might need to borrow that visor, so I'm not blinded by those shorts," replied Todd.

"I think you look cool, Mom."

"Thanks, sweetheart."

"For your age," Rebecca completed the thought.

"Just try and keep up with me at the beach," Liz said, then gave the group a quick assessment. "That goes for everyone."

"Ron, did that sound like a challenge to you?"

"Most definitely," he answered.

"Well, what do you think we should do?"

"In the words of the immortal Marvin Gaye," Ron looked at his daughter and nodded.

"Let's get it on," Jennifer said.

"Oh, one sec," interrupted Todd. We've got one more who should be joining the fun at any moment."

Briana Douglass skated into the room. The thirty-year-old African American beauty wore a tight purple two-piece workout set with a yoga sports bra tank top that was more than amply filled.

"Ron, I'd like you to meet, a dear friend, Briana Douglass," said Todd. "Briana, meet Ron."

"Very nice to meet you, Ron," said Briana.

"Same here," Ron replied sheepishly, then gave a quick look at Todd, who smiled and glanced at his amused wife.

Jennifer also looked at Todd, giving him a quick wink.

"Well, time is wasting," remarked Todd. "Ladies first to the car." The girls and women leave. Ron and Todd remain behind.

"Really?" asked Ron.

"What? She's a friend. Thought it would be nice to invite her and have some fun."

"That's it? Fun?"

"Well, I'm having fun," said Todd. "What's the matter, don't you like the color purple? I thought it looked nice on her." Todd left, leaving Ron alone.

He looked around, then smiled and quickly joined the group.

They arrived at Venice Beach, where they skated until sunset, ate sausage with fried onions, pepperoni and pineapple pizza, extra hot Buffalo wings, frosted cinnamon buns, and had the time of their lives, despite their upset stomachs.

And, oh. Ron and Briana had a wonderful time and Jennifer invited her to come over for Sunday dinner which her father thought was a splendid idea.

A LETTER FROM THE AUTHOR

Dear Reader,

My heartfelt gratitude to each of you for investing your time in reading my novel, *The Stolen Girls*, and more importantly, my sincere appreciation to you for supporting the literary work of writers everywhere.

If you would like to join other readers in hearing all about my new releases and bonus content, you can sign up here:

www.stormpublishing.co/jeff-stetson

Writers, if honest, leave a little bit of their soul on each page so that the reader will better understand that writer's truth as well as their own. I'd love to hear your truth, so I hope we will remain in contact and if you find *The Stolen Girls* merits your support, I invite you to provide reviews and hope you will recommend the novel to your friends and colleagues. Regardless of your decision, I wish you unlimited wonderful novels on all your future reading lists.

The Stolen Girls, as well as all my previous work, explores our shared humanity; the goals, aspirations, and dreams that make us human, regardless of our perceived differences and any obstacles to overcome. My story is focused on two men: one white, the other Black; one wealthy, the other struggling financially; one well-connected, the other alone, without support. And yet these two men are brought together because they will both experience the terror no parent should ever face, the abduction of their young daughters.

I thought about writing this novel for many years because I wanted to find a way to adequately convey the emotional pain of having a child taken away from their father, placed in harm's way, without ever knowing if they'd ever hold their daughter again or ever know her fate. I also wanted to demonstrate the courage and faith required to overcome fear and a debilitating sense of desperation.

But the reason it took so long to finally commit to begin this journey was that I needed to be convinced that I could write this novel without exploiting the girls, creating a story that, despite their potential jeopardy, would have them become empowered, never losing faith, and discovering a strength they never realized or believed they had.

In the middle of their horrific set of circumstances, two men and their two daughters transcend their own differences, to find the moral strength to persevere, and in the process not only find friendship but the undeniable power of love.

I hope you find, at least, a bit of yourselves in the struggles and victories that Todd and Ron experience and that you begin to care about Rebecca and Jennifer as much as they begin to care about each other. Most of all, I hope that you rejoice in their mutual commonality, as well as our own. And, finally, that we come to understand that the things that separate us, whether class, race, social status, politics, or wealth, do not and never will define us or limit our potential to see the best in each other and defeat the worst in ourselves.

Thank you for reading *The Stolen Girls*. I sincerely hope you enjoyed it.

Jeff

KEEP IN TOUCH WITH THE AUTHOR

facebook.com/jeff.stetson.5

x.com/JeffStetson

instagram.com/jeff_paul_stetson

linkedin.com/in/jeff-stetson-356b7818

ACKNOWLEDGMENTS

An author writes alone but once finished depends on others to bring his work to life. Special thanks to Claire Bord for her editorial vision, assistance, and ongoing support as well as to the entire team of Storm Publishing for providing an environment that nurtures writers and creates opportunities for them to flourish.

My deepest gratitude to those who have supported my work throughout the years, whether theater, film, television, or novels. I left education in order to educate. If I've managed to accomplish that, and at times inspire, then that will be my greatest reward.

Continue to support the arts and fight those who would restrict or obstruct the right to do so.

Made in the USA
Las Vegas, NV
01 March 2024